I0847467

THE ROAD OUT OF NOWHERE

M. WRIGHT

*Dedicated to Abigail my daughter,
for whom these stories were originally told,*

to my wife, who has been a constant encouragement,

and to L.S. whose talents, taste, style and patience were invaluable.

I

―――

CONFRONTATIONS

he crow listened and obeyed.

It lifted heavily off the ground and then drew itself up, through the rain, into the flock above.

If anyone had been there who understood crows, they would have been amazed at the way they had gathered; tens of thousands, arrayed rank upon squabbling rank, and all unnaturally close.

The crow dodged through the crowded air. Rising into the very centre of the mass, it rasped out its orders.

Instantly, the flock wheeled, screeching as if a single, powerful beast, and rose until it almost merged into the belly of the storm that growled above. Lightning arced, gorse and heather burst into flame, and with gathering momentum, the storm and crows moved across the Moor; they moved purposefully; they moved toward the Road.

Not far away, a man stirred in his bed. The thunder was close now, but the man paid no attention. He looked up with a grin, apparently sharing a joke with the rough boards above his head.

He smiled, sighed, and getting up, pulled on his clothes. He strapped on a sword, picked up his staff and prepared to leave the hut.

On the slope below the Moor, the Village slept under heavy skies. The early morning had been wet, and now a summer storm was threatening to break from the north. The flashes and peals of thunder rolled over the dull, wet buildings: the white washed walls seemed to press themselves into the ground in anticipation of the onslaught.

In their bedrooms, the Walkers stirred. Jill turned to hear a low groan from the next room. "Mum?" She called, glancing at the clock: its numbers glowed, burning '5:30' into the air.

Jill's Mum had not been sleeping well since the sickness started. Jill would lie awake and listen to her mother's movements, and try not to worry. It didn't work and, even though there were no more sounds from her mother, she rose and walked to the window. The storm was closer now; the lightning could clearly be seen. She was still only half awake, but something odd caught her attention. *What were those birds doing, underneath it?* She squinted through the glass, staring up at the towering anvil shaped cloud, fascinated by the activity of the dark birds.

"Are you getting dressed for school already?"

Jill's Mum had clearly not gone back to bed. She was standing at the door frowning. "Are you all right, dear?" she asked.

Somehow, the question irritated Jill; *it was Mum who was ill, not her.* Jill stretched a tired smile across her face. "Yeah, I'm okay. Just watching the storm."

"Try to get some more sleep won't you dear?"

"Yes, *I* will, Mum."

The storm was rolling forward quickly now, and the crows were no longer circling, but flying determinedly, keeping position under the centre of the storm. They moved along the moorland Road and closed on the escarpment. The escarpment was where the Moor ended and where the Village huddled beneath. The yellow sandstone track of the Road was bright in the gloom and on it stood a man; a staff in hand; a sword at his side.

The man raised his staff.

He was standing where the Road turned to go over the edge of the slope, just out of sight of the Village. The cloud was almost upon him now, the lightning raining down in torrents of power, the birds solidifying in an arrowhead formation.

If anyone who understood lightning had watched, they would have thought the man very foolish, because he was standing tall with his stick raised in the air, like a lightning conductor waiting to be struck. He shouted into the storm, his voice booming against the wind.

"The Lord of the Way does not permit you access. Disperse! Return! There are those who yet wish to travel the Road. Times and seasons are not yours! You cannot have your prey. Return!"

Lightning arced down toward the Road. The murder of crows turned and started to spiral toward the lone figure.

Jill turned back to the window. She could not see clearly because the first squall of rain had smeared the window, but it seemed that lightning from all over the cloud was focused on one spot. That wasn't possible, was it?

The staff remained aloft, and instead of being struck, the lightning turned aside and scorched the turf to left and right. A continuous barrage of power assaulted the Road, but never touched it. Instead, the lightning forked horizontally only feet above the ground, making arches of branching light.

"Return! You have no right!" His voice boomed, even over the thunder.

The girl yawned, stretched and decided to lie down. The rain had become heavier, and it was difficult to see anything now, so she decided to ask a teacher about the storm. Jill groaned at the thought of school, but the rain continued to pound the glass, and enjoying the feeling of being warm and secure, she drifted toward sleep.

"Time to get up!" her Mum called. Was Mum losing track of time again? Surely, she had only just lain down. Jill frowned, *what was up with Mum?*

The crows were now pouring down, diving from the cloud and funnelling themselves on to the point where the Road allowed access to the Village, and their prey.

The man was unmoved as he watched. Sweat and rain mixed and ran into his eyes, and he wiped his forehead with the back of one hand. With the other, he lifted his staff once more.

"The seasons are not yours! The cohort must disperse! You will return to your master!" His voice did not waver. "Must I show you reality again? Will you never learn the lesson?"

Then, quietly he glanced at the ground and grinned. "No, I don't suppose you ever will." His smile fell away, "But you can still serve a purpose of sorts." Looking up, his eyes filled with tears as his dark curls streamed back in the gale, and he extended his arm once more.

"No further!" came the command.

Lightning sprang from the staff upward into the avalanche. Crows on the front line exploded, a cascade of bright power rippling upwards. Others behind simply ceased to exist, swept away in the shock of light. Only a few stragglers managed to twist away on singed wings.

The lightning continued upward, fingers reaching into the cloud and tearing into its core. With a roar of thunder, sheet lightning illuminated the Moor for miles around. Then, abruptly, all noise stopped.

The rain continued in flurries but the cloud was breaking up.

"It was a long time ago, but your master did not want to learn then either," muttered the olive-skinned man. He had turned to watch three crows that he had allowed to live continue on their way unscathed.

"Do what you came to do, but if you harm a hair of their heads . . ."

The first of the three crows alighted on the Walkers' roof. Jill was getting up and preparing breakfast. She had made toast and coffee and was getting her mother's favourite spreads out. Mum had got the time wrong, and although Jill decided not to mention it, she pouted.

Jill's Mum walked in, dressing gown tied tight and her footfall heavy. "I haven't slept at all," she said, and reaching for her coffee, murmured a thank you.

Jill looked at the clock; it was almost six. *I haven't slept either,* she thought with a sigh, and spread some toast with honey.

"You're looking tired, dear." Mum sounded factual and 'in-charge'. Jill had found this comforting at the beginning of the illness, but now that Mum was too tired to do much and Jill did most of the housework, Mum's tone of voice irritated her. Of course, Mum could not help being sick, and Jill was smart enough to know all this, but that made her feel ashamed of herself, which somehow made her even more angry.

"Make sure that you've got some fruit for morning break, and take a coat."

Jill had to stifle a rising desire to argue. If Mum wanted to be in charge, she should be looking after her.

Jill stopped her thoughts and corrected herself. She tried to smile, but it faded on her lips.

The crow cocked its head to one side as if listening, then dropped in a steep glide down to a rhododendron bush outside the kitchen window. It looked in.

"Are-you-sure-you're-all-right-dear?"

It had become Mum's catch phrase and it was driving Jill mad, almost as if it was Jill who had something wrong. Jill stared at her toast and chewed slowly, refusing to talk.

The crow stared at Jill and cawed softly.

Jill shifted uneasily; thoughts swirled and rose; anger and tears pulled at her mind. "This is stupid," she muttered, "I can handle it." Several really nasty ways to start an argument suggested themselves. She bit her lip.

The crow stared at her, still unseen.

"What was that dear? Did you say I was stupid?"

The crow cawed again.

The thoughts were Jill's, but she had mastered them until this moment. Now something was pushing them forward into her mind. She tried to put them in order, to keep them in place, even though her face twisted with the effort.

"Answer me Jill; I'm not used to being ignored."

Jill's thoughts jostled her. Her mind was tired; it teetered, like an old Grandma leaning on a stick, barely able to stand, unable to control the squabbling brats around her. She stood, red faced, and glared at her mother. The old woman inside her was beginning to fall. The stick snapped.

"Just leave me alone, you never do anything around here!"

Mum's eyes widened and she went pale. She opened her mouth as if to say something, then closed it again. As it was, Jill was not listening. Her rage was continuing to rise as her anger poured out.

Outside, the crow chuckled. It cawed, still ignored by the arguing people, and then flew up on to the roof. Fat with pleasure, it perched on the ridge and preened itself.

The second crow perched as well, and looked down through a skylight on the roof of the industrial building upon which it had landed. The workshop was to the east of the Village and, "Sponsored by Reckit's Oil," was emblazoned down one side in curving writing, as if a giant hand had signed the wooden boards. The building had clearly been there for some time. Although a new glass and steel reception welcomed visitors into a 'space-age', air-conditioned greenhouse, only fresh white paint had been used to cover the rest of the huge, wooden shed.

Noises came from inside: banging and cutting of metal; the roar of an immense flame; and the sound of a rivet gun all reverberated and spilled out into the green countryside.

Abruptly it all stopped. Four men in blue overalls walked out of double height doors and over to a new temporary building, one of them carrying a lunch box. A fifth man in a suit followed, but then paused and shouted back into the building. "Do you want anything? Shall I bring you back something to eat?" A muffled reply drifted on the air. The man shrugged, turned and then walked across the new shingle path with nothing but the sound of the wind and stones for company.

The crow flew down to the massive sliding door, which was just far enough open to allow a pickup truck to be parked half in, and half out of the building.

It hopped inside the shed.

The man inside could not be seen. Amid the cables and confusion on the floor was a laptop, quietly humming, and behind it, in the middle of the space, a huge metal object was suspended on padded supports. It was cylindrical, with a point at one end, and seemed to have been carved out of a solid silver.

The crow waited, not yet seeing its target, then as a dull banging noise emerged from the silver object, it tilted its head slightly and skipped behind the pick-up's front wheel.

A wiry man in a neatly pressed white coat emerged from a hatch in the middle of the huge cylinder. He muttered to himself and pushed his greying ginger curls back across his head. Clambering down, the man walked over to the laptop and called up a technical design on the screen. Bending over he compared the image to the heavy object in his hand.

"It should fit, now why on earth . . . ?"

The crow watched carefully, his hard, black eyes gleaming silver in the reflected light. As the man walked away, the crow moved to the computer. With tensed wings, it over-shadowed the laptop and gave a rasping shriek. The screen flickered and went out. Directing its gaze at the silver machine, the crow swore low inarticulate curses. From inside the metal shape, a roar of frustration erupted and the crow flapped lazily out of the door. It spent the rest of the afternoon, after the lunch break, gazing through the skylight, its crowing accompanying the growing sound of argument from inside.

Jill had eventually apologised. Her mum had crumpled into a weeping mess and repented for all her failures as a mother, wife and person in general. Jill felt awful. This was a new experience for her, and not one she liked. Part of her wished just to be sent to bed for the rest of the day, and to come down and find that she was eight again. Mum would be well and she would be grounded by the awe-inspiring person who had always controlled her life. Jill used to think she could even control the weather.

Jill knew, of course, that this would not happen, but she still longed for it with all her heart. It was not that she did not enjoy freedom, finding out things, exploring, it was their lives falling apart that she hated. It felt as though she was suspended over a chasm, just waiting to fall.

Jill cuddled her Mum, stroking her hair. "I love you, Mum."

"I love you too."

"I'm sorry; I didn't mean to say all that, it just . . ."

Jill's Mum interrupted, "I know, I know." She held up her hand and looked straight at her. "I know it's hard for you; just me and you and all this." Her mother's face pulled tight and she looked like she might cry again, but she coughed and continued. "I can't tell you it will be all okay, and I wish your father was here, but I am trying dear. I am trying; really . . . I don't want to . . . It's not that I want to be ill . . . I want to see you finish school . . . to get to University . . ." At each pause, Jill's Mum had looked in agony and when, at last, she burst into tears, Jill wept with her. It helped Jill to know that her mother had not given up, but *What could Mum do?* she thought. *What could anyone do now?*

A cold future without her mother rose up before her mind's eye. Her stomach turned and she looked away from it. Jill had to go to school; it was time to get ready now, and she kept telling herself that everything would be okay. *Things would get back to normal soon. The doctors will know what to do.*

The crow stopped preening and chuckled to itself.

The boy watched from the window as Jill walked up the main street of the Village toward school. He lived in an old house on the south side of town, although they had not been there long. He stared out of the dirty window, wondering what it was like to have her life.

Mus' be all right. Her clothes are mint.

His own clothes were piled in the corner, the sheets on his bed had not been changed for a month and he had not washed for two days. Although he could not have told anyone that he was doing it, he fretted about his torn shirts and the broken bed slats. It hung over him and made him gloomy and sour, and it showed on his face. There was a knock at the door. He went downstairs.

At the door, the boy found himself staring at the shiny brass buttons of a blue uniform. The muscles in the boy's neck tensed and his hunger turned to sick tension in his stomach.

"I'm Officer Merrison." Some sort of black wallet appeared with a metal badge inside. "I'm looking for Mr. Williams. Is he here?"

The boy stared at his feet, shifting his weight from one side to the other. The policeman crouched down, and looked up into the boy's face. "Where's y' Dad, Kyle? You know he's in trouble for violating parole." The boy said nothing. He stopped moving altogether. "When did you see him last?" The boy pulled a face and shrugged.

"Dunno."

"Speak up. I just need to know when you saw him last."

Kyle looked into the officer's eyes. "I'm hungry. You got

anything to eat?"

Officer Merrison squinted at Kyle. "Your Dad's not in, is he?" Kyle shook his head. "He wasn't in all yesterday either, was he?" Kyle sniffed and a tear rolled down his cheek. He quickly wiped it away, embarrassed.

Officer Merrison could not stop himself thinking of his own daughter, Catherine. She was only two years older than Kyle. "Come to the patrol car, son. I've got a pie, and a candy bar, even some fruit if you like. You want some?" Kyle nodded and then started to cry, quietly, with as much dignity as a hungry, lonely boy could muster.

"This is Officer 3-0-2," the policeman said into a radio headset, leaning on the car. "I've got an eleven year old juvenile: Williams, Kyle, and an absconded parolee, Over?" Kyle heard radio hiss, and then a voice that sounded like it had been boiled and canned said something he could not make out. The policeman responded with jargon and code that Kyle could not much understand either.

Kyle's stomach rumbled. "I'm hungry."

Still speaking into his microphone, the officer leant in the window and pulled out his lunch. Kyle devoured the pie, the chocolate and was half way through a banana when he started paying attention again to what Officer Merrison was saying.

"Transport directly to the Facility for the processing? Roger that." A moment of hiss and garbled words, then Officer Merrison spoke again. "A key worker will be there to evaluate needs, confirm our assessment and countersign? Good. Can you clear the rest at your end? Over."

Transport directly to the Facility? Kyle's heart began to beat. He'd lived in the Facility before. The staff weren't unkind, but the other children beat him, and it had taken months for his Dad to reappear and claim him.

The third crow landed on the patrol car's roof lights.

As the policeman talked he swatted at the crow. He cried out in pain, wringing his hand. "It's all right base; I just got the most almighty static jolt off the car. Over?" Somehow, the laughter came back over the radio loud and clear. The crow stared at Kyle, made an ear-splitting cry and flapped over to a nearby bin, before Officer Merrison was able to deploy his nightstick. The crow kept calling, rummaging in the trash and glancing over at the patrol car.

Kyle's panic spiralled upward. Dad was gone. How long would it be this time? How would Dad find him? He became hot and flushed and his insides knotted. Kyle was going to be miserable and afraid all the time; he knew it. He could see the days stretching into weeks. Kyle pictured being at the Facility, the large boys, the violence. It felt as though he were already trying to twist out of the reach of their fists. He could see himself lying beaten, bruised, bleeding, even dead, while the big boys and the staff laughed. He thought about the first night and the things they would make him do. He really began to scare himself, and decided to stop the flood of images for a moment, his mouth parched with panic.

The crow had stopped rummaging, and focussed on Kyle. It was at that moment that Kyle realised that Dad had run. Kyle could run too. He was good at it; he could hide for hours at school and never be found, not even by the caretaker.

The police officer was still finishing his conversation.

The crow mumbled and then cawed softly. Kyle looked up at the crow and met its eye.

"Kyle, you're going to come with me. We'll find somewhere comfortable for you tonight," Officer Merrison said.

A simple plan dropped into Kyle's head as he stared at the ragged bird, a simple plan that left him cold and numb, but clear-headed. Now, for the first time in days, he knew what to do.

"I'll just get my coat and stuff from inside the house, okay?" Kyle spoke softly and carefully, in as natural voice as he could manage.

The policeman gave him a sideways glance and paused for a second, trying to weigh him up. Officer Merrison narrowed his eyes, but nodded.

"Okay, quickly then, and just your coat, son, just your coat. Don't try any tricks; I'll know if you're hiding something." The policeman smiled in a friendly way and Kyle walked past the crow and into the house.

Jill was feeling more positive as she walked to school.

After she had wiped Mum's tear stained face they had had the best conversation she could remember, while they both got ready for the day. Mum had told her some of the details of the treatment she was going to have in hospital, and that she shouldn't worry, even though they both knew that Jill was too much like her Mum not to fret.

"Come here, lovely girl," Mum had said. Jill did and was enveloped in a hug. For a moment, Jill thought her Mum was crying again, but when she let go, Mum lifted her chin and her eyes were full of warmth, not tears. "Never look down, always look up. Go on, smile, I love to see you smile." Jill strained to produce a grin. "Have a good day at school. You can do that for me, can't you?"

Jill left wrapped in her mother's words; they hedged her in, hiding her somewhere safe. The crow followed from house to tree to bush. It was cawing and ducking all the time as it cast about, as if watching for an opening.

She was nearly at the school gates when the light caught the corner of her eye. It flashed in the ditch by the side of the road, like a diamond in a spotlight. She stepped down off the road, but even as she reached it, the light faded. Jill bent down. Where the light had been was a small chunk of yellow sandstone. Jill picked it up and examined it. It was a small rock, flat on one side with most of a carved 'a' engraved on its surface. Jill stroked it, cleaning off the dirt, and stared at it as she turned it over in her hands.

"Just like the Road," she said, "I suppose it must've been wet to glisten like that."

The crow screamed and flew quickly back to Kyle Williams' house.

Smoke was billowing from Kyle's house and Officer Merrison was entering the building looking for the boy. The crow could see

Kyle running into the small wood behind the house, and it slowed to a lazy flap. It swooped down to join his companion on the roof of the patrol car. They listened for a moment to the worried shouts of the policeman and then, flew off, squabbling. Kyle's crow headed to the school, but the crow that had been following Jill now turned toward the east and the large white-washed shed. It returned with the third crow and found Kyle's bird stationed outside the school, unwilling to enter. The three grey faced birds sat staring at the gates.

Black wrought iron, topped with gold tipped spikes, stood heavily, barring the way, but it was the gate-posts that held the birds' attention. The brick pillars were edged with sandstone blocks and on their surface were the carved weathered remains of ancient words and letters. These blocks had clearly been taken from some older construction, reshaped and used in building parts of the school. The crows eyed the gates cautiously, but Jill's crow lifted into the air, and hovering and pecking, drove the other two in through the side gate.

Jill had an extraordinary day. She swung from highs of hope to low despair, and grew increasingly agitated by the racket of three squabbling crows outside. She tried to hang on to her mother's words. It seemed everywhere she went there was the noise of argument and discontent; yet, there were also the stones. Sparkles and splinters of light caught her eye all the time, even inside the building, and she wondered why she'd never seen them before. Jill ended up finding four more fragments of rock, and at lunch sat on a low wall in the playground arranging their letters to see if she could spell something.

"What you got there?" came a familiar voice.

Catherine Merrison, Cathy to everyone who knew her, was one of Jill's best friends, and Jill was pleased to see her, though she showed it by looking only a little less sour than before.

"Nothing really, just some old stones I found."

"Yeah? Let's have a look." Cathy sat next to her and looked over her shoulder. "A-G-A-P-E. 'A gape.' What's that about? Is that the best you can do?" She leaned over and rearranged the stones to read, 'A page.' Jill swept the stones up and put them back in her pocket, stared out into space and said nothing. "Where'd you get them? Off that moor road you love?" Jill looked the other way, still refusing to speak. "I don't know why you spend all your time hiking on the Moor, especially when yer Mum gets so annoyed about it." Cathy looked at her and tried to lean forward and catch her eye. "Okay, get all silent then, it doesn't matter to me." Cathy stared down, and then squinted sideways at her friend. "How's yer Mum anyway?"

"Okay, I s'ppose," said Jill, her arms folded.

"She still goin' away tomorrow?"

Jill nodded, and started to sniff and cough a little. Catherine handed her a Kleenex and tried to catch her gaze. "You should take some time off, it's nearly the end of term, no-one would mind." Jill started to smile, controlling her face with an effort.

A crow landed in front of them, and screeched at Cathy. Without thinking, Jill threw one of the lettered stones at it. She threw it as hard as she could and caught the bird square in its chest. It shot backward, propelled half way across the playground, tumbling as it went. It seemed to be coughing as it gathered itself up in a crumpled heap of feathers and then it retreated.

"Why did you do that?" Cathy was staring at Jill as she retrieved the stone from where it fell.

"Don't know," she said and shrugged her shoulders, "something about it just really annoyed me, I guess."

The bell rang, lunch finished and it was not until Jill was walking home again that she could properly examine the stones. She strolled, lonely and thoughtful, examining one of the strange objects in her hand.

Without warning, a crow dived on her and pecked at her head.

"Ow! Get off!" Jill dropped her bag, and looking up, spotted the bird as it banked and turned back towards her. "You asked for this," she muttered and with more feeling than she realised, she threw the stone again. It seemed to her that the stone swerved slightly in the air, but however it happened, the stone struck the crow hard. There was a momentary rustle of leaves in the bush underneath the bird, a cloud of feathers and the crow was no longer there. Jill frowned. *Where did it go?* She watched the bush, listening for movements, but she decided that it must have limped off, or be hiding quietly. Jill felt much better and although she tried to feel guilty for attacking wildlife, she found herself grinning. "It was a stupid bird. It shouldn't have pecked me," she said out loud. To her surprise, the stone had somehow turned up on the tarmac of the road. As she reached for it, it faded from bright gold to yellow. She frowned again, and turned the stone over in her hand. What was going on? "Maybe you're not going to lose these stones, only your marbles girl," Jill said to herself, then smiled at her own joke. "It's got to be getting bad when you only want to talk to yourself."

Jill decided to go home, but found her feet heading up the slope toward the Moor and the knuckle of bare rock where she liked to sit and think. There was no point having another row before tomorrow. She'd sit, think, and work it all out before she saw Mum.

2

Nowhere and the Road

From up at the outcrop, the Village seemed almost perfect.

"I don't know why we came in the first place," muttered Jill, "It only seems perfect from up here."

Looking down from her favourite spot, the houses looked neat, the atmosphere was relaxed and the people friendly. People looked as if they cared about each other; certainly, everyone knew everyone else's business. Jill didn't really mind people knowing about her Mum's sickness, or that Dad had disappeared years ago. The extra slack she got for homework; the blind eye people turned to her explorations on the Moor—these were fine, but they did not fix anything. Mum was still sick. Dad was still gone.

What really bothered Jill was this—in spite of all the care, it was still only *almost* perfect.

Jill's eye traced out the path of the old moorland Road as it descended from high behind the Village, wound its way through the houses, and then dipped out of sight. Below lay the Town, constantly busy with hurrying people, and behind, the modern highway curved toward the easterly haze and the City's smokestacks. Beyond that was the Capital at the Coast, which was even bigger than the City. She knew all this because, not only did she half listen in the geography class, but she had also been to the Capital twice: once when very small when her parents had been together; and again, more recently, when Mum had become sick.

The Capital was where her Dad had got his job and where her Mum started becoming really unhappy. Dad might have been happy or sad, but since she had never got to know him, she had not been able to tell. Jill could not even remember his face and she was not sure she wanted to; even though it was his money that made sure they were comfortable. Jill hugged her knees tighter, as she remembered leaving the dirt and the noise behind to come to the peace of the Village. Things had looked like they were going to be a lot better here, just her and Mum, but then they had visited the Capital again and she had been told that Mum was sick.

As she thought about it, Jill realised that it wasn't just her family that had problems; it was everyone, every house she could see. 'Dealing with issues' was what the teachers would say.

"All those smart people, and no answers," she muttered, "no *real* answers anyway." She felt completely miserable. The wind caressed her ear, a cold comfort. Jill wiped away a tear and found that the wind was picking up. The smell of coconut from the gorse bushes was intense as she sat looking over the Republic of Nowhere, the land of her birth and the extent of her expectations.

There was one particular puzzle that her mind would drift back to in situations like this: the Road.

Up from the town, a black-topped road tarred the spur of the Moor that the Village stood on, picking out the ridge of the hill. It laboured its way up into the Village, just like any country road around here. This was how it should be. However, on the other side of the Village, the Road emerged and climbed the hill as a speckled yellow ribbon that draped itself across the face of the escarpment. Jill stared at the Road. *It's pretty against the hillside,* she thought.

The Road may have fitted into the landscape as it ran up onto the Moor, but in almost every other way it was quite wrong. Jill had examined its every detail on her occasional 'days off' from school when she explored the Moor. She always managed to get permission for these expeditions afterwards; no one at school liked to use the words 'playing truant', so they had turned her hiking into a Geography project. The Road above the Village was made from compacted sandstone pebbles, sand and dirt, and was raised up with a grassed hollow on either side. No one seemed to know where it went or who had made it. Instead of the usual ditches or drains, manhole covers and stagnant water, the Road was clean. She could not think of describing it any other way.

Walking up to the Moor Jill would have the chatter of a beautifully clear stream on her left, while the ditch on the right side was warm and dry, and oddly, free of both weeds and wind. This was where her thoughts always began to race.

That it was warm was not surprising, as it faced south-east downhill and caught whatever heat the sun could give. That it was dry, always puzzled Jill. *The ditch should be permanently damp; it takes away all the rain and run off.* The ditch was broad and wide and, although the Road was raised above the surrounding land, the air in the ditch felt too still, as if the atmosphere was holding its breath. This was what Jill had told herself anyway, when she was lying comfortable, crooked in the dry hollow, watching summer clouds scud off the westerly Moor.

But even more puzzling to Jill was this; no weeds had choked the ditch. *Why hasn't gorse and heather worked up the bank long ago, just like other disused tracks? Who keeps it so neat?* There were never any workmen on the Road. She never saw anyone travel it and no one ever mentioned it in particular. Nobody in the Village denied its existence; they just appeared to look past it when pointing up to the Moor. *Why is it here?* Jill thought. *It should have disappeared years ago.* It was this highland moor-road that was *the* Road, not the bitumen strip down to the town. Jill stared at it wondering where it went and, turning the puzzle over in her mind, rose to go home.

She raced back and found that the Town doctor was visiting her Mum. Jill liked the doctor, and he gave the impression that he liked them. He was sitting in the old winged armchair drinking tea, refusing biscuits and insisting that he could sit for only five minutes and he could do that only because they were last on his list. He would leave in twenty minutes' time as he always did. Jill knew what to expect.

Every time he visited, he was kind, clever and trustworthy and knew just what to do. Mum would then become worse. The pills would do their job, but something unexpected would have happened to stop her body getting better. All that knowledge never seemed to be able quite to sort out the problem. Jill felt sorry for the doctor sometimes. He gave the impression of carrying people's problems in his bag, just next to the anti-depressants, or whatever those blue pills were that Mrs. Varney took. The bag appeared extra heavy as he left. Jill hugged Mum as the doctor's car drew away and kept holding her till the sound of the engine and the memory of that bag had faded.

"What's the matter, dear?"

"Nothing, Mum."

This felt like the old days, for a moment. Mum was sitting on the sofa and Jill on the floor and Jill buried her face in her Mum's fashionable jumper. Jill smiled at the idea of 'fashionable knitwear' and sighed.

"You are a funny one!" said Mum, and ruffled her hair. As she smiled the dark rings under her eyes diminished. "What are you thinking about?"

"The Road."

"Have you been up there today Jill?" said her Mum, sounding strained.

"No, but I was looking at it from the outcrop and thinking how odd it was. Where does it go, Mum?"

"For the last time, I have no idea, and I don't want to know either, there are more important things in life."

The sharp tone hurt Jill. She didn't want to argue; it wasn't supposed to work like this. *We're just a bit tired*, Jill told herself, *like this morning*. Mum stood up as Jill lifted her head and breathed an apology. By the time Mum had reached the kitchen sink, Jill saw the silhouette of her shoulders sag. Jill sat still, waiting, hoping that they wouldn't have another row.

"It's all right darling, I'm sorry, but I really don't know why you persist with your clambering around up there. That Road is odd; I wish you'd stay away from it, especially while I'm away."

Jill's heart started to pound, "Why's that Mum? What's wrong with it?"

Her mother paused, uncertain what to say. She frowned, then turned, and leaning against the sink looked straight into her daughter's eyes. "I watched the workmen last year, when they repaired the pot holes in the Village, and tried to extend the bitumen over the first sandy part of the Road. You know, just as it leaves the houses by the Beck's place, a few yards from Mrs. Varney's." She paused.

"Go on." Jill had not heard this tone in her Mum's voice before; she was quiet, confidential, as she toyed with the dish-cloth.

"Well, they tried to dig out the stones and mud, and then shovel it all away. They worked all morning. At first, you couldn't notice anything odd. But . . ."

"But what?" Jill tried not to let her impatience show, but her voice was beginning to thin out, letting it through.

"Well, it was the oddest thing, I wouldn't have believed it if I hadn't seen it myself from Mrs. Varney's front room window . . ."

Jill cut in, "Seen what?"

"I'm getting to that, don't be funny with me." Jill's Mum hesitated again, finding her words, "It was as if the hole the workman dug never got any bigger, and neither did the heap of stones they dug out. After their tea break there was some loud swearing because the hole and stone pile had got smaller. 'Turned the air blue they did,' as Mrs. Varney said." It was one of their friend's catch phrases. Both mother and daughter smiled.

"No one had seen how it happened. They spent some time searching around, looking for kids. The same happened over lunch, and Mrs. Varney said it happened overnight, just as if it was water and not rock that had flowed back into the hole. They tried that next day too."

"The stones must have been rolling back in, right Mum?" Jill was leaning forward, her whole attention riveted.

"No, I watched closely and there were no stones rolling around. They would have had to roll uphill anyway."

"So what happened?"

"Well, they came back that next morning, saw the hole almost filled in and scratched their heads. They left someone to guard it, went away, and two men in suits and hard-hats arrived that afternoon to look at where the hole had been. They talked to the worker who had been left behind and then they left as well. A tarring crew arrived the day after. They only lasted a few hours. A large crowd of Granddads and Mums had gathered to see what might happen. The tar didn't stick. It sort of rolled off, crumbling as it went."

"What pushed it off then?"

"No one saw. You just turned around and it had moved. They got really mad and then sold the load they hadn't used for driveways. They haven't been back since."

"You're having me on, Mum."

"Now you're asking for trouble, young girl." She paused and looked out of the window again. "Some people talked about government experiments and aliens. One or two about the drains, but most of the people who saw it didn't want to talk about it at all. Even Mrs. Varney went off the subject."

"How come I never heard?" Jill was a little indignant.

"Look, if you don't believe me, ask Mr. Jones—he'll be able to tell you more. He's the only one I've ever heard talk about the Road" Jill immediately stood up. "And if you go, grab my shopping list for Martha's Store on your way out." Jill's Mum tried to talk to her, but Jill had gone. "So tell me where you're going . . ." Her voice trailed off as she heard her daughter move swiftly through the house, ". . . and remember to come back and talk to me later." A smile quickened on her lips. "Oh, she'll be all right," she muttered, turning back to wash dishes.

Jill did not stop, either to ask or answer questions. "Okay

Mum!" she shouted as she grabbed a coat and the list from the hall table and headed out the door and into the still bright summer evening.

Mr. Jones was a local man, retired, and had an immaculate garden on the corner of one of the few side streets in town. Jill turned left out of her lane, along past the five new 'affordable' homes with their stray cats, skipped past "Martha's Convenience Store"; past the Post Office, and right, up the second side street. The Hangman's Arms was there, and as usual, she idly wondered what was so special about his arms. However, pubs did not interest her yet, so she had never bothered to get to the bottom of that puzzle.

Mr. Jones was in his garden, weeding as usual. He looked up as Jill pushed the gate open.

"Hello dear, can I help you?"

She sat down on the earth bank as he looked up from his kneeling pad. "You got something on your mind? Your Mum know you're here?"

Jill nodded.

"Well, come on in and I'll make a cup of tea," he looked about at the slowly dimming light. "It's about time I stopped. How's your Mum doing?"

Jill shrugged. "Okay. She's going to the Capital for treatment tomorrow. She'll be fine." Jill found that as she said this, she did not believe it, and her stomach turned over as she ducked in the kitchen door.

"And how are you?" Mr. Jones enquired. Jill tried to stretch out a smile on her lips and stood taut and uneasy. Mr. Jones brushed mud off his hands, put a kettle on, and got the cookie jar out. "Fancy a biscuit?"

Jill took one, although she often pretended to be too old for them in front of her Mum. Mr. Jones made the tea, and motioned toward the lounge, where they both sat down.

"So, what is it young lady? What can I do for you? Your Mum need some help?"

Jill hesitated, then rushed out her words. "Well, Mum says that you know about the Road."

"The 'Road'? Which road might that be?"

"What other Road is there? C'm'on Mr. Jones, please." Jill pleaded, and looked a lot younger than her years as she said this. Jill was aware that she probably did, but did not care. "Please!" She tried using her most winning smile, which was a mistake, as it now looked childish.

Mr. Jones appeared slightly surprised, "What year of high school you in? You've been there two years now, haven't yuh?" Even though he raised his eyebrows, he sipped his tea and decided to play along. With an amused smile, he settled back into his chair. "Well, you've come to the right man for that anyway, if nothing else." He sighed, sipped some more and then looking over his mug, fixed his audience with piercing eyes. "The legend is not often spoken of now, but it runs something like this," and Mr. Jones commenced to tell his tale.

"The Road, in its present state, has apparently been there for as long as anyone can remember, but from what I've found out, it's not always been like it is now. There have been times when pilgrims and traders have crowded the Road, and it's been fought for on many occasions. In fact, its history has almost as many twists and turns as the route it takes. The history books in the Town contain maps of the Road from over the years; I've spent many hours with dusty documents and magnifying glasses, trying to find out where it came from, who built it and why."

That this old gardener should have done this surprised Jill, but as she thought about it, she was not sure why that was. *I suppose,* she thought, *that old men could be interested in more things than gardens and beer.* She dismissed the idea as stupid; it made her feel uneasy, almost as if old men were normal, like her friends. Mr. Jones coughed and Jill remembered to listen.

"As I was saying, it is a legend that goes back in time long before the Republic of Nowhere ever came to be. The king who reigned at that time had become very concerned with exploration, and became rich from trade. He invited many powerful princes and ambassadors to visit the Capital, there was always some trade delegation or state visit. They wrote songs about him you know; for years afterwards he was a hero. Anyway," the old man waved his hand, as if to shoo away distractions, "this went on for many years until one of the furthest flung of the trading posts sent word of strange tales, told them by merchants from lands even further afar. There was, they said, a country completely unlike any other; a wonderful land full of wealth, power and wisdom. It was ruled by a mysterious prince who was known as the "Lord of the Way". Mysterious because he wore the plainest clothes that any poor traveller or pilgrim could have. Everyone wanted to know him, but he would disappear at the most inconvenient times. He was always exploring they said." Jill was leaning so far forward that she slipped off her seat. She blushed, sat up again and decided to finish eating her biscuit. The chocolate chips were melting.

Mr. Jones coughed and continued.

"Would you like a cough sweet?" said Jill hopefully, remembering the sticky packet in her coat.

"No my dear, thank you. Where was I? Oh yes, the prince. Well, the king was filled with curiosity about how he might meet this 'Lord of the Way.' It was clear to him that they had common interests, but no one, it seemed, knew how to find this prince. The king never visited other rulers but the great King of Nowhere decided to find this 'Lord of the Way' himself. A great fuss was made in Nowhere and the king took a great feast on board a fleet of twelve ships, to show how great Nowhere was." Jill's mouth was open mid chew. Mr. Jones paused, "I haven't lost you have I? Most people have glazed over by this point." Jill remembered to close her mouth, and gave a gentle grin. "I'm not boring you? You want to continue?" Jill shook her head, then nodded, then giggled. *Was this what it was like to have a granddad?*

"Okay, I suppose you asked for it." He put down his mug and leant forward. "The voyage contained many adventures and when they reached their destination, they found it beyond all they had imagined. Some of the stories tell of buildings built from gemstones, with amazing powers. The gifts they had brought to impress the prince seemed quite ordinary in this land; nevertheless, in front of the Palace of the 'Lord of the Way' the king set out the great banquet in silk pavilions and invited the Prince to come."

"In the middle of the festivities, the king presented his gifts, and to his relief, the 'Lord of the Way' was overjoyed at his generosity. The now humbled king pleaded with the prince to visit the Capital and to advise and help him." Mr. Jones' voice dropped to a gentle low murmur. "The Prince simply said, 'I will do more than that. I will make a Way for you and any of your Kingdom to come to me whenever you wish.' Then, right in the middle of the feast, he vanished." Mr Jones waved both hands outwards, with his palms open, like a magician who had made a coin disappear. Then he sat back.

"So what happened then? Where did the Prince go?" Jill asked.

Mr. Jones shrugged. "No one knew. After a further two weeks, the feast came to an end and the king returned to Nowhere, crestfallen because he had not seen the Prince since the promise had been made."

Mr. Jones paused and swallowed the last of his tea. "Still want to hear the rest?" Jill nodded. "You've got something stuck to your cheek," he said. Jill found a small lump of chocolate on her face and now turned bright red. Mr. Jones was clearly enjoying himself, and he fetched a damp cloth. They settled back into their story.

"Two years later, strange news came from the northern borders of Nowhere. A large army was slowly advancing from the far northern wastes. The king arrived within days and camped with Nowhere's army, roughly where the Village later came to be, just out of the winter's blast beneath the high ridge. The force on the horizon advanced slowly. Day to day, the banners and flashing steel appeared closer and eventually, as spring broke in on the Moor, the king's patience also broke. He would ride out to meet this strange new opponent, and see if peace was possible."

"As he readied to advance his cavalry, he was greeted at the entrance of his tent by a familiar face. It was the 'Lord of the Way', his friend, who greeted him with much joy, and before the king could recover his surprise, invited him to inspect the new road he was building. So the party rode out and met a royal procession they had never seen the like of before: road diggers in velvet;

labourers in royal furs; masons and engineers with golden measuring rods and the most amazing scribes recording their progress."

"Well, the king was delighted and appointed his own body of men to guard the workmen, as the prince would not let anyone from Nowhere work on the Road. It was to be a gift he said. There was a great feast when the Road reached the Capital, "To finish off unfinished business," the king had said. He then asked what he might do for this travelling Prince, and the 'Lord of the Way' had replied that the King might keep the Road clear and guarded throughout all his Kingdom of Nowhere. He was to repair it up to the point where the king had camped on the edge of the high northern Moor. After that, the 'Lord of the Way' promised to take the Road permanently under his protection, for although the prince's lands lay far across the sea, he promised that if whoever would take his Road, would 'find him or be found'. The king said he was honoured and agreed."

Mr. Jones stopped, staring at his new friend. "Well, that's the story, the Road was built."

"Is that it? What happened next?"

The old gardener frowned. "Well, all sorts of strange stories were recounted over the years about the king's adventures, many of which bear the marks of exaggeration."

"So you think that some of the story is true?" Jill's eyes were bright with the question.

"Well, the Road is a very peculiar thing, and no-one has an explanation for its strange properties."

"You mean the fact that it can't be dug up?"

Mr. Jones smiled and leaned forward again. The chair creaked. "So you heard about that did you? Most people gave me the impression that they were embarrassed to talk about it, but I must admit that it simply sharpened my interest. That's why I investigated some of the records in the Capital."

Mr. Jones leant even further forward, and whispered. "I believe that a fortified gate was built over the Road by that ancient king, right where the Road left his territory, and he probably built a small castle to protect the approaches to the gate itself, just as he promised the travelling Prince."

Jill looked blank, not understanding what Mr. Jones was driving at. "What does that have to do with not being able to dig up the Village road?" she asked.

"Well, there are the stones." He stopped and stared at her, a quizzical smile playing at the corner of his mouth as he sat back again.

"Mr. Jones! *Please,* tell me."

The smile remained and the old story-teller continued. "The stones that are built into the school and that almost certainly came from those old ruins near here. Some archaeological digging was done at the ruins in my Grandfather's day; the story goes that they found stones that would get up and walk at night. They'd find them on the Moor-road next morning."

"What did they look like, these stones?" Jill said, turning her stones over in her pocket.

"Small. Usually they had letters carved on them, fragments of inscriptions, as if someone had broken them up."

Jill held out her hand. "Like these?"

Mr. Jones froze and stared at the pebbles in Jill's hand. "Yes, just like those. Where'd you get them?"

Jill recounted her day and Mr Jones listened intently. "What do you think these stones are?" Jill asked as she finished her story.

"Part of an enchanted castle," Mr. Jones said and winked. Jill rolled her eyes. "Well young lady, they found that the ruins were what was left of a very ancient castle, almost as old as the oldest part of the Capital Tower. You know the Capital Tower?"

Jill shook her head, because although she knew a little about it, she felt wonderful listening and wanted the story to continue.

"The Capital Tower was the ancient kings' fort, down at the Coast. That would make the ruins here older than the Town's written records and about the right time for the travelling Prince, if he came."

Mr. Jones' caught her gaze and grinned at her. "Well, I found that the oldest records for the Village related to a market for ponies and sheep farmed on the high Moor. There was an ancient charter for the market that talked about 'The Keeper of the Gate'. The gatekeeper was to announce the market days, settle disputes, dispense the King's Justice and that sort of thing. I also found that the oldest house deeds identify properties as so many yards from the 'Field of the Gate' or, later, the 'Market Square'. "

Jill interrupted, "So the Village was built next to the ancient king's castle."

"Yes," said Mr. Jones, "I think that the Village grew up around the old fortified gate: this Village is the gateway. The gate must have fallen down and been built over, but it would have been where the Road officially passed out of Nowhere." He paused dramatically and then continued in low tones. "Where it turned away from the Capital; the City and the Town, left all civilisation behind and headed into the wilds and the Prince's protection . . ."

"And that's why it can't be dug up from the edge of the Village onwards!" Jill exclaimed excitedly. "He's still protecting it! That's why it's so perfect, and no-one ever needs to fix it, he fixes it . . ." Jill had jumped up, kicked her second glass of cordial over, and stumbled sideways.

"Now don't get over-excited. Where's that cloth?"

Mr. Jones wandered out and left Jill wide-eyed and thinking. Ideas, possibilities surged through her head. *If the Lord of the Way could repair the Road for thousands of years, what else could he do?*

The old gardener came back in. The mood for stories having lifted, he mopped up the spill and met Jill's stare, squarely in the eyes. "Do you want those stones?" Jill quickly pocketed the carved pebbles. "I see you do. Perhaps your stones will walk, or perhaps they like you!" The old man winked "I don't need them, but I see I've stirred your interest. It's a fine tale isn't it?"

Jill looked surprised. "You think it's more than that, don't you?"

"Well, that would be telling now, wouldn't it? Don't you go spreading wild rumours about me filling your head with old fools' tales. I'd be in trouble with your Mum and others who aren't so . . ." he searched for the words for several seconds, ". . . so friendly to the Road as you are."

Jill glanced at the clock, said thank you very much for his time, smiled bashfully, and said she had to get her Mum's shopping and that she would like to come back soon. Mr. Jones said that it was a pleasure to make a better acquaintance of such a polite young girl, and the two new friends parted company as the early evening lights in the Village started to come on.

Jill stepped out into the street fingering her Mum's shopping list, nervous and excited. She looked up the hill to the Road again, to where the crows would circle over the ridge and the wilds began, and started planning.

3

REAL LIFE

Jill bought the shopping and then, as she did on every Thursday, dropped in on one of her friends. Catherine Merrison lived down the road from the shop, at the other end of the Village towards the Road. Jill was a regular guest at her house, and so when she burst in from the porch, Mrs. Merrison sang out up the stairs, "Cathy!"

"Mrs. Merrison, you know I'm going to stay at Mrs. Varney's most of the time Mum is in hospital over this Summer. Can I stay here for a few days with Cathy when Mum's away?"

"What for?" A smile creased the corners of Mrs. Merrison's mouth.

"Me and Cathy could plan our route for the 'Tour of the Moor', you know, the hiking competition."

Mrs. Merrison cast a glance over her shoulder as Cathy thundered down the stairs.

"Well Cathy, what do you think? After all that you told me about that stone Jill threw around today, do you think we should let such a dangerous *individual* come and stay?" Mrs. Merrison rolled the word 'individual' round her mouth as if she was savouring the taste of honey on her tongue.

Cathy grinned and slid up to her Mum, cuddling her with both arms around her waist. "Oh, you can handle her, can't you Mum?"

"I think so—maybe?" she grinned, her words deliberate and slow. "But only for a short time, let's say a month or so."

"Oh, thanks Mum!" Jill had always thought Cathy was one of life's enthusiasts, and this was what she liked about her, most of the time.

"I'll phone your Mum just now," said Mrs. Merrison and strolled off to the low beamed kitchen. Half a telephone conversation drifted into the hall. After a few seconds, the girls let it float over their heads.

Jill started the conversation. "I'm sorry about today; I was in a real mood. Mum and I have been arguing."

Cathy glanced to one side and then at her fingers. "It doesn't matter," she sniffed. "When is she coming back? Do you know?"

Jill shook her head.

"It'll work out. Things *will* work out. It'll be fun you being here." Cathy almost bounced. "When can you come over?" she asked.

Jill frowned, "I'll settle in at Mrs. Varney's. I could come over after the weekend for a day or two. I think Mrs. Varney is looking forward to seeing me." Jill rolled her eyes. "She's been talking about it and I don't think I could get away before then." Jill was not sure this was exactly what Mrs. Varney thought and felt distinctly uncomfortable saying so.

Cathy smiled, "That'll be great. School's breaking up on Tuesday for the Summer Vacation, so we'll have plenty of time. What do you want to do? Hey, listen, I've got a new CD. I'll put it on—want a coke?"

Jill knew that life around Cathy would be loud and fun.

"Okay. What is it?"

The two girls disappeared upstairs, and spent time talking, although the conversation was a little one-sided. Jill soon knew all about Cathy's music, gossip and the fire at the Williams' house. "And you know," Cathy continued, "my dad was saying that his dad ran off and left him for two days!"

"At least he's had a dad. Is his mum going to die as well?" Jill snapped.

"That's not fair, and you know it. His life is nothing like ours."

"Not like yours, you mean—things are pretty cool for you." Jill stopped and looked at her shoes. "Look, I'm tired, I'd better get going."

"Sure." Cathy searched Jill's face, "I didn't mean to upset you. You okay? Maybe you should talk about it."

"Yeah, if I could get a word in edgeways." Cathy had not meant to sound quite so like an adult, so she stayed silent, and after a few seconds, Jill softened. "Look, I'll see you after the weekend." She faked a grin. "You can hit me then if you like."

Jill walked back up the little lane from the Merrison's house and turned up the Road toward the Moor, needing to make one more visit before she went home.

She slipped quietly up to Mrs. Varney's door in the twilight and knocked. The door swung open and a worn, kind face appeared in the bright wedge of light. Mrs. Varney was kind, gentle and always wanting to feed people. Jill considered her a wonderfully professional grandma.

"Step inside little one," Mrs. Varney said, "Do you want some candy?"

Even professionals can overdo it, thought Jill, not unkindly. She stepped in upon worn carpet, into a narrow hall with an ornament shelf containing some of the most highly polished objects in Nowhere. "Now, what does my little pumpkin want?"

Jill gritted her teeth. Mrs. Varney had been a family friend for years and, although Jill's Mum took deep comfort in her companionship, Jill always ended up wanting to be somewhere else whenever Mrs. Varney turned up, professional Grandma or not. At this moment, that desire had almost become a need.

"Mrs. Varney, would you mind if I spent a lot of my time at the Merrisons' place? I was hoping I might go there tomorrow for a few days." Jill studied Mrs. Varney's face and, much to her surprise, found relief.

"No dear, stay as long as you like. Just let me know when Mrs. Merrison has had enough," she smiled. "Is that all?"

Jill nodded in dumb shock. Mrs. Varney didn't want Jill to come around. Mum would not be so happy with the arrangements if she knew Mrs. Varney was so relaxed about where Jill would be. However, a grudging admiration for Mrs. Varney slipped in.

Fancy her being quite so sly, letting Mrs. Merrison take up the slack, Jill thought. It suddenly struck her that Mrs. Varney might not always enjoy her company, just as Jill found Mrs. Varney hard going. This was a novel thought, but before she could fully take it in, Jill was saying her 'thank-you's and 'goodbye's and 'see-you-soon's and then kisses and hugs and goodness knows what else. Jill found this all unbearable and quickly slipped away.

The alarm screeched. Jill was jerked out of her sleep. She lay there the next morning in a drowsy haze; refreshed, content, and unconnected to the rest of the world. Warm feelings rose within her as she remembered the Road and the story Mr. Jones had been telling her. She remembered that that story was very important but she could not recall why. A thought pushed in that she had to pack and quickly too. Jill was aware that there was a terrible reason behind this last idea and did not want to bring it to mind. She lay still, hoping that she could remain happy.

Jill heard her mother packing and then remembered; Mum was going today. Mum was ill and probably would die. Unhappiness poured over her; grey heaviness like winter skies and twice as cold swept over her imagination and settled bitterly in her guts.

Jill rose and dressed, but her arms and legs were leaden and she hung her head as she ate breakfast, staring at the plate. Somehow, the waffles, peppered bacon and syrup did not taste like they normally did.

"Why have you got your boots out, dear?" Mum was looking at the walking boots next to Jill's unusually full bags. Jill remembered the story that had seemed so important the night before. She looked up at her Mum, needing an explanation, and one came.

"Project I'm working on Mum. I've got to take all my camping things to school, to draw and stuff." Jill was not lying. They had to bring in objects representing their favourite hobby for an end of year art class. When Jill wanted to escape from people and the Village, she headed for the Moor. Jill wrapped her arms around Mum's shoulders, started sobbing and clung on. "Don't go . . ."

Her Mum held her, rocked, and patted her gently.

"I'll be back soon, don't worry. Look," she held her at arm's length and fixed her gaze intently on Jill's red-ringed eyes. "I will be at the best hospital the Capital has. It'll be all right," but Jill just kept hanging on. "I will be having some difficult treatment; it's not going to be pretty. It's best if you stay here with Mrs. Varney for the moment — and Cathy, of course." Jill's Mum winked. "See you soon, pumpkin." The taxi engine rumbled outside.

Finally, Jill let go.

"Bye, Mum. See you soon. I love you." She watched her Mum get into the taxi.

The taxi drew away and Jill leant against the doorpost and wept. Everything seemed to have come to an end and, after a minute, so did her tears. She visited the bathroom, straightened herself up and went to school. Jill knew that she would not be missed too much if she didn't go. However, she wanted something, anything, to do. Then she remembered that she had something very definite to do.

The school was a small 'Rural Community School' at the Village's edge. It was one of those old-fashioned schools that had started to try out all kinds of new ideas. Children came to the school from several other local communities and the classes were housed in old red brick and slate buildings. Yellow sandstone blocks framed the windows and gable ends, and were covered in the curious writing that marked the stones in her pocket. The classes were small and were of mixed ages. There were private study rooms and, best of all for Jill, each child had a desk in these study rooms and time in each day to use it. Jill enjoyed the freedom, and liked the individual attention teachers often gave her. This was unusual even for the progressive state of Nowhere, and Jill was vaguely aware that this was a much better and friendlier school than her cousins had to endure. She whistled as she walked up the school gates. Such solid, familiar things took her mind off home and her Mum. Jill noticed the stones built into the gate. Somehow the story Mr. Jones had told her now seemed ridiculous, as if someone had told her that one of her friends was really Snow White. Jill felt embarrassed by the heavy bags and walking boots she was carrying, and hoped no one would notice. As it was, she needn't have worried, and she reached her first class without a problem.

The first lesson was history and each child whose individual plan of study required it filed into the class. Mr. Banister came in and the lesson passed quickly as he let them explore the internet about local history. The voice in her headphones droned with all the passion of a bored tennis umpire, but when she delved into a website on the Capital Tower, she suddenly sat up. What had gained her attention were not the images of the strange looking castle, but what the voice was saying about one of its most ancient rulers.

"Jacob was known as the 'Great Explorer' and his reign is associated with the development of many legends and myths surrounding his expeditions. He is supposed to have befriended the rulers of all the great empires and cultures of his day; discovered an overland route through the far north to a mythical easterly kingdom ruled by a 'Lord of the Way'; and established a library of 'living books'. He is also thought to be responsible for turning Nowhere from the worship of the stars and the gods of war to the Cult of the Way. More about these legends and myths can be found in the Anthropology and Mythology section of Munster's Exact Repository . . ."

To find something so similar to Mr. Jones story in a history lesson was a shock. Her mind wheeled through the possibilities. *Could the king Mr. Jones talked about be King Jacob? Could the Road be Jacob's Road? Could 'myths' be real? Who decided what was 'myth' and what was history anyway? How did anyone decide what was real or not?* Mr. Jones clearly believed in some of them, maybe because he had experienced the Road himself. *How did Mr. Jones decide which stories were true, and which not?* Her head throbbed as if it might explode, her chest was tight, and her hands had become sticky and damp, but she did not mind, it distracted her from the knots in her stomach. Jill feared that this was not going to be an easy day.

Calm down and think about it all later, when you're at Cathy's. The knots tightened in her belly; would she go to Cathy's? "No, think about it later," said Jill to herself in her firmest voice.

"Jill?" The voice's sharp tone made her jump. She realised that the teacher was calling for the class to log off and take the next rotation. Jill packed up and headed for the school lab, where Science was the next lesson. She was not looking forward to the class, it was not her favourite. However, today was to be different from the normal boring lesson. It was to become the most unusual lesson of her life.

"Today the theme is going to be the nature of reality." The teacher's smile was crooked. Mr. Gilmour was in an odd mood, but the eighteen students who had settled around the desks and benches of the lab did not notice this. Mr. Gilmour did not normally make much of an impression on them and they anticipated little change today. He was a young teacher and had not tried anything adventurous, but since this was the last science lesson they would have before the summer, he had decided to be experimental.

"What is the nature of reality? What's real and what's not? How can we tell?" His desk lamp lit his face from below making it appear quite odd, and his teeth shone as he spoke.

Jill sat up and listened.

The teacher pulled away a cloth covering a mask. The mask sat on a stand above and behind the lamp on the front of the desk, so that it was lit from below. "Now which way is this mask? Is the nose coming out of the face, or is it going in? Is the face a hollow shape, or does it stand out?" They all stared and blinked. "Who thinks out?" It certainly looked as if it were a normal mask.

The rest of the class began to notice Mr. Gilmour and their eyes fixed on him and the mask. They raised their hands, almost in unison.

"Who thinks in?"

The quiet bespectacled boy at the front raised his hand. "You've seen this before Greg?" asked Mr. Gilmour. The boy nodded.

Mr. Gilmour reached into the mask, where the nose should be. The mask was hollow! It was the inside of a face they were really seeing. A murmur of surprise ran round the group.

"We only ever see faces that are turned out, so that's what we expect to see. Even when we see the inside of a mask, a face turned *in*, we cannot recognise it. Our minds interpret it as a face turned out, so we cannot see it as it really is. Sometimes reality is far different from what we expect." Mr. Gilmour turned off the low lamp on the front of the desk, and the shadows on the mask began to look a little like a folded-in face. "How we choose to illuminate something will change how we see things as well."

The blond, bespectacled boy at the front of the class put up his hand. "But doesn't science help us know what's going on?"

"Yes, Greg, but you do have to be careful. Tell me, what's a hypothesis?" Several hands went up.

Jill's thoughts drifted. What if people were so used to seeing a particular way that they couldn't accept anything else? What if there was something behind these things, that people just looked past? Was this what was happening with the Villagers and the Road?

The teacher's voice floated by. He was pulling out answers from students who normally stared glumly at him.

Suddenly the questions stopped and Mr. Gilmour reached behind his raised lab bench, searching and organising for a few moments.

"Okay." he stood up. "Let's test a few hypotheses on the basis of our normal experience."

The teacher produced a large dark brown jar with fluid in it, produced some metal tongues, and fished something out of the bottle. The something was silvery, dull looking, and Mr. Gilmour dried it off on a paper towel. "What do you think will happen if I start to burn this metal, then throw water on it?"

Greg frowned. "It should go out, sir."

"Hands up first, Greg. Who agrees?"

Most people agreed and the curiosity of the class deepened as they watched Mr. Gilmour set up a thick glass bowl with a flat bottom behind a stiff transparent screen. He put on his lab coat and safety glasses, then placed the little sliver of metal on a small stand in the bowl. From under his desk, he produced a fierce little gas burner, lit it, and heated the metal. It began to burn brightly. He then threw a beaker of water on the metal. The resulting explosion shattered the class' quiet concentration. Several children visibly jumped. Jill was amazed, what would Mr. Gilmour do next?

This was just the effect that the teacher was looking for. "You see, you can't always trust your experience, even in science. Hypotheses that should work on the basis of your ordinary experiences sometimes don't." A buzz of relief ran around the room, but not through Jill.

She put up her hand. "Is medicine a science?"

"Yes, it is and doctors have to be good scientists to enter their profession." Mr. Gilmour was used to Jill asking unusual questions; moreover, he knew about her mother's illness and was nervous of how well Jill was coping. This was because Mr. Gilmour, in his turn, did not cope with crying girls.

Mr. Gilmour tried to direct the class back to another demonstration. "Look at this," he said as he pulled out a large object from under his desk. It was covered with a black cloth and clonked metallically as he placed it on the desk. The noise seemed to quieten the class. Mr. Gilmour had never given them a lesson quite like this, and the fascinated children watched him remove the cloth and reveal something like a TV aerial on top of a large metal box. Next, he lifted a car battery onto his desk, to which two wires were attached. The aerial was that old-fashioned kind that sits on the TV and points two rods up, nearly vertical in the air. Two eager helpers pulled the classroom blinds as Mr. Gilmour prepared his next shocking revelation.

"Right—is everyone sitting? Good, I'll just complete the circuit." With the flourish of a stage magician, the teacher connected the wires to the box. There was a bright flash and a loud crack as a huge spark leapt between the steel rods. Mr. Gilmour was clearly enjoying the lesson and some of the rowdier boys were now very interested. Greg on the other hand had ducked down in his seat, and others, like him, were finding the lesson more stimulating than they liked.

"Now calm down class, no more surprises I promise."

Mr. Gilmour's voice was smooth and confident; his end of term spectacular was going extremely well. "Well, no more new equipment any way. What do you think happened, Greg?"

"Well, the electricity goes into the box; and then it is turned into a large spark at the wires." The bespectacled boy was concentrating hard.

Mr. Gilmour grinned, "Yes, and how do you think that happens?"

The rougher boys persuaded the class, by much hand waving and noise, that the metal box stored up power for a spark. "There's a build up of electricity in the box, and then it jumps out!" said one called Pedro, nearly falling out of his seat in order to get Mr. Gilmour's attention.

"Okay, who agrees?" Mr. Gilmour's delight was unconstrained. "Who would like me to disconnect the power supply, before it happens again?" Several voices murmured their approval, and a vote was taken to decide the matter. It was decided to disconnect.

"I am taking the wires off the battery, NOW!" Again, a bright spark instantly lit the teacher and class. The blinds were raised and most of the children sat blinking and a little stunned. "What a shocking experience," said Mr. Gilmour. The class groaned and Mr. Gilmour spent the next few minutes teasing the answers he wanted from the class, but Jill was not listening, she was thinking.

Mr. Gilmour summed up. "The object that changes the electricity into a spark is a special kind of transformer. The spark didn't come from a build up of power, but from connecting or disconnecting the battery. You could leave the battery connected all day and it would never spark," he continued, "it's the sudden change that triggers the release of power, not a slow build up. Next term we shall start using equipment like this for many of our lessons, but not quite as we have done so today. Sometimes we need to be shocked out of our expectations. The history of science is littered with such surprises and I hope that you have enjoyed our surprises today."

A 'sudden change' Mr. Gilmour said, had 'triggered the release of power'. Jill could see her Mum's sick face, her weakness, and suddenly she felt as powerless as her Mum. Mum needed a sudden change. What was she thinking? "I need a sudden change," she muttered, "but what does that mean?" Thoughts surged upward like butterflies, the questions flapping around her mind. Her hands were sticky again and her throat dry, but she decided to not to cry. She would have to distract herself quickly. She chose one of the fluttering questions and put up her hand. "Sir, I used a history programme today, an interactive one. If I can't always trust what I see or what I think will happen, how can I trust what it tells me? What anyone tells me?"

"Well, I don't know about history, but in science we test it out. We use an experiment, a fair test."

"How can you test history? It's already happened. There's got to be a way of knowing what's true, what actually happened."

Mr. Gilmour struggled to find the right words.

"These things take discipline, honesty. If you ask Mr. Banister, I think he'll tell you that you've got to get to know your source of information. What do they believe? Are they trustworthy? Can you rely on them to get things right?"

Tears started to prick Jill's eyes so she grabbed at another question. "Yes sir, but what about people? Can you test them in experiments?"

Mr. Gilmour disliked being put on the spot, although he thought that he was always clever enough to know what to say. He answered in a measured manner. "People are a little difficult to pin down; too many little things can change that would make the test unfair. Everyone responds differently. The same lesson can go very differently for different classes. You just have to try things out, personally weigh things up."

Jill couldn't stop; she could feel herself losing self-control. "But what if people miss things with someone the first time, and don't get things right . . ." her voice was beginning to rise, "What if things never go right? How can you know what's going to happen? How do you know that the scientists or doctors aren't missing something? What if they get really sick?" Her voice was catching in her throat, but she continued anyway. ". . . and the scientists can't sort out what's happening? What if . . . ?" Her voice trailed off and she turned her face away, which was just as well as she had become very red-eyed. The teacher looked awkwardly around, not knowing what to say.

"Right let's pack up, go on to your study period." The class cleared and Mr. Gilmour moved to Jill's desk. "If you want to, we can talk in the library at lunch when it's busy, plus there's always the school counsellor." He paused. "I'd like you to talk to someone. Is this about your Mum?"

Jill nodded. "It's all right sir." She ran for the door, found a quiet corner, and wept for the second time that day. Every time she closed her eyes she could see her Mum's face, every time she raged at the idea that she would never see her again. Once the crying subsided, she talked to herself. "You either give up girl and die, and let her die, or you fight. Maybe Mr. Gilmour's right for once, maybe things aren't the way they look. There's got to be a way out of this."

She was definitely going to do something, but what? Without thinking, she turned the stones over in her pocket and bit her lip. She smiled. All her thoughts settled; the last part of her plan fitted into place. Relying on what other people said was not going to be good enough; she was going to put reality to the test herself.

4

The Plan

Jill used the rest of their free study period to straighten out her locker. She did not want to see anyone for a while. The lockers were in a side corridor, away from the classrooms and private study areas. She looked around a little nervously. The one thing worse than being in school when you did not want to be, was being sent home when you wanted to stay. Right now, after her outburst in science she feared Mr. Gilmour's pity might get her sent home early. That was not a possibility Jill relished, not today, not now; she needed one more opportunity.

The next lesson was uneventful and lunchtime arrived quietly. Jill was with her usual friends, but had other things to do, things to do with food. The cheapest and best food could be obtained from the kitchens just before the weekend. On Fridays, the dinner ladies were allowed to get rid of anything that would have to be thrown out by Monday. The money went into an unofficial 'Friends of the School' fund, which the Principal thought was a great idea. Jill walked up to the counter, and asked for Mabel. "Mum would like anything, especially if it will keep."

"Why's that dear?" Mabel was cheerfully inquisitive, in an

off-hand way.

"She's away for a little time and wants me to get anything I can, to make sure there's enough in the fridge and larder, even if it's going out of date." This was true. Mum often used this unofficial grocer's to make the budget stretch.

Mabel sucked through her teeth. "What's going to be out of date by Monday?" She spoke out loud, as much to herself as to anyone else and cast a proprietorial eye over her kitchen. She was a good cook and a large lady, but Jill had never noticed the connection between those two things until that moment.

"Can't say I haven't heard about your Mom, I'm sure it will be all right," she said, glancing sidelong at Jill as she leant on the counter. "I suppose I had better do her a favour and keep my eye on you," Jill's heart stopped. "Don't want her coming back and finding you all skin and bones." Mabel laughed, and Jill breathed again.

"Well, let's see. There's that peppered bacon you like. We have too many eggs to use up on Monday, and there's bread that won't last over the weekend. Oh yeah, I can give you a special rate on some tins of Boston Beans, but don't tell no-one, okay?" The dinner lady winked, in that oddly deliberate way some adults have. Jill packed her already overloaded bag with as much as she could fit and then some more, thanked Mabel and got her rather small lunch from the serving counter.

"What's up Jill, not hungry?" asked a chubby faced girl from across the dinner table as Jill sat next to Catherine.

A second girl chimed in, "No, she'd rather cry instead of eat."

"Just leave her alone, all right?" Cathy was in no mood to let anyone upset Jill again. "Let's go outside, Jill," she said and the two friends rose and left the hall. They found a quiet green corner and stood staring at the high Moor; it was bathed in full sunlight.

"I don't think I can face Physical Education and Art this afternoon," said Jill. "Will you tell them I've gone home sick?"

Cathy pulled a face and started nervously to chew a fingernail. "I don't lie well; you'd only get in trouble." Cathy's eyes widened and she pointed her now shortened nail at Jill. "I think it was going to be a run this afternoon, an open ended one, where Miss says we're competing against ourselves. No one will miss you in art if you can think of an excuse, not with Miss Bates anyhow." Both girls giggled and turned to walk across the play area, knowing that their Art teacher did not notice anything, except what was just under her nose. Jill wrinkled her forehead in concentration. "What can I say to Miss in PE? She's laid back, but she's not stupid."

The girls sat down under a tree quietly enjoying each other's company and trying out different reasons that might convince the sports teacher until the bell went. The run was next, so Jill sighed nervously and hurried to the changing rooms.

"Can I make my own run, Miss, a really long one? I have a free study last lesson, so it won't matter." Jill had lied. She felt the unaccustomed pain of guilt as she did so, but ignored it.

The teacher scrutinised her face. "Well, it's the last day of lessons this year," she said. "You've had a bad year, haven't you?" Jill wondered where this question was leading. "You've never given me a problem though . . . always performed well for the cross country team . . . Well, I suppose . . . on you go, see you at the fair," said the teacher, walking around the corner to her office.

Jill changed into her walking clothes without another word spoken, slipped her boots on and headed for the changing room doors.

"Funny running kit, girl." The teacher had returned and Jill froze.

"I was hoping to check out a route for the school orienteering team." It was the first thing that had come into her head. Jill winced inside. This was so close to a straight out lie that she thought she would be caught, but the teacher laughed and shook her head.

"You must really love that moor." The teacher was smiling. "I didn't see anything unusual. Just remember to sign out and use my name for your authority; you're training for fell running if anyone asks. See you on Monday then?" Jill grinned and waved, then left. Her plan was actually working, this far at least.

The School was on the south side of the Village, away from the houses slightly, and on the road that led down to the Town. She could reach the Road if she walked back through the Village, but Jill didn't want anyone to notice where she was going; so swinging a large semicircle around the east side of the Village she walked along the edge of the moorland spur on which the Village sat.

Jill looked down on the Town beneath. It was a hazy day, and the Town was partly obscured by the light smog. She loved being above this dirty air, and it always shocked her to think that you could not see the filth when you were in it.

Swinging along an old hiking path, the weight of her pack and the hot sun might have made you tired, but Jill felt happy for the first time that day. She was away from people, arguments, sickness and lies. Jill was going to leave it all behind and she felt wonderful. Mum had come here to 'get away from it all', but whatever she was running from seemed to have followed her here. "I'm going to get away from them all, finally be free," Jill said to the scattering sheep. The sheep just stared back, with its long stupid face. Jill smiled at it. By the time Mrs. Varney thought of checking on her at the Merrison's place, she would be long gone. That was, of course, if she managed to check something out for herself.

Jill was now scrambling up the escarpment, cutting off the corner between the bottom of the hill and the diagonally rising Road. Her path took her straight up the steep pitch and she was sweating. *No need to join the Road too early*, Jill thought. People would spot her on the track if she was low down near the Village. *Just keep going straight for now.* No one seemed to scan the higher part of the Road as it rose to the ridge. She felt secure from detection up there.

There was one thing that could make this a short walk, and as she reached the ditch by the Road, she paused. Her heart was racing. What if Mum and Mr. Jones had cooked all this up between them, just to distract her? She had not appreciated all that deception over Christmas and the 'Man-in-Red'. It still rankled with her to have had her hopes and beliefs built up and then knocked down, even though she had been just a kid. It then occurred to her that she too was lying and being deceptive. *That was different, I've got a good reason*, she thought, though she could not think why her reasons were different. *Maybe lying was all part of growing up?* Jill turned the idea over a few times, then decided she did not like it. "Concentrate on walking up this hill," she said to herself.

She reached the Road and crossed the ditch. The rucksack was hefted over her shoulders, and from the top of the bag she pulled out a rock hammer, the kind that has a wedge shaped head.

Now to test it out. Could she make a hole in the Road? "Time to test your metal," she said to the hammer. Dust and pebbles flew everywhere. *That was easy.* Jill worked quickly, embarrassed in case anyone found her. What would she say? It was a good five minutes before she decided to check her work.

Now she looked at it, she was not certain that it was getting any bigger. Jill stared at it for a few moments and decided to renew her excavating. Stones came out with each blow, but after a few minutes, she twisted around and examined her little pile of pebbles. It had not grown, Jill was almost certain of that. She frowned, and perspiration trickled into her eyes.

Jill decided that the Road had not let her make the hole bigger; the stories must be true. She had tried to make it bigger and it hadn't worked, had it? Jill convinced herself, but as she left the hole thoughts started to follow her, like annoying little children clamouring to be heard. A crow could be heard crying far above her, and she looked up as she walked, shading her eyes and frowning.

"What's wrong with me?" The question came out loud and it surprised her to hear how annoyed she was. Jill had reached the top of the rise now but still her doubts pressed in on her. Maddeningly, they all made sense. She was just running away from a difficult situation. She had seen it on TV; 'denial' was the word the lady had used. Any sensible person would just go back and 'face it'. Had she seen any stones go back into the hole? Why hadn't her lettered stones walked back to the Road on their own, if it was all true?

"Jill, you're an idiot!" she shouted. She stopped, frustrated with the thoughts and angry with herself. She would pack the stones back in the hole, like any sensible hiker, and leave the Road as she found it. Jill could see herself bravely facing the future without a mother and safe in the bosom of the Village with her friends. She would be 'adult' about the whole thing. She just needed to fill in this hole and there would be no evidence of her erratic behaviour.

Turning around, Jill walked back the few hundred metres to where she had started on the Road and spotted the gorse bush where she had climbed up; it was very large. Where was the hole? There was only a scrape of loose stones where it should be, just deep enough for her fist.

Jill spun round. There was no loose gravel lying around, let alone all the dirt she had dug up. She could see nothing moving and could hear nothing but the sound of grit under her boot.

Jill had been away for only a few minutes. The Road was so straight that she would have seen anyone moving even down to the Village. Jill was sure that the Road had been clear when she left the hole. She examined it and bending over, Jill could hardly get her knuckles in it now, much less her fist. Who had filled it in?

Sweeping her eye over the moorland slope her heart beat more quickly. There was no one there, and the hillside was flat for a couple of miles in any direction. There was no one on the high Moor either; she had had a good look for other hikers before deciding to turn around. Besides, Jill had been walking back toward the hole for five minutes; she would have seen them run away.

Who would run away from filling in a hole, anyway? They couldn't have read her mind, so as to know what she was planning and then try and trick her, could they? This thought scared her a little. Another thought followed. *Perhaps the stones moved themselves?*

"Keep calm", Jill said out loud, but her palms had become very sweaty.

She glanced down at the ground again. *Where was the hole now?* No evidence was left of the few stones that had remained. This was simply too weird. She scoured the Road up and down for evidence of her fifteen minutes of hard labour. It just wasn't there. Her heart started to beat really fast, and her impulse was to run down the hill. Her knees felt odd, but she stood her ground, and stayed upright.

If the Road had fixed itself, then perhaps Mum's story was true. If Mum's story was true, then maybe what Mr. Jones had said was true. If the Road could fix itself, it was possible, no; it was probable, that 'The Lord of the Way' was able to protect the Road even now. Then he would be real, really in charge, really Lord of this Way. Jill felt exposed, naked before this invisible person with whom she wanted to deal. Or did she? She had desperately wanted him to be there, but now his reality was looming in her mind, she was scared. Her knees gave way, and she sat nervously on the Road.

"I'm sorry for hitting the Road," she said out-loud, feeling foolish. Deliberately speaking into the air, even in this empty open space, made her very aware of her own voice. It was rather like talking to herself in a wardrobe when she used to play 'hide-and-seek' — her voice was far too loud and she was afraid someone might hear her.

Someone might hear me? Of course I want him to hear me! What's wrong with you Jill? She swallowed hard, and spoke again. "I had to find out. I need someone to help me and I think you might be the only person who can. Where are you? Will you help?" She did not know whether it was the Road who heard her, or this Lord of the Way person, but she immediately felt a lot better. "Err, how do I find you?" The question hung in the air, but no response came. "I guess the myth said that was what the Road was for," she muttered, "if it was a myth. Time to go."

Jill stood up. She had started hitting the Road only half an hour earlier, but the world had changed completely for her in that time. This Road was different. This Road went 'Somewhere', she was sure of that now. The kind of fear that gripped her now was different to all she had experienced in the last few days, but in spite of this, Jill decided to find out who or what was at the end of this Road, no matter what the risk.

She started walking.

5

ROCKET

For the second time that day, Jill looked forward to exploring the highlands before her. The first few miles were familiar to her because she had walked the edge of the Moor many times before, using the sheep and pony tracks, as well as the occasional hikers' trail. Jill had hardly used the Road on those occasions and she wondered why.

The Moor ran far to the north, beyond the confines of settled lands. Maps that Jill had looked at the night before had showed it as a plateau that continued for huge distances, beyond which it gradually sloped down to half-frozen grasslands and eventually to an infinity of ice. This was the land of bears and rabbits. Moving into the wilds was a real adventure.

If Jill had known what else she might meet, then finding bears would have been the last thing on her mind. She stopped and pulled out her best and largest map when she was just below the ridge. The map showed the Road as a dotted yellow line with a label in old curving script saying, "Ancient Trackway."

"I had worked that much out," Jill mused.

The key at the map's margin marked yellow as meaning,

"unsuitable for motorised traffic or unofficial highway." The dotted line said that it was, "unfinished/unmetalled road." Jill stared at the Road. This was no more information than she could see with her own eyes. The map's dismissive phrases hardly did the Road's properties justice.

"How could they mark, 'Tougher than you think'?" wondered Jill. The dotted line petered out in the middle of a featureless section of the Moor.

Obviously, this map was going to be of little help.

Jill loved maps. She had learnt to live by them, and it was disconcerting to have so little help from this one. She put it away, and did not think it would reappear for the rest of the trip. As Jill started off again and she felt the warmth of the sun on the back of her head, and the afternoon was wearing on now and the sun had dropped in the sky. She decided to rest only when she had reached the high lookout point at the top of the escarpment.

As the Road reached the summit, its gradient eased and it turned from heading north-east to due north. Any hiker who walked it would slowly swing from ascending diagonally to climbing straight up the hill and, as a result, it always seemed like the path was going to level off before it did, no matter how many times you climbed it. Jill remembered not to expect it to get easier, but just kept walking, pushing through this first difficult stage and wanting to put as much distance between the Village and herself as possible.

Re-climbing this stretch was irritating, but after six or seven minutes of sweat, she had ascended beyond the visible ridge that could be seen from the Village. Jill relaxed and took in the Moor's expanse and new horizons.

She then noticed the little sandstone path that branched off to the right of the Road. It led up to the slight knoll known to the more adventurous members of the Village as the 'Lookout'. After one last look back, and a five-minute break, she clambered up the path.

The view was breathtaking as always, and despite the heat,

the day was crystal clear.

Funny, it was hazy earlier on. I wonder where the mist went? Even the town looked clean, every detail was picked out. Maybe there were some answers in Nowhere after all. So Jill shaded her eyes against the lowering sun, and gazed out.

That's odd. Jill took her hand away from her brow. She returned it again. It hardly made any difference. She looked long away to the City: the tall smokestacks rose majestically through the air in front of her, every detail picked out.

"What a day this is, what a view," she whispered.

She tried gazing even further, her eyes drinking in the flood of light, every sense sharpened.

"I think I can see further than anyone has seen before." She paused, and then bit her lip in delight. *There must be a new theme park beyond the City! I can see the Capital Tower.*

The Capital Tower was far too small to be seen at this distance. In fact, she knew it was a long way over the horizon, even from the Lookout's high position.

It didn't look quite right for a theme park. What was that grey smudge next to it? Jill concentrated on it and found she was looking at wave crests. The Sea and the Coast! Her head swam and she felt peculiar, as if her body was made of helium balloons.

"It's only the effect of the climb. It will settle down in a minute. That can't be right," she said to herself.

She looked again, her curiosity drawing her on. There were the ancient harbours, there were the Freedom Gates over Ivan's Basin and there was the Dome of Sparrows that glistened silver and gold in the afternoon sun. Inside she became cold and sick: this was unnatural. Jill was looking at an exact replica of the Capital and suddenly realised why it looked odd. It wasn't flat.

It is a hard thing to describe, but even through binoculars, distant objects will look like they are cardboard cut-outs, painted in pale blues and greys and propped up like scenery in the theatre. The Capital she could see was gloriously three dimensional and full of colour. Her jaw dropped; she could see people moving about. Nausea began to rise in her throat, and she screwed up her eyes and swallowed hard. When she opened her eyes again she was hovering at a great height and looking down. Now she really felt sick.

Whatever this is, just keep clam. The reality of the Capital's urban bustle broke on her; sound, smell, and the feel of the sea breeze. "Those small moving colours are cars and buses and trams and people," she muttered as the adrenaline took hold of her. She wobbled and her head spun. "Keep calm; it will go away. You just have to wait a second or two." Every muscle in her body was rigid as anxiety fluttered inside her.

But then, she noticed someone in the crowd that Jill thought she knew, a flash of recognition focussing her attention. Without thought, she leant forward to see the people more clearly. She could see hats, coats, and faces . . .

"Mum!" She shouted out-loud, then shock overtook curiosity. Quickly the view receded back to the hill. Jill staggered, dizzy for a second.

"That must have been some climb. Maybe I really did over do it," she said to herself.

Jill was not sure that she had seen Mum now and certainly did not want to try again. However, as she cautiously looked round wondering what to do next, her eye was drawn again by the freshness of the landscape. It only took seconds before Jill realised that she could see through smoke and behind hills, and everything looked so *clean* and uncluttered. The scenery was amazing from this vantage point and the strangeness faded as Jill started to relax. Peace began to steal over her, coaxing her to stay with the experience.

"Whatever it is, it will probably never happen again. Nothing good ever does," she whispered. But contrary to her expectations, the incident did not fade. Jill found she could change what she was looking at just by wanting to, and could view it from any position she desired. She flew across fields and lakes, through mountains and under hills, dizzying herself with sheer speed.

After a while, the wind tickled her nose and she sneezed. With some regret, Jill decided to start moving again, and noticed three things almost simultaneously.

First of all, she was stiff. She had cooled off and needed to keep going to find a suitable camp-site. More remarkably, there was a silver column rising into the air, suspended on a pillar of shaking fire and heat. It was far away, but close to the east of the Village.

But what captured her attention was the little hilltop she was standing on. It was actually paved with sandstone the same colour as the pebbles on the Road. The stone slabs were laid out as the petals of a daisy, and she was standing on the central, circular slab. Random lines of letters, all of different sizes, shapes and directions were cut to into the rock, as if a powerful explosion had flung words from across the universe and embedded them here. However, it was the fact they were glowing that really jerked Jill back to the here and now.

A loud rumbling and growling noise made Jill look up to face the direction of the Village. The noise was coming from the silver object. Her vision fell towards it and the noise increased; she was now able to see that it was a rocket, shining in the sun, fins and nose cone reflecting the light. Alarm took hold of her, for a second she forgot about the shining words under her feet, *they* were trying to find her.

If she had been thinking clearly, she would have known that school had only finished for a couple of hours and no one was expecting her to come home tonight, nor, on the other hand, did she know anyone who owned a rocket. However, enough odd things had been happening to her that she started to run anyway.

Sprinting as fast as her boots would allow, without a thought she hurtled back down the little sandstone path and fled north. The sound stopped as she left the fiery slabs behind, although she could still hear a distant rumble on the air. The rumble started to swell in volume. Why was it getting louder? She glanced over her shoulder, and saw to her horror that the rocket had fallen away from its vertical climb, and was veering around toward her.

The terror of pursuit fell on Jill. She ran, feeling like she was flying for the second time that day and looked round desperately for somewhere to hide. She willed her limbs to move faster, but her muscles filled with weight and she slowed and looked back.

"Idiot, you can't outrun a flaming rocket!" She stopped, panting hard. The rocket was now dropping toward her and wobbling in a frightening way. Jill's stomach turned — it was not hunting her, it was going to crash and crash near her; *far* too near her.

Jill started to sprint again, glancing back. The rocket loomed closer, louder, as loud as it had been on the Lookout. There was a huge crumpling noise behind her, accompanied by a hiss and a terrible rumble. Jill did not dare look back now. Tearing and screeching noises increased in a crescendo; she could feel vibrations and blasts of air from the impact. Her limbs felt paper light as panic surged through her and she hurled herself forward.

Without warning, Jill found herself lying on her face while dirt and rocks flew over her head. She tensed her body as the sounds got even louder, but nothing else happened. The noises ceased; the dirt and stones stopped falling. Jill relaxed and started breathing and coughing. Her mouth was full of the Road, and she spat and checked herself as she sat up. Nothing bleeding or broken and not many bruises. She stared into the clouds of dust.

From the shapes showing through, the rocket had ploughed diagonally through the Road and thrown a good deal of it into the air. One of the fins of the rocket was reflecting a shaft of light through the muck, and showed that it was now on the west of the Road, several metres from where Jill was. She stood up, and brushing herself off, felt relieved that after the futility of trying to out run her pursuer, she had managed to out run the crash site. But why had there been no explosion? Why had she not been burnt alive? Jill decided that she better take a look.

The Road was cleaved down to its core. She could see huge foundation stones in the hole, and reckoned that if she stood at the bottom her head would be below the surface of the road. The Road, underneath the gravel, was made of layers of paving. The shattered slabs became thinner as they got closer to the top, and they were all the same mellow yellow stone. Jill thought she saw deep gouge marks on the foundation fill, heal over and disappear while she watched. The air was thick with dust so she was not absolutely sure of it and she started to sneeze and cough, her eyes streaming with tears. Jill decided to move to clearer air.

Jill carefully picked her way around debris strewn down the bank and crossed over the western ditch (which was dry at this point) and then up to examine the rocket from the southern side.

The rocket had ripped a rich chocolate brown scar through the Moorland. Gorse bushes and heather had been scattered to either side and the rocket lay twisted and buried to about half a metre in the earth. Bushes and top soil were heaped up black and peaty by the shiny, crushed, steaming tin-can nose of the rocket. Some bits gently smoked, while other parts groaned as it cooled. It looked broken. It sounded miserable.

There was no cockpit she could see, nor were there any wounded to help. Jill shuddered at the thought of blood and wondered whether she should leave now.

Then she noticed a porthole, about two-thirds the way up the rocket. It had come to rest slightly more up than down. It looked oddly familiar to her and somehow old fashioned with a riveted retaining ring surrounding the thick window. The whole thing reminded her of something she had seen before. She stared and puzzled. Then Jill remembered Saturday morning TV with its nineteen thirties black and white films and grainy heroes in spark spitting rocket ships.

How peculiar, she thought. The scene was so exotic and her sense of the normal so stretched that she forgot to be frightened and moved closer to the ship. Sharp smells assaulted her nose and caught her breath, and light beamed off distorted mirrors of polished metal. Now that she was closer, she noticed that the porthole actually formed part of a door, the gap between the opening surface and the fuselage so small as to be hardly noticeable. She reached out to touch the incredibly fine line, which was partially hidden amongst scratches. Jill leaned forward. The door flew open with the speed of a champagne cork and then stopped short. She withdrew her hand and was now very frightened indeed; her feet frozen and her heart skipping. A head appeared.

"I say, that wasn't supposed to happen. You wouldn't know where we are would you?" The man's head, for it was most obviously a 'he', was striking in appearance. Jill thought she had never seen anyone like him before. Tight ginger and white curls had randomly popped up as he hurriedly pushed his heavy goggles back. He had a modest number of wrinkles, lively hazel eyes, a sharp nose and freckles. The man's skin was quickly developing bruises to complement the gallant graze stretching from his left cheekbone back to his ear, where small earphones dangled like tribal jewellery. He was wearing a flying jacket (the sheep's wool lining showing where the collar turned back) and a white lab coat underneath.

While his rocket and jacket belonged to a man of action, the rest suggested that this action man would have trouble locating exactly where the action was. He somehow reminded Jill of a confused red squirrel. It was the funniest thing Jill had seen for days, and she gave way to giggles.

In response, he produced a clipboard and took a pen from the collection in his top pocket. "Excuse me young girl, but I really need to complete my observations. Where are we?"

Jill managed to control herself and held out a helping hand toward the stranger. She braced her foot on a slight fold in the metal and helped him descend. He slipped, then stumbled, and finally, he fell on her.

"Excuse me, I am sorry. Oh, I don't normally do this. I am sorry, oops!" said the man falling again and temporarily trapping Jill's legs. Jill could not contain herself. A small jab of rage swung around to hysterical laughter, and when somehow the pair untangled themselves, Jill tried to sit up. She was shaking with silent laughter and, although Jill cannot remember how long it took, it seemed several minutes later that she finished wiping her tears. She felt oddly blocked up in her head and her stomach muscles hurt. Jill rubbed them and then blew her nose. She stifled one last chuckle, and looked up at the now bemused man. No, she had not imagined it; he *was* wearing old-fashioned flying gear, and he *was* leaning on a rocket.

"Feeling better are we? Well, I don't know whether I should ask for an apology or give one."

Jill just stared at him. She grinned broadly. "It was you who nearly ran me down in that, that . . . tin can thing. What were you doing?"

"I'm not sure I want to tell you, if you're going to be rude about my rarefied atmosphere vertical elevator."

Jill, still smiling, looked puzzled.

"It's a vertical height gaining device powered by a thrust generated by an impulse of hot gases downwards," he blurted.

As he said this, his chest swelled, his forehead furrowed, and he started to lean back and speak with a distinct flourish. "I like to call it an R.A.V.E., or RAVE for short." There was a pause and then another fit of giggles from Jill.

The stranger's shoulders sagged and he blushed. "Okay, it's a rocket."

Jill immediately felt a little sorry for the man who seemed now quite dejected, one hand rested and almost stroked the skin of his previously very impressive machine.

"To answer your question, we are now just above the Village on the edge of the high Moor, and you nearly killed me."

The man started to write down something on his clipboard, filling in various parts of his paper records with energy, then he blushed bright red. "I'm so sorry. Things went a little wrong. It was meant to go up, not across. I have a little research lab near the Village, maybe you've heard of it? Sponsored by Reckit's Oil?"

Rocket politely smiled and waved his question away. "No, well never mind. I hope you're all right. May I ask your name?"

Jill looked blank. Inside she was panicking; of course, he was from the Village! Jill had seen where he had taken off, she could not allow this man to tell people where she was, and neither did she want him to hang around to see where she went. Another possibility flashed across her mind. He might come with her. Uggh! That would be *unthinkable*. Jill thought about lying, but like Cathy, she wasn't much good at it. She would always blush at the wrong moment in a way that always made adults suspicious. "I wonder if that is why the PE teacher came back to check on me?" she thought.

"Jill." She stood up and extended her hand again, shaking his hand vigorously. "And yours?"

"Rocket. To be precise, Rocket Propellant Precipitant Scientist the Third. Please don't ask." Now Jill really did blush, crimson with embarrassment, as she struggled not to laugh in this man's face. "My parents were unimaginative. Everyone just calls me Rocket."

Jill was thinking furiously. *There **must** be a way of getting rid of this man.* "Let me show you exactly where you . . . Er . . . landed." Jill turned and took a few steps back toward the Road. As she did, she noticed two things. The first was a rocket fin, ripped off against the foundation stones on the far side of the Road and embedded vertically in the ground. The second was that the cut through the Road looked to be shallower than it had been.

Rocket looked up and seemed to read her mind. "That's odd. The impact furrow appears to be less deep where it crosses that old track-way."

He was inquisitive, very inquisitive! Jill decided quickly that if she could distract him, maybe she could slip away. What she said out loud was, "You still haven't told me what you were trying to do."

"Simple. I wanted to develop a cheap, high-level ionosphere observation platform. I was trying a new approach, but the experimental . . ." Jill was staring at him, not understanding a word. "I was trying to get higher so I could see more and discover more," he said, a little more quietly.

"Was that all it was about?"

"Science is a noble pursuit young girl. It is important that we are able to know more, find out what the world is about. Even if it entails risks, even risks to ourselves. That was why I built my vertical eleva– . . . my rocket. I say, where are you going?"

Jill was scampering back to the Road. "If you want to see more, come with me," she called over her shoulder. For someone who wanted to discover more, thought Jill, what could be more distracting than the Lookout?

Rocket watched Jill duck into the cleft in the Road and then quickly clamber up to the top of the bank. He stared after her, until his curiosity got the better of him and he started to follow. He was still unsteady from the crash and Jill easily outpaced him. When he caught up with her on the Road, Rocket was red and kept pulling at his collar as if it was too tight.

"Were the gorse bushes comfortable?" Jill asked.

Rocket pulled out a piece of something sharp and green from his collar and, for a second, his face almost stopped scowling. "What did you say was up here?"

"I'm not sure yet. Follow me," said Jill with a grin, and skipped back along the Road and up to the hilltop.

The white in Rocket's hair seemed more apparent the more out of breath he became, and by the time he had reached the little knoll he was gasping and scarlet. "Now look here!" Rocket began to say.

"No, you look here," Jill was standing in the centre of the sandstone circle and reached out her hand to Rocket. Stooping over, he allowed himself to be drawn across the stone. The letters under their feet started to glow.

It was at this point that Jill had hoped to run while the scientist was out of breath and concentrating on the view from the Lookout, but she decided that it would not be safe to sprint away until she was sure that he was taking no notice of her. Jill stepped back and let go of his hand, and watched for her opportunity.

The letters shimmered and glowed white and gold, their shapes flickered like flame, and Jill took another step back to get a better view. Enthralled by the beauty of fire under her feet she smiled in spite of herself. Then she remembered the rocket builder, and looked up.

His gaze appeared focussed on images that Jill could not see and his face was filled with wonder. Clearly, whatever this place did, it was an individual experience.

Good, she thought, now I can go without being noticed. But as she turned, she heard the rocket builder's voice drift toward her and stopped, thinking that he was talking to her.

"The Capital . . . I wonder . . . yes I can . . . where else can I see?" Jill turned back to see him still looking away. Had he seen her leaving? Staring at his face Jill saw that a wildness had entered his eyes, unlike anything she had seen before. His speech became louder now, more forgetful of himself. It reminded Jill of walking into a room where someone is reading and does not notice you come in, so that you can see their thoughts in their face. Now she could *hear* him mutter as well, she was fascinated. She decided to watch a little longer, just to see what happened.

"Just think what could be discovered with this device. Who would need any high altitude platforms? Just think what progress could be made! I wonder what the old fools at the institute would think of this? Well now, why should I wonder? Let's see, shall we? There he is. I didn't know he was involved with the money. Why the old goat! — and *he* had *me* kicked out for budget irregularities. He's taking that money for himself, I'll bet."

Rocket's face had a hungry look now. Several different emotions chased across his features. Surprise was driven out by anger, followed by the hard determination of rage, but what followed was a sickly smile. "Whoever had access to this device could bring to light not only new discoveries but expose certain administrative problems in the systems of academia, problems with money that is. Of course, they would need someone on the Institute Council to prevent this happening again; someone who could see what was really going on." He laughed.

Jill paid closer attention to the old man's face. His expression was relaxed now, but unpleasant. He was having more ideas about the jobs he would have and what would happen to the 'old goat'. Pleasure played about his lips and eyes. His lips were not moving! With a sudden shock Jill realised that he was not speaking; she was actually hearing his thoughts. She was beginning to feel giddy again. But now Rocket's thoughts boomed into her head.

"They would need someone whose newly published work would open doors in every place of learning in Nowhere."

The central disc had started to glow brightly, not just the letters, but the plain stone too. Its intensity was rising with every second. She began to feel heat radiating from the disc, but Rocket gave no outward signs of noticing. This was not good. Something was wrong. Something had to be done. Now.

Jill gathered herself up and wished that she had stayed in bed this morning. She breathed hard, and flung herself at the now brightly-lit figure, feeling his light frame buckle sideways as they rolled off the pavement together. He pushed Jill off angrily and was about to shout at her when he noticed the smoking soles of his feet, even as he saw the glow in the stone fade away.

"Ow, my feet are on fire!"

Rocket kicked off his shoes and then banged the smouldering boots on the ground.

Jill stood slightly to one side, nervously eyeing this old man whose thoughts she had read on the sandstone disc.

"I'm sorry," Jill said swallowing her words, "I nearly got you killed, this time."

Rocket looked up and fixed her with a stare.

"What was that? How does it work? Did you know it was dangerous? Why did you knock me over?"

"Why did I knock you over? You were about to be burnt to a crisp, that's why! It didn't like your thoughts, and I don't think I did either. I think it has something to do with this Road that I am travelling on. The one you sliced across with your vertical elevator thing. Oh, and it wasn't dangerous before *you* turned up." She dropped her gaze. "Oh, and another thing, you didn't look very nice; your face looked horrible when you started thinking about that 'old goat'."

Rocket sat stunned and looked at the stone disc trying to work out what had happened. His eyes widened and he looked up at Jill again. "You mean that as I could see all those wonderful things, you could hear my thoughts?"

Jill nodded.

Rocket rose, brushed himself off, and changed the subject. "I saw the light dim away. Do you have a time limit on the central stone?"

"I was on for a lot longer than that, and it never did anything to me. I don't think there's a time limit; I just think it knows how to protect itself."

"Ridiculous!" Rocket blustered.

"I don't think so," Jill replied, "It only started getting hot with your thoughts of your old friend, like it was angry or something. And I agree with it; what you were thinking was pretty ugly."

"Well, yes." Rocket dropped his gaze. "Maybe so, but if we were to ever use this stone for research we would have to place certain limitations on its use; protocols, procedures and other restraints." He looked up sideways at Jill. "Maybe we could examine its mechanism, and see what caused it get so overheated?"

Jill cut in, "So you could be welcomed into every place of learning in Nowhere?"

Rocket looked ashamed. "You have the advantage over me; I haven't heard your thoughts today."

Her thoughts? Jill decided to stop feeling angry with him.

"I'm not sure it's a machine. I think it might simply be alive. Come with me and you'll see what I mean."

Jill was getting used to giving orders, but Rocket was now less certain of following Jill's instructions; however, with a little coaxing, she led him back to the ditch, and the metal fin.

"Before we went up to the Lookout, I scratched a mark on the fin to show how deep this hole was. Look, here it is."

The Road was now at least fifty centimetres higher than the mark Jill had made on the fin, and the hole was becoming narrow, even tight.

"Well, how very scientific of you," Rocket slowly trailed off into thought. He held his right elbow with his left hand and chewed on a pen he was holding to his mouth. He stopped and jabbed the pen in the direction of the twisted fin. "Why did you do this?"

"I tried making a hole in the Road myself earlier today. I had less success than you, but it did the same thing for me then. I thought I might like to check it myself after you'd gone."

Jill remembered too late that she was trying to avoid telling this stranger about her escape plan. She suspected that she had already said too much.

"After I have gone? What are you doing up here then?"

"I like rambling." Jill looked distinctly uncomfortable.

"What else do you know?"

Rocket was holding his head over to one side with an inquiring smile. His curls bobbed with every energetic movement but he met and held her gaze.

"The Road's repairing itself quite quickly now," Jill said with a weak smile. Rocket continued to stare her out and what felt like ten minutes of silence passed. "Okay, okay," said Jill. "I suppose I like people to level with me too. How can I put this?" It took a few minutes, but in the end Jill told him everything that had happened to her since she had had her argument with her Mum. When she had finished, Rocket let out a low whistle.

"Do you think this 'Lord of the Way' might have use for an old researcher?"

Jill frowned. "Why?"

"Well, it might take me months to get this thing to fly right and, even if I can, I don't want to go back and report just yet." Rocket tapped the fin loudly. "Then again, up here I find a self repairing road and an 'observation at a distance' hill. Who knows what might be ahead? It might be worth a few days' sally forth."

"What!? You come with me? You'd never make it. So how old are you then?" quizzed Jill.

"Old enough to be your father I'd wager."

"You mean my grandfather," laughed Jill, "Anyway, I don't want company. Mum told me to watch out for strange men. And to be honest, you're one of the oddest I've ever met."

Jill looked up at the lowering sun, thinking hard about how to rid herself of this intruder. "Well, if you're coming, you'll need to go back for camping gear. Don't want you catching hypothermia, *old* man."

Rocket became animated, almost cross, jabbing the palm of his hand with his finger to make each point.

"Less of the '*old*,' my dear! I'm still fit enough to have survived a crash at over 30 metres per second into this igneous formation with no serious contusions or traumas." Jill blinked as he drew breath. "I don't need to return. Besides, I'm only about ten miles from my lab and it's a wonder no-one has come for me. They should have been here some time ago. There's no helicopter, no one's calling me on my personal radio. Maybe they can't find me; maybe we're somehow cut off from them. I suspect your Road has affected us more strongly than you think, as I've never heard of that knoll having strange powers before. If I leave you now and go back, I don't think I'll ever find you again." Rocket paused and became a little calmer. "I have discovered, young lady, that in this life I need to take my chances when they come and in this case that means going with you, now. Of course, I'll have to let someone know where you are if I go back. I am supposed to be a responsible adult. If you're right and I could get home and then back to here, others will be able to follow too, and will almost certainly want me to show them where you are." He raised an eyebrow. "However, in the interests of science, I could stand in as the adult chaperone on this trip."

Jill did not agree, but Rocket argued determinedly for some minutes.

He was stopped in his tracks by an outburst of shouting. "There's no way you're coming with me, and I'm not going back!"

Rocket seemed to be taken aback for a second, and then much to Jill's surprise changed tack. "All right *old* girl. I hope you don't mind me calling you that, but you seemed to like the description. You might have a point, *old* girl, about my need for better camping gear, in order to investigate this road"

"Yes," said Jill, her voice wavering a little, "Yes, I do."

"And you would be able to suggest where I might be able to obtain this equipment?"

After a moment's pursing of lips, Jill replied by describing the locations of the two best camping stores in the Town.

"Well, in the interests of safety and other considerations I'll go back." Rocket was chewing the end of his pen again. "I'll be seeking to catch up with you, shall we say, in two days?" Rocket raised his eyebrows as he suggested his plan.

Not if I have anything to do with it, Jill thought. What she said aloud was, "Err, yes . . . that's very sensible."

"Can't have a young girl wandering, unprotected out here on her own. But then, being accompanied by an old man . . ." Rocket paused, then seemed to make up his mind. "Lightweight modern stuff all gaudy, not woollen tweeds?"

"What's 'tweeds'?"

"The finest material when you're on a grouse shoot. The colour of gorse and heather, with a rough woollen texture."

"Err, no, stick with the modern stuff," Jill replied, not sure what he was going on about.

Jill bit her lip. "You won't mention this to anyone in the Village?"

"Now, would that be sensible?" Rocket grinned. "Well, not for the moment." Rocket turned, and started to walk off. He smiled and waved goodbye.

What is he up to?

Rocket had long disappeared back down the Road before she took her eyes off the horizon and continued. The shadows ran off to the east far beyond her view, as Jill turned and walked away.

"I think I should reach that group of low trees on the horizon before I camp." Jill often talked to herself when lonely. She picked up their pace and arrived at the landmark, with about half an hour of light remaining.

Below her was a small valley with a wood and a thin wisp of smoke rising from a chimney pot jutting above the treetops.

"Well, that looks like a welcoming house," said Jill, pitching her tent and then scanning the expanse of the Moor around her.

The light finally failed and Jill sank into a lonely, dreamless sleep.

6

Mrs. Lazybee's B and B

The next morning Jill awoke to the delicious sting of a cold dewy dawn. During the excitement of the previous day, Jill had not eaten well and she was ravenously hungry. The stove was set up, beans opened, and eggs and bacon cooked. Jill had been going to ration herself, but had not had to do this on her own before and was not used to self-discipline. She stared at her supplies. Less than twenty-four hours into her trip *and* she had eaten more than a quarter the food she had got from the dinner lady. Food was clearly going to be a major concern. The walking at least should be good. "Let's get on, old girl," she said to herself, "and make sure that the old man can't catch up, even if he tried."

The Road swept down the valley side as a gentle curve, cutting across the slope. It turned slightly more sharply as it entered the wood below and then disappeared out of sight. Whether Jill was moving more quickly than normal, or whether the path was shorter than it looked, it was certain that the morning hardly seemed to have got going by the time she reached the wood's edge.

Jill walked happily, arms swinging in the bright sunshine, and keen to see what was ahead. The wood was bright, its margins festooned with wild flowers. These were not the gaudy displays of florists' windows, but Jill thought they had the relaxed air of plants dressed for a good friend's party.

The Road had no overhanging branches and the wood contained lots of beech trees, which cast a golden-green hue across the sandstone pebbles as the sun shone through their leaves. She had walked for several miles and the sun was beginning to feel warm as it climbed higher in the cool air. The thought of water was about to draw Jill to the stream in the westerly ditch, when she suddenly noticed a clearing and signs of a house ahead.

"That must be the cottage that I saw from the Road higher up," said Jill. Now she could smell smoke from wood stove. It was delicious, and she became hungry as she thought of camp cooking. She walked more quickly as she entered the clearing.

"Wow, a picnic!" Jill exclaimed out loud. "Whose is it?" Jill had not been on many picnics and somehow now felt a little left out.

The picnic was on a large table with benches on either side, large enough to seat about eight people. There was a red check tablecloth; basket and a feast laid out with proper country fare. The food looked enough for at least sixteen people and after the morning's brisk walk and a night in fresh air, Jill wondered whether she might not be able to eat most of it herself. *I'll try anyway.* She wandered over to the table.

"I say Jill, I wouldn't touch that just yet, we don't know anything about whose it is," came a familiar voice from over her shoulder. Jill spun around.

"What are you doing here?" she screeched at Rocket.

"Excuse me, but I was serious about not leaving a young girl unprotected."

"But I saw you walk off!"

"Yes," Rocket stuttered, "but I couldn't get back to get the equipment, even if I had wanted to."

"What do you mean?"

"Let's just say I scouted around as I let you get a little ahead. I found that there was a disturbance as I started to walk down the

Road. It was just by a large gorse bush, on the hill."

"Did the bush look like it had been struck by lightning, real big?" Jill asked.

"Yes. Why do ask?"

"No reason," said Jill looking down. "So what happened?"

"I kicked a stone. It seemed to pass through some sort of layer, like water, but vertical and in front of me. I didn't hear it land. So I threw a few more through and couldn't hear them land either. I became convinced that as soon as I stepped through, I wouldn't be able to return."

"So you sneaked after me!"

"Well, I used to be a boy scout, and I got some stuff from the wreck to bivouac with," he tapped the bundle at his side. "You were up at dawn, but I had risen long before that."

Jill's Mum had often called her a mouse because she could not help but nibble bits of cheese whenever it was out in the kitchen. It was a matter of seconds before Jill commented, "This cheddar is delicious, you should try some."

Rocket groaned. "I still think you should ask whoever's this is before you start playing 'finders-keepers'. I do hope that whatever happens next isn't as eventful as yesterday. I could do without those kinds of days."

Jill rolled her eyes. "You just can't see when things are going well. Relax, *old* boy, this is great. Anyway, now you're here, we could do with all the food we can get." Jill picked up a roll, took a bite, scooped up a curl of butter with her knife and proceeded to construct a generous, 'Ploughman's Lunch', with cheese, pickles, fresh lettuce, tomatoes, and cucumber and as much of whatever else was available to fit on the plate. Rocket held back.

"Are you really sure that it's all right to eat? Isn't this the bit in most stories where the food turns out to be drugged?"

Jill looked up at him grinning. "I didn't think that scientists read many stories," she said. "All the boys at school who are good at science have soldering iron burns and car magazines, and are pale and boring." In Jill's school, this was in fact true, although she had only assumed them to be boring and had never taken the time to find out for herself. They were pale because they spent all their time soldering together electronic components indoors, and never got onto the Moor. If Jill had known what one particular boy had used his electronics for, she would have been even less friendly to scientists.

Rocket's face finally broke into a smile and he was about to tell her that her top lip was covered in flour from the fresh bread roll, when a voice from the cottage opposite distracted them both.

The voice came from a woman in a curiously old-fashioned costume at the cottage door.

"Coo-eee! Do help yourselves, my ducks."

Jill, who was sitting with her back to the cottage, stifled a surprised cough and sprayed some salad and cheese across the table.

"That's very kind," Rocket called, "is this your picnic?"

The lady's good-natured smile broadened.

"Yes, I puts it out for all the travellers who come by. I'es enjoys a little company. Come on in and say hello when you're done and finished." The lady disappeared for a moment inside the cottage, re-emerging with a large glass jug that looked as if it was full of home-made lemonade.

Jill swivelled around. "Thank you very much," she said as the lady approached. "My friend was a little worried about the food. He hoped that he wasn't err . . . trespassing."

"Don't be silly my dears," said the lady and carried on in such endearing tones that Rocket found himself a little ashamed not to be eating. He started to nibble at some freshly baked trout and some potato salad at the far end of the table, poured himself a glass of wine, and surveyed their lady host. She was by now cutting another chunk of cheddar from the large round cheese and encouraging Jill to sample the delights of her lemon cake.

Jill was pleased to meet her. This professional Grandma could be a useful ally in getting rid of Rocket, again, and in the meantime Jill was enjoying the food.

Maybe I could try screaming, and blame him for something, then get the local authorities to delay him. I wonder who watches over this part of the Moor and the Road? Somehow, Jill got the feeling that the police were presently out of reach. *But this is where I'll lose him for sure.* Jill looked up at the lady and smiled. *What is it about her that is so familiar?* she thought.

The lady was plump, rounded and very jolly. She sparkled with delight as she fed Jill, and her red cheeks crowded in on a knot of small friendly features. Tiny eyes, turned up nose and plump lips all smiled down on her. Steel grey curls sprung from under a hat that looked like a gathered lace handkerchief and more lace crowded around her neck and collar, which flowed down into the freshest looking cotton blouse, embroidered with flowers. Below all this was a long dark wool skirt. A blue, flower-covered apron covered most of this, and a crocheted shawl lay over her arms and swagged around her back.

"I'll just take this back," said the lady and picked up the lemonade jug that Jill had moments before emptied into her glass tumbler. She walked back across the Road to the cottage and disappeared into the low door.

Rocket also followed her with his eye. *What was she up to?* He stared at the house for any clues.

The cottage looked like the sort of building you might see in the west of England on holiday or in tourist books. It seemed to sleep under a heavy down quilt of straw thatch, smoke curling from a fat chimney and lime washed walls. Rocket could already imagine the wood burning range that had produced the many baked tarts and cakes on the table. Roses crawled about the doorway and the walls were heavy with scented flowers. Woodland flowers bloomed in beds in front of the tarred strip at the bottom of the wall. Swagged curtains winked from small lead light windows, and Rocket fully expected to find that small talking animals peered out from behind over-stuffed chintz couches.

"You've stopped eating, my dear. Do have some more."

Rocket was brought back to reality by the inquiry of the cuddly cook, who had sidled up surprisingly close. He decided at that moment that the old lady seemed to be an extension of the fat white walls of her cottage.

"Oh, excuse me, I've been terribly rude. My name's Rocket.

No, just Rocket." Rocket extended a hand and sought to smile as broadly as he could. He pumped her hand as she said she was pleased to meet him, and then Rocket turned to Jill, at the other end of the table, sweeping his hand out and away with a dramatic turn.

"This is Jill, The Adventurer. In fact, I have rarely met a bolder young lady." The woman almost bowed as she shook her hand and said that she was sure it was a pleasure to meet so grand a young lady. Rocket, sharp eyed, now fixed the cook in his gaze. "Whom have I had the pleasure of addressing, may I ask?" The woman looked slightly bewildered for a moment as the focus shifted to her.

"Well, I don't rightly know what you mean, er, I suppose you're meaning me, aren't you?" She blushed bright pink in confusion.

"I am sorry, I didn't mean to cause you any embarrassment, I simply would like to know your name." Rocket was gentle in his insistence; however, Jill noticed a certain sharpness still in his eyes.

Their host smiled and recovered herself. "Why didn't you just ask, my dear? My name's Mrs. Lazybee and has been time out of mind. Now, won't you have a slice more of the smoked ham, or do you prefer the honey roast?" Seemingly satisfied, Rocket visibly relaxed, took several slices from both plates and tucked into the meal with real pleasure.

The picnic continued for quite a while with much scurrying to and fro by Mrs. Lazybee. It seemed impolite to turn down her request for a little company by the fire before they moved on, so they both entered the cottage, despite Rocket's misgivings. Jill was relieved, as she had thought Rocket would want to press on, but he seemed curious about the old woman. *As long as you focus on her old boy, I'll have an opportunity to disappear.* As it turned out, Jill nearly got her wish.

The cottage was as Rocket imagined; minus the talking mice and moles, and both he and Jill sank into comfortable high-backed chairs. The fire flickered in the grate, and it was well stoked. The cooking range was radiating heat as Mrs. Lazybee prepared scones, and the warmth at first felt smothering. Mind you, they had just eaten a fine meal and Jill said that it would be rude to open a window. She yawned and nodded off. Rocket was wondering when Mrs. Lazybee would sit down and chat as he examined the crowded ornaments and low ceiling of the room. As its cluttered neatness embraced him, he began to realise what it was that was bothering him about the whole scene, but just now he had a headache and felt too tired to think, he would consider it later. What a feed they had had! Mrs. Lazybee certainly knew how to make one feel at home. *Just time for one more stretch and yawn and then a nap.*

That was the last proper thought Rocket had for some time. He slipped into a deep sleep. He and Jill slept all the afternoon. Some people talk about a dreamless sleep, but it is hard to imagine an afternoon nap quite so complete. The day wore on and the pair remained motionless, without a single movement except the rising and falling of chests. No dreams chased across their eyelids. No snores disturbed Mrs. Lazybee's cooking and the chimes of a distant clock. The flower prints at the windows, dust-free ornaments and old-fashioned furniture cradled them securely. The mixed odours of wax polish, pot pourri and fresh cakes somehow created the perfect anesthetic. Time passed, then it was evening.

Rocket woke with a start. He stretched, sluggish and content, and while unwinding backward, he looked for a clock.

"Oh, I *have* slept. What time is it?"

Jill stirred. Rocket looked out of the window, and was startled to find that it was pitch black outside.

"What the . . . !?" Rocket frowned, "Jill, wake up," he strode over and shook her.

"What's up?" came the mumbled response. "I'm asleep! Go away."

Rocket wanted to leave straight away and probably would have, except that Jill was taking some time coming round, and in spite of his sleep, he now had the worst headache he could remember.

She stretched, blinked then sat motionless with nothing but a vacant look in her eyes.

Rocket was watching Jill and looking toward possible exits, when in came Mrs. Lazybee.

"What time is it?" said Rocket a little sharper than he meant to sound.

"Oh, my dears, did you want to leave today? You were so fast asleep it seemed a shame to disturb you. Sit down and rest your weary feet."

"What's the time, Madam, if you please?" Rocket was becoming rude.

"Well sir, about nine o'clock if I'm not mistaken. Yes, there's the chimes." The distant sound of a grand hallway clock floated in from the interior of the cottage.

Jill looked up, still half asleep.

"Here, you don't want to be going out on a night like this. It's not safe you know," the first frown that Rocket had seen on Mrs. Lazybee's face furrowed it into a crumpled mess. "You'd better stay here for the night. I'll just fetch supper." Mrs. Lazybee whisked about on her heels and with great rapidity left again.

Rocket had been about to object, but somehow the decision had been neatly taken out of his hands. He stammered and sat down.

Jill was amazed. What had happened? *She just told him what to do, and he obeyed! That was power!* Jill was beginning to like her more and more. *Oh, why have I got a headache?* She winced and held her head. *There's more to this old granny than meets the eye, but I'm not sure I care to find out. Just so long as she feeds me and I can get rid of the 'old boy', who cares if she's hiding something, I can hardly complain.* Jill winced again, and then yawned. *Maybe all this walking has made me tired. If I take a good sleep here, maybe . . .* she yawned again . . . *maybe I'll get rid of this headache.* For a moment, a thought popped into her head. *I wonder what all this is about? Why is she feeding us so much food?* Jill frowned. "Who cares, so long as it works?" she said out loud.

"Pardon?" said Rocket, "did you say something?"

"Uhh, no. Never mind me." Jill smiled broadly in a way Rocket could not quite make out.

Then the food came in, which did not taste poisonous. Rocket had to admit that he had rarely tasted more wholesome food, and certainly never more delicious.

He ate and tried to remember in vain what it was that he had been thinking about earlier in the day. It buzzed about in the back of his mind like an annoying fly, just beyond his reach. What was it that he had begun to realise? It would come to him tomorrow. He would eat this fruit and cheese and go to bed. Yes, that would help.

Mrs. Lazybee led the two upstairs. Jill had enjoyed her sardines on granary toast, a delicacy she had never tasted before. She was wondering where she might be able to buy these fish at home, when led by their ever-efficient hostess, they both thoughtlessly tumbled into the billowing wastes of huge eider-down quilts.

The next morning both awoke in good time for breakfast. Their iron bedsteads were in a low ceilinged room. Above, there were dark wood beams spanning the worn Persian rug, and below wooden boards, beds and old timber furniture. Light shafted through the small window, the room glowing with the dawn.

"Good morning Rocket," said Jill.

"Oh, morning," he mumbled. "I don't remember being put in the same room as you. Most improper. In fact, I can't remember much at all. She didn't give us anything except hot chocolate to drink, did she?"

Jill paused. She couldn't remember anything about the previous evening either. *That can't be right; there must be something to remember.* For a second her mother's face came to mind. But then her stomach rumbled, and her headache had returned. "Could you? Would you mind?" Jill's face combined a question and a plea. "I'd like to get dressed so I can eat breakfast."

"Oh, all right," said Rocket who grabbed a towel and headed for a bathroom himself.

Several minutes and lots of steam later, Rocket re-emerged to find that Jill had washed and dressed.

"I wonder what's for breakfast?" Jill mused. With the lightest of moods, she bounced downstairs. Rocket thought it sounded uncommonly like thunder, and followed.

Breakfast did not disappoint.

Eggs, bacon, mushrooms, tomatoes, toast, black pudding and other sausages jostled for space with omelettes, waffles, pancakes, croissant, fresh rolls and bagels. Rocket momentarily wondered where all this could have come from, but since Mrs Lazybee appeared with muffins, that thought was put to one side. Fresh coffee and blueberry muffins were more than enough for his early morning mind to consider. Jill was trying Earl Grey's Tea with her Full English Breakfast, and rather enjoying the experience.

"This is rather good stuff. Eh, what?" said Jill. She meant to mimic Rocket; however, since her mouth was full of bacon and mushroom dipped in soft egg yolk, it came out more as "Riss is rarrer 'ood suff, ey wut?" Rocket, stopped and stared, which in Jill's present mood made her giggle in embarrassment. For a moment, she stopped and thought; she could not remember why she was laughing. *How did I get here in the first place? Well, who cares anyway?* This place was too good to be true and she did not feel like thinking. *I can work out how to get rid of the 'old boy' some other time.*

Rocket, on the other hand, had that buzzing in the back of his head again. A thought was trying to gain his attention, but so was a new headache. *What was it? Something to do with Jill's question and stuffed mouth?* No, it was no use, it was gone again.

Rocket smiled in an embarrassed way and noted his surprise that there was no steak or kippers on the table, until Jill pointed them both out.

"Quite remarkable," he muttered. He stopped again. *Yes, it was quite remarkable. Why was that? What* was *the reason? Things always had reasons! What was Jill's and his reason? What was it about Mrs. Lazybee?* He nearly caught the thought this time, but his head started to ache almost as badly as yesterday. *Then again, why not just enjoy a waffle followed by an omelette?* Yes, he would pass the toast Jill had just asked for and eat. If it was important, it could wait 'til after breakfast when he could give it his full attention.

Jill was still watching him and waiting for an answer, but when it did not come, she simply shrugged. *Hey, when things feel this good, who cares?* Jill was not bothered now either by headaches or questions.

The two now ate in a halo of delicious comfort. More breakfast was eaten than seemed sensible, which Jill thought very funny. Mrs. Lazybee asked for help with the dishes and much time was spent cleaning up. Rocket asked her what she had meant by the danger of travelling in the dark and she responded with comments about not twisting ankles on a night road.

"Not safe my dear," she said in much the same way as the previous evening, and for a second, like a flare in the night, Rocket knew that she had meant more than just turned ankles. Equally suddenly, he had to pass the drying cloth, clean the frying pan and put the cutlery away. The flare guttered out, the thought died, and he was in the dark again. The end of washing up left him hanging out wet clean laundry as Jill learnt some basic baking. A nap and morning elevenses left him praising Jill's fresh coconut cake, and then Rocket remembered part of what he had been going to say.

"When shall we set out again?" he spoke suddenly, with relief, and then frowned at the sharp jab of pain across his forehead.

Jill frowned, what was it she had been going to do? She needed to get to the Lord of the Way. Oh and yes! She was going to get rid of this annoying old man, and get out of this odd little cottage. Why had they stayed so long? But he wanted to go too! *I need to distract him, if he stays, even for a few hours, I could slip away unnoticed and be free of him.* "Oh," she said out loud, "let's stay till tea time, please?" Mrs Lazybee looked at Jill with mild surprise, and Jill thought she saw her nose twitch. Jill was furiously thinking of an excuse to slip out the back door, and was standing up to leave straight away, when Mrs Lazybee fixed her with an angry stare.

"Pass the tea towel, there's washing up to do, dear. It's your turn." Jill was startled by her fierceness, and seemed confused. Mrs. Lazybee smiled broadly. "Sorry dear. Now, with such a journey on your minds, maybe you should at least get some strength up over lunch. Let's sort out the kitchen. Maybe we could get a few things together after that? What do you think?" There was a momentary pause. Rocket's mind cramped up. Jill's face looked blank again.

"Well that's settled," said Mrs. Lazybee swinging back into action. "Where did I put that apron?"

Lunch came and went, conversation flowed, and although Rocket was aware that, "things needed to be addressed," as he might have said, all urgency was gone. He said later that it was as if he was a football that had rolled to a stop. He was waiting for a kick. Nothing in this place seemed likely to jolt him and so it proved for the rest of the day.

Jill appeared to be happily forgetful again. Nothing seemed out of place to her, and by the end of the second day, all she did was nap and cook. She talked of nothing but the delicious food. High tea, dinner and supper all passed by and Jill and Rocket's sleeps slowly stretched out.

The next day was a little overcast, and as Mrs. Lazybee could not risk hanging out her wet washing on a drizzly day, Rocket fixed a pulley on the old-fashioned slatted 'airer', which hung over her cooking range. The clothes above toasted while Dundee cake and Danish pastry cooked below.

They almost missed elevenses, as they both dozed so long, and somehow, by turns, the day was used up. When supper arrived, they felt more tired than ever, going to bed with yawns, hot chocolate and heavy eyes.

The next four or five days passed in much the same way, with later and later breakfasts, earlier bed times and longer naps. Mrs Lazybee remarked that they must have had remarkable strength to keep so busy, but this time even this did not stir their suspicions.

These two might have remained in their state of waking sleep for a very long time, except that someone started to snore.

It was early on the tenth day of their stay and both were asleep. Jill rolled over and complained, half to her pillow, "Rocket, stop snoring."

"I'm not snoring," Rocket replied as he blinked sleepily at the bright morning sunlight.

Jill insisted, "Yes you are, and it's the middle of the night too."

"What are you talking about?" Rocket sat up against his mound of pillows, scowling. It was certainly not the middle of the night, although he felt as if it should be.

There came that noise again.

"Will you please stop that?" murmured Jill, and rolled to face the wall. "It's not fair," came her sleepy voice, which tailed into the faint wheeze of sleep.

But Rocket, now with a fierce headache, concentrated on the regular sound that had disturbed Jill.

Mrs. Lazybee slept downstairs near the kitchen. She had explained her need to tend the ovens on their first evening.

This noise that Rocket could hear sounded as if it was upstairs and very close. Rocket suddenly realised that there were other bedrooms, which he and Jill had not looked into. He had assumed that they were empty. They had certainly not seen anyone else staying with Mrs Lazybee. There it came again, with a slight catch of a snort. No, it had to be someone snoring, and it wasn't him or Jill or Mrs Lazybee either. His mind swam sleepily, but he shook his head and forced himself to focus.

There, that was better. Invigorated by the exercise of his will, he decided to do something. He was Rocket, a scientist, and he would investigate this peculiar sound.

Rocket threw the bedclothes back, swung his legs out and strode across the room. He opened the door, his heart beating wildly, and was relieved to find the corridor empty. In the moment of opening, he had been gripped with a momentary terror that Mrs. Lazybee would suddenly appear and block his progress.

Rocket listened for a second, caught the sound of a rasp, and turned right down the corridor, away from the cramped twisting stairwell. The sound was not coming from the bathroom, first on his right, nor the bathroom behind him by the head of the stairs, but from the fourth door along the upstairs corridor. He walked along, gently placed his hand on the doorknob, and pushed the door open.

It was a room just like theirs, with two beds. One was neatly turned back. The other was rumpled mess. At first he could see nothing in the bed, however seconds later a pillow snored. Rocket's heart leapt as the sound seemed far too loud, and he momentarily wished to be back in bed. He shook himself again, *Pull yourself together boy!*

The situation reminded Rocket of wandering into his aunt's room when he was very small and being caught about to drink her perfume. He did not enjoy feeling like that again. He took a second look at the pillow and found that he could now make out a hand that hung out of one side of the bed, and that a head was wedged underneath the pillow. Since the sheets and pillowcases were a bright crumpled whiteness, he had not noticed at first that one of the pillows was a boy in a white night shirt. He was lying face down and small flecks of tousled dark hair protruded from under the pillow. About where his waist should be, he disappeared into the vastness of the quilt.

Rocket stood motionless, wondering if the boy could breathe properly, but the next hearty snort settled any fears. He would not try to wake him. He must have arrived late last night, Rocket told himself. The scientist in him, however, had received quite a jolt and was on a roll again.

What if there are others, in other rooms? He held on to this idea, and decided to investigate, moving somewhat unsteadily to the corridor again. He tried the next door. Two beds, sunlight and neat sheets. The next door after that also opened on an almost identical scene.

Relieved, Rocket confidently pushed open the third door. It was a peculiar sight. An older man and woman were breathing evenly, laid back with folded arms in neatly made beds. Dust lay on their foreheads, and sparkled in the shafts of sunlight, and no crease or other sign of movement appeared in the bed or their neatly pressed pajama tops.

Rocket quickly tried the next door. A lady who could have been his mother lay cradled in quietness, still, except for gentle breathing.

He glanced down the corridor. As in many cottages, the floor was uneven, and within a few feet the corridor bent around, following the curved contours of the house wall. This lack of straightness meant that no part of the corridor could be seen more than a few feet away. He looked back. The stairs had already dipped out of sight behind a wall bulge.

Well, there cannot be more than a few doors to try, Rocket told himself. The sleepers he found were fascinating to look at, and some had unusually long hair, as if they had needed a cut a few years ago. He was absorbed in trying to figure out where they had come from, when he realised with a start that this must be the twentieth that he had opened. He stopped and looked down the corridor. No, there was no end wall. It simply twisted out of sight. The light and sound in the corridor suggested that it continued for several feet more.

This was absurd, as he should now have walked out of the cottage, and the spot he was standing on should be suspended over the garden. He checked between his feet. It seemed solid enough. He walked briskly along trying to find the end wall. Rocket glanced out of a window and saw the picnic table, the Road and the front garden, so the corridor was still at the front of the house. He started to run, his own nightshirt flapping as the corridor twisted, but the corridor continued without any sign of coming to an end. He stopped, panting, and pushed open a door. The light was inexplicably dim in the room, although the curtains were open. The sleeper looked wrinkled, and ribbons of perfectly or-dered hair cascaded to the floor. Rocket started to panic. There was no end to this corridor. *It goes on forever!* he thought, recovering his breath. A night terror started to force itself into his thoughts. *Perhaps it goes on forever in both directions?* He started to walk back. *Walk calmly. Don't give in to the fear old boy.* Perhaps the corridor wouldn't let you go to its end. Perhaps it wouldn't let you go anywhere. Maybe he would not be able to walk back to the stairs end of the house either. He felt the fear closing on him, and started to pick up his feet, stumbling into a sort of trot. *Stop thinking about it!* He glanced over his shoulder and the twisting walls behind now seemed full of menace. Somewhere, a shadow moved, he was sure of it. Rocket broke into full fright and ran for his life.

He fled until his lungs felt like they were bursting and his throat burned. His run should have brought back to the stairs.

Still the corridor did not finish; still he could not find his room.

Rocket squinted to hold back tears and whispered a plea to the air, pushing the walls away as he ricocheted down the passage. He unexpectedly missed his grip and fell down, panting loudly in the almost silent corridor. There was the sound of snoring again. What a wonderful sound!

Rocket's red and angry face was covered in sweat, and he looked up thankfully to see his and Jill's room.

"Jill, get up, we've got to go." Rocket was still gasping and his nightshirt was wet with perspiration. Jill did not even stir. He shook her shoulder. Her hand ineffectually swatted his own. He tried again, but nothing worked.

Rocket left the room for a few moments, and returned with a full bucket of water that he had found in the bathroom. The quilt was flung back across the room. The water was launched and found its target. Jill finally woke with a furious yell.

Her first clear thought was that she *really* had to get rid of this man. "What are you doing!? It's the middle of the night!"

"No it's not, look out the window; but it should be. By the way, here's your towel, and come with me, if you please." The towel was hurled at her. Jill wrapped it around herself and chased after Rocket, not quite sure what she would do when she caught up with him. She had not seen Rocket like this and was unsure what was going on. He showed her the snoring boy, and when she began to shout at him again, Rocket led her firmly by the arm to the second set of sleepers.

"Ow, that hurts, stop it." Rocket pushed the door open, while he checked that he could still just see their room's door, down the corridor. Jill peered in. "What's going on? Who are these people? Why are they so . . . asleep?"

"There are hundreds, maybe thousands of them up here. Get dressed and we'll ask Mrs. Lazybee."

Jill suddenly looked very afraid.

"Yes, why should an old lady make anyone that frightened?" Rocket asked, more to himself than Jill. "Come on. I'm going to wake the boy if I can. Please get dressed."

Jill hurried back and dressed, but when she returned Rocket was upset.

"I can't wake him. I saw others. They looked like they'd been asleep for years." He paused and then, much to Jill's surprise, said, "Let's go to breakfast, shall we?" Jill's stomach felt queasy, but she followed him down.

"Mrs. Lazybee. I have found a guest in the room next door." A mild ache started in the back of Rockets head.

"Really my dear?"

"He was snoring." The headache was definitely returning.

"I hope he didn't disturb you."

"I'm rather glad he did. He was able to wake me, but I can't wake him." Sharp stabs of pain flashed across Rocket's temples.

"Oh, I expects he needs his rest."

"How long has he been asleep?" Rocket was by now gritting his teeth, and his thoughts were becoming confused.

"This last week, I think, or maybe longer. Got here just before you, dears. He seemed quite tired though, poor soul."

A week asleep! Jill was horrified. So people really did go asleep here, perhaps forever. Her mind went back to all the people in the Village. *Quite a few of them would really fit in here,* she thought. Jill realised that if she had not had all her problems, she would have never left herself. *How could you have fallen for this weird old witch? Why's Rocket gone quiet?*

Rocket had turned pale, gathered his thoughts and launched out again. "I really think that a week's sleep is enough for anyone. We should wake him."

"Really? I don't know. He was so tired when he got here, and so comfortable after he dropped off it seemed a pity to disturb him. Rest is good for you, wouldn't you agree?" Mrs. Lazybee's bright eyes fixed him and for a moment, confusion crowded his face.

Jill panicked. *No! I need him to stay awake.* She thought quickly. "I think a week is far too long. That boy needs to wake up. Ummh, he must be ill or something."

Mrs. Lazybee's face grew concerned. This idea had apparently never occurred to her before. "Do you think he might be unwell dear?"

To Jill's immense relief Rocket spoke again, his eyes regaining their old firmness. "Yes, I suspect that he is in critical danger. We must wake him at once."

Mrs. Lazybee, after several changes of mind, was slowly persuaded by both Rocket and Jill to come upstairs. She had no trouble waking the boy, but was quite at ease when they mentioned to her the other guests.

"Mustn't grumble, I suppose. They all needed some peace and quiet. They come to me for peace and quiet, so I don't disturb them. Let them rest; easier that way."

Jill took the still groggy boy downstairs.

"Is he all right do you think?" Mrs. Lazybee asked Rocket.

"It is my opinion that he will make a full recovery, madam," Rocket replied, "but I hope you will wake any others who contract this malady."

Mrs. Lazybee's face brightened. "Well, I'm sure if any good gentleman like yourself tells me that a child is sick, I'll be glad to help. Mus'n't disturb anyone else though, they needs their rest." Mrs. Lazybee bumbled off down the upstairs corridor and quickly disappeared.

For a moment, Rocket felt the recent paralysis of thought returning. He shook himself and shuddered. He changed out of his nightshirt, quickly packed up their little bundles of equipment from their room and hurried downstairs.

Jill was sitting at the breakfast table; propping up the drowsy lad, and helping him sip water. *I could have been like him. I may as well have been dead. I may as well have been back in the Village.*

"Why aren't you two eating?" Rocket was sounding very much the grown up now.

"I thought you said the food was poisoned?" said Jill.

"I think this *place* is poison, not the food. I'm sure it would have killed us by now otherwise. It's my thoughts that have been deadened here, not my body, and I've only had headaches when

I've tried to ask her questions. Can't think of a drug that could do that. You two been having the same headaches?" Jill and the boy nodded. "I thought so, so eat all you can; we're leaving in the next couple of minutes."

The two ate as heartily as they could, Jill enquiring where 'that witch' was and Rocket rebuking her for her rudeness while he explained that Mrs. Lazybee had pottered down the sleepers' corridor. He told her about everything else he had seen. Even their new friend sat up and took notice at his tale.

"I've been bothered by something ever since we arrived," said Rocket. "There were no apparent connections for this place, no community to support and no talk of friends or family. There seemed no sense in what she was doing. Who puts out a meal for nearly twenty people each day if there's no reason to do so? Why have a guest-house and no house guests? Now we know why she never talked about her previous visitors. She's stacking them all upstairs, in storage."

"Why would anyone want to do that? It's sick!" Jill pulled a face, "Uggh!"

"Whatever her reason for all this is, she's hiding it. Who would capture people like this? What would they want them for?" Rocket said. He stopped for a moment to sip his Earl Grey tea. "Have you noticed how hard it is to think here, especially when *she* is around? And have you noticed the headaches come and go only when you try to think, especially when you want to ask difficult questions. And she never talks about things."

"Huh," said Jill, "I thought she never shut up."

"She never talks about anything that matters, though. It seems to me now that this is some sort of honey trap for travellers on the Road, like those plants that lure insects into their petals. They have sweet nectar in the centre, then, bang, it's all over." Rocket concluded with a dramatic snap of his hands.

"Yeah, but who would want to do that?" Jill wondered to no one in particular. The boy picked it up.

"I suppose whoever persuaded Mrs. Lazybee to be like she is, and equipped her cottage with bottomless food and bedrooms. I started out in the first bedroom, not where you found me. By the way, I'm Kyle."

"Kyle Williams from the Village?" Jill was wide eyed.

"Yes, you've heard of me?"

"You lived near to "Martha's Convenience Store" in those rentals. They said you ran away after the house burnt down last Thursday."

Kyle looked embarrassed. "Yeah, well. Didn't feel like staying. Once the house burnt down, wasn't much point in sticking around. I took to the Moor on the old road and then ran into this old dear. I thought I was in heaven."

"You left the Village the day before me," said Jill, "how long do you think you've been running away?"

The boy frowned. "Only three days. I spent two nights on the Moor, shivering, but you said "last Thursday," so what day is today?"

"Saturday, ten days," Jill replied.

Kyle whistled. "I guess I must have slept longer than I thought."

It was Rocket's turn to frown. "Well, let's not sleep our lives away; fill your pockets with food, we're leaving. Have you got anything upstairs Kyle?"

The three cautiously ventured upstairs, and fetched his thin coat, sleeping bag and a picture of a man, smiling cheerfully. Without another word, all sorts of greasy meat, hard-boiled eggs and breads were wrapped up in the handkerchiefs that Mrs. Lazybee had insisted they all use. Jill slipped into the kitchen and reclaimed her food from the cold store.

"The bread was stale," Jill said," So I grabbed another loaf. My bacon and stuff seems okay though."

They quickly moved outside and rejoined the Road.

The day was a little overcast and humid. They started to walk and glanced nervously behind. Through the still, moist heat, they heard a voice call out behind them.

"Don't leave just yet my dears, the day's still young."

All three broke into a run together, and did not stop for a good ten minutes.

7

THE WAYFARER'S HUT

Kyle Williams, Rocket and Jill all stood panting in the heavy air, sweat running uncomfortably under their clothes. Rocket cocked his head to one side, as if listening. "I can't hear her any more," he said.

The other two were standing watching the trees. They glanced around, scanning the scenery as if part of a wide game. Jill turned to Rocket; "Do you think she'll follow?"

"Only if houses can walk," Rocket said.

Jill looked up at Rocket. She was still annoyed at the way he had added himself to her trip and now it seemed, thanks to him, she was landed with a boy too. Rocket was bent double with the exertion of running and seemed content to watch his own feet for a short while, while Jill watched him. *The old odd ball saved my life, though. I'm glad to be out of that evil cottage.* Jill still kept a suspicious eye on the Road behind them, as she was not as confident as Rocket that they were really free. She was tense, with a sort of nervous sickness in her stomach again. *What am I going to do about Rocket? What about Kyle, come to that? I'd stopped there to get rid of 'the old boy', now I'm landed with another guest.* Jill had met him only once

96

or twice at school, and disliked him every time she had. Some of the other children had said that he smelled, and she mostly believed them. Kyle himself looked a little green. He was glancing nervously at everything, including Rocket and Jill. *He's feeling worse than me,* she thought as she stared.

"The wood seems friendly enough, but I'll be glad to be out of it as soon as possible," Jill said. "Anyone want to go back to the Village?" she asked hopefully.

Rocket smiled. "You don't get rid of me that easily."

Kyle shrugged. "Nothing to go back to," he said and glanced about as he said so, not meeting her eye. The three started to walk on, still breathing hard and little shaken.

The wood, it turned out, was bigger than they thought, and although none said so, each kept fearing that it was like the cottage's endless corridor. Every corner that promised open country, simply turned out to reveal a wider than normal clearing. Although the trees were as bright and fresh as ever and the flowers as friendly as before, the dull light and a heaviness of mind led each of them to suspicions that things were nowhere near normal.

Kyle said it first.

"Where's the birds?" He stopped, partly turned to Jill, and repeated the question. Rocket stopped too and listened intently.

"It's *too* quiet," Rocket said in a whisper, and then he grinned. "I've always wanted to say that, you know."

"Say what?" Kyle queried.

"You know in films, the hero gets to spot things no-one else does. 'Look, there's the way out,' or 'I've found the diamond,' or 'It's too quiet' and then something dramatic happens." Rocket found this amusing, but the children couldn't see why.

"When do they say 'It's too quiet,' then?" said Jill.

"Well, usually when they're about to be attacked," said Rocket, "but I don't think there's any need to be alarmed, it's just . . ."

The other two did not wait, but sprinted off. Both kept glancing back and it took several minutes before Rocket persuaded them to slow down.

A minute later found Rocket staring into the treetops and he started to talk again. "You know, it would be unusual if some natural predator had eaten *all* the birds," he said. "Perhaps they have been hunted out by people. I mean, if it were a natural predator, it would have to be big and agile to be able to kill all the birds. I suppose it would stand a better chance of catching all the birds if it could fly. Or maybe, there were huge numbers of the predator. You know, something with sharp teeth, or even sharp beaks, and an appetite for meat. I wonder if that's what Mrs. Lazybee was talking about, with that talk about it being too dangerous to travel at night? If that were so, maybe it would sweep down on its prey from up there, or maybe it doesn't need to wait for night."

Jill frowned in concentration as her gaze followed Rocket's finger to the trees. She started to tremble slightly. *Could something even stranger, even more dangerous, than the old witch be out here?* The shaking took hold properly now. *Think on one thing at once, think about Mum, think about the good things.* Her stomach turned over. Jill stopped and stared at him. "I don't want to talk about it all right? Not until we're out of these woods." Jill's voice was unsteady but something about her glare brought Rocket to a faltering pause. "All right?" The question hung in the air as Jill stood her ground, shivering against the light.

Rocket stammered. "All right old girl. I didn't mean to upset you. I was just thinking out loud . . ." He coughed and looked away.

"We've got enough to worry about without *inventing* things to scare ourselves!" Jill spat the words out.

"I'll not mention it again," Rocket mumbled.

They continued to walk.

After a while, they passed the burnt out hulks of two other cottages, and a third more mysterious stone building, similarly blackened. They all peered momentarily at these landmarks, and then quickened their step once more. By the third ruin, Rocket had muttered something about the interests of science and finding out what had done this, however a sharp look from Jill had brought colour to his cheeks and no more was said.

By the time that the Road started to wind uphill again, the

afternoon was well under way. The sun shone dully where it could be seen as the clouds raced past it, a moon like disc. They laboured up the side of a steep hill, still deep in the woods, as the Road snaked back and forth on itself with hairpin bends. As they got higher, it got hotter. Sweat trickled down their faces, oozed through their clothes and tickled their legs. Silence fell on the walkers; their only extra movement came from knocking the small flies away from their faces. This was no change for Kyle who had not said much all day but now seemed very uncomfortable as well as dumb. Grimacing and blowing harder than the others, he dragged his feet.

Jill broke the silence; "Anyone got any water?" They had eaten some bacon sandwiches earlier and they now all felt very thirsty.

"Yes, thanks," said Kyle as he drank the last of his own supply and insisted on a break for a minute. Jill stared at him and his empty water bottle, but Rocket got them moving again very shortly. None wished to be in the woods after dark and discover what made them unsafe at night, especially after Rocket's thinking out-loud.

As they resumed walking, Jill was fuming with anger. *One of them wants to scare me to death and the other is prepared to let me die of thirst!* But being this angry reminded her of her mother and arguments, and her rage leaked away into thoughtful calm.

After about half an hour, the trees began to thin. This cheered Kyle up to no end and he began to talk about what he wanted for tea, and what they might do tomorrow. They could see that the wooded hillside they were climbing would soon break into the open before they went over a ridge. A sound like distant water drifted on the air from above and the trees around them stirred with a momentary breeze. It was the first fresh air of the day and very refreshing. Kyle looked at the open sky and flinched, almost as if the extra light hurt his eyes.

Jill had watched him all afternoon. *Something's definitely not right with him,* she thought for the tenth time that day. *Some thing's definitely not right with me for letting him stick around!* And Jill wished, not for the first time, that she had actually been able to leave everyone else behind.

They emerged from the trees into gorse bushes and still warm air. The Road straightened out, and the slope eased, and they soon rounded the crest of the hill. The relief of the breeze made them all stop.

Rocket scanned the horizon.

"What are you looking for?" asked Jill.

"Ways down; shelter; anyone else."

To the west, the wood swept round in a low depression, an impassable tangle. To the east, the Moor ran a large distance away to the boulders and jagged teeth of cliff tops. The hilltops behind were smoother, but Rocket pointed to swirling dots above them. "There will be cliffs or very steep hills there too," said Rocket, "the birds are riding currents of air that drive up from below." Beyond that edge, grey sky hid any view of what lay behind. They watched the silhouettes for some minutes. To the north, the Road ran straight and clear.

"I think the Road will look after us," said Jill. Now it was the others' turn to stare at her.

"I hardly think it helped us last time," Rocket said.

"What? This road? How can a road help anyway?" Kyle asked. They started to walk again.

"It's a long story," Jill said, and bit by bit, with many a doubting question from Kyle and occasionally from Rocket, she told her story again, beginning when her mother told her about the Road and up to the moment Rocket had appeared. "So I'm here to find this Lord of the Way guy, and that's why I'm headed down this path. I need to . . . to find some answers," she concluded.

Kyle said out loud, "I thought this Road was weird," What actually ran through his mind was that it had to be better than the Institution. "So why's the old man here?" was what he actually said.

"The *old man* has decided to investigate the Road's weirdness, as you would say, *young man*." Rocket said, "I'm trying to find out what's behind all this, but I'll tell you what I think in a few days.

After that last episode, it maybe my duty to take you both home."
Jill turned to Kyle and grinned as he rolled his eyes. They had
been wandering along the top of the high moorland plateau, and
Rocket had still been casting around in every direction. He suddenly
let out a low whistle as the sun broke through clouds behind them.

"Lady and Gentleman, I give you Nowhere," he said.

The view behind was amazing. As sun and breeze dispersed
the mist, the whole of the land of Nowhere lay picked out like a
three dimensional map.

Kyle broke the momentary silence.

"Now, that really *is* weird."

None of the strange powers of the Vantage Point were present,
but it was clear that no normal view could look like this.

"It really is quite a place, this land of Nowhere," said Rocket,
shaking his head.

Jill bit her lip, and kept quiet before putting her hands in her
pockets. The stones prickled with heat and she had the queerest
feeling that they burned hot against the land behind her. All
Nowhere's lies came to mind; all hers too. All the disappointments
she had known seemed to lurk in the shadows that picked out
every hill and tree. *There's got to be something better.* She thought
about how a few days ago she had been taken in by Mrs. Lazybee.
*There's got to be someone who can help Mum, but they're not back there,
that's for sure.* Jill then turned back up the Road. "Well, I'm going
on. You two can do what you like, but I'm finishing this," she said,
and with flick of her hair Jill strode forward again.

Rocket simply shrugged and resumed walking while Kyle
trailed compliantly behind. Kyle was used to things being done to
him, and to other people telling him what to do. But nothing ever
really happened to him, nothing that really mattered. Trouble would
always happen, and he would still be miserable after it happened,
so it did not matter what he did. Something else was bound to
come along eventually, just not anything that would really change
things. He kept plodding head down, following Rocket; just as
Rocket, in his turn, tried to appear not to be following Jill.

Rocket kept searching the skyline all afternoon, but there was no one else on the Road or the Moor that they could see. Jill looked around as well, but there were only miles of empty windswept bracken and gorse. No other soul was to be seen. They had stopped for a late lunch and had finished off Jill's remaining food. As they sat and talked they fell quiet, each to their own thoughts. Even after they resumed walking, no-one seemed to know what to say, and uneasy silence fell.

Everyone said that Jill saw it first; a small square box on the horizon, just to the right of the Road.

"That could be our shelter for the night," said Rocket, and although Kyle remained unconvinced, the party's mood became less sombre.

The breeze had become stiff and the clouds were allowing shafts of sunlight to brighten the late afternoon. High and lonely birdsong seasoned the air and even Rocket began to quote some poetry about sweet, sad longing. The desperation of their situation had taken on an almost heroic quality, and as Jill said, there was nothing else to be done. They strode toward what quickly resolved into a hut.

Jill's thoughts swung wildly from one extreme to another.

This could be my opportunity! Maybe this time I'll get it right and lose both of them, would be followed by, *But Rocket saved my life,* and then *Yeah, but I wouldn't have needed to eat the old witch's food if he hadn't eaten mine,* and *I'm not that different to Kyle, but at least* **I** *bathe.* Finally, she settled on the theme of, *I'm not going to let these losers keep me from reaching the Lord of the Way.* In the midst of all this, it occurred to her to wonder to whom the hut might belong.

"Doesn't look like much," said Jill. "What do you guys think?"

As they walked, more details became apparent. At first, all they could see was that the hut was made of dark brown wood, and that the roof spread wide, Swiss style. It became apparent after awhile that it had a timber-shingled roof and that a small yellow sandstone path peeled away from the main road to meet it.

"It's no palace," said Jill.

"Looks really rough to me," said Kyle.

Rocket squinted, and the freckles around his eyes seemed to all join up as he did so. "Doesn't quite look normal, in my opinion. Let's see what we can, before we get too close," and they stopped at a safe distance to survey their target.

The hut stood facing the Road, a stone's throw away from it, and now Jill could make out all sorts of great stuff hanging outside from its walls, eaves and just about any available point on the temporary building. They were still some distance from it and the other two travellers could only dimly make out what the objects were. Jill, however, was in no doubt. "That's fantastic! Maybe we could get whoever owns this stuff to sell us some. This is exactly what I need for a really long hike."

"Now hang on Jill, let's not go through this again," said Rocket.

"Through what?" said Kyle.

"She has a weakness for cheese," said Rocket.

"I can't see any cheese, is it inside? I'm hungry." Kyle was apparently serious, but Jill did not miss a beat.

"He's referring to the picnic table at Mrs. Lazybee's," said Jill, "and to his own lack of adventure."

"I simply would like to stay alive and awake," said Rocket.

Kyle had heard a lot of arguments in his short life and did not want to hear another. "We don't have any choice, sir. There isn't anywhere else to go, except back to Mrs. Lazybee's, so let's check it out." Kyle blushed deep red, but managed not to look at the ground.

After a few tense seconds, Rocket sighed, stared up at the still, heavy clouds, and then looked straight at Jill. "Well I suppose you have a point. But let me do the talking this time." With that, they started walking again.

What Jill was excited about was an amazing array of hiking and camping equipment. Jill could see boots, walking sticks, oil skins, tents, ice picks, camping stoves, blankets, hats, rucksacks and much else she couldn't yet identify hung, pinned, leaned, trailed, tied or otherwise heaped up in amazing profusion under the eaves. The wide roof allowed the merchandise to be displayed under shelter and the hut itself sat on small, mushroom shaped stone pillars and was larger on closer inspection than it had seemed at a distance. Rough sawn boards ran horizontally, each one overlapping the boards beneath like slates or tiles might, and it could have provided ample space to sleep, cook and eat for more than three.

As they reached where the path split from the Road, Rocket asked the question that had been bothering them all. "Who would leave all this for anyone to take?" No one answered.

Jill altered course and followed the path out. Kyle, who had been trailing behind, sprinted past her and arriving at the flimsy door, banged it hard. Nothing happened. The wind whistled underneath the hut, and tousled their hair. They stood, stared and considered what to do.

As Kyle stood back, Rocket started to wander around the hut inspecting its structure. It was surrounded by short grass and Rocket put his head down to look underneath. "It's sitting on more of that same stone the Road's made of, Jill."

Jill grunted a reply. She was examining the rainbow of boots hanging just to the left of the hut door. They were made of fine oiled leather, suspended by silken laces from hooks on the wall, and were of every possible colour combination. The laces were shot through with gold, and glints of gold also shone out of the stitching. Kyle stopped staring at the door and then decided to slide up to Jill, kicking a small cloud of dust from the stones. "The door's padlocked, so there can't be anyone inside," he said.

Jill was oblivious to his words, having moved onto silk, cotton and leather waterproofs, which rustled as she stroked them.

Rocket reappeared having completed his circuit of the hut. "What do think of the equipment?" he asked Jill.

"It's gorgeous. It's not made of anything I've seen before, but it feels like it would do a wonderful job, and some of us came really badly equipped." Jill scanned them both up and down. "Whatever its quality, you could use all the help you can get," she said with smile that made her look just like her mother.

Rocket fidgeted and stooped to examine a curiously made lamp. Kyle scowled and Jill in turn sighed. Looking up, she noticed that, tucked underneath the eaves, high upon the wall, there was a sign that would be impossible to see if you were standing out from under the roof. Its golden lettering was painted on a circular slice cut from the end of a log, and looked like leaves and branches tangled and woven together. Jill pointed up, "Can you see what that says?" she asked Kyle and Rocket.

"It's all jumbled," said Kyle.

Rocket shaded his eyes. "I think I can make something out though," he said.

After a few minutes discussion they agreed that the letters said something like this: -

"If the journey's end you do desire,
No payment from you will I require,
Take all that you need, it is mine to give,
Now heed my words and you will live."

"We can't just *take* it," mumbled Kyle.

"Well, we don't know if it's safe," said Rocket, "and I don't like the sound of that threat at the end."

"I don't think it's a threat though," Kyle said, "it sounds more like a *warning*."

"If the owner was here, we could ask him," said Jill, "but it's all locked up. There can't be anyone for miles."

"But we need the owner to turn up," said Kyle, "he can't be too far away."

"Well, where would we find him?" said Rocket.

"Wherever you need me," came a voice from behind. Rocket jumped and turned around so that all three could see who had just spoken.

Leaning against the hut's corner was a wiry man. He was over six feet tall, and was wearing walking gear. A crimson waterproof jacket covered the top of what looked like chocolate moleskin trousers, and his boots were jet black with crimson laces. Jill thought she could smell flowers, and he certainly had sprigs of flowering heather tucked into his coat and bootlaces, and without being able to say why, Jill immediately liked him. *A good looking guy who appears out of thin air and smells great!* The man broke into smile that made her feel as if the sun had just come out. *Careful girl, you weren't your best when figuring out the last stranger.*

Rocket took a step back. He looked confused, and Jill found herself speaking. "Excuse me, but are all these things yours?"

"They certainly are," the man replied. His smile was remarkably open.

"We would like to buy some equipment, please. My friends need to replace their coats and tents and there seem few places around here to get anything." Jill was trying to be at her most mature, partly because she was already imagining herself wearing a sapphire blue coat and also because she was trying to give a good impression.

"It's not for sale." His voice was gentle and warm.

"I'm sorry; we simply assumed that such a display invited commerce," said Rocket, who on the other hand, sounded unfriendly in a polite, adult sort of way.

Kyle said, "Sir, could we borrow some of the equipment and return it later?"

"No, I never take gifts back." The man had a rugged face, and lines radiating from the corners of his eyes seemed to laugh.

"Gifts? You give this stuff away?" Jill's voice was rising.

"And why would you do that?" said Rocket.

"It is mine to do with as I like," the man said, "have you not read the sign?" He pointed up to the plaque.

It was at this point that Jill noticed his hair. It twisted into brown, stiff waves and, as the sunlight caught it, they glistened a rainbow of colours. *Stop checking him out! This is too good to be true girl;* she closed her eyes momentarily to regain her own thoughts. *Remember the old witch, don't walk into this blind!* She opened her eyes, in charge of herself again. Kyle was talking now.

"It was hard to read and it does really weird things with your eyes," Kyle replied.

"It would be easier to make out if you knew me better," the stranger replied, "but that will come." This seemed to get Rocket's tongue moving again.

"Sir, we have had a very unfortunate encounter already on this Road, why should we trust you?"

The man extended his hands wide. "I can offer no proof of my good intent, but be assured, I won't put you to sleep, rather I intend to wake you up."

Rocket made a stifled snort, and the man glanced up at him.

"I can see from your eyes that you have met the eternal maid already. Her self-sufficiency will not last, but that is not for your journey. Unlike her, I journey this Road, and indeed, I am here to help all who seek to journey this Road, so some call me the Wayfarer." With that, he smiled and extended his hand to Jill. "I am at your service, if you will have it." He shook her hand, and then smiled, leaned over, and kissed her forehead.

What's he on? Jill went pink.

He turned to Kyle, and simply held Kyle's hand between his own hands. Rocket refused his offer of a greeting with a curt 'no thank you' but seemed a little less stiff.

"Please," said the Wayfarer, "come inside."

Slipping out a small golden key and chain from under his shirt, he unlatched the lock and opened the door. Sweet smells of spices, oils and leather wafted out and Jill could not tell which she liked best. They tickled in her nose like the scent of gorse bush flowers and raced into her brain, and everything seemed more sharp, more real than normal. She stepped in, closely followed by Kyle, whilst Rocket leant against the door frame looking in.

The hut was surprisingly big inside, even with the large frame of the Wayfarer. In between the shelves and the piles of boxes, there seemed plenty of space.

"Here, have something to eat," he said, tossing a fresh, floury loaf to Jill who broke off a chunk and reluctantly passed it around. Nobody ate it. He took off his waterproof and busied himself searching amongst all the boxes and racks of equipment.

While this was happening, Jill was able to observe the Wayfarer's appearance more closely. He had olive skin and deep brown eyes, and seemed immensely strong, his arms had muscles like steel rope, and his shoulders were much broader than his waist. He was wearing a white linen shirt; richly embroidered with interwoven patterns that looked like they might be pictures of real living things, but none that Jill had ever seen. A sharp, strong nose set off a chiselled face, and he was weathered but unworn. Jill felt relaxed, almost at home, as she watched him. *This isn't exactly normal, but I don't think he's dangerous. I don't feel sleepy at least.* In fact, her mind was awake in a way that she occasionally experienced when hiking, as if the Moor's wind was blowing away the dirt of the Town. *Well, I don't think he's going to hurt us anyway,* she thought, and *I don't see any sleepers here. I don't think anyone could sleep with him around.* She looked at the loaf in her hand and realised she was hungry. *I suppose that must mean that the food's safe then.* The Wayfarer was definitely not in a hurry, and as he busied himself, Jill started to nibble the bread. The other two watched her carefully.

Apparently satisfied with his searches, the Wayfarer pulled out several stools, sat down and indicated for Kyle and Jill to do likewise. "Tell me, what did you read the sign as saying?"

"Well, all the things are free if you want to follow the Road all the way," said Kyle.

"And do you?" said the Wayfarer.

"Do we what?" said Jill.

"Want to go to the end," said the Wayfarer and stared into Jill's eyes. Jill found herself unaware of anything else except his eyes and wondered if she was falling in love.

"No my dear, you're not. Not as you've been taught to think." It was the Wayfarer's voice that brought her back to the present moment, but how had he replied to her unspoken thoughts? Jill decided that she must have muttered something out loud, so she looked away, blushing bright red.

"Well, do you?"

"I'm not sure," Jill said, "how do we know we can trust you?"

"How do you know when to trust anyone?" replied the Wayfarer.

"Feelings I suppose," she said. Then she remembered her science lesson, "Maybe when you get to know them and find out if they don't lie."

"I will not hide things from you little one. In this I want you to test me." The Wayfarer laughed, "By your measure then; what do your feelings tell you, *really* tell you?"

Little one! He thinks I'm just a kid! "That's not fair!" Jill was very tired after their escape that morning, and all her mixed up feelings of the past few days rose within her. Tears welled up in her eyes.

"Why are you on this journey then? What or whom do you seek?"

Jill paused for a moment and answered slowly and carefully. "I want to meet the Lord of the Way, and I don't want to say why, not just yet anyway. Is he still alive?"

The brown skinned man laughed very hard. "Yes, yes he is, although many wish it weren't so."

Jill's mind spun. *I knew it! How do I find him? Can I really trust this man?*

He paused, and fixed his gaze upon her face. "If I am to be of service to you, it's an answer from the heart I require. Do you want to go to the end of the Road?"

The turmoil inside Jill didn't go away, but in spite of all the strange things that had happened the answer came to her quickly. "Yes," was all she said.

"A good answer." The Wayfarer turned to Kyle. "And what do you want?" He grinned and threw a few grains of wheat, one at a time, at Kyle. Kyle, ducked, and fended off the little missiles. He started to grin too.

"I want to go home."

Jill looked up in surprise and Rocket's eyebrows shot up.

"Now, where is that?" The Wayfarer's attention was focussed completely.

"I don't know. I . . . I don't have one, it . . . it burnt down." Kyle stopped smiling.

"Really? Is that how it happened? Where do you want to go then?"

"Not back."

Jill followed his eyes as they darted about. *He's hiding something.*

"What about the Road? Do you want to go to the end?"

"I'm not sure. I don't think I want to go anywhere."

"Well, I can help you only a little." The Wayfarer faced Rocket. "You, sir. What do you intend?"

"I will finish this walk, it's *interesting,* shall we say. I simply would like proof of your good will."

Now Jill's attention had switched to Rocket, she thought he sounded cold somehow, and felt awkward listening to him. The Wayfarer wasn't upset and took a leisurely moment to reply. "It will take more than interest to finish this Road," he said his eyes lingering on the man before him, "but as to proof of my good will, you shall have it. A proof that shall take a new form for you, and also take some time. You are an honest man; you shall have all that you can bring yourself to receive."

"Which will be as little as possible."

"As you wish."

Jill's plan of the last few days started to take real shape again. *Maybe these other two will want to go back after all, this Wayfarer looks like he really can stop them if he wishes.* Unexpectedly a new thought crowded in, *Should I be leaving them behind?* And then almost as unexpectedly, *What would **he** want me to do?* This last thought was more disturbing than the first, because although Jill was convinced that she could choose whether to leave Rocket and Kyle, choosing to not like, or listen to the Wayfarer felt impossible. *No one will tell me what to do! I do what I want!* The cold rage that had suddenly sprung up in her took her breath away. It frightened her to feel like that. She sat shaking and wondering what to do.

Suddenly the Wayfarer stood, and turned into the hut, and the tensions of the moment dissolved. The wood stove quickly blazed, and the smell of sweet sauces and potatoes wafted through the little building and even Rocket relaxed and helped prepare some of the vegetables. Jill set a small pine table with simple silver cutlery, and within half an hour, a rich dinner was set out. There was a dish of sharp and sweet beans, fresh steamed spinach, and boiled potatoes with butter. As the hungry travellers were finishing their meal, the Wayfarer reappeared with coats, tents, boots and sleeping bags.

"Here, take what your hearts can bear."

"Don't you mean our backs?" said Rocket.

The Wayfarer made no reply except to start giving things out. Jill was soon dressed in a sapphire blue waterproof, and was wondering what to do with her old equipment. "Could you look after my stuff?"

"Of course." The Wayfarer exchanged her tired boots and camping gear for new. He pointed to a changing booth, and Jill was soon trying out new linen and wool garments from the seemingly endless supplies. Kyle found himself drifting outside, unwilling to take anything. Rocket took only a tent and new boots, and joined Kyle outside, wanting to give Jill space.

Both the boys thought Jill's outfitting was taking a ridiculous length of time and in fact, this was the first thing they had been able to easily agree upon, and they ended up talking like old friends. The door was open and every now and then snatches of conversation floated out of the hut, cutting across their own talk.

Kyle stopped mid sentence and looked up at Rocket. "Do you want to stop here tonight? Only the food is good and it'd be warm."

Rocket sniffed. "Not with him around. Anyway, after our experience with Mrs. Lazybee I'd rather keep going."

"You wondering what they're talking about as well?" Kyle asked.

Rocket stared at him awkwardly for a second. "Well, er . . . yes I am. Why do ask?"

"I'm good at listening at doors, without being noticed, you know, had a lot of practice. I'll just wander over casual, sir, and see what's keeping her, okay?" Kyle's head was cocked to one side and he was grinning.

Rocket looked embarrassed. "All right, it might be prudent, go on then."

Kyle sauntered over to the door and leaned toward it for a good minute. He then shot back over to Rocket's side.

"Well, what was that chap talking about?" whispered Rocket out of the side of his mouth as Jill stepped outside again.

However, Jill's new appearance stopped all conversation. She now resembled a kingfisher, so brightly coloured were her clothes. Emerald green flashed underneath her sapphire blue coat, and her skirt was the colour of red Devon soil. Her boots were the kind of blue you see in a deep tropical sea, with laces the colour of an island lagoon. The rucksack matched the colour of the coat, except for straps and trim that looked like they had been made from fresh willow leaves, with a light green that almost glowed. Jill now had a beret on her head the same colour as the straps, and a delicate gold scarf around her neck. She also held a staff in her hand, which looked like any plain walking stick until you inspected its bark. In its silvery fabric, mottles and stripes caught the light with an odd regularity. After a second, your eye recognised them as pen strokes and brush marks. They formed strange looking words, all lying one on top of the other in translucent layers.

Aside from this last peculiarity, she looked fit for fancy dress, and looked as excited as a child at Christmas. Kyle laughed out loud. Rocket's eyebrows disappeared under his fringe. "Quite a delightful ensemble my dear," he said, "Where's the party?"

"You look weird," said Kyle.

Jill appeared to ignore them, and immediately started to walk off. She turned and waved a friendly goodbye to the Wayfarer and was immediately several steps ahead. Rocket waved stiffly at the hut's owner and forced a smile. Kyle simply glanced back and then looked up at Rocket, who shrugged.

"Well, we seem to have got away lightly there, old boy," Rocket said to Kyle quietly, "but I think we need to watch Jill. She's been quite affected by that charlatan. There's more to this than meets the eye I'll wager. What were they talking about anyway?"

Kyle glanced first at Rocket and then Jill striding ahead, and then shrugged back. "Dunno. They were talking like, real serious, but he seemed to be teaching her poetry."

"Poetry!? What sort of poetry?"

"Dunno, didn't make any sense to me. 'Pose they both like that sort of stuff."

"He'll be trying to brainwash her I'll be bound, mark my words" Rocket replied and looked so serious and grand that Kyle didn't know what to say, so he tried to nod in an intelligent way. He looked back at Jill. She certainly looked fine against her surroundings, but if that's what "brainwashed," looked like, that's what she must be.

"We'll have to watch her closely," Rocket said.

"We'll have to start walking faster if she's not going to disappear out of sight," replied Kyle, and both he and Rocket started to jog for a few minutes.

Nothing more was said for a few miles, mainly because Rocket and Kyle's cynicism was exhausted by their lack of breath. They had previously not had any trouble keeping up with Jill, now they were quickly blowing hard. They stopped for a few minutes as Rocket and Kyle regained their breath. "Those boots must have wings on," Rocket gasped with a forced grin.

"Yes, let's see if the rest of the Wayfarer's stuff works as well," Jill replied.

Rocket rolled his eyes. "We'll see," was all he said.

The day was closing to an end. The sun shone red on a clump of yew trees, and in between gasps, Rocket suggested that they should stop here for the night. The travellers decided to camp, as the trees made an excellent shelter and as was often the case, there was a convenient stream in the western ditch.

It became their habit to use this ditch as a wash-room, and the Road's raised surface provided privacy from the easterly camp. That evening, Kyle was dressed in his underwear, inspecting a foot blister when a black crow landed nearby.

"Hello, bird." He clicked his tongue. The bird cocked its head on one side. It hopped closer. Kyle was very pleased and kept making encouraging noises, throwing out breadcrumbs from crumpled pockets. It ate up the crumbs. Kyle quickly rummaged around in his bag and pulled out a roll from the morning's breakfast table. The bird tilted its head the other way, took several hops forward, took the bread, and throwing it to one side, started to peck Kyle's hand. Kyle thrashed out, shouted and backed away. The crow proceeded to follow, ducking and weaving to avoid the blows that were being aimed at it. Kyle yelled loud and long and Jill, who had been waiting her turn, tumbled down the bank, and almost caught the carrion eater with her stick. The bird turned, screeched and flew off. Both watched the creature fly away.

It turned out Kyle's hand was bleeding badly, and Jill produced a bandage from her new equipment.

"I hate this road," said Kyle, sulking.

"We can always take you back," offered Jill. Kyle stomped off to the tent Jill had put up for him and the incident seemed to be over. They finished washing, ate from Jill's supplies of bread and bean stew, and slept.

8

———

THE CROWS

The day started with birdsong and bright light.

It turned out to be a cheerful awakening for a new start. Sunlight slanting under the dawn cloud illuminated the canvas roofs. Inside their tents, the oiled silk inners glowed, bathing every one of them in light.

Jill lay in her tent staring into the brightness. *Now what did he say?* She recalled words and rhymes to mind. *It's not going to be easy believing all this.* She lay listening to the other two outside, busy already. *And do I really have to look after the other two?* Then she remembered his face and what he had said. *Well whatever it all means, I can't get there without them, so they're coming whether they like it or not.* For the first moment, Jill felt real weariness, an unwillingness to see the whole situation through. *It's all so strange, this Road, but what could happen today that was worse than everything so far?* Jill got up and decided to face the day.

Rocket was cooking breakfast on Jill's new stove and as he saw her come out of her tent, declared it most efficient.

"What fuel does it use?" Rocket asked in a friendly voice.

"The Wayfarer said that it wouldn't need any fuel added as

long as we stayed on the Road," Jill answered.

Rocket rolled his eyes in disbelief. He seemed to think of a reply, hesitated, and returned to frying whilst whistling tunelessly, which nearly ruined the whole mood.

Jill decided to ignore him. *We'll see who has the last word.*

The bacon and eggs smelled delicious and bread was brought out to mop up the corners of the plates. They broke camp quickly and, determined to make good time, swung up onto the Road and into their stride.

Jill was by far the quickest of the three now, however she seemed to make it her business to gauge her pace so that Rocket and Kyle could almost keep up.

"Oi, slow down Jill!" Kyle was panting. "How come she can leave us for dead?" he demanded from Rocket. "This place is weird!"

"At least at this rate my tired limbs will be warm," grinned a red-faced Rocket. Kyle panted and frowned.

Jill glanced over her shoulder. *Yeah, it is 'weird', but great 'weird', especially when I could really leave you two behind. I could be on my own at last!* She grinned to herself and then looked at Rocket. Her smile faded. *He didn't abandon me. Can't abandon him now anyway.* Jill sighed, let them stop for a moment, and, annoyed with herself and Rocket, decided to enjoy the view.

From here, she could see birds circling above the rocks that marked the edge of the gorge, which was now three or four miles away across a dish shaped piece of Moor. The forest lay thick and solid behind her and everywhere else the Moor swept on, uninterrupted. Clumps of wind-twisted trees and the occasional rock outcrop pushed up like islands from the undulating gorse and bracken. In the calm air the dew sparkled, and shadows were long and sharp.

"Wow, what a great day to be up here!" The other two looked at Jill with blank expressions. "Don't you just love hiking?" Kyle stared back at her blankly. The sweat still sparkled on Rocket's forehead and he frowned to himself and checked his watch.

It was as Kyle decided not to argue with Jill that a thin veil of cloud dimmed the bright sunlight. Kyle looked up to check the sky.

"I think that crow from yesterday is back," he said. High above, a black, ragged bird circled, dark against a wispy sky. It looked uninterested but Kyle's stomach was twisting, and he felt the same sickness that made him run from the Institution rising from his guts.

"It just a bird," said Jill, watching Kyle out of the corner of her eye.

"That's all right for you to say, it didn't go for you," he grumbled. They squinted upwards for a few more moments, and then walked on.

It was a little later that Jill looked up again. *That crow seems to have brought a couple of friends along with him.* She peered upward, hand over her eyes.

"Yes, odd isn't it?" Rocket said quietly. "They stay straight above us, and it seems that every twenty minutes or so, we collect another. We're due the next about now." His voice was restrained, and she watched him check the sky with an understated manner that she had not seen before.

"Oh well, they're not bothering us at the moment," said Jill, "look, let's not pay any attention to them."

"No, old girl, I think that on this occasion we need to keep an eye on them. Nothing has been ordinary so far. I'd be quite relieved if it was ordinary this time, but why should crows keep pace with us?" Rocket's soothing voice began to sound a little forced. "Don't you think that's a little odd, Jill?"

She frowned. "Perhaps they think we've got some food. I think you're being far too gloomy; I'm sure there's nothing to it," and her face brightened, "They're only birds after all, what difficulty could they be?"

Rocket glanced down at his watch and then looked up again. "Here comes number four, right on time."

"Anyway," said Jill, "back in the wood, you said that something big and nasty had eaten the birds. If these crows are here, there can't be anything bad, can there?"

Rocket raised his eyebrows and said nothing.

The new crow flapped and wheeled his way to the group, making for the nearest bird. The two seemed to be on a collision course, then both turned to fight. There was a momentarily tumbling through the air as each pirouetted around the other. The new bird broke away and was chased off with raucous cries, and the disturbance over, the four crows settled into long circular glides.

Jill spoke slowly, "I've never come across punctual crows before."

"Well, as long as they only watch," said Kyle, as he glanced down at his hand. It had started to throb.

Jill was still stealing glances of Kyle, and realised that she had never seen him smile. "You okay?" she asked.

"Yeah, of course," said Kyle pushing his bandaged hand out of sight and into a pocket, "you ain't my social worker, and I don't need another one."

"Sorry," said Jill. "What's bitten you?"

"A crow, yesterday, all right?" Kyle moved off and Rocket shook his head to tell Jill to drop the conversation.

Jill shrugged. *Why can't things stay positive for once in my life?*

Jill picked up the pace and the walkers moved more quickly now, in spite of Rocket's and Kyle's previous complaints. They, however, did not seem to mind. Upward glances became more frequent as the tattered masters of the air increased. Time passed; no-one talked. Kyle noticed that the bandage on his hand was becoming slightly sticky inside with blood, and sweat had started to sting the open cut. He and Rocket were red and panting.

After about another hour a crow landed on the ground just to the right of the Road. It studied them with unblinking eye, and stood still as they passed. It cawed loudly as it ascended and Kyle thought that it looked as though it talked to the others as it rejoined the other carrion birds. He tried to forget the idea; it was obviously silly, but his apprehension was rising. He stopped and panted.

"I'm getting tired now, but I don't want to stop too near those birds," he said in a tired mumble.

"We've got to find some cover to rest," said Rocket.

"A great idea," said Jill, "but I think you're overreacting about those birds, I'm sure they'll go away if we ignore them."

"I'm not so sure. We'll see how it goes when we make camp tonight," said Rocket.

Kyle remembered the crow on the police car, but stayed silent. He still did not understand what had happened himself, and could not bear to say anything that made him look stupid, or tell *them* too much.

Across the Moor, a few hundred metres away on their left and slightly ahead, three huge rocks stuck up from the ground. Two of them leant together, forming a rough arch and shelter. Rocket signalled to the others to follow and they hopped over the lively stream in the western ditch. There was a sheep track across the heather to the stones and they made quick time towards them, sitting side by side with their backs against worn granite on the far side of the boulders.

The lean of the rocks was such that they could not be seen from directly above and the mid-morning sunlight made their hideaway bright and warm and helped to restore a cheerful mood. Food was gratefully eaten and Jill's drink bottle was passed around. After the usual pleases and thank-yous and 'you're-sitting-on-my-coat', the group fell silent, thoughtfully staring at the horizon.

A crow suddenly dropped down in front of them and then did not move. It croaked loudly. A second landed by it, the flurry of wings sounding like flapping sheets in the quietness. The three friends sat very still.

"Perhaps they get fed too much up here," said Jill, "You know, by people passing along the Road, like us."

The first crow cocked its head. It then turned its head to one side to allow it to look directly at Jill; one eye fixed on her.

"Do you think it can understand us?" said Kyle, sounding a little nervous.

"Don't be ridiculous," said Jill, "it's just a crow." *At least, I hope it's just a crow.*

The lead bird turned to its neighbour, rasped a low call and then looked straight back at Jill.

The second bird hopped forward, ripped the bread out of Kyle's hand and started to peck at the bandage.

Rocket immediately swept it away with his foot. The bird calmly lifted in the air, barely uttering a croak, and then settled beside its companion. Both crows stood still and watched.

"Don't move," Rocket hissed to an obviously scared Kyle.

The first bird turned to the newcomer, cawed twice, and then made a rasping shriek. The second bird lifted itself on its heavy wings and flew low and straight to the north west, barely staying above the gorse prickles.

"Here, let's put the food away in my bag," suggested Jill, and without taking their eyes off the bird, what remained of their bread and fruit was returned to the rucksack. The bird was motionless, staring, waiting.

"What do we do now?" asked Kyle. He picked up two sharp rocks, one in either hand.

"Wait until it goes away?" wondered Jill.

"No. I think that crow is waiting for something to happen, other than us throwing it bread," said Rocket.

"Why?" asked Jill.

"Need you ask?" retorted Rocket, "My suspicious nature, and the fact that here nature acts suspiciously. So far, nothing is quite what it looks like, or should be."

"Do you think that this is where strangeness starts again?" asked Jill. "Only I really don't think the Wayfarer had crows in mind."

"I don't remember it easing up much, my dear," said Rocket, and laid a hand on Kyle's shoulder.

"Don't worry, I don't plan to throw bread at it this time," said Kyle. Kyle looked around back through the arch made by the two stones. "Look at the shadows behind us, there must be about twenty of them circling just behind our heads."

Rocket suddenly frowned, "What do mean, '. . . didn't think the Wayfarer had crows in mind . . .'?"

Jill had no time to explain. The crow in front immediately let out a long, rasping call. Quickly, the crows started to descend in ever-tighter circles. With wordless speed, the travellers found their belongings and their feet and made to leave.

Three crows swept in from the front. Kyle shouted a high, frightened kind of yell. Rocket fended off a sharp beak from his face with his hand and cried out in pain. Kyle was backing away from the other two crows as Jill brought her staff down cleanly on a crow's back. It disappeared in a small explosion, leaving a foul smell. There was second of shock for everyone.

Then battle commenced in full.

The last crow on the ground flew at Kyle's hand and tore at the bandage. Kyle fell backwards. Jill swung again and the Wayfarer's stick clipped the attacker's wing. Cawing loudly, it hopped out of the way, around the rock.

"Back to the Road!" shouted Rocket. They started to move through the rough arch back the way they came. Immediately five crows landed in the grass to block their route. The sound of wings beat behind them.

"Forward!" urged Rocket.

Kyle glanced behind as four more dark shapes seemed to fill the triangle of sky behind them. He pushed to the front, eager not to be trapped. This time one of the crows went for Kyle's head while two others hopped in front of him, weaving and bobbing clumsily. Kyle panicked: he closed his eyes and ducked. He heard Jill's stick whistle past his ear and choked on the stench of ex-crow as a flurry of feathers landed on his shoulders. Looking up, he hurled a rock at one of the lead crows. He missed. The next rock made a satisfying thud as it struck home. The other crows moved forward to take the place of fallen comrades, hovering and wheeling low. As Rocket moved the children forward towards the Road, the lead crow went for him. This time it was met with Rocket's pocketknife. It bellowed and flew off.

The flurry of dark feathers and bird cries would have completely confused the two children, except for Rocket's cool head. They pushed through whirling wings as Jill started to take accurate aim at any bird that came too close. With the occasional lucky shot from Kyle, only about ten crows remained to harass them by the time they reached the Road. They all hovered and hopped in front of them at the edge of the ditch. Jill took great delight in stepping forward.

"Out of my way you mangy birds," Three crows exploded into sulphurous smoke as Jill scythed through them; the other birds scattered.

This is going to be easy, even with the other two.

"Which way?" shouted Kyle as they clambered up on to the Road.

"Back to the hut," Rocket said.

"Back to the weird guy?" Kyle was amazed.

"What for? Why not keep going?" Jill asked.

Rocket ducked as the regrouping crows dived on him.

"It's the only guaranteed shelter and I'm not going anywhere till I understand more about these blasted birds and that walking stick of yours. And I'll take some convincing to trust this Wayfarer chap. Seems all too plausible to me . . ."

The discussion ceased temporarily because of the crows. Jill was kept busy and several showers of black confetti rained down onto the Road. As each feather struck the sandstone surface, it disappeared with a boiling hiss, not even leaving a smell. Seeing this, Rocket swung his bag into the path of one of his tormentors. It careered through the air and landed on the Road. The crow hopped from one foot to another as a sound like frying eggs could be heard whenever its feet touched the Road. Jill could not help herself, giggling as she watched the wretched animal bounce hurriedly down and across the ditch.

"That's the last one I think," she said, leaning on her stick. Still smiling, she heard Kyle whistle low. Kyle had been looking up.

"Don't laugh yet," he said, "reinforcements have arrived."

They all looked round. The Moor was almost flat here; it gently sloped to the horizon and the Road ran slightly downhill, clear and straight for miles. There was no shelter anywhere ahead and now the sky had become black with crows. They were streaming in from the north west, and blotted out the light over the Road for as far as they could see.

"I agree with Rocket," said Kyle, "There's no way we'll get

through that lot."

"Okay," Jill conceded, "but you two need to have a serious conversation with the Wayfarer . . ."

"Don't worry," cut in Rocket, "I have more than enough questions for him to answer."

"Can we go now?" Kyle said nervously, looking up again.

High above, a large flock of crows seethed; more arrived all the time.

"We'll know not to leave the Road this time. It obviously affords some protection," said Rocket, now bandaging his own hand with a handkerchief.

"We can't hide underneath it though," moaned Kyle, "they'll pick us off like beetles on a rock."

"We can make good time if we start to move before they attack again," said Jill, "and they don't want us on the Road, so I think Rocket's right, it's the best place to stay."

"Good girl; let's get moving," Rocket started to lead back the way they had come. Kyle followed him, trembling.

Jill found it depressing, doubling back on their steps. *I am getting farther away again! Why am I the one having to protect them? Why didn't they take a staff? I never wanted them along anyway!* She was trailing behind having to take frequent swipes at birds that came too close: if it had not been for her new speed and strength the other two would have left her behind, such was the fright that had gripped them.

Although the attacks had become fewer, the strain of watching out as they alternately walked and then ran was very draining. Kyle's bandages now had a growing red stain even though he was looking greener by the moment. He was always glancing about, sick with fear. It was he that first noticed that one of the crows was acting oddly.

"Look at that over there." Kyle did not point up, but flat across the Moor. Far to their right a crow flew back and forth, low across the ground. Below him, running in from the north west, long grey shapes bounded through the heather.

"What are they?" Kyle said, "And what is that bird doing?"

"Well, they look to me like wolves. I think that crow is fetching them," said Jill. Rocket did not argue, for it did look uncannily as if the crow was doing just that, shouting out directions as it banked back and forth.

The three humans started to run again, eager to erase the six or seven miles remaining to the Wayfarer's hut.

Suddenly it came, a torrent of black sweeping down on them from the east. Jill was ready and had seen them coming. She swung wildly but made little impact on the mass of birds. Rocket was momentarily knocked to the ground and was slashing with his pocketknife for all he was worth. Kyle Williams was borne down and across the wet western ditch, the crows goading him with sharp beaks and claws. His cries were nearly lost in the tumult. Jill saw what was happening and loped low towards Rocket, shielding her head with her coat as she reached into her bag.

"Here, use this!" She shouted through the noise and thrust her camping light into his hands "Turn it on! Quickly!" Rocket fiddled blindly with its controls as Jill dealt death left and right, and then the lamp lit. A blue flare of light flooded the Road, even at mid-day. The crows scattered. Rocket and Jill, though dazed, came to realise that they were now under a dome of light; as if they were figurines in a life sized snow shaker.

Jill came to her senses. "We need to get Kyle," she insisted.

Kyle was at first unaware of anything except the pain in his hands and the horrible churning of the flock. Every time he tried to turn and see where he was he would have to cover his eyes, instinct urging him to protect his sight. Kyle spun around, striking blindly at the assault. He could find no escape from the torture. He stumbled, fell and lay sobbing like a small child, hoping it would just all end.

With a shock, he realised that the birds were not just cawing. Now he began to hear meaning in the noise. They were screaming accusations and swearing, their strange thin voices fading in and out of his understanding.

"You never loved your father . . ."

"You are a failure . . ."

"You've betrayed everyone who tried to help you . . ."

"Even your social worker thinks you're an idiot . . ."

"You'll never finish your journey."

"You're ours now."

"It's your fault your father left you."

"You're worthless, give in."

"You only know how to destroy, to burn . . ."

"Give up . . . give up . . . give up . . ."

Their voices became a rhythmic chant, reverberating around him.

Terror seized him. Struggling to his feet again, he tried to ignore the madness. But how could he? The crows were right!

I burnt the house. I'd burn anything, I'd burn anyone. I'll never see Dad . . . they've thrown me away 'cause I wreck things . . . he's not coming back . . . he went because of me . . . I'm no good . . . nothing matters . . .

Darkness started to close over Kyle.

A cry, a yell, cut through the ghastly choir around him and in fear, he thought at first that there was some new enemy. To his amazement, he realised the sound was Jill; an extremely angry Jill. She had nearly reached him now, her stick weaving awful arcs through the air. Crows were shattering under the force of her anger and Kyle was glad not to be one them.

Jill had heard the crows starting to caw together, and though she could hear no words, she was convinced that no good could come from it.

"You're not having him. Not my friend! Get away! I'll kill everyone of you if I have to!" Kyle would have smiled but for the pain of constant pecking. He passed out, and fell headlong under the weight of crows.

Jill had led Rocket down the bank after Kyle and had been able to vaguely make him out, stumbling and fending off attackers. He had looked as if he was sprouting angry feathers and beaks. She had seen him fall. With all the force she could muster, she ploughed forward. The air around her looked thick like glass; glass that shone with light from within and the flock boiled around that radiance, held back by the light, except for a few, that blindly stumbled in to meet their death.

Once she reached him, Jill turned him over, and started wiping away the blood with a cloth. She was scowling and biting her lip. *Idiot, try to remember what the Wayfarer said, before this all gets too much. What did he say . . .?*

"Is he alive?" asked Rocket.

Kyle was a mass of scratches and bruises, especially the back of his hands, which had been covering his face.

"I think so, it looks superficial, nothing a First Aid Kit couldn't handle." Jill sat him up and was about to tend to him, when Rocket shouted.

"Beware attackers! Wolves!"

"What?!" Jill's words exploded out. *Surely it's not meant to be like this?*

Low shouldered grey shapes pushed out from behind a clump of gorse. Deep growls vibrated through the air, fangs were bared, and manes of fur bristled. Their pupils gleamed like polished black marble in a graveyard. Jill felt the twist of fear in her belly, but she stood, her face drained and white with rage.

Kyle had regained consciousness, but did not like the world he was seeing much more than when he had passed out. He was now half-blind in smothering light, almost unable to breathe in its weight, and he could still hear the crows' words. Moment by moment they became clearer and he was agreeing with them. Second by second his heart sank, and he began to hate the light. Why not let the crows finish him? At least then it would all be over. Kyle could see three long grey snouts, sniffing at the edge of the dome and the crows flapping furiously, trying to cut off any retreat. He gave up on hope completely.

Jill heard herself say, "Not my friends, not here," as if someone else were speaking. Her gaze however, was fixed and steady, and she held the staff tightly to herself. Jill stepped back nearer the lamp, to stand over Kyle, ready to fight. The lamp began to weaken; the circle of light shrank. The wolves circled around their prey, looking for weakness, for darkness that would let them enter.

"What's going on?" said Rocket.

"Do you remember what the Wayfarer said about the stove? It doesn't need fuel whilst it's on the Road. I think the lamp's like that too—fine on the Road, but will only shine for a short time when we're off the Road. We need to return."

"I'll get Kyle to his feet," Rocket said.

A wolf nosed into the light, squeezing its head and shoulder through the radiance. Jill only hesitated a moment, then brought her staff down. The wolf yelped and shot backwards. The lead wolf yapped three quick barks and then all the wolves started to break in at once from every side. The light dimmed even further.

Jill drove the first wolf back as before then opened a gash on the shoulder of the second. She pivoted around to face the third. Its eyes were nearly shut against the light but it was already well inside the lamp's protective sphere.

It crouched low, a snarling, coiled spring, casting about from side to side trying to locate its target, ears forward listening, lip curled through pain. The light guttered for a second and the wolf could see clearly: it had its mark and began to move.

Jill blocked its way. Without thinking, she lowered her staff and pointed it directly at the wolf.

"No!" she yelled. The staff vibrated gently in her hand and the wolf was pushed down. His ears went back; anger gleamed in the red of his eye.

"NO!" This time the stick shook violently, and the wolf was flung out of the retreating circle of light.

Rocket had one arm round Kyle and with the other he carried the lamp. He started to move to the Road.

"Care to let me in on the secret of that trick?" he said.

"I didn't know I could do that till a moment ago," Jill replied. Without meaning to, she stopped, overtaken by her thoughts. "So that's what the Wayfarer meant . . . I get it."

"Get what?" mumbled Kyle.

No one bothered to reply, as, at that moment, the light went out.

Three wolves in front of her howled in triumph, between them and the Road a host of crows descended. Jill nearly lost her nerve, but the travellers were only a few paces away from their objective now. Jill lowered the staff again, planted her feet and filled her lungs.

"By right of the Wayfarer, let us pass!"

Crows were shredded as though by a shotgun, the wolves cowered: this they had not expected.

"We are travellers in the Way, we must pass!"

A rising sound, like the note of an ancient bell, started to come from Jill's staff. Words embedded in its bark shone moonlight silver. The wolves whined and backed away, the crows started to fly higher. Jill thought she could push through like this, but as the power started to surge, she decided to see what it might do.

"You must yield. He is our protection!" A shower of lightning shot like flame from the end of the staff. When Jill opened her eyes again, the wolves were no more and clouds of black feathers marked where a few of the birds had remained. Smoke rose quietly into the air.

Rocket eyed Jill's staff for a moment and made a mental note not to make her angry. With Kyle, he walked straight ahead through the smell of singed fur and once they reached the ditch, the protective light returned. Jill, although stunned for a moment, gave a loud victory yell and then joined the others on the Road.

Kyle was by now dangerously ill, he was barely awake and kept mumbling, "They're right you know, it's no use." Neither Jill nor Rocket could make out his meaning.

"I think he's in shock," said Rocket, "Do you think you could get rid of a few more birds while I see if I can bring him round?"

A crow was flying low and calling just above Jill.

Jill just grunted, staring at her delirious friend. She felt suddenly drained of energy and very foolish. *What am I doing here? Who did I think I am anyway?* She was sure that if her friends could see her they would laugh at her new clothes and this upset her more than anything else. All this time, the large crow kept circling her and cawing loudly. Jill looked up in shock; it had called her name. Surely, that was not possible?

"What's the matter dear?" Rocket asked.

Jill looked up uncertainly. "Nothing, I think." She looked at Rocket sideways, "I thought I heard something that's all, from the crow."

Rocket's face darkened. "I think that Wayfarer's got a lot to answer for," Rocket said. "Filling your mind with all sorts of nonsense."

"But the staff, the lamp, my new strength, even the crows, don't they tell you that he's been true, that the sign outside his hut is true?" Jill spluttered.

"I don't know what's going on, but I'll guarantee that that staff of yours contains some complicated mechanism. It's a machine, like that seeing stone at the Vantage Point. I knew I should have dismantled it: this is all hokum. Let me have that staff, I'll show you," and Rocket reached out his hand toward Jill. She backed away.

"No way! You're not breaking this, it's keeping us alive."

"How do you know this Wayfarer is not sending the crows? How do you know this is not some sort of game, a trap, like Mrs. Lazybee's? How do you know the stick isn't calling to them?"

Rocket was controlled but enraged, for a moment he almost seemed to snarl like the wolves.

The crow was circling low and cawing quietly now; two or three others were flying to join it, their soft squawking not loud enough to distract the arguing pair.

"I . . . don't know", Jill's mind tottered, "he's not like that I'm sure . . ."

"Where's your proof? If he's so good, why didn't he tell us about these crows? Why isn't *he* here fighting with us?"

Jill stumbled sideways dizzy, and as she did, leant on her stick.

Power seemed to well up from it into her arm and heart.

"I don't know," Jill finally answered, "but what you're saying is just wrong. I can *feel* he's true. So I feel dizzy, kind of confused, and I guess you are too; something to do with those horrible birds. But it's his words, his gifts that are keeping us alive, so I'll use them . . . on you if I have too."

Rocket walked toward her.

"Back off, I mean it."

The crows called softly above.

"You can't trust him," Rocket hissed, his face twisted with anger.

Jill paused, and then without a word swung at the lowest bird. There was a small explosion and a crackling like static electricity and the crows scattered noisily.

Rocket's face seemed to clear, and he stopped moving towards her. "Oh . . . , yes, no . . . that is an odd effect. Well . . . I still don't trust him."

"Well I do," Jill said, "It's you I don't get. You're travelling with me remember, and we're going to trust him. Okay?"

Rocket, frowned and shook his head. "Maybe you're right, maybe not, but I suppose this is not the time to argue about it," he hesitated, "we'll talk later."

Jill had sounded firm, but in reality Rocket's words had left her shaken. In the next few minutes, Jill attempted to clear the skies of their enemies, but at best the staff now only pushed them slightly further away. She shook her head and concentrated. *Stop trying to kill things and just get back to the Wayfarer. Whatever's going on, he'll make things right.* "I don't know why it's not working now," she said to Rocket, "I suppose we had better get to the hut."

Looking embarrassed, but much more normal, Rocket stood panting propping up the slumped shape of Kyle. "Here, help me carry Kyle then," he said, "I don't think he can walk any more."

Jill caught Kyle under his left shoulder and helped him along. His unconscious weight dragged them both down and they stumbled. It was then that Rocket pointed out a small downy birch tree. "Keep me safe my dear," he said and plunged down the bank. He returned unharmed carrying two stout branches. The branches were straight and with a little experimentation, a neat stretcher was constructed with a ground sheet.

"You are sure you can manage?" Rocket stretched his voice in concerned tones as he watched her lower Kyle onto the litter. Rocket went first, carrying Kyle's feet, while Jill's staff lay across the stretcher in front of Jill, the lamp swinging from it. Jill's strength was less than before but it was still Rocket who strained. They stopped to rest, while Rocket regained his breath.

All that time the light shone. All that time the crows harried and cawed safely from above. Jill looked up at the boiling menace and felt her confidence seep away. She kept feeling dizzy and confused, but every time she did, Jill shook her head and focussed. "No, I'm going to get help, *he'll* help us."

Kyle was only barely aware of who people were now. Shapes blurred above him in the painful haze of light. Motion was undefined and sickening. The calls of the crows sounded like school friends and had the familiarity of a recurring nightmare. Occasionally the voice of Jill broke in, over the birds, but it was easier to agree with the crows; it seemed he had talked with them so often before.

Rocket pointed west. Jill glanced over to see five grey hunters prowling the Moor. They sniffed the bank, but the Road seemed to repel them completely. Jill was not worried, although she noticed Rocket's pace increase.

"Hope that staff starts to work again," was all he said. Jill turned her thoughts to the one who had given her the gifts. She tried to remember what he said and even managed to smile again. Slowly Jill felt her confidence returning.

This labour continued for over an hour. The strain of being guarded wore on them. Frequent stops and drinks did little to relieve it. Jill stopped thinking about how far they had to go and focussed only on the moment's sweating and chaffing. Hands were sore and legs ached. Although during breaks, her shoulders felt deliciously light, when she picked the stretcher up again she was convinced that it was closer to the ground than before. Could her arms actually be getting longer? She tried not to think about it.

Kyle was unconscious now. He muttered fitfully; random snatches of dreams and nightmares spilling out of his lips.

It was early afternoon before the hut finally came into sight. They paused for a few seconds to rest. Without warning the flock poured down, piling in between them and their destination, determined to halt their progress. Several birds at a time burst like feathered rocks through the protective wall, flailing blindly. Jill stopped, put down the stretcher and set the lamp on the Road. She dealt with the first two crows with a practised aim. Then, she let out a scream. Two crows, as though pecking at a red-hot stone, were trying to drag the lamp off and raining blows down on the glass. She crushed the first crow into the Road with her foot; the second received the butt end of her staff. Now the crows were gone, but they had done damage. The glass was cracked and the light inside was starting to dim.

"If this goes out, we've had it," Jill said, panic rising in her voice.

"Put the boy on my back. We'll have to move quickly."

"What will I do?"

"You put the lamp on one of the stretcher poles and I'll carry it. That will leave your hands free to use that magic stick of yours," Rocket said evenly, "and you'll be occupied full time if I'm right - do you think you can run?"

Jill nodded.

"Well, let's get Kyle on my shoulders then." Rocket paused as another crow burst the bubble and Jill struck it down. "We'll have to run to the hut before the light splutters out."

The light was starting to look a sickly yellow, but Jill and Rocket could not pay attention to it, being distracted by the crows' unnatural hovering and weaving. Confusing as this was to the travellers, it also seemed to leave their enemies tired. The birds were constantly colliding with each other, allowing the travellers to press on with what remained of the light, the flock parting, giving way for the moment.

Wolves howled nearby.

Rocket looked particularly uncomfortable. He was bright red and blowing but still pushed gamely on, Kyle sagging like a rag doll on his shoulders. The slowly moving shell of light was shrinking and crows flew closer, bursting through the low roof. Rocket stumbled to his knees. The lamp swung, clattering against the pole. It wavered and became slightly brighter, like a light bulb about to burn out.

"Give me a moment," panted Rocket. "Must . . . catch . . . my . . . breath," he insisted between gasps.

The crows rained in more densely.

"It's no use getting our breath if we lose it to these beasts!" Jill was calmer now. She was flushed and her rib cage was pumping air hard into her own lungs. "We must keep going. It's just a cross-country run."

Rocket groaned, "I used to hate them at school."

Jill wielded her walking stick in tired sweeps and Rocket swayed. Although the light was now brighter; somehow, the visible thickness of light at the dome's edge was thinning out—the goldfish bowl that had kept them alive was evaporating. Rocket nodded and started forward.

They were almost at the hut now and moving quickly again. Jill was completely absorbed in her task. Then the light became blindingly bright for a second. Then, it went out.

Rocket fell, sprawling from the sudden onslaught of darkness. Jill clenched her teeth, standing firm against the crows.

"Get off them, they're mine." Her words transmitted power and several birds vaporised. She pointed skyward and shouted again and again. Holes opened in the darkness swirling about her, but she did not have the strength to keep this up, there were just too many of them. Holding tightly to the staff, she planted the staff straight down onto the Road. The walking stick sank six inches into the hard compact stones as if finding a slot.

"I will finish my journey, by the Wayfarer's rights. You cannot stop me."

Jill's hands became numb as light cascaded through the stick.

Lightning arced outwards and upwards. Still she held on, the bark's symbols were now aflame, words burning like the sun.

Her mind was filling with the sounds of voices singing. Strange new languages poured through her till she could not hear her own mind. Jill strained to hold onto her own thoughts, but ideas flowed through her, surging through her mind in a wild torrent. She struggled to breathe, to keep her head above water. She clung to her mind, concentrating on just remembering who she was. Power raged through her. Jill could bear it no longer. She let go. She lost her grip. The staff fell.

Looking up, there were fewer birds, but the sense of menace remained.

Rocket had struggled to his feet. "We can make it," he said.

Together they lifted Kyle up, but Rocket could hardly take his weight.

Then the darkness fell again.

The renewed attack was just as fierce as before and Jill was flailing the stick about. Rocket covered Kyle with his body. Despair and anger filled Jill. *It wasn't meant to be like this! I was going to leave other people's trouble behind, but not to this!* Without knowing why, she shouted out and up, into the air, "I'm sorry! I can't do it, all right?" she sobbed, "Would you leave us to die? I need your help!"

The air sang around her. It was hard to describe in any other way, but in all that long day, it was the first truly beautiful moment. A rich musical note, strong and valiant, pierced the air and made it throb with power and wonder.

The shrieking of the crows diminished as the sound increased; they were becoming more transparent by the second; their reality was simply fading away. The moment the last feather disappeared, the note ceased. Jill stood and looked around, stunned. Underneath the eaves of the hut stood the Wayfarer, with a ram's horn pressed to his lips.

9

———

EXPLANATIONS

Later that day, in the hut, their cuts and bruises were being tended. Hot sweet tea had been made, blankets were draped around shoulders and the stove was roaring in the corner. The Wayfarer had not yet said anything. It was now raining outside and the percussion on the roof and windows was a soothing music to mix with the crackle of firewood. Kyle was still asleep on a low bed in the corner.

"Will he be all right?" Jill asked.

"Yes, my little storm maiden," the Wayfarer said, "if you trust me. Do you?"

"Yes."

"Then I have permission to tend him?"

"Of course."

He turned to Rocket. Rocket had been deeply shaken by the way the Wayfarer had rescued them, but he still sat hard faced in the corner. Eventually Rocket nodded his head, hand outstretched to indicate that the Wayfarer was welcome to start.

The Wayfarer stepped up to Jill and held out his hand.

"I believe that you have something which I need."

136

"I do? What could I have that would help Kyle?" asked Jill.

"One of the lettered stones from your pocket. Together they have the sum of the Road's power, but one will suffice for this situation." Jill searched her pockets and fetched out a pebble. "It's only an ordinary looking sandstone rock," she said, reaching out a dirty hand.

The Wayfarer took the stone and placed it on the boy's now ragged shirt, resting in the centre of his chest. Then the Wayfarer stepped over to the stove and stirred the cooking pot.

"Aren't you going to do anything, else?" Jill was indignant.

Rocket looked at her. "I thought you trusted him?" he asked with a slight smile.

Somehow, although his back was turned, Jill knew the Wayfarer was also smiling, although all he did was continued to stir the pot.

"Hang on, I do, but you said —" Jill stopped as Rocket caught her eye. He motioned to the couch. The stone had started to glow cool and bright, as if it floated in a pool of moonlight. The pebble brightened, flaring rapidly to shine like a light bulb and then brightening further still to blaze like a small star. Stark shadows were thrown against the wall, and the raindrops on the window were picked out, silver-edged. Their faces were all brightly illuminated, but no heat could be felt. Jill could not look directly at the blazing source of power as the Wayfarer stepped forward. He knelt by Kyle's head, with his back to Jill and started to speak softly.

"Awake, O sleeper, the light has dawned on you."

One-half of the Wayfarer's head was brilliantly lit, the other seemed as black as jet, except for the glistening colours where the light caught his dark curls. Jill could hardly look at him and she wondered why the light did not hurt his eyes. She kept squinting, watching the Wayfarer from behind the shade of her hand.

Kyle stirred and murmured.

"Forget the dream, reality is here," the Wayfarer said, "your injuries were not your invention, but they are in your charge, you are their custodian. Give them to me, and I shall take away the lies too. Give them to me. You must not agree with the birds of the air: they come to steal and destroy. Listen to me!"

His voice grew stronger, the light still increasing and pulsating with his voice. Kyle started to moan and move. It looked as though his body was a puppet with someone else holding the strings.

"Arise and come with me, don't sleep any longer. The Spring is here. It is so good outside. Come with me."

Kyle started to cough, and shook, and then opened his eyes.

The light dimmed and faded. The Wayfarer bent over him and kissed his forehead. Kyle remembered his father doing that, when he was small. The Wayfarer wiped his forehead and face with a cool cloth, then returned the stone to Jill.

"Keep it to remember me by."

The Wayfarer turned around. "He'll only need a few hours rest, you can continue tomorrow." He walked back to the stove and continued to stir the pot. Jill sat stunned, opened her mouth, and then closed it again. She repeated this several times.

"You would like to know what happened?" Looking up in surprise, Jill found that the Wayfarer was talking to Rocket. Rocket nodded slowly. "Firstly, do you trust me now?" The cabin was filled with a few seconds of total peace.

"No, I'm not sure I do."

"What could I say that would help you?" the Wayfarer asked.

"You could explain how those staffs work for a start. What is their mechanism, their fuel?" Rocket was agitated as he spoke.

"Would you like to take one apart? Here, take the stick Jill used today. And use my knife. Cut it in two." The Wayfarer passed him the objects and stepped back.

With surprising ease, Rocket cut the stick in half, and peered at the ends. "But I don't understand." He showed the cut ends of the staff to the Wayfarer, two pale circles of creamy wood. "Where's the power supply, the regulator, the electronics?" His bewildered eyes peered over his glasses.

The Wayfarer stood still and gazed steadily at Rocket before replying. "There are no electronics, no need for fuel cells. The Road supplies the power, and my words are their regulator."

"But, but . . ." stammered Rocket.

"Have you any other explanation? If you had the power to do so, and split the Vantage Point in two, you would find only stone there, my friend." Rocket stopped trying to reply, but looked uncomfortable. "Who had the power today? And who had to be rescued? And how did I eventually save all of you?" The Wayfarer paused, and then chuckled. "If you don't believe my words, try my actions. Now, are you going to trust me?"

"Why weren't you there on the Road with us? Why didn't you tell us about the crows and their attacks?" Rocket sounded as if he had been insulted.

"Would you have believed me if I had told you? You would not receive what I had to give."

"Well, I never thought about it like that before . . ."

"Do you believe I'm real, that I'm genuine?"

Kyle started to snore gently and Rocket nodded his assent. "It appears I am going to have to," he conceded.

"Then it appears that you will have to act on that."

"Yes, I shall, if I can understand a little of what happened today," Rocket said. He shifted in his seat and looked down, studying his boots.

"It won't take you long," the Wayfarer said. Rocket looked up at him, side long. "Life, *real* life, is the power in the Road. The Road has life because it flows with truth. Anything that is true echoes through its bones, and the Lord of the Way has commissioned me to care for all those who travel it."

"So you're the boss?" Rocket asked with quick and sharp words.

"So to speak, and what you speak makes all the difference," replied the Wayfarer, smiling.

"Explain then, what was going on with Jill's walking stick?" Rocket said.

"Let the little storm maiden tell you, she and I had a good conversation yesterday, and she seemed at home in the battle today." The Wayfarer chuckled and walked away to the wood stove, stoked it, and put some onions on to fry. He turned around and all eyes fixed on Jill.

Jill coloured up, and started falteringly, looking at Rocket. "Well, yes—yesterday, when I was getting the equipment, the Wayfarer," she looked over to the cook, "well, he showed me how it worked, told me all sorts of things, and said I had to protect you two. I didn't like that bit, to be honest . . ."

"All in good time, old girl," said Rocket.

"Well, okay," said Jill, "I suppose that can wait. To tell you what you want to know Rocket, the lamp and the staff draw their power from the Road. They work like ordinary objects until you need to get out of trouble." The Wayfarer nodded and smiled. Jill continued, "There was something about the Road wanting to get you to where you needed to be, but I can't remember that bit clearly. It was all summed up in a rhyme anyhow: now what was it again?" she paused; closed her eyes and with words stumbling, half chanted the verse.

When you trust the words you say,
Which he has taught you to obey,
That which seeks to block your path,
Will not endure his fiery wrath,
For from the truth all power flows,
Speak it well and they will know,
The gifts you bear are his alone,
Like the Road they'll bring you home.

"And what is the truth?" said Rocket and, not waiting for a reply, continued. "It seems to me, that this requires us to trust your view on things entirely,"

The hut's owner spoke, and his quiet words filled the room. "Don't you trust me by now? Haven't I shown my good will in saving a boy whom you struggled to wake? I have called him back from deception and unnatural sleep, as you did at the cursed cottage."

Rocket stumbled, "How did you know?—Where were you?—

Who are —" and stopped, staring at the figure in the corner.

"I saw you when you fell out of the rocket and when you tried to save Jill's life at a picnic," the Wayfarer said quietly, "and I know who you saw from the Vantage Point, when Jill saved your life. You might like to know that the 'old goat' did not lose you your job and when you meet him once more, you'll find a good friend." His words hung in the air, solidifying the silence.

Rocket's eyes became wet. He said nothing more for a long while, other than, "Yes, I do believe I trust you," which he repeated to himself several times.

"Well then, that's settled. Let's eat," said the Wayfarer. The awkward quiet of the moment was broken by the clatter of metal plates, the clunk of heavy wood furniture, and the sound of wooden spoons doling out more soups, stews and vegetables than they could possibly eat.

Questions came fast from Jill and Rocket.

The Wayfarer's response was to offer them more butter, or to point out how delicious the butter beans were, and serve them some more stew. When every last morsel was gone, they pushed back their stools and listened once more.

"You need to know that the staff releases the Road's power when you are truly convinced of what you say. You cannot say just what you like; it has to agree with the truth that flows in the Road. Even if something sounds good to you, or seems to give you a convenient way out," he said, looking straight at Jill.

Jill interrupted, squirming in her seat, "What about those words in my head, coming from the Road, and why couldn't I get rid of all the crows? How will we finish the walk with them about? How did my staff sink into the Road?"

"And what is this all about truth and life and staves? It still all seems like, like . . . magic and nonsense!" exclaimed Rocket as he waved his hands in the air.

The Wayfarer smiled holding up his hands to stop the rush of words. He fired off answers quickly, bending a new finger back on his right hand for each fresh point, "You simply heard what was in the Road," he said turning to Rocket, "it is not a magic, but the staff works in obedience to laws that you have not yet discovered. The lamp works by the same laws and when you know the Road as well as I do, then you will understand life like I do." He ran out of fingers. "Just remember what the sign says. It is these gifts and my words together that will keep you alive on this Road."

The two friends both tried to press more questions but the Wayfarer held up his hands again, "Enough for now! Just trust me."

It was dark now and the Wayfarer brought out bundles of equipment for Rocket and Kyle. Their host insisted that each staff be only for the use of the person it was given to, to serve their need only. Both were rough branches like Jill's and were a metallic, purplish grey. Rocket's had rough brown stripes raised from the surface, whilst Kyle's was smooth, but both had the unnatural writing woven through their bark.

 Choice of colours for coats and other things, however, was allowed. Although it seemed unkind, Jill insisted that Rocket looked like a cockatoo, and said as much. They compared their 'plumage' and their laughter woke Kyle.

He was groggy, but after they had quickly explained what had happened, he sheepishly thanked the Wayfarer for all that he had done. "It's all right. Now, will you take what I offer this time?" chuckled the Wayfarer, and pointed Kyle at the piles of oilskins and equipment.

Kyle kept saying thank you and rummaged wide-eyed and yawning through the piles, while the Wayfarer kept telling him it was fine and tidied up behind him. In the end, Rocket and Kyle had both chosen plain black boots but there the similarity ended. Kyle had gone for greys and browns, with an occasional dash of vibrant black. Rocket, however, had a red broad brimmed hat, a yellow and red knee length coat and bright green trousers. His royal blue pack finished off the effect.

While the man and boy searched, Jill looked up at the Wayfarer. "I have been wanting to ask you some things. Why was it so hard today, and what did you mean exactly . . ."

The Wayfarer held up his hand. "Explanations sometimes take a long time. I have told you some things now, but the rest will be understood further down the Road, and even then you will have only just begun . . ."

Jill interrupted, "But where can I find the Lord of the Way?"

"What were you told?" The Wayfarer held her in his gaze, and after a few moments Jill found a memory floating to the surface.

"Mr. Jones said that the Lord of the Way said travellers would, 'find him or be found.' But what does that mean?"

"What it says. Now look, your companions return," the Wayfarer said. And as Jill looked, a somber Kyle and brightly coloured Rocket strode over to them. Any more questions died on her lips.

The Wayfarer looked intently at all three of them. "Promise me," he insisted, "that you'll start anew, so that you can finish this together, no matter what happens, right to the very end of the Road, wherever the truth leads you."

All three nodded and a quiet seriousness descended. Jill felt the same peculiar feeling she had had when she had attacked the Road, a sense of someone else being there.

Perhaps I am getting closer to the Lord of the Way now. She looked sidelong at her friends. *Whatever happens, it looks like I've got to enjoy the company.* She grinned as she found her bunk, *I wonder what Mum would think of these two?*

10

THE LODGE

They woke to find the hut empty. The hut was still crammed with every possible good thing, but the Wayfarer was not there and that made all the difference. They dressed and found notes everywhere pointing out the best place in the hut for food, to take this book or that, and to pick up a bow from the stores because they would have to hunt food on the way.

Jill pulled faces at that idea, but Kyle was already hungry and thumbing through a small, leather bound recipe book. He read a bit out. "'First shoot your hare . . .' hey, most of these recipes start with something like that. What's this? 'To gut your hare, turn to page fifty four to find . . . 'Cleaning, Gutting and Hanging.' That should be worth trying." Jill said nothing, but was in fact thinking of a pet rabbit that she had once owned when very small.

The most impressive note was set on the rough dining table. It read:

The Wayfarer, Warden of the Road,
By the authority of the Lord of the Way bids you a safe journey.

In token of his permission, authority and favour, bear this note and receive all his gifts.

Use them for the mundane task, but remember that their power will conquer in time of need.

Underneath were three knives, leather sheathed and with bone handles and a small extra note saying, "These might be useful for the time being."

"I wonder what he means, '. . . for the time being . . .'" said Jill, and picked up the knives to examine them. Their blades were like a dagger's and were etched with the same pattern of words as the staves.

"I don't know, but with all these gifts, it's like all our birthdays come at once," said Rocket, but no one smiled.

Rocket picked up the note on the table, folded it and placed it inside his coat.

"I'd rather have him with us," said Jill.

"I still haven't looked at our other gifts properly," said Rocket, "and I think it would be good if you could teach us that rhyme again."

"Okay, there's nothing to it really," said Jill, "But can we do that later? I'd like Kyle to tell us what happened to him. I haven't had the chance to ask him since he woke up yesterday."

"Yeah, I'd like to know what's going on too," said Kyle, "I was asleep for most of it. Why don't you finish what you were saying, I didn't get it all last night."

"Well, yes, let's sort things out while we talk," said Rocket.

Jill described what she had experienced, putting in all the details that she had left out the previous night, with Rocket interrupting and shaking his head occasionally. Kyle would not say much about what he had heard and felt, but was amazed to hear how the previous days' battle had gone. The others managed to wring the main points out of him eventually, but it was clear that he did not want to talk. They eventually turned to their new equipment. The fitting of belts, packs, tents and cooking equipment took much longer than they had anticipated.

"I say, this is all rather awkward," said Rocket struggling with a will to get on his overloaded pack.

"Here, let me help," said Jill.

"I don't see what's your problem, old man," grinned Kyle. He, in his turn, looked quite smart, almost military, with his black wool ski hat pulled down over his head. "Special Operations Kyle at your service," he said and pretended to spray machine gun fire with his staff.

"It doesn't work like that," sniffed Jill. Kyle shrugged. Jill started to giggle. "You've got leather patches on your coat elbows, Rocket!"

"Yes, doesn't everyone? It makes the sleeve last longer, don't you know? All my jackets always do. Most practical." It was at moments like this that he seemed his most old fashioned and least energetic. He stood cupping one elbow in his hand while he chewed the pen in his other hand. Jill glanced at Kyle and they both burst out laughing.

"Time to go I think," said Rocket, "come on." And without much further conversation, they packed up and left.

The day was uneventful. The crows were seen early on, although only in one's or two's. At about midday, one boldly swept down and around them, cawing all the while. The friends talked in worried tones at first, scanning the sky and looking to the horizon, but the crow soon left, and no others appeared again. After a while, they began to speculate as to why it might be that their attackers had changed their behaviour.

"Perhaps there aren't enough crows left," said Kyle, who was looking hopefully upwards.

"I doubt it," said Rocket, "I think it likely that there are always more than enough. In fact, if we were being left alone because of a lack of crows, I guess our walk would get very tough later on, when they had found ways of increasing their strength again."

"Do crows breed that fast?" asked Jill, feeling slightly embarrassed.

"Normally? No they don't," said Rocket, "but these are not

normal crows."

"Maybe it's because we're all wearing the new jackets and clothes," said Jill.

This sounded hopeful to Kyle. "How do you mean?" he asked.

"Well, they attacked you, Kyle, and you were the least committed to the Road: you didn't have any equipment or weapons. That could be the secret. Perhaps the crows know when to stay clear." Jill talked quickly and waved her hands. "Perhaps when they have got strong, well-armed opponents they leave you alone."

"Or at least they wait until they've got a better opportunity," Rocket interjected.

Jill could not think of a reply to that, and things settled into an uneasy quiet.

Over the next week, Kyle lost several arrows trying to bag his first quarry, as the rabbits seemed to know exactly where he was and how to avoid him. He eventually learnt to shoot straight, and by the eighth day, they were eating rabbit stew. Jill was now hungry enough to eat it, the constant exercise and outdoor air giving her an appetite. She had started to learn the names and uses of the wild plants from one of their small books and enjoyed using the beans, spices and wild herbs to cook with. Although they still hunted, Jill noticed that the packets of spices and beans never decreased much.

She mentioned this to Rocket who snorted at the idea of everlasting beans. However, he did not argue, which was most unlike him, and this may have been because of the change that was coming over the group. Although they were no longer suspicious of each other, being forced together had worn away at their politeness. All their little habits had started to become hateful to one another, like splinters of personality pushed under each other's skin. They began to joke all the time and to irritate one another.

Rocket generally led, and spoke little. He was watchful, but apart from their blisters and sprains, there was little for him to do or say. The Road was straight now and always north. The terrain hardly changed. The Moor would occasionally roll over gentle hills of heather, or through small woods or a copse or two, but mostly it was broad and open. Two peaks rose in the far distance: a dark one to the north west, and another straight ahead and white. The mountains never looked closer and the group felt like they were going nowhere.

Kyle would say things like, "Nothin' to see round here," or "Don't know why I came," and the other two would do their best to ignore him, which grew harder each day. Each time an argument looked likely Rocket made the comment, "Uh, this is how it starts, you know," and once or twice Jill nearly slapped him for his trouble. It had begun to rain all the time.

The only thing to cheer them up was talk about the Wayfarer and what had happened, each time retold with more drama. This replaced discussion of precisely what kind of rain was falling on them now, or which wild herb or root improved the taste of the dried beans and rabbit the best.

They slept with the tents almost on the ditch, with the lamp hanging from the top of one of the walking sticks, for protection. Jill took to falling asleep with her head out of the tent on the warm summer evenings, watching the rainfall through the dome of light, and wondering what lay in store for them.

By the twentieth day, they were ready for a change and a rest. Rocket was playing another round of, "I spy, with my little eye, something on the horizon beginning with . . ." when Kyle named a something beginning with "h".

"Hordes of crows," said Jill.

"Nope," said Kyle.

"Half a tree?" suggested Rocket.

"Nope."

"Wild horses," said Jill.

"No, I've already done that one nine times today," said Kyle.

"I'd counted ten," Rocket said.

"A hurricane," said Jill.

"Nah. Plenty of rain though", he said and blew off some drops from his coat's hood.

"We give up," said Jill with a sigh, "what is it?"

"A house," said Kyle and spent the next ten minutes thoroughly enjoying the others' excitement.

It appeared through the mist bit by bit and Kyle's sharp sight had located it as a slightly less grey form against their even greyer surroundings.

"I like the way it's set off by the dirty yellow of the sky," said Jill sounding like her hairdresser.

"Yes, it's really cheerful up here when the sun comes out," said Rocket, completely missing the joke. The other two looked at the glowering sky, then at each other and giggled as they kept walking.

They reached the house that evening and camped in a low, semicircular grove of dark hollies. The trees were just by the house with their open side to the Road. Sheltered and out of the wind, a lawn of rabbit-nibbled grass lay between close-planted trees. They were all tired, cold and wet, and Kyle wanted to know why they did not try to break into the house straight away, and spend that night inside.

"Because we're not invincible, young man," said Rocket, "and we've had problems at strange houses before. It's stopped raining, for the moment anyway. We'll wait till morning."

Kyle grumbled and went to find something to kick.

Before they went to sleep, Rocket carefully checked around their camp-site, and after a while called Jill over. "Take a look at this," he said, pointing to a moss-covered slab of stone by his feet. It was the same stone as the Road and only a small part was visible. They started to scrape away the growth and discovered that the slab extended beyond the moss and underneath the fine lawn that they were camped on. The roots all peeled back like carpet, revealing a bright, brown speckled stone. It looked familiar.

"It's just like the Vantage Point," said Jill. They had only uncovered one of the outlying petals of the paved area, but the same jumble of letters as at the knoll had become clear.

"Our tents must be pitched on the far side of the circle with the trees ringing its edge," Rocket said surveying his surroundings, "Jill, I wonder whether we can plant your staff into the sandstone to light the camp-site tonight? It might give extra power to the lamp."

Jill walked across the turf to the tents and struggled to push her walking stick into the ground. The turf was soft and slowly gave way. Then, as if locking into a well oiled machine, the staff slipped smoothly and evenly into the ground, straightening up as it did so: at the same time, a high and lonely song pierced Jill's mind. She released the staff, and the beautiful lament stopped.

"It would appear that we can," said Rocket with some satisfaction. "Are you all right, dear?"

Jill nodded and smiled weakly, but tears stood out in her eyes.

Rocket's hand rested briefly on her shoulder, then he walked across to the tent. Jill hung the lamp, which shone tonight like a small star. Kyle stomped back into sight.

"It's your turn to cook," Jill started to say. Kyle scowled. "Never mind, I'll do it tonight," she relented. Jill unhooked the stove and cooking pan from the back of her rucksack. The pan was shaped like half a pear, the point acting as a pourer, while the stove's stand was intricately worked to look like curling branches of ivy. In the previous weeks, she had marvelled at the beauty of such a mundane thing and it had cheered her up frequently. Jill stared into the little blue flames reflected in the iron and bronze and began to wonder who had made it. Sighing, she prepared the rabbits Kyle had shot earlier.

The evening passed uneventfully. Jill went to bed, her head angled slightly in the direction of the Road, and watched the sky flicker light over their camp. The clouds were skimming low over the Moor, kissing the ground in places, their vapours colliding with the light, but Jill lay feeling alone and abandoned, and unable to sleep. The feelings that were keeping her awake found their way to the front of her mind in the quietness, so she spoke them out into the gloom.

"What's the point of all this?" Emptiness waited just outside the corner of her eye up on this Moor and there seemed so little she could make a difference to, so little to do, except endlessly follow this Road to find the Lord of the Way.

How long would it take? How long did Mum have?

The flickering light played across all she could see and her eye was drawn from the sky to the Road. She had to tilt her head back, watching the shadow and light race across the bank.

What? Jill strained her head back. There was a pair of feet on the Road, at the edge of her vision.

Who was it? She wrestled in her sleeping bag, all rustling feather down and padding and rolled over. The Wayfarer appeared, briefly illuminated by glancing light, and then he was gone. Another sweep of light revealed an open Road, and Jill was disappointed, but strangely, her worry had left her. She rolled over again and went to sleep.

The next morning they got up and skipped breakfast.

"Let's check out this seeing stone apparatus before we look around the house," said Rocket, "Do you think it still works? It looks very unused."

Jill looked at the sandstone and nodded. "I'm sure it still works," she said in a far-off voice.

Rocket looked at her quizzically. "Let's clear the turf then. We could do with knowing what's ahead, don't you think? Maybe there's a short-cut."

"What's the point?" said Kyle, "And what are you going on about? It's just a huge, crazy tombstone. How's that going to help?"

"That's the last thing it is," said Jill, "and to prove it, you can test it."

Kyle frowned.

"We think it's a viewing platform like the one that allowed us to see all over Nowhere," said Jill. "We could suddenly see things we couldn't before. You know, it's like I told you, after Mrs. Lazybee's? I found one just above the Village, just before I met Rocket."

Kyle's frown was replaced by a thoughtful look and a quietly muttered, "Cool." What he actually thought was that it sounded crazy to him, but he was too embarrassed to say so in front of his new friends. They worked purposefully for about half an hour, mostly with their hands, until only crumbs of soil were left. Kyle was stripped to a black cotton tee shirt and his black canvas cargo pants and boots, and stood radiating sweat and anticipation as he waited to be told what to do next.

"What now?"

"Well, you stand on the central circle and look," said Jill.

"Look at what?" asked Kyle.

"Look at anything, really," Jill replied, "Just don't worry. All right?"

"Yeah, uh, yeah, right." Kyle rubbed his hands on his trousers and tried to smile.

"Find out what you can about the house and see if there's anything ahead," Rocket commanded, "If that's all right of course, old boy."

Kyle smiled weakly and stood on the central stone. It immediately lit up with flame in the stone runes underneath him, although he appeared not to notice.

"It *is* impressive," said Rocket, "Ready to knock him off if things go wrong, like you did me?"

"Sssh," said Jill, "just watch."

Already the whole slab was aglow, and although no heat could be felt, the patches of damp were steaming. Lumps of soil dried and crumbled, their dust blowing away in seconds. Soon the stone looked new.

Kyle, meanwhile, had casually glanced at the house. "I wonder who built it?" he said to himself.

A purple and crimson-robed man stepped around the corner gave Kyle such a shock that he had to bite his lip not to shout out and his heart beat sickeningly. *Where'd he come from? He's not a cop is he?* Then he realised that no policeman he knew of would ever dress like that. A new idea occurred to him. *I wonder if this is the stone working? Not bad if it is.*

The man walked away and Kyle's interest followed him around the back of the house. Kyle's view moved up until he was gazing down on the man's head. Someone dressed in royal blue velvet joined him, and the two looked at a map. The first man pointed at something and Kyle's gaze followed his finger.

He could see the Road, but nothing of the house or the others. This was a shock and it was then that Kyle realised that he could not remember walking or moving and that he was actually floating above the ground. Dreams will often rob you of your common sense, and this was much like that. Everything was fascinating and happened as fast as he could think about it. The view that he could see was of where the house should be. He looked back down and saw that the two men had pulled out a house plan. It flew up, out of their hands and into his face. Kyle struggled to get it off, but had the curious sensation of melting into the paper; or did the plan dissolve into him? His view cleared and as it did so, the scene had changed.

The two men beneath had disappeared and there were others running around digging by the Road. They were also dressed in furs and velvet. No, they were not running but walking very quickly, like sped-up film. They dug trenches and placed huge sandstone blocks in them. There were others digging a circular hole and laying slabs in that too. He watched them plant a semicircle of little bushes by the slabs and he gasped.

"It's that seeing stone, where I'm standing."

Something about the experience appealed to him and he controlled his rising panic. The men finished building the Vantage Point, and the words 'The Lodge' echoed through his mind. The men started to move even faster as the house grew from the ground before him. The builders faded from sight and soon the Lodge had been finished, but it seemed smaller than the one Kyle had seen minutes earlier. It was low, sandstone yellow, with a slate roof and small, friendly windows. Travellers came and left, the seasons of the year passed, and all seemed well. The house pulsated with movement, the walls almost breathing in and out. In seconds, night fell, and a storm blew in, but still, lightning fast, visitors came and went and the windows of the house glowed in the dark.

Without warning, a bolt of lightning leapt down from the storm and ran through the house, as if searching for something. It briefly lit one room in particular, and then went out. The visitors stopped leaving. Fields of crops instantly appeared and the spring behind the house became a well. Extensions were added to the house, grand and ornate. It became a square building with a courtyard inside. Brightly lit windows showed glorious luxury in the new hall that faced him.

The storm grew.

It boiled up into a monstrous cloud above the new hall and crashed downward, lashing hailstone and lightening onto its target. The lights went out. Windows were smashed and then the house became completely still, as if dead. Out of the central window of the grand hall nearest to him, a mist rose and moved through the storm. It came towards him, snake-like and unaffected by the weather. A thin voice hissed at Kyle. "Who disturbs my nest?"

Kyle froze.

A voice answered from inside his own head, "We do, my master."

Terror swallowed him and he felt himself plunge headlong. Everything went black.

Jill and Rocket had seen him lean forward, and had heard a few of his thoughts as he marvelled at the house, but things had gone quiet for quite a while before he'd collapsed. The flame in the stone blew-out, and both man and girl had rushed forward to see if Kyle was well.

Cold sweat stood out on his forehead. He awoke and sat up.

"Weird," said Kyle.

"What's wrong?" said Jill.

"Nothing, nothing now anyway." Kyle glanced at the house. "I thought something was trying to get me. It was weird."

"You've said that," Jill snapped.

"Tell us everything; from the beginning; just as you like," said Rocket, and helped Kyle to stand.

They led him across to the bank of the Road, and before they sat down Kyle had started to explain his vivid picture. It took him several minutes to finish and when he got to the end, he stumbled.

"Then this fog hissed at me, and . . . and . . ."

"And what, old boy?"

"And it all went black and I woke up here."

"Nothing more?" asked Jill.

"Nothing," Kyle said firmly.

"Are you sure?" said Rocket, searching Kyle's face.

"Yes," said Kyle, but looked down.

"Thanks Kyle," said Jill, "Are you sure you're okay?"

Kyle nodded.

Rocket let this rest, but was chewing the end of a pencil he had found somewhere, and he was muttering to himself. "So, nothing of the Road ahead, but a history of the house. Uhmm, interesting . . ." He looked over his shoulder. "Quite a monstrosity it is too, and if you are correct, presently empty. We could do with a rest from the weather. Why don't we look inside? Are you up to it yet, Kyle?"

"Uh, yeah, I think so."

"Let us explore, then," said Rocket with a grin, "but with caution, as always." With a flourish, he stood up to lead the way.

The Lodge was low, long and ancient. It stood facing the Road and was constructed from the same warm stone, with its own little sandstone path, leading to the front door. Deep blue slate covered its roof, and a tall tower rose from the middle of the roof rather like a huge chimney. Flat metal collars ringed the tower outside, like polished circular shelves. The house wall had arrow slits high upon it, and lower down there were small, arched windows with gem-like glass. The path led to a large central doorway.

The door was studded with iron nails, and the hinges across it looked like three branches, each with a leaf at its tip. Like the windows, it was arched and surrounded by columns, worn soft by time. The door stood slightly ajar.

"It looks like a defensible house," said Rocket.

"What's that?" said Kyle.

"A house that can be defended from attack, what else?"

"What, you mean a castle?" Kyle said, "It doesn't look like a castle to me."

"Well, a defensible house is meant to be lived in, not to be fought from like a castle. It's built by people who aren't looking for a fight, but think they might have a battle all the same."

"Umhh," said Jill.

"Let's have a look around from the outside to see what we can," said Rocket. "We can't be too careful. Look out for any old ladies or big black birds. Everyone agreed?" Kyle shrugged and Jill nodded. "I'll go the long way round with Kyle, to check every approach from that side, and Jill can take her walking stick around the other side. Have you got your knife as well?"

"It never leaves my side," said Jill.

"Good luck then. All right old boy, let's go." Rocket ruffled Kyle's hair, nodded at him and winked at Jill.

Jill moved around the corner of the house. Short grass grew next to the Lodge and it was easy to walk toward the back. The windows became more ornate and the stone a dirtier grey the further she walked. By the time she reached the back of the house, neatness had been exchanged for decay.

Jill looked in at one of the oddly shaped windows. The floor was wooden and falling in, but what was left of the wall coverings and furniture looked as though they had been very rich and expensive. Obviously, no one had lived here for years.

She continued around the corner, examining the wreck before her. The rear wall was as black as soot. The windows were made up of tiny diamond shaped panes of glass, many of which were missing. There was a large family crest, high above the windows where two stubby cannons poked out on either side. Jill noticed that in places the top of the wall had long gouges, as if some powerful claw had ripped off the top edges of the stone.

The walls rose high over her head and she backed slowly down the grass through the thorny shrubs and wild flowers. In a second, she had dropped to the floor, and was peering at the sky intently. A crow hovered, trying to grasp the weathered stonework with its feet, and drove its beak into a hole. Small chunks of masonry scattered loosely upon the grass and the crow started to fly off. It saw her. Jill raised her staff.

"Be gone!" she shouted, and, an instant later, only black feathers remained. Jill looked and saw that the wall was covered with many beak-sized holes.

She checked the sky again and cautiously finished walking the back section of the wall, meeting Kyle and Rocket at the far corner of the house.

They had found nothing more than she had, so she told them about the crow she had seen and showed them where it had pecked.

"If the crow returned each day, it might just join up the holes and cause a lump of wall to fall out," Jill thought out loud.

"Why would the crows attack this place?" Kyle asked.

"I don't know, but it must have been some place to live once," said Jill.

"Let's see what's inside, shall we?" asked Rocket. Kyle grunted something about taking their time, and they moved to the front of the house while Kyle slouched, grumbled and thrust his hands deep into his pockets. Jill watched him closely and wondered what might have changed his mood.

The door was still open and all three stopped on the smooth flagstones in front of the entrance. The sun had come out and stained-glass windows brightly illuminated the scene as they peered in.

Inside was almost entirely natural stone, clean and fresh. Arches looking like the ribs of some gigantic animal, or the trunk and branches of a tree, held up the roof. It reminded Jill of an old church. Two arched doorways stood at the back of the side walls, opening to the right and the left, and from the way the floor was worn, this was the main passageway of the house. Jill lifted her staff and pushed open the door with its tip. As the walking stick touched the door, the staff sang with a pure high note and the sound hung in the air. It seemed almost too special a place to go inside.

"Cool," said Kyle.

"Stone is inclined to be," said Rocket as they slowly stepped in. Surprisingly, the air was not cold, but warm; a deliciously dry smell teased their noses with the promise of indoor comforts. They stood and waited, soaking up the atmosphere, listening to that peculiar indoor silence that a building makes when no one is in it.

"I don't think anyone is at home," said Jill.

"Why don't we 'ave a look around? What we waitin' for?" Kyle said. He was suddenly alert and friendly and both Jill and Rocket looked at him. "What? I was just tryin' to be helpful."

"I think it's a very sensible suggestion," said Jill and glanced at Rocket with a shrug of her shoulders. Rocket decided that Jill and he should start off exploring with Kyle watching the door. Kyle protested loudly.

"That's ruined any element of surprise," Rocket said. He grimaced as the echoes faded. They all agreed to check out the rooms on either side and then return.

Jill and Kyle went into the left room, which was empty except for an old cupboard and a curtain against the wall. Instead of a hallway, they could see that the room they were in opened directly into the next room through another low arched door way. Kyle pulled aside the curtain to reveal a brightly lit stone staircase. They were discussing how to continue exploring when they heard Rocket call, and found him pulling an iron ring in a heavy timber door, tucked just behind the front door.

"It's locked," he said scratching his head.

"There's no use us trying to get in there then, is there? Look, we found a way upstairs," said Jill, "I think we should split up and explore. Kyle can look around upstairs, you can search the courtyard and I can finish looking around downstairs."

Rocket pursed his lips and raised his eyebrows, Kyle shrugged with a smile, and so, Jill's plan was adopted.

Jill moved north. What Jill saw as she explored the house reminded her of a very badly kept museum. At first, nearly all the exhibits were missing. She walked back past the cupboard and through two quiet empty rooms. The only thing filling the space seemed to be the sound of sand crackling under her boots. The next room had a huge table and benches, with a fireplace large enough to walk into. Large metal hooks hung down from the ceiling and inside the clean fireplace. The passage continued as an arched tunnel squeezed in on the right hand side of the huge mantle piece.

This looks like some old fashioned cottage kitchen, but bigger, she thought. The passage led to dimly lit and empty storerooms and ended abruptly with an arched doorway on her right.

She pushed the door. It opened smoothly onto a room with another door opposite. "The house turns a corner here," she mused, "This must be the north side."

Jill stepped into a very different room. Here the museum had exhibits, but they were all decaying. Cool, moist air wrapped around her. The room had paintings on the wall; fine timber ran underneath her feet and embroideries covered fine plaster walls. There was polished wooden furniture that might have graced a castle when it still held soldiers. Everything was covered with patterns and pictures from old stories, long forgotten. Even the people pictured in the windows stared into the distance as if waiting for a bus. Jill thought they looked funny but guessed that the windows told stories too. She wondered why it all looked so lifeless.

"I suppose stories are meant to be lived, not trapped under glass," she muttered to herself, "I bet they would take a bus out of here if they could."

A breeze blew cold from the next room. It whistled around the misshapen door in the far wall and for no apparent reason, Jill felt a surge of fear. Even so, she walked to the end of the room and grasped the ornate brass knob. The damp had warped the mahogany door and she found she had to yank on the handle several times before it juddered open across the floor.

She looked in. This was obviously the end hall where the crow had attacked the wall; she recognised the windows. Cautiously, Jill entered.

The room was high, with a balcony around the base of a barrel-shaped ceiling far above her head. The ceiling was covered with pictures of almost naked men and women. Even though parts of the ceiling had fallen off, what remained told a story. Paintings spiralled around through love, jealousy, envy, pride and hatred. Jill liked picture stories and this tale started in the middle of the roof and spun out above her head, until it reached the balcony. She suddenly noticed a very familiar face amongst the paintings. Jill started with fright; the face had spoken to her.

"Hello," it said.

"What are you doing up there?" she asked Kyle as he peered over the balcony railing. Jill had almost forgotten that anyone else was exploring.

"Nothing, but I should watch your step, this whole end seems rotten. It stinks too." His foot caught some rubbish, which fell through a hole in the balcony floor, kicking up dust and dirt, and made both of them cough.

This hall did indeed reek. The plaster had fallen off the wall in clumps, and damp patches of red and white fungi appeared everywhere. The hangings here must have been truly magnificent when first made, but the old military glories, the geometric designs, the gods and mythological creatures, were all now tattered shreds. Corroding metal objects lay all around. Cushions and carpets were faded and decaying, parts of the floor had fallen in, and the ragged gaping holes in the outer wall lent the whole place a feeling of instability and danger. Much of the east wall was an expanse of broken glass and last Autumn's leaves still lay where they had blown in.

There was only one perfectly preserved object in the room, a huge portrait of an imposing man, dressed in an old-fashioned military uniform, all brass buttons and gold braid. It hung against the rear wall facing the sunrise. He had a long blue frock coat, white silk breeches, and square silver buckles on his shoes. He stared out imperiously. *What a proud man, and such strong eyes!* She examined his face, letting her eyes linger on the detail.

After a second, it seemed that nothing else in that room mattered; the face seemed to pin her to the spot. She was no longer sure that the face was just a painting: she felt herself falling, being drawn up into those eyes, those horrible eyes. Jill could see mist in the air.

"Your eyes are dead," Jill said out loud.

Kyle shouted, "What was that?"

In a moment the spell was broken. Jill quickly looked elsewhere. "Nothing, see you back at the front door." Jill hurried back through the southern wing, which was a mirror image of the north side. She had temporarily lost her desire for exploration and not looking at anything, scurried to be away from the painting.

Kyle, however, had seen Jill shout and decided to find out what had frightened her. He had been hating this part of the building, but decided that this might change his opinion. Kyle found a stair that led down to the floor of the hall and looked up at what she had just seen. He smiled. He had just about decided to steal the painting to scare Jill later, when Kyle reached up to touch it. Mist appeared. His mind clouded. A crow flew into the room, and he heard something howl. He twisted around sharply. *Where was it? A crow? A dog? They must be there somewhere.* The room was spinning now, and as he stumbled, he looked around wildly. Panicking, he looked up again.

His eyes met the painting's. He could not look away, no matter how hard he tried. The mist thickened and he heard a hiss. Kyle was flailing with his arms, trying to stop the room lurching around, when he heard voices in his head.

"Who disturbs me?"

We do, master.

"Bow before me, and I will give you power," came the hiss again. "You are nothing, obey me. The others hate you. When they know you and what you have done, they will destroy you. It is because of you your father left, you are worthless. You never loved your father, you are a failure . . ."

Kyle felt his knees buckle and he sank down, the weight of the eyes crushing him. His staff struck the floor loudly. Crows cawed around him and he heard their screams once more. He stared at the ancient picture. *It's growing!*

He heard the voice speak again, "You will eliminate her."

"No," said Kyle. His voice was shaking, but his walking stick shook in his hand in a very different way. Of course! He brought the staff around and pointed at the painting as best he could.

The hiss spoke, "Do not try to . . ."

"NO!" Kyle shouted and there was a loud cracking noise, like a firework, and Kyle was flung onto his back. He lay still, and all around was quiet and black. Quiet was good, but why was it black? Then he remembered to open his eyes. Kyle breathed again in relief. The mist, crows, and voices were gone and the room was still. The painting hung undisturbed.

What was that voice in my head? It had talked with that man thing in the painting. *Was it me speaking with that thing*? Kyle was still shaking. Still, he had beaten it. He would not tell the others, they did not need to know, they thought he was odd already. No need to give them proof.

He got up, and with one last glance, ran upstairs to leave the hall.

Jill, meanwhile, had reached the end of the southern wing and was glad to see a low arched door just like the one she had left on the northern side. She opened the ancient oak door and stepped into a large room.

This one was by far the most welcoming she had seen yet, for a huge circular window illuminated velvet-lined shelves covered with every kind of brass navigational instrument. The window was an explosion of colours, casting shards of rainbows about the room. Jill thought that some of the instruments reminded her of things she had seen on films with old sailing ships, one she definitely recognised. It was an old telescope, sitting collapsed on one of the higher shelves. Jill took it down from the shelf and weighed the compact cool metal in her hands. She slipped it in her pocket. The next two rooms held nothing except window seats and a fireplace, and after a short arched tunnel, Jill found herself back at the entrance.

Kyle Williams arrived shortly afterwards, and asked where Rocket was. They found him combing the flowerbeds for 'something interesting'.

Rocket insisted on 'ladies first' and Jill told them all that she had seen.

"That picture in the end hall gave me the creeps," she said, as she finished.

"Yeah," said Kyle, "It looks so old that whoever the painting's of must be dead by now."

"Well that's one good thing," said Jill, "I'm glad about that."

"You can't say that," said Kyle, feeling nervous, wondering if the painting could hear.

"Why not, it's what I really think."

Kyle thought quickly. "I . . . I don't know," he said, "It's what I said about my Great Gran when she died, and I nearly got killed for it. You should have heard Dad; they could've heard at the police station the way he was going on. In fact the cops popped round later that night, so they might have." Kyle was giving Jill a lopsided grin, which somehow irritated her immensely.

"Well, Kyle's right of course, it's not normally considered polite, but I've never been one for politeness myself," said Rocket.

"Well, what did you find Rocket?" Jill asked.

"Me? Nothing much," Rocket mused and looked around. "There's an ornamental fountain that can't have had anything in it for years. Nothing has grown in here since the year dot, as far as I can tell. That end hall is rotting from wetness, and yet the ground in here is bone dry. Perhaps it has to do with the way this place was abandoned. It's pretty odd, just to run away and leave half your stuff, even if the crows were having a go."

It was Kyle's turn next, and his eyes drifted over their surroundings as he spoke. "The downstairs sounds pretty much the same as upstairs, empty and clean, then damp and horrible, with that nasty oil painting in the end room," he hesitated, not sure what to say. "And it *is* creepy in there . . ."

"Especially if you sneak up on someone," said Jill, who had not yet quite forgiven Kyle for giving her such a surprise.

"Yeah, that was a laugh," Kyle said, "the best for days."

Jill narrowed her eyes and Kyle pretended not to see, glad to let the talk move on.

"I did find one useful looking thing; a short guitar with four strings and a really fat bottom bit."

"Looking a bit like half an onion?" Rocket cut in.

"Yeah, I s'ppose so. It was in the corner room just above the place where you found all those brass bits."

Rocket took charge, "Kyle, you go up and check out that room again, and I'll look at the brass instruments. There may be something we can use there."

"What about me?" Jill did not like being left out.

"Try the cupboard in the first room," Rocket said, "it could turn something up, old girl."

Jill found the cupboard locked. She rattled it. It was locked and solid. Then she remembered her knife. Taking the blade out of its leather sheath Jill slipped it between the double opening doors. There was a slight resistance, and then the blade sliced down and the doors popped open. She pushed them back and looked inside.

There were staves and coats much like her own, and boots on the floor, all looking brand new. It smelt fine, all oils and leather. She pushed around the coats not looking for anything in particular, and then she thought she saw a blue umbrella in the corner. There is a thrill to finding something that is really special, and although she did not know why, Jill felt the hairs stand up on the back of her head. She looked again. Yes, there was a slim, tapering object with a gold top flashing at her. Was it an umbrella? She pushed the coats to the right and then smiled.

It was a sword. Its hilt was made of waves of gold and silver. She picked it up, its belt swinging and clattering, and saw that the sheath was made of stone and was shot through with veins of glistening gold.

"Such a beautiful blue," Jill said. It had the intensity of the sky on a summer's evening, and Jill expected it to feel warm to the touch.

She tried the handle. It was as if the hilt was made for her hand, the blade slipping out as she gripped hard. It seemed light and then the next second twistingly heavy; it waved around with a will of its own. It bucked around in her hand, and she tried to control it, now using both hands. The blade surged and Jill began to worry that she could not control it. Spinning around, she stumbled forward.

"Stop, stop, I didn't mean to," the blade wavered for a moment and then bucked again. It pulled Jill towards the door, and then swung up and struck the stone door arch. There was a loud bang; a flash and her hands were stung into numbness. The sword clattered and spiraled across the floor, while smoke and stone dust filled the air.

"Ow, that *so* hurt!" Jill said out loud and cradled her right hand as she was doubled over in pain. She sucked in air over her teeth and rubbed her hand, then coughed out the smoke she had just breathed in. Both Rocket and Kyle stumbled in as the vapours were clearing.

"What happened?"

"Are you all right?"

"What on earth blew up?"

"I found a sword," Jill said.

"What? It exploded?" said Kyle.

"What is it with you and pyrotechnical weapons? You didn't shout at anything and point your staff did you?" queried Rocket.

"What's pyrotechnical?" asked Kyle.

"Oh will you just be quiet?" Jill sat down with her back to the wall. "That sword over there has a life of its own and when it ran into that doorway it exploded."

Rocket looked at the sword and then the wall. "It's left a deep notch in the stone work, although it seems unharmed itself. Now where are the bits that would have been blown out?"

"Oh, all over the floor," said Jill.

"Funny, I can't see any," said Rocket.

"Me neither," said Kyle Williams.

"Oh, what a surprise," Rocket had turned back to the door as the last wisps of smoke cleared. "The notch seems to have almost disappeared too."

"So this place is part of the Road too? Great," said Kyle, "maybe we can hang out here for a while and relax out of the way of wind, rain, crows and Jill's cookin'."

Jill stuck her tongue out, pausing in her rubbing of her right wrist.

"That still hurts, doesn't it?" Rocket looked concerned.

"Uhmm, it gave me quite a jolt." Jill winced as Kyle straightened her hand out.

"Well, it would if you use it against its own ally," said a voice from the entrance room, and every head turned.

The Wayfarer poked his head around the corner. "Would you like some help with that wrist?"

"It's not my fault; I didn't know it would do that."

"Well, you picked it up." The Wayfarer's voice was gentle, even as he corrected her.

"Yeah, but I never knew that would happen," Jill whined.

"It was still your choice. Maybe you'll be more cautious next time." The Wayfarer grinned as he leant against the doorway. "Let me at the patient, please."

He stepped forward and, taking her hand, said, "Your wrist is out of joint, here." He applied some pressure with the palm of his hand over her wrist and looked down at the hand intently. "Now get back where you belong," he said.

There was an audible click, and the Wayfarer let go of Jill's hand. Jill frowned and peered at her wrist, "It doesn't hurt any more. Thanks." She looked at her hand in bemusement and kept turning it over in front of her face as if she was checking a new manicure.

"Now this," the Wayfarer picked up the sword by his finger tips, "is how to hold it unless you want to go to war. Grip the hilt and it will come alive, and it will bring life too."

"Oh, I'm not going to go anywhere with *that!*" Jill said shaking her head.

"Pity, because it is yours now."

"I never take anything that's not mine," she retorted.

"Well, then replace the telescope and we'll talk about whether you need the Sword."

"How did you know about that?" Jill's voice was slightly hoarse.

Kyle was trying to move the lute he was carrying behind his back. Everyone stared at the bulge sticking out behind his knees.

"You may keep the lute, but I think you'll find it hard to carry in addition to your tent and bow. You may try, if you want." Kyle looked uncomfortably shy.

"Go and replace the brass instruments, and I'll see you in the kitchen."

"I've only got one telescope," said Jill.

"I think he means me as well," said Rocket, accompanying Jill back to the Instrument Room, and producing three complicated looking metal devices. Jill addressed him with awe, "I never thought that you had it in you."

"Well, *he* at least, knew that I had it 'on' me."

"I wonder what he wants this time?" said Jill.

II

THE SWORD

The Wayfarer led them back to the room with the large table and fire place and they found that it was now a working kitchen. Kyle had helped the Wayfarer get food and furniture out, and teased Jill as she entered.

"You didn't look very well. The Wayfarer helped me to get these things out of the store cupboards."

"But I looked . . ." Jill turned to the Wayfarer, "and there was nothing there."

"They were not yours to find," said the Wayfarer, "Kyle's a little hasty. Let's just say I know how to find things."

"I'm with you then gov'nor; this is loads better than Jill's cooking!"

"So this was all back there?" said Jill, pointing to the passage next to the fireplace.

"In a manner of speaking."

"I suppose that's where you got the fire wood from too," said Rocket.

"That was burning when we came in," said Kyle, "you had to 'ave seen it Jill." The fire did look like it had been burning for a few hours, with a deep bed of ash and hot yellow coals.

Jill stared at it and said nothing.

"My generosity can take many forms," the Wayfarer said, looking at Jill directly. She turned pink and felt foolish.

"Why did I have to put the telescope back?" said Jill after a long pause.

"First, let's eat. There's plenty here," the Wayfarer said. The table was laid out with steamed fish, hot bread, cheeses and wine.

"So where'd the hot food come from, Kyle?" said Jill, watching him closely.

"Dunno, es jus' 'ere 'n de bots. Es good," he said spraying some of his fish over the table. Jill pulled a face, brushed some fish off her sleeve, and started to eat.

"Why couldn't I take the telescope?" Jill had returned to her topic after a few minutes of contended eating. Kyle and Rocket listened with interest.

"Why did you want it?" said the Wayfarer.

"Well, it was beautiful; it felt good, and I've always wanted some binoculars for walking on the Moor," Jill said.

The Wayfarer looked at her and picked up a bread roll, and offered her the basket.

"Well . . ." Jill looked away from the Wayfarer at the wall, "it's just been abandoned here. No one wants it."

"It's my job to strengthen what remains, not to weaken it. It belongs here." The Wayfarer was stern, but not unkind. "Do you need it?" the Wayfarer asked, gently.

"Yes, well I suppose so . . ." she drew breath and looked down at her food, "No, I suppose not. But it would be good to have, don't you think?" Jill looked up at the Wayfarer, the question in her eyes.

The Wayfarer paused, and then replied slowly. "All that you need for this journey is mine to give, and you only have to ask. You've already got enough. But if you need more, then there needs to be a reason for it. What's your reason?"

The Wayfarer sat very still, and stared at the young girl, more intently than ever. Jill squirmed. *What do I want? I don't really want the telescope, but there's got to be more than just a walk in the rain. I want to help Mum, but it's not just that . . .*

Jill went red, and started to lose her temper. "If I can't have the telescope, tell me what are we doing here? When do we get to meet the Lord of the Way? I mean, do we just have to tramp through the rain till we get there?" Jill was staring back at the Wayfarer now. The other two had stopped eating altogether and were watching closely. "Well, what about other people?" Jill said. "What about other places? There has to be a point to all this. Why is it taking so long? These last weeks have been almost as bad as the Village; it's all so pointless!"

The Wayfarer smiled. "Why did you start walking?"

Jill looked down, then back up into the Wayfarer's gaze, "I needed to find the Lord of the Way. I need his help. I think he's the only one who can help."

"You need help?"

"Well, me and Mum." She would not cry, she decided.

"Well said! Now we're getting closer to your reason. Was that all there was to leaving the Village?"

"It was all phony," Jill said quietly.

"Phony?"

"Everyone was just pretending. No one could help Mum. No one could help themselves, not really. It was all so stupid . . ." Jill was tearing up again, and speaking very quickly, ". . . and there were so many lies that I couldn't stand it any more. Everyone pretended they were all okay, but it was just a put-on, so I had to get away from it. I couldn't stand it."

"You wanted it to be genuine."

"Yes! Really real!" Jill looked up again, into the Wayfarers face.

"Well, were you genuine?" The Wayfarer asked quietly.

"What do you mean?" Jill dropped her gaze again.

The Wayfarer let the question hang in the air.

"Does it matter? I'm here aren't I?" Jill said, staring at her plate.

The Wayfarer remained quiet.

Jill shrugged, "There wasn't much point to anything."

"Ah, a point! A purpose. A reason. That telescope has purpose when it's held by someone who needs it, but when it's in someone's pocket just because it looks nice . . ." The Wayfarer shrugged. "Purpose and belonging go together. You could say that everything needs to find its true owner."

Rocket cut in, anxious to break the tension, "By the way, talking about true owners, what did actually happen here?"

The Wayfarer turned to him with a quizzical smile.

Rocket continued, not needing a reply. "From the state of this house and what Kyle saw on the Vantage Point, I deduce that an attack by someone like the military-gentleman chap in the painting, with the help of a few thousand crows, drove off the inhabitants of this house."

"Yes, but there's more to see here than that," replied the Wayfarer. As he spoke, Jill could see all the people in the stain-glass windows in her mind's eye and she felt sad.

Rocket frowned in puzzlement, apparently having run out of words.

"Let me explain," the Wayfarer began. "The Warden of the Road cares for this house, but not all of it. These walls are a part of the Road. This Lodge was built to give travellers rest and food because the Warden had need of it, but no more than that. That was its purpose."

"Were the cannons yours then?" queried Rocket.

"No such crude thing would belong to the Road! No, in fact, only this side of the courtyard has ever been truly part of the Road, the rest does not belong. Hopefully it will be removed." With this, the Wayfarer looked meaningfully at Jill.

Jill was not at all comfortable.

"So what happ'ned?" Kyle asked.

"There was a series of battles. Some travellers grew weary and decided to stay here a long time. Soon they had children and settled, but in doing so, their enemy had stopped them moving down the Road, and then he wanted to get rid of them altogether."

"What enemy?" asked Rocket, who had taken to chewing a pencil again.

"He was once a servant of the Lord of the Way, someone who controlled access to his throne room, but hated the building of the Road. He thought that it would ruin his prestige if everyone could get there."

"So that's where this Road actually goes." Rocket chewed even harder, and muttered to himself, "Interesting, most interesting."

Kyle glanced at Rocket, then back at the Wayfarer. "So, like I was saying, you said the Lodge was only here so they could have a break; why were they allowed to stay then?"

"We do not fight travellers, we help them."

"Who's 'we'?" asked Rocket, suddenly leaning forward again, his eyes narrow.

The Wayfarer paused for a second, and then ignored the question. He turned to Rocket. "They took gifts from this enemy, and those gifts spoiled the Lodge. They thought things were going well for them. They felt strong, were feared by their enemies and their enemies gave them gifts to keep them from attacking."

"Sounds like things were going great," said Kyle, "no-one got in their face, and they got rich as well. Wish someone would give me gifts."

"Well, they thought it was good too, but the Road was less and less their life. In fact, the extensions were built by this enemy, but it was all a trick."

"A trick?" Rocket asked

"What you build is always yours, after a fashion."

Rocket smiled, "Ah, then it was a gateway for him to get at travellers."

"The military gentleman in the painting," shouted Jill, "I bet it was the old military gentleman!"

"Yes, yes, you are both right, and that's as good a name as any, although I would not count him as a 'gentle-man'." said the Wayfarer, "Yes, he's the one who drove them out."

"About the painting, what's . . ." Kyle began.

Rocket's eyes had widened, "The crows and the painting chap go together, so if the crows are still attacking people, then do you mean that this painting chap is *not dead*?"

"Most perceptive, young man, 'not-dead' is a good description," said the Wayfarer, "but he is not truly alive now either."

Jill pulled a face, "Uggh!"

"The military gentleman, as you call him, still commands those he can bend to his will, those whose minds accept his lies. If you surrender to obey him once, you become his slave. Did anyone look long at the painting in the far hall?"

The question hung in the air. Kyle blushed to his collar, "Well, er . . ."

"Yes, I did," said Jill, "it made me feel sick. I ran away from it."

"Good," said the Wayfarer, "when the travellers received his final gift, they hung it in pride of place. Hopefully it will be gone soon."

Kyle was struggling. He wanted to talk about what had happened, but couldn't think of any way of saying it that left him looking good. "This is confusing me," said Kyle, "I'm off to find the lemonade."

"It's in the back cupboard," the Wayfarer waved his hands descriptively, "the far corner, in a stoneware jug."

"It wasn't there earlier," said Kyle.

"Believe me, you'll have no difficulty finding it. Well," the Wayfarer continued, "so few have travelled the Road of late. The military gentleman has effectively blockaded the road, but now, someone had taken up the Sword again." The Wayfarer fixed his gaze on Jill once more. "Your frown does not suit you. What bothers you, my little storm maiden?"

Jill found such pet names irritating, especially when she was trying to concentrate, and was puzzled to see an amused look on the Wayfarer's face.

"The Sword, which now belongs to you," the Wayfarer continued slowly, "was made to defeat the military gentleman and set his prisoners free."

Jill's expression was turning from a look of confusion to alarm. "No, that's not my sword: I found it, but I don't want anything to do with it. I'll put it back as soon as I can. Shall I go and do it now?" Jill twisted even further around in her seat. The idea that she had to do something to help in defeating some undead monster seemed so beyond her — and all because she had picked up an antique sword!

It's so unfair! First these two and now this Sword! She folded her arms and refused to think about it. It would all just go away. Jill quickly pushed her chair back; it made an awful scraping noise, which echoed around the hall.

At this point Kyle returned with tumblers and a stoneware jug, and started talking over the conversation.

"I didn't see it earlier, but it looks like that really good stuff those posh supermarkets sell. Anyone want some?" No one spoke to him. Kyle looked at the way the Wayfarer was leaning over the table and then looked at Jill. She sat opposite, scowling, and had turned away from his attention. "What, did Jill get in trouble? Did I miss somethin'?" Kyle never liked missing out, especially when it was not him that was in trouble. He put the tray down and poured Rocket and himself a drink. Rocket put his fingers to his lips to show he should be quiet. Kyle shrugged his shoulders and grunted an, "Umf", and slowly worked his way through the rest of the jug.

As Jill stood up to go, the Wayfarer said, "I said that the Road was open before you and that you have your weapons, so the crows will not stop you, but the military gentleman may be able to, especially if he still has access to the Road. You can outmaneuver him, but your weapons will serve only your journey, no-one else. Why are you walking this Road, Jill?"

"That's not fair! Leave Mum out of this!" Jill was almost shouting, "You said that the Road was open and clear to walk."

"It is. There is a way around, but even then, he can deceive and lead astray."

Rocket stood up too, "You don't mean that this young woman has to take on some ancient ghoul?"

The Wayfarer stood as well; he did not shout but his voice cut through the din.

"The Sword was made to defeat him and it will do so, because it has power, life, in itself. It was rejected by those who first had need of it, but will only respond to its true owner, to someone with whom it can fulfill its purpose. The Sword's mine to give, and its purpose is found in someone who wants to open up the Road again, someone who needs to reach the Lord of the Way. What's your purpose Jill?" He stared at her.

"This is weird," said Kyle, who was casually leaning back and enjoying the scene, "there's another way around, right? Let's take that way." Kyle finished the lemonade and returned his glass to the table with a thump.

Jill said nothing; her gaze was being held by the Wayfarer's eyes.

"But why do I have to? I just want to get away from the trouble. Why do I have to get involved with all these other people?"

"To leave those things behind you need other people, you need to serve a purpose. Without that, you'll never finish the journey; you'll never find your answers. Do you not feel anything?"

Jill glanced down, "I don't know."

"Will you do it? Will you do it in spite of your fear? Will you do it for someone else?" he spoke quietly, but it was as though his breath filled the room.

"You need to think this through, young lady," Rocket began, "It will need commitment and . . ."

The Wayfarer cut through Rocket's words, "It's your choice Jill."

"I'm not sure . . ." Jill hesitated, "I can't decide, not yet. Can I think about it?"

"When will you give me your answer?"

"By tomorrow's breakfast?" Jill asked.

"Yes, that's good. Let's eat and think, then, as long as the gentlemen have no objection?"

Rocket and Kyle both shook their heads and the group fell quiet.

As he ate slowly, Rocket kept looking sidelong at the Wayfarer, while Kyle frowned and munched loudly. When they had finished eating, the three travellers sat looking at their plates, each chewing over their thoughts.

12

A Living Library

The Wayfarer looked up at Rocket and a broad smile covered his face. "Would it help you, my friend, if I showed you what was behind that locked door?" the Wayfarer asked, "the one you were wrestling with?"

Rocket nodded, "That would be good."

There was the scraping of chairs as they all stood up and returned to the entrance. The Wayfarer produced a large iron key, turned it smoothly in the lock and lifted the handle. As the door was pushed open, bright light spilled out, shadows stood back from them and they blinked as they stepped into a brilliantly lit room. They entered into warmth and the smell of wood polish and the first thing that they noticed was the wall. The room was perfectly circular and every inch of it was lined with books. Jill's gaze followed the shelves of multicoloured leather-bound volumes up and up until she nearly fell over. Right above her head the light was so strong that she could hardly see, and as she squinted against the brightness, she bumped into a huge round table the middle of the room.

"How do you like my Living Library?" the Wayfarer asked.

"Like on the computer," whispered Jill, "Like King Jacob's."

The Wayfarer nodded, although Jill did not notice.

Rocket's eyes were as round as saucers. "What's the light source?"

"It's a series of mirrors that trap and focus the light down into this room," the Wayfarer said. "The books need it to grow."

"To grow? What, they're plants?" Jill said, as though the idea was ridiculous.

"No, but they need the light nonetheless," the Wayfarer smiled.

"Are the mirrors those metal projections ringing the tower?" Rocket was leaning back and shading his eyes from the light, "And how do you get up to the higher shelves?"

"To answer the first question, yes they are," the Wayfarer said, "and to answer the second, watch this." There were four cupboard doors where the corners of the room should be, and from a little triangular room behind one of these doors, the Wayfarer produced a short pair of poles. He placed the two ends on the floor next to each other and then, a quick flick, no one saw quite what he did, and there was a rail between the two poles like a step. Above it, the poles were spanned by what looked like the back of a wooden chair. He placed this step by a set of shelves, stood on the rail with his thighs against the chair back, and said, "Up!"

Immediately, the poles lengthened and the Wayfarer shot upwards, as if on an elevator. When he had nearly reached the top of the shelves they heard, "Stop," and then after a faint, "Down!" he reappeared, book in hand. "Try this one; I think you'll like it."

Rocket took the book from his hands and examined its spine. "My word," he muttered. The book was little larger than a folded newspaper and covered in bright red leather. He placed it down on the central table and opened it. Diagrams and equations covered the pages. Rocket rapidly flicked the pages over and when he finally stopped turning, Jill was standing by him. The page he stopped on had a fine picture of a rocket.

"It's just like yours," said Jill.

"It is *mine*," said Rocket.

"Really? How many were there of those, what was it, RAVE

rockets?

"Just the one, and I had only just completed it. I hadn't let anyone see it. Did you get this off the net? How did you get past my firewall?"

The Wayfarer paused and looked puzzled, "I didn't get past anything and I don't have the Internet. The book gets the information. As it soaks up the light, information grows on the page."

"How?" Rocket looked up from underneath his bushy red eyebrows.

"The light and the Road carry echoes of the Truth and the books turn those echoes into writing. They're alive with the facts that race about inside the Truth. When the echoes change, the books do too," the Wayfarer said.

Kyle sat down and stared upward again, and said in a far-off voice, "I think my brain hurts. Are you lot going to keep this up all day?"

The Wayfarer stopped, passed Kyle a book from the lower shelves that looked like a very fast car, and then turned to Rocket again. "Look at the title on the spine."

Picked out in gold pressed-letters were the words,

"The Life and Works of Rocket Propellant Precipitant Scientist the Third,"

And then in smaller print,

"Sometime resident of Nowhere, currently travelling on the Road of the Lord of the Way."

Jill said, "So you keep records on everyone?"

"No, the facts that talk about Rocket's life are strong, and the book about his work is fat; however, not everyone's life has that much truth in it, so the echoes of their lives are only heard weakly here. I'll show you. Wait here a moment."

Jill's attention wandered, her eye's scanning the spines of the books all around her, looking for clues. *How do you get truth in your life then?*

The two short poles were repositioned; the Wayfarer rocketed up and then returned.

The book he placed on the table was thin and blue; they opened it with interest. All over the pages were little, finely scripted, entries. They were in the 'b' section and Jill read,

"Joe Blow, Average height, build and weight.

Present Actions: Cautious pursuit of a mediocre job in a small town; wants a quiet life.

Original Purpose: To solve the problems of lack of water in the province of Qui'itichin and save approximately 1.3 million people from an early grave.

Present State of Heart: BORED AND UNHAPPY"

Jill read on, fascinated.

"Wow, I never realised people had a purpose until today. Why's this entry so small?" she asked.

"Because there's so little that's true in his life; and because the book is true to the Lord of the Way, it only tells you what is good and necessary to know."

The Wayfarer was moving rapidly around fetching various books while Jill curiously watched. "So I won't find what I did to Jemma in these books?"

The Wayfarer stopped and looked straight at her. "Was it a good thing?"

Jill giggled slightly, "Er, no, it wasn't."

He leaned forward and talked quietly in her ear, so no-one else could hear. "Then it will be recorded as part of a very simple description, but not in every juicy detail of how you humiliated her in front of her boyfriend and mother."

Jill stopped giggling and turned pale.

The Wayfarer stepped back. "Oh, it's all right, I won't tell anyone else, because it doesn't concern them, and it doesn't really reflect the Truth about you, does it? I mean, about what you should be doing, or who you're meant to be?"

Jill looked up, determined to be honest, "No, I suppose it doesn't, but it does say something about me, doesn't it?"

"Yes, but I've dealt with that elsewhere," the Wayfarer said, "and I don't want to recall it." The Wayfarer had been piling up books in the centre of the table and now called them all over. "Now," he said, "there are some books that will be more useful to you than others at the moment. Look at these."

Rocket was still absorbed in the book of his life works and was muttering about how he might watch the text form and grow on the page. He did not move, and did not seem to have heard the Wayfarer. Kyle sighed, and putting down his own book, marched over to Rocket. He took the red book out of his hands and placed it on the table next to the other books. The scientist followed like a naughty schoolboy.

"Could you put it back for me?" the Wayfarer asked Kyle, and pointed up to the very top shelves.

"What, you mean I can . . . that lift thing over there . . . what do I do?" Kyle could not believe his luck.

"Just speak firmly and clearly and keep your feet on the bar. Now go on."

Kyle needed no more encouragement and there was a faint whistle of air as the poles whisked him upwards.

The Wayfarer spread open two tomes in front of them.

"This one," he said, pointing to a thick, green leather book, "contains a history of what has happened here and in the realm the Road travels through. This one," he pointed to a slim, blue book, "tells you about the kind of travellers the Lord of the Way looks for."

"He looks for travellers?" said Jill, somewhat taken aback.

"Well, yes he does, but it's not quite as you might think; you still have to look for him, if he's going to look for you."

Jill looked as though she might say something else when there was a soft 'whump' sound and Kyle came back to the table, looking rather grey.

"It's a long way down from up there," he said, "and I didn't feel too well." He frowned, held his breath, then blurted; "Do these books talk to you? Because if they don't, I think heights must do strange things to my ears."

The Wayfarer waited until Kyle looked at him, then said, "You are honoured, my friend. What did they say?" The Wayfarer was wearing his gravest face, but Jill thought that his eyes still twinkled.

"'Take us, we'll show you the way,' or something like that," said a concerned Kyle.

"That will be the maps," said the Wayfarer, "they're always too keen to get out. I've caught them jumping down before. Let's see," he cupped his hands and called up, "If you want to be of help, come now."

Two fluttering packages floated down and landed in the middle of the table.

"They are not allowed to speak normally," the Wayfarer confided to the three humans, and then spoke straight at the maps, "I don't want to hear that you've been talking in the ranks; is that understood?"

There was a barely perceptible flutter and then the maps lay flat.

"Good," said the Wayfarer, then he swept his hand over the four books. "These are all alive, and will reveal to you the nature of the things you will have to face. The military gentleman deals in lies and deception; these will help you see through his words. One of the maps," he pointed to an old, slightly crumpled, worn parchment, "will show you how it was, and the other," there was a shiny sleek green package, "will show you how it is. Read them carefully, they will help you. Now," he smiled, "I need no maps to show you your beds." Rocket groaned out loud and kept on glancing around. "Fear not, my friend, you can come back later and explore the library."

All this time Jill had hardly paid any attention. The same words kept coming back to her, *Joe Blow . . . BORED AND UNHAPPY . . . no purpose . . .* She followed on behind the others to see where her bedroom was.

The Wayfarer took them upstairs and small cupboards yielded beds, mattresses, sheets and blankets. Rocket hung around while this was happening, then when he had almost helped enough, disappeared into the library again. Jill propped herself up on a bed and started reading the thick green book. Kyle spread himself out on his bed and read the maps with great interest. Jill wanted to read the maps first, and felt like she was sitting on grass burrs for all the time Kyle Williams was reading. She eventually immersed herself completely in her book, trying to forget her jealousy.

Jill was surprised at how much she liked the book, and she turned it over to check its title. "The History of the Road's Foundation" it read. *It's supposed to be a history book, but it's more like an adventure story. I wonder how it ends?* Jill read of people who had done great things, of their hopes and desires. There were pictures of faraway places, descriptions of grand buildings, battles, victories and eventually, disasters. It seemed depressingly familiar. *Why do people always do things like that? Why can't they get it right?* She reached the last page and found that the writing just faded out. She turned over blank page after blank page and realised that the book was unfinished. *The light must still be causing words to form on the pages. Maybe what we do will write the next pages.* Her eyes widened at the thought, but at that moment, the call to dinner interrupted her thoughts.

Dinner and supper passed in the now usual way and as their latest meal was ended, the Wayfarer asked Jill to fetch the Sword, which he had propped up in the first room.

"What is this Sword made for, storm maiden, what have you read?" the Wayfarer seemed serious, but Jill thought his eyes were dancing, alive to joy. *I don't believe he's ever depressed,* Jill thought, but then she remembered to reply to his question. "To destroy the military gentleman's lies, and all that he does against the Road," she said, as she held the scabbard and hilt level before her.

"What did they do when the Sword was given?"

Jill looked around the hall, looking for echoes of the past.

"They put it away and chose to accept the gifts of their enemy instead."

"What were the enemy's gifts?"

"All the fancy halls, the fountain, and the cannons."

"What were these things in reality?"

"It said they were a, 'false comfort'; a 'dry well'; and 'futile weapons'."

"You have read well!" the Wayfarer seemed to weigh Jill up for a moment. "But..." he paused, watching her. "Have you found a purpose?"

"You said I had until breakfast!"

"Yes, I'll ask you tomorrow," said the Wayfarer and turned away.

"Wait! Does it involve other people?" Jill was looking up at the Wayfarer.

The Wayfarer stopped and turned back slightly. "What do you think?"

"I'll do it," said Jill uncertainly. She looked again into the Wayfarer's eyes. "I'll do it for you," she said quietly.

The Wayfarer shook his head, and then surrendered to a smile. "That's good. That's where it starts, and it is good enough for now," he said.

Both Rocket and Kyle looked dumbfounded.

The Wayfarer tuned back to face Jill fully, and Jill began to smile very gently.

"Will it be hard to control? How do I use it?" Jill could not break his gaze.

"It will obey its purpose, and if you give yourself over to your purpose then it will obey you and you will know what's going on. Remember this in the battle, let go of the confusion, hold on to what you know. In due order, we will strengthen what remains by removing what weakens it. We will destroy the enemy's stronghold, and you will learn about the Sword."

The Wayfarer asked no more questions and no one asked him any either. They all ate quietly; a sombre mood had descended on them. Just before they all went to bed the Wayfarer stood up and said, "Tomorrow, we will see what the Sword can do now that someone has chosen to receive the gift. It shall be a good day."

13

What Remains?

The Wayfarer had woken them early, and they were outside in the open air so that they faced the wreck of the easterly wing, the part of the building called the "New Hall". Jill was close to the hall, while the party of spectators stood quite some distance back, on a small hillock looking down on the House. On the Wayfarer's instructions, Jill drew the Sword. It bucked in her hands as it had the previous day, flicking around as though alive.

"Speak to it, Jill. Ask it what the Lord of the Way is saying." The sun had almost risen; the sky was crimson and pink; and birdsong velveted the air.

Jill's voice was nervous, but steady. "What is it that the Lord of the Way says?"

Suddenly, on the hilt, words in gold fire shone and the Sword became still. Now that she did not have to hang on so tightly, she could adjust her grip and read the writing as it cast shadows over her hands.

At first, it quivered and flickered and she could not read it, but then as she concentrated, it resolved itself into letters that Jill could recognise.

She read it out loud.

Weapons forged against you shall not succeed,
Words exultant against you shall not proceed,
Those who serve me victory inherit,
I myself shall proclaim their merit.

"What does that mean?" Jill called back.

"What things stand in your way?"

"The military gentleman, I thought you said," Jill shouted over her shoulder.

"And how did I say that he had power on the Road then?"

"Through the stuff they added to the Lodge" There was a slight pause, then even as far away as the Wayfarer, Rocket and Kyle were standing, they saw Jill's face register his meaning. "Ohhh, am I supposed to attack the building in front of me with this Sword?"

"Why do you think we're back here and you're over there? Now speak out loud: agree with it." The Wayfarer's instructions rang clear in the crisp dawn air. "Speak out and follow as it will lead."

Jill's mouth was dry. "Is it safe?"

"Not for the military gentleman it isn't," called the Wayfarer, "Are you sure you want to do this?"

Jill set her face in a stern expression and faced the wall. "Nothing can stop me," she said, unconvincingly. The Sword made a gentle sweeping motion, but failed to make contact.

"Be more specific, more confident, agree with the Sword." The words floated on the morning breeze, seeming to hang in the air like billows of breath. Jill shivered; she was becoming cold and damp with dew. She stiffened her arms against the wobbling movement of the sword and her arms.

"I'm going to win," she said, this time, almost as if she meant it.

The Sword lurched forward and impacted the black stone in front of her, nearly pulling her over. The mark made on the stone was unimpressive. Dust settled on her and she shouted over her shoulder at her friends, still gripping a dangerously alive sword with both hands.

"This is ridiculous, how can I hack this place down, even with a special sword?" Jill's temper was beginning to show.

"Persist, my little storm maiden."

Jill turned around to see three amused faces. She already looked embarrassed and angry and this deepened into piqued fury. "Look, will you not call me that! I'm trying to concentrate and you're using that silly nickname." With this little outburst, she flung her arms out and the tip of the Sword struck the wall. She was knocked flat by the blast. Pieces of stone showered around her.

"I see you still have your touch with pyrotechnics, dear," said Rocket.

"Shh," said Kyle and the Wayfarer together.

"What happened?" Jill exclaimed, dusting herself off with her free hand, and gingerly hanging onto the now more passive blade.

"You said something you meant, and struck with the Sword." The Wayfarer said, grinning broadly.

"What, I just need to get a bit steamed up?" said Jill, incredulity all over her frown.

"It helps. Do you hate this place?"

"It stinks, and I don't like the look of that guy in the picture."

"I agree. These additions give him entrance to the Road. They are a weapon against you. Without removing them you will find life very hard."

"What, he really can get onto the Road because of this?" she held the Sword pointing at the cracked windows.

"Yes, especially his image in the hall of vanities."

"Right, that does it." She brought back the Sword. "No creep's getting in my way." The Sword smashed down through the window. "And this place is not going to let him."

As Jill brought her sword down for the second time, it swung down vertically into the hole she had already made in the window. Without warning, light and fire swept out from under the Sword edge. There was an explosion, and smoke and fragments rushed up past either side of Jill. Her hair flapped wildly, but she was unmoved, rock-like, as though surf was breaking over and around her. The window and central wall had disappeared. Jill stepped inside.

"It is best if you remain outside," called out the Wayfarer; seconds later, the southern wall blew out. Jill re-emerged, dusty and rubbing her head. She picked out fragments of brick from her hair.

"Agree with the words on the hilt; use your passion, and your head," the Wayfarer called, "but not to catch the falling stone." Kyle giggled and it felt like he was cheering his school soccer team from the sidelines.

"Weird," he said.

"No weapon that comes against me shall succeed," Jill bellowed and, in response, the Sword swung. This time all along the edge of the Sword white flame leapt, cutting the view in half with brilliance. More wall collapsed as the cannons disappeared into a billow of dust. Rock whistled past the spectators' ears and only the Wayfarer remained upright.

"Remind me not to get her angry," said Kyle.

"That's what I thought when she only had a stick," Rocket muttered.

"Ssh," said the Wayfarer.

"No lies will stop me!" The Sword was coming back on the reverse stroke, lightning struck out from the tip and skewered the picture on the far wall. The oil paint melted and it burst into flames. "He says that victory is mine!" The Sword was held high above her head and brought down on what remained of a windowsill. It buried itself deep in the stone. There was a rumbling sound, and the noise of falling masonry. Sparks leapt from one stone to another, and the stones started to shake. Jill held on to the Sword, feeling the noise surge through her. She could hear words singing in her ears, the words on the sword hilt, repeated over and over again. There was song and other poetry she could hear behind it, all in harmony with the main words.

This is beautiful!

She started to hear how it all fitted together, and began to add her own words, each line becoming louder and louder:

Living words and living stones,
Truth and beauty clearly honed,
Break the bonds of your decay,
Spring up and sweep the dark away,
Darkness flees before the light,
Flow once more against the night,
Reject the gifts of compromise,
Restore the victory over lies!

Within the sounds of Jill's last line, a noise, a note started to hum and seemed to hang in the air. It was neither far nor near, but saturated the air quietly, as if there were millions of invisible insects, humming and blanketing the Moor. Rocket and Kyle glanced around. With the increasing sound, the building started to shake, and then to crumble. The sound faded from the air, but their feet tingled from the song, now in the earth. The remaining added buildings started to collapse, first the east wing she was facing, then the north and south sides of the little square surrounding the withered garden. Stones and glass fell in as the buildings collapsed like a row of dominoes.

They could see into the courtyard, and without warning, the stone fountain in the centre exploded. Its foundation shattered and a crystal column of water surged high into the early dim blue sky.

The sun came up.

The water flashed blood red and the rays of the dawn set the dust and mist on fire.

After a few stunned moments, Jill removed the Sword from

the ruins and returned to the onlookers under a fine drizzle of spray. The fountain of water was broadening out and becoming lower, but was still throwing drops high into the air. The stonework surrounding the garden was hissing and dissolving on contact with the spreading deluge.

"How long I've waited for the fountain to be restored," the Wayfarer sighed. He turned to Jill. "Feeling better?" he asked. A red-faced and grimy girl nodded. Her hair was plastered down with dust, dirt and water, and everything about her needed a wash. "That's good, very good. Now we must prepare for the rest of your journey." Jill and the Wayfarer started to walk back to the original hall of the Lodge.

Jill admired her handiwork. *It looks so much smaller without the other buildings, but somehow it's better like this.*

However, Rocket and Kyle were in a state of shock as they watched the unlikely pair walk away. Kyle finally found his voice, "Was that a nuke, or what?"

"No, apparently it was an angry woman," Rocket replied.

"I hope she tells me what the trick is with that magic sword of hers," said Kyle.

"Yes, as I said before, that's what I said when she only had a stick," Rocket observed. "However, I'm not so sure I want to know now. Look at that! The wreckage has disappeared."

Where there had been decaying wood and stone, there was now churned up ground, like a freshly ploughed field. Some stones and timber seemed to be sinking into the ground; other parts were dissolving and running away in the water. The water had become a broad spring, which was bubbling up to knee height and was beginning to carve out its own channel. The sun's new light was pink and the Moor was overflowing with bird song: it all seemed so peaceful and alive.

Rocket breathed deeply and admired the view. He pointed so that Kyle would look. "There seems to be an old river bed that the water is running into — look there, a heather bush is being washed away." The bush was bobbing on peaty black water, thick like treacle, and there seemed to be no end to the head of water surging up.

Kyle started to walk back to the house. "I'm going to my room, just to check it's still there," he called out to Rocket.

Rocket watched for a few more seconds and then followed him in.

Inside Rocket found Jill and the Wayfarer in the Living Library.

"The first task is to strengthen what remains. More is left of the Road than what you can see at this house." The Wayfarer was speaking, explaining things to Jill as they both leaned over a map. "This is where the river used to run, and if all goes well it will cut off the military gentleman's forces from the east. You have done more than you realise. People will be able to use the Lodge again and, in time, things will be renewed. Before this, wolves had been able to run on the Road north of here. Things will be different now his image has been removed. He had been used to much freedom and so now, our enemy will be angry." There was a pause, and he became much more deliberate in his manner.

"Listen. Be careful of the wilds to the North West, he has many allies and he will attack from there." He pointed to the words 'The Mansion House' on the map. "Lord Bygone's people are besieged here, and they have been deceived into staying still. You will need to lift the siege before things can get better. Use the Sword to deal with that situation."

"You must reach the Tower beyond the Mansion, or you and others will not be ready for your second task, which is to raise the blockade itself. You will receive a gift that you must use at the Tower. Press through to it, no matter what your friends say. Restore the light to Lord Bygone's people."

Jill tried to interrupt, but the Wayfarer held up his hand. "You will be told how to do this when the time comes. Here and here and here are where the blockade has been imposed by the enemy." Jill looked over to three spots a little further north that had been indicated by the Wayfarer. "You will break the blockade together, you are all needed. The enemy will try to split you apart. Press through, especially for those at the Mansion House, for the enemy has long wanted to keep those there isolated and afraid. He cages them in a false security."

Jill marvelled. The Wayfarer sounded so confident in her. She stared at the blockade. The Road split and disappeared only to continue again further on.

"I still don't understand," said Jill, "Why could he block the Road because of what happened here in the past? I thought it was impossible to damage the Road?"

"You yourself have seen the Road damaged temporarily. If someone with responsibility chose the military gentleman as an ally, then the old deceiver can steal that authority and use it to block your way, as he did here."

"And as long as the halls were joined to the house the permission for the military gentleman to interfere still stood," Jill continued.

"That's right, until someone with a true purpose returned. The Sword was given by The Lord of the Way to put things right. It gives authority to deal with the mistakes. You are the first in a long time with a true purpose to travel, so the Sword belongs to you. It belongs to whoever needs it. You must handle that authority carefully lest you repeat other's mistakes."

The Wayfarer paused and looked at Jill hard. "Even those who carry my gifts have the right to temporarily invite him back. You must all be careful not to allow that. He will seek ways to make you invite him back onto the Road. He will try to use you against each other."

Jill frowned, "I don't see how he could if I only agree with the Sword hilt. It does the rest."

"Be careful. He is a deceiver, a twister of words and feelings. Believe me, there are ways for him to do it. Keep reading, be on your guard, and don't be tricked as you were by Mrs. Lazybee. And always do what the Sword says, no matter what."

Rocket interrupted, "Er, I say, now that you mention her, shouldn't we have breakfast?"

Jill ran over and hugged Rocket. She turned back to the Wayfarer. "Where will you be? Won't you come and help me?"

"I am needed elsewhere. I will be with you soon, where and when you need me. Rocket's right though, I'm ready for a meal too."

Jill ran off saying something about getting it ready.

"Is it really that dangerous?" said Rocket.

"You will need to be her advisor and encourager, my friend, that is your task." The Wayfarer's attitude was uncommonly solemn.

"Well, I was thinking of my own danger, actually, not hers," said Rocket.

"I know," said the Wayfarer, to which little could be said in reply.

Breakfast was the usual feast, hot strips of bacon, eggs and muffins. Once the cleaning up was done, the hiking rations were replenished from the stores and the party prepared to walk again.

They stepped outside and Jill, who had disappeared for several minutes, returned bright cheeked and clean.

"Where have you been?" asked Kyle. "And how come you're shiny?" he said with half a squint.

"I've had a bath, something you should try, scruff." Her shoulders were back and her arms swung easily. Kyle started to say something, but glanced at her sword and decided not to.

"Did you bathe in the fountainhead?" asked Rocket.

Kyle was about to ask what a fountainhead was, but figured out that he meant the new river and so managed to keep quiet. This made him feel very grown up.

"Yes, and I filled up our water bottles from the spring. You should try it, it's great." Jill passed out the bottles and much to the Wayfarer's amusement various sounds of "Mmm" and "Ooohhh!" were heard for the next minute as the ice-cold water was swigged. There is nothing quite like the water from that fountain. I have often heard Jill comment that she could really do with a cup of water from the Lodge.

The Wayfarer promised that he would be around soon, but that he had other business to attend to and bid them farewell, for now. Kyle nearly asked why he was going but somehow that did not seem right to ask, but this left him irritated and undid the feeling of being clever that he had had before. The group left again, spirits high but somewhat apprehensive. As they walked off, Rocket turned with a concerned look to Kyle.

"Are you all right old boy? You seem very quiet."

Kyle just nodded, grinned and tried to knock Jill's hat off: it all ended with a wrestling match. Jill won with two submissions.

The Road now had a river running away from it to the north east. Small hollows kept filling out as the water found its way into old courses, and the travellers were constantly pointing out new flashes of silver light on water, each one more distant, as the day wore on. The rain seemed to have stopped, the sky was a hot deep blue and swifts and swallows filled the air. They passed the day uneventfully and agreed to camp early so as to be able to read easily before they lost the light.

Kyle got out the maps. He unfolded them and was about to smooth them out when the paper rustled and lay as flat as a billiard table. This became a habit for the maps and was the only odd thing that an outsider might have noticed about them.

"Tomorrow we should reach the Mansion. Look, it's not on the ancient map, but it is on the new one." Kyle pointed to the identical line of the Road on both and bent over closely, to read the maps. "'Residence of the Lord Bygone,' it says here. It seems to be marked as a friendly house."

"We'll see," said Jill, and lifted out her heavy green leather bound volume. "Lord Bygone," she read, "was one of the residents responsible for transforming the Defensible House." She was reading from a chapter where she had left a bookmark before. "He also led the people away on the day of the last great attack. After that it doesn't say much."

"Perhaps he's with the crows and this military gentleman then," said Kyle, "and he's best avoided. He'd have to be about the same age as this military gentleman — it gives me the creeps."

"The Wayfarer didn't say anything about that," said Jill, "but he didn't give too many warnings about anything, except to be careful of tricks."

"Perhaps he's still under attack from the crows," said Rocket, "and has learnt to defend himself better. Still, him being as old as Methuselah doesn't bother me too much any more. It's all very odd here. I think I'm rather beginning to enjoy it."

"Weird," Kyle said.

"I still don't know who he means when he talks about 'his people' either," Jill was frowning.

"I suppose that must be people like us," said Kyle.

Both Rocket and Jill turned and looked at Kyle.

"What did I say? What's the matter?" Kyle pleaded, shrugging and lifting both hands helplessly.

"Nothing old boy," said Rocket; "you were most perceptive, that's all." Jill agreed and ruffled Kyle's hair. As the light faded, they put up the lamp for the night.

"Sleep well, my little storm maiden," called Kyle as he headed for his tent. He never saw the clod of earth coming and was picking crumbs of soil out of his ear for several days.

The next day was clear and bright and the party rose early, ate breakfast and started their hike. Kyle led the way, pointing out every bend on the map and indicating where things used to be and were indicated on the old vellum.

"Here was where old food store buildings used to be," he said when they passed low stone ruins, "and over there was the armoury."

They stopped and stared at the outlined village that had once belonged to the Lodge. The walls stood several feet high in places and in others there were heaps of stones. Bracken sprouted through the tumbled down buildings and nibbled grass filled the interior spaces looking like civilised islands in the middle of rough ocean. A sheep tumbled out from a fireplace and everyone jumped.

"It must have been sheltering from the wind," said Rocket.

"Poor thing, it is cold up here today," Jill looked sorry for the sheep and the sheep looked sorry for itself. It bleated, plaintively.

"We need to get on if we're to reach the House by tonight, otherwise we'll be as miserable as that sheep," said Kyle.

As they walked away, Kyle glanced back. He saw the sheep bound away, a long, grey blur.

That's odd. I've never seen a sheep move like that.

It was out of sight in less than a second and he did not see it clearly. He frowned, but kept silent. As they kept walking, they came across small derelict houses on both sides of the Road.

"What does the map say about these?" said Jill.

"They must have housed small families or groups of travellers," said Rocket, "Well, read it out, boy. What does it say?"

"It doesn't." Kyle squinted at the brown vellum, folded it up and got out the modern looking map. He unfolded it. He twisted it around, held it upside down, coughed and then let out a little cry of triumph and twisted it around another three-quarter turn. He started to talk, muttering and wrinkling his face, "It doesn't have any writing, I think it says something though. Weird . . . no, there's writing here, it's all squiggly." He brought the map up close to his nose and then held it away. "It's really difficult to read, ahh, that's better," the map was now at his finger tips and he had a really strange stare.

"I thought you said that the writing was really small?" Jill was starting to laugh. Even Rocket could see the funny side of Kyle's behavior.

"It is . . . oh, I've lost it," he brought the map up close and then held it further away again. "I almost could make it out when I relaxed and it went all fuzzy, so I thought it might be like one of those '3D' pictures. You know, you let your eyes go fuzzy and an object jumps out of the page, and I . . ." his eyes almost crossed, "There! Got it."

The other two stood still and listened with intent, and Kyle started to read,

> *"There were once communities of travellers here,*
> *Scattered and divided, driven far and near,*
> *They longed for somewhere their quest to start,*

Through wrestling their questions they found their heart,
Braving the fog of unknowing."

"Where's all that written?" enquired Rocket, looking over Kyle's shoulder.

"There," said Kyle pointing to a small yellow mark, "inside the buildings next to the word 'Ruins', just underneath it."

"I hope these maps get better at poetry as they get older," said Jill. The map rustled aggressively, which gave Jill a start. She mumbled a hurried, "Sorry!" And then, as much to herself as to anyone else, Jill added that she'd never hurt the feelings of a piece of stationery before.

"Do you think it means the people who used to live here, or us?" asked Rocket.

Jill looked up. "Well, I suppose they are living maps, it could be either."

Rocket ignored this and poured over the map. "Oh, yes, quite remarkable," he said, "I wonder what the 'fog of unknowing' is?" He stared hard, mouthing words under his breath and then turned a funny green colour.

"You know you wanted to know what the 'Fog of Unknowing' was? Well, do you think it could be *that*?" Jill was pointing at a wall of mist that was hanging gloomily in front of them, covering the Moor for miles on either side and blocking the Road, and as a result, did not notice the sickly colour that Rocket had turned. The day had quickly turned cold. The breeze had dropped to a chilly trickle. None of them had noticed the cloud bank appear and all were certain that it had not been there five minutes before. They didn't move.

Jill frowned and gripped her Sword more tightly. *This must be where it gets nasty again, but I think I'm ready this time. Hope these guys know what to do.*

Rocket looked up. "I can't see any crows yet."

Kyle stared up too. He saw something faint and high up, just visible beyond the edge of the mists. It looked like a bat. "Can you see anything else?" Kyle asked, his voice nervous.

"No," said Jill and Rocket together. Kyle swallowed hard. He was still afraid of the voice in his head that had answered the painting, and was not sure what to admit to.

"Well, can you see anything?" asked Rocket.

"Er, well . . ." Kyle heard a hiss. ". . . no, nothing. Nothing at all," he concluded hastily.

"Do you think we should wait here till the fog goes away?" said Jill.

"No, I definitely do not," said Rocket, "we should press on now. Get the lamps out. Every one, hands to weapons, lamps on staves, full bad weather gear and forward." Rocket's commanding mood continued for a few minutes as they shuffled things around. Kyle quickly did as he was told.

The fog had started to roll around them now and flowed damply around their ankles. Kyle finished fixing his lamp in place and a milky dome of light surrounded them.

"That's better. Well, the map had a little more writing on it than Kyle had read. When it jumped out at me from the page I felt quite queer, although the message itself was peculiar enough."

"What did it say?" interrupted Kyle.

Rocket continued, "It said that the fog of unknowing crept upon unwary travellers and caused them to start forgetting things."

"Sounds like the perfect excuse for school," said Kyle, "Sorry Miss, I forget my home work 'cause I was mugged by a cloud on the way home." The fog was impenetrable around them now and Jill and Rocket turned on their lamps too.

"No, the text said that the travellers would be in danger of forgetting themselves if they remained too long in the fog. It also said that we should not camp if the fog was down. Did the old text say anything Jill?" Rocket was actually longing to read the books himself but never borrowed a book before the other person had finished it. Maybe Jill was a slow reader, he thought.

"There was a bit about the, 'mist of no-meaning' but I thought it was just a bit of fantasy."

Rocket gave her a 'you-should-know-better-than-that' look. "What did it say?" was all he actually said.

Jill sighed, slipped off her rucksack and got out the heavy green book.

"Oh, that's odd," she said opening it up, "it's fallen open at just the right spot." Jill started to read, "'A foul vapour of forgetfulness is the mist of no-meaning. Life's tasks are remembered no more, then the path is abandoned. Corrosion of the wits follows, where neither truth nor beauty is any longer discerned. At the end, the poor wandering wretch that was the traveller forgets himself, no longer having an identity separate from the fog. Even in their tents, dreams have been stolen; even the lamps of the Warden of the Road may not defend you from such malfeasance."

"Weird," said Kyle.

"Most cheerful I must say," Rocket, "but in agreement with the map's general outline." He looked up in time to see the paper white disc of the sun disappear behind an extra wisp of cloud. The confluence of light around them eliminated nearly all of the damp taste of the air; the bright, scattered light from the fog obscured anything beyond.

"There's another bit straight underneath it, marked 'Dragon of Confusion'," said Jill, still reading.

"Dragon?" said Kyle, "does it have wings?"

"Yes, there's a picture. It says here that, that . . ." her face showed real concentration and effort. "Well, just listen to this, 'Those who come under this beast's power must fight to survive. Using both of its heads it devours its prey, it surrounds itself in mist of no-meaning.' I think I preferred a good straight fight with crows," said Jill.

"Don't worry," said Rocket, patting her head in an infuriating way, "we can safely assume that bit is nonsense. Everyone knows there's no such thing as dragons."

Jill put the book away, shouldered the bag and they moved on.

The Road was straight and flat. If it had been rough they might have been tripping constantly or would have had stretched their nerves looking out for their feet. As it was, they strained eyes trying to spot anything coming ahead. Fear was pressing in on them and although none of them said so, they could all sense each other's panic. Their voices became hoarse as they sang anything they could remember, trying to keep their courage up. They struggled to think clearly. They could see nothing but the fanciful monsters that leapt out of the swirling fog. The wind picked up: they became cold. The curled talons of the cloud whipped around them. There is nothing quite so demoralising as walking without seeing any progress and they were on a consistent gentle incline so soon only the ache of their legs indicated the ground covered. They kept walking.

Eventually the pale white of the fog turned deep grey and then coal black. They had given up singing some time before and they were all now wiping their noses, except for Kyle.

"Here, use my handkerchief old boy," said Rocket.

They stopped as the Kyle accepted the cloth with a look of resignation.

"Don't look so glum, it can't get worse," said Rocket as Kyle noisily cleared his nose.

From far above Kyle thought he heard a piercing scream. Fear seized Kyle by his throat.

"What was that?" said Jill.

"What was what? I didn't hear anything." said Rocket.

It started to rain.

"I thought it was impossible for it to rain like this in a fog," said Jill.

Rocket shrugged and peered into the falling wetness.

"Well out on a moor like this, at least we're not caught out in a thunder storm, with all the problems of lightning strikes and such like," said Rocket forcing a grin across his face as if the corners of his mouth were stage curtains that he had just hoisted up.

A dull flash was followed by a muffled roar, like a thousand giant bowling balls demolishing something nearby. The ground shook.

"Please be quiet," said Kyle and handed back the sodden handkerchief. He put his head down as if leaning into the breeze, and started walking again. He looked like he was walking toward his own death.

"I think he needs to be watched," Rocket whispered to Jill. Jill stared after Kyle and nodded.

A minute later, something howled.

Kyle jerked his head up. Golden eyes, shining through the mist burnt into his. The fog rolled; the eyes disappeared.

"We're not going to get out of this," Kyle mumbled. He heard a hiss in his ear, and spun around to find his tormentor. "It's not blimmin' fair!"

Jill could not see what was causing Kyle's terror, but realised that what Kyle was experiencing was real enough. She stopped and caught his shoulder. "Remember what the Wayfarer's sign says, Kyle, 'Heed my words and you will live.'"

"Yeah, yeah," said Kyle, meaning the opposite.

"Remember what happened with the crows, and how the Wayfarer helped, old boy?" said Rocket.

Kyle focussed on him, his eyes blurry and far off. "Yeah, I do, what about it?"

"The Wayfarer said that the Road will get us there," Jill added.

Kyle calmed down. "Where?"

"You know, to the end, to the Lord of the Way."

"Where are we going?"

"Has it slipped your mind, old chap?" asked Rocket.

"More like his mind is slipping," muttered Jill to Rocket.

"It's the effect of the fog, dear boy," said Rocket to Kyle, "We need to help each other." He held his gaze.

Kyle stood still. He dropped his head into his hands.

Jill walked up to touch Kyle's shoulder. *Something's going to happen, and I need to be near him when it does.*

The fog swirled. There was a sound like the flapping of huge wings, a roar of rage and they struggled to keep their feet in the sudden blast of air. Kyle shrugged away from Jill. "They're coming to get me! It's no good," his head was still in his hands, "it's no good!" Jill looked up and listened. *The wings seem to be further away for the moment.* She turned to Kyle.

"Calm down Kyle; we can fight it, but you've got to trust the Wayfarer," Jill tried to shake him. A body of darkness seemed to be filling the air above them; massive, without form, but coming closer. Kyle screamed as waves of turbulent air swept over them. "Kyle listen, we've got to stay on the Road, you've got to focus!" It became darker, and darker, till claws and shadow swooped through the air close enough to touch. His lamp fell from his staff and went out. "You've got to listen . . ." Rocket was crouching, trying to see which way to point his staff.

Kyle ran.

"No! Not again!" The Sword was bucking in its sheath. Jill drew it and fire leapt from its tip, upward in to the fog. There was an ear-splitting cry of pain and a confusion of sound followed. Heat washed over them. Both Rocket and Jill covered their ears and after a few moments, their immediate danger was over.

"What was that?" Rocket spoke in stunned tones.

"A dragon, maybe? I don't know. Which way did Kyle go? We'll need to find him quick," shouted Jill, struggling with the Sword.

"Dragons can't exist, I'm sure they can't." Rocket pointed down the bank, staying out of the way of her blade. "And . . . I think he ran away from the Road."

"Not again!" She hesitated, staring hopelessly up and around. "Oh, it's no use. Whatever it was that attacked us, we'll still have to go after him. I'll leave my lamp here so we can see our way back." She lowered her staff to the ground with her light and ran after their friend. Rocket groaned and followed.

The night was dark, and with Rocket's lamp not much could be seen. They trotted along for a minute before Rocket caught her arm.

"Stand still and listen," he said, and put a finger to his lips, "Shhh!"

Through the mists, a sound of weeping could be heard.

"I think it's that way," Rocket said.

They walked and found themselves amongst a dozy flock of sheep. Jill was concentrating on walking toward the noise, and the fog had become so thick that it was impossible to see more than a few steps ahead, so it was no surprise when she tripped on one of the animals.

The sound of a growl was heard.

"Was that you? Because if it was, it's not very funny," Jill was looking straight at Rocket, "I'm trying to listen and if you're trying to frighten me again . . ."

"I've no idea what you mean, but I think that's Kyle ahead." Rocket lifted his lamp up higher, and a few yards ahead, the prostrate form of a weeping boy could be seen.

"It's no use," he repeated between sobs, "We'll never make it out . . ."

"Come on old chap." Rocket knelt besides Kyle. "Jill's explosive touch drove that thing away, whatever it was." He started to pick him up and Kyle too responded.

Both Jill and Rocket got under his shoulders and started to help him walk back, but the flock of sheep seemed restless, and now everywhere they turned, white animals seem to get under their feet.

"Rocket?" Jill's voice was tense. "I don't like these sheep."

"Well, their traditionally meant to be stupid."

"No," Jill was speaking from the side of her mouth now, "it's the way they turn grey and have long bushy tails when you see them out the corner of your eye."

"Trick of the light, dear girl. I can't see anything clearly in this weather."

Jill realised that Rocket's attitude was bothering her more than Kyle. *No, I'm going to get this right.* She drew a deep breath and said, "Well, then it won't matter if draw my sword," and then stepped away from Rocket and Kyle. There was the sound of steel against stone as she drew the Sword and held it by both hands over her head. She read the flickering letters and then spoke loudly. "Be seen for what you are, and get lost!"

The blade blazed with light and Rocket gulped at what he saw. The white shapes changed in an instant and became long, low and grey. It was brighter than day and the wolves cowered, closing their eyes against the light and then ran. "Well, most remarkable. I thought I was getting used to this, but I don't think I am"

"Well let's hurry and get him back to the Road, before they regroup."

They moved rapidly, and after several stumbles, manhandled Kyle over the ditch and sat down on the friendly sandstone. All three were panting. They steamed as the rain continued to soak them.

"Let's keep moving," said Jill, who stood up and offered her hand to Kyle. He took it, and they started to walk again.

The night and fog seemed to last forever, a constant dripping and "I'm not sure he's going to make it." Kyle had been stumbling for a while, and although he had started to walk on his own, his eyes were glazing over. Jill had started to despair.

"We need to find shelter and get him out of this fog," Rocket stopped and steadied Kyle, who was not really in charge of himself. "Any ideas?"

"No."

"Anything from the Sword of destiny?"

Jill glared at Rocket, drew the Sword, and stared at the hilt. "That's not what it's called and it's not funny. No. There isn't."

Rocket smiled gently. "Well, nothing for it but to keep walking and hope something comes up."

That's what I hoped when I met you, Jill thought with a grin, *let's hope we have more success than I did.*

They plodded on with nothing but the cold, dark and constant dripping for company.

It was near midnight when, with frozen fingers, and wet beyond what they thought possible, they noticed that the Road had sprouted a side shoot, a small path.

"Wait here," said Jill. She walked down the path quickly, while the other two stood and waited. They watched her dissolve into the night, the light of her lamp first forming a distinct halo, then a general glow in her direction, and eventually even that glimmer dimmed and faded.

It felt like no one or nothing else existed in the entire universe. Kyle glanced at Rocket to check if he was still there. He then looked at the stones around his feet, luminescent in the wetness and lamplight. His gaze drifted out towards the edge of the lamp's dome, and his mind wandered. *Where have I been? What I am doing here?* The question failed to find a counterpoint in his memory; even the hissing he could now hear clearly could not gain his attention. *I'm so tired.* He focused on the drips from the peak of his waterproof hood, and studied their shape, colour and flight. He was fully absorbed in a physical world, one of intricate detail, but was rapidly forgetting everything else, even himself.

"Here she comes," came a voice from far away. He heard it, but the words failed to find anywhere to land. Once they had entered one ear, he felt them slither out the other and disappear into the fog as though they had never been.

"Kyle, Jill is coming back now. Come on old boy, pay attention." Kyle became aware of someone calling him. "Kyle Williams, pay attention, you're not going to fall asleep on me again." Kyle slowly realised that Rocket was talking to him. Treacle-thick tiredness held his mind back for a second, then he focussed on the ginger hair in front of his eyes.

"Oh, uh, yes, yeah, right. What were you saying?" He was given oatmeal, honey and raisin biscuit. He ate, his mind still drifting slightly.

Rocket spoke to Jill. "He's not looking too good. I think he's been getting worse since the fight. What's down there?"

Jill had drawn the Sword, which glistened in the rain.

"There's a set of sandstone steps that seem to be the same material as the Road, and after that there's a big hollow. It feels as if there is something big in it, but I couldn't see anything. I think it's worth checking out."

"Absolutely," Rocket mused, "The quicker we can find some shelter the better; even I'm beginning to lose my focus."

"Ugh!"

Rocket and Jill looked around with a start.

"It's gone all soggy," Kyle had spat out the biscuit and was staring in disgust at the uneaten half in his hand.

"I thought you said he was getting worse," said Jill.

"Who'd have thought soggy biscuits would help?" murmured Rocket, "Well, I suppose it all depends on what you consider important."

"Come on, or do you enjoy the rain?" Jill said. She had started to walk back.

The path seemed to become more gravelly and they reached the top of the steps that Jill had talked about. The air rang damply with six boots on the wet stone steps and the rich cacophony turned into the crunch of deep gravel. The path divided into three—a crossroads with gently curving arms. There were dark shrubs on either side.

They crunched forward, their sound soaking into their surroundings and creating a curiously indoors feel. The bushes gave way to flower beds and they passed through another intersection of paths. Suddenly Jill lurched sideways and down a path on the left. The Sword was pointing ahead of her and Kyle had the impression that he was watching a dog owner being taken for a walk by an overly-large pet.

"Quick, follow her," said Rocket.

They tried to keep up but passed several dark masses of clipped bushes and three gravel crossroads before they finally managed to find her. Jill stood panting on a much wider path than before.

"What were you doing?" Kyle said. He was out of breath too.

"The Sword was pulling me," panted Jill.

"Weird," said Kyle.

"Can't you think of anything else to say?" Jill asked with an annoyed voice.

"Well, I think I can," began Kyle but was interrupted by Rocket.

"I think it's dark in front of us."

"I'm tired but even I can see that," said Kyle, "Isn't it dark everywhere at the moment, and wet?"

"No, it's even darker ahead than elsewhere," Rocket insisted.

"Then I'm going back," said Kyle and turned to make good his words.

"I think the Sword brought me here for a reason," Jill said, "let's go forward."

"Yes, and whatever the reason is, I don't want to fight it," said Kyle. "You two can get on with it, I'm off."

However, the other two moved forward and Kyle watched in disbelief. He rolled his eyes and followed.

"You'll be sorry," was all he said, adding a few rude words under his breath.

As they walked forward, the faintest glimmer of light appeared in front of them and quite high in the air. It was about the height of a fourth story window. They noticed one or two other points of light quite close, the brightest of these being straight ahead. Even in the fog, they could hear their feet echo as they tramped across a very large expanse of gravel. The lights started to resolve into squares and vague shapes and the darkness ahead became more solid and much less grey. In moments, they could see the vague outline of a grand house. Far above, dark curves and pinnacles pierced into the grey black rain. The images in front were still indistinct, but they could see enough to recognise a huge mansion. They stopped.

"Do you think they would mind if we called in this late?" said Kyle. The other two turned and stared at him. "Okay, okay, so it's not like we're popping in on my favourite aunt for tea and biscuits, but I just thought I wouldn't want to meet anyone this late on a night like this."

There's something about this I should remember, Jill thought, and the realisation that her memory wasn't working gave her a start. *Don't worry girl, you're tired,* and Jill sighed. "Let's just get on with it."

They walked forward, the mist faded completely, and all at once, the details of a grand house appeared before them. Windows illuminated the stone walls with a warm glow. A huge flight of steps ended in a deep paved area like a stage in a theatre, and led up to a large panelled door. The door was just as you might see in front of rich houses in the middle of London, the dark red paint glistening in the wetness. The windows were tall and broad and the whole house seemed at once to be immovable and soaring into the night above them.

They all stared upward.

"Who's going to knock on the door?" said Kyle, and Rocket was about to step forward when Jill strode up and struck the door with her staff three times. The sound echoed with a deep boom.

"Careful, we don't want to take it off its hinges," said Kyle, "I'm just glad the stick wasn't loaded—a great way to make yourself known at midnight, blowing the door off its hinges . . ."

Kyle continued to mumble, so Rocket walked back across the top step and looked up, sheltering his eyes from the rain. He noticed a dim flickering light move down from the window that they had seen first. It traversed diagonally across several of the large central windows, and then disappeared near the door. He was pondering the way the old glass was bending the light when he realised that it was someone coming to answer the door. He scurried back to the others in time to see the handle turn and the door open. A shadowy figure stood inside. Kyle fell quiet.

A deep voice boomed out, "Who calls on me at this time and disturbs the House?"

14

—————

Lord Bygone's Mansion

"Told you so," said Kyle, to no one in particular.

The figure held a candle up higher to shed light on the dripping forms, as the rain continued to pour down.

"The Wayfarer sends his greetings," said Rocket, "and we seek shelter from the fog of unknowing." Rocket was not being his usual cautious self.

Jill's eyebrows rose high on her head and Kyle was about to say something more when Jill, who was standing next to him, allowed the end of her staff to swing lazily in front of Kyle's nose, just like the end of a frustrated cat's tail. He studied it for a moment, thought about what he was going to say, and then decided that he did not want to say anything after all.

With Kyle silent, it seemed like several minutes before the stranger responded. "If you really are of the Wayfarer, how do you come to know him?"

"We found his hut and received his gifts," said Jill, "just look at us."

"That would be common knowledge for anyone who had

210

started travelling the Road," said the stranger. "Has he done anything else?"

"Err, yes. He woke me from a sleep after I had been attacked by the crows," said Kyle, glancing between the staff's tip and Jill. Jill looked straight ahead, but seemed to smile.

"So you've fought the crows and survived." The lamp holder seemed to waver for a second, then spoke again. "How did this happen then?"

"We used the weapons he gave us," said Jill, "and we're not afraid to use them now if we need to." Kyle misunderstood her and backed away while Rocket squeezed her shoulder.

"Really my maiden, I see you talk with fire. How then do these weapons, that you claim are the Wayfarer's, actually work?" The friends exchanged worried glances. "Don't be afraid, what could I work against the Wayfarer's tools?"

Jill took a deep breath, "When we agree with him and speak it out loud, power flows from the Road into our staves. Then we deal with anything that might try to stop us."

The stranger slowly smiled and asked, "And what might you have seen that would tell you the name and nature of this fog?"

"He has shown us the living library," said Rocket in a clear ringing voice.

"A Living Library? Now you go too far! They no longer exist," the man seemed offended, but continued in a quieter tone. "Can you prove your close association with the Wayfarer? All this information is known to my enemies, and the Fog does not normally come this far south, not without some sort of attack. How can I be sure of your good intent? After all, it is late, and I really have no idea who you are."

Rocket reached into an inner pocket and pulled out a folded document.

"This is a token of our authority to travel this Road, and if you doubt it, inspect the staves we carry." Rocket strode forward and allowed the stranger to take the note that the Wayfarer had left at the Hut. An amused smile crossed his face. "And, just for your information, my hot-headed friend here would be able to enforce her right of passage, if it comes to that, as several hundred crows have discovered."

The man at the door read the note, and then eagerly leaned forward toward Rocket. He brought the candle close to the staff, as he chuckled and muttered. "Several hundred crows, indeed. Whatever next?" The markings glistened in the light and he peered at them, scrutinising the weapon closer still.

"Upon my word," he breathed and seeming to make up his mind, straightened up. He handed back the Wayfarer's note to Rocket and smiled.

"Well," came the voice from under the candle, "if you've been with him that recently and fought that bravely, you'd better come inside, no matter what other nonsense you're talking. Can't have you lose your wits out there." He sighed. "Come in," he said, making a sweeping bow, "Please."

They stepped into a cool, sheltered hall, as high as a small cathedral. It had a pair of marble staircases running down the back wall from a high balcony: everywhere gold leaf and oil paintings encrusted the walls like barnacles and the floor shone like sea-polished stones.

The stranger rang a small bell and placed it on an ornate side table. In almost no time at all a rather sleepy butler appeared, his buttons done up crookedly and his powdered wig twisted as if it was a baseball cap.

"See to it that a supper is prepared and brought for these weary folk. Rouse Mildred to prepare rooms and instruct Joanna to bring fresh vestments for our wet friends. That is all," The butler turned to go, "Oh, and Jennings," Jennings paused mid step and listened like a statue, "straighten your apparel, especially your piece and the waistcoat vest." He waved a hand and sent him away, "On you go."

Turning to his guests, their host seemed to relax, although it was hard to tell from his stiff posture if he ever fully relaxed. "I apologise for the lack of hospitality I have displayed. I might not have opened the door at all to you except for the fact that the Wayfarer was here earlier in the day and told me to expect you. He said you were carrying a note of authority and to recognise you by such. He also anticipated that you would stir the pot a bit." His bushy eyebrows rose and fell rapidly and he looked quite serious. "He did not talk of details and it does not pay to open your door to all travellers here. Some come only to cause trouble. Please, let us find somewhere warmer."

The stranger turned and walked away, his long flowing night-gown and tasselled nightcap flapping in the still air. He showed them to a large side room and proceeded to light the candles and stir a smouldering fire into flame. The travellers dripped quietly onto the stone floor and Jill sneezed.

"Who have we the pleasure of addressing?" said Rocket.

"Excuse me, sir," the old man seemed painfully embarrassed. "I normally receive visitors in more convivial circumstances. I apologise for my egregious lack of manners, let us make introductions. I am known by the title of Lord Bygone. May I enquire as to your titles?"

After introductions were made, drowsy ladies in crumpled frocks brought in a wonderful array of cold meats, pickles, salads, breads and cheeses. The group ate quietly and politely and answered all Lord Bygone's questions regarding the state of the Road and the journey so far. They found thinking easier now that they were inside the mansion house and away from the fog and it felt wonderful to be warmed by rich food and wine. Once they had finished eating, they were shown to hot baths, fresh clothes and crisp linen beds. They had their wet clothes taken away and fell asleep, content and exhausted.

Jill woke to a breakfast tray in her room and sat up. *Lord Bygone's Mansion; that's where we are!* Jill breathed a sigh of relief, *My memory's working again.* Jill liked breakfast in bed. *I'll eat and admire the view at the same time,* she thought and rose to draw the curtains. The view stretched far across the Moor, and she could see the gravel paths they had stumbled through the previous night. Beyond the clipped trees and neat flowerbeds, there was an earth bank. It was topped by a wall almost twice as high as a man, and on this wall there was a broad walkway and battlements, which were obviously a powerful defence. Jill could see only one small doorway piercing the bank, rather like a small tunnel, and beyond that, the Moor rolled away speckled with the same blanket of bushes and thorns as ever. The sky was clear, except for a small cloud rising in the west over the dark and distant mountain.

Jill dressed in the bright clothes the maids had laid out the night before and went downstairs. She found the others in the same room in which they had eaten the previous night. They looked odd in their new outfits.

Kyle sneezed, "Dey say dat dere washin' my clodes but," he exploded again, "I dodn't trus 'em, not afder dey made me take dat bath."

The miserable looking youth was interrupted by Lord Bygone. He was resplendent in a scarlet frock coat, waistcoat, white shirt and pantaloons. He wore a silk cravat at his neck, silk stockings and black leather shoes with silver buckles. In his hand he held an ebony walking stick, which flashed silver top and bottom.

"Allow me to make a better acquaintance of you, sirs, madam," said the grand figure. He made a low bow with a flourish of silk from his wrist. "I am the Lord Bygone, steward of this house, protector of the people of this community and humble poet of the Lord of the Way." The two children blinked, Kyle stifled a giggle into a handkerchief, and spluttered, which allowed him to clear his nose. Lord Bygone partially straightened up. "I would be glad to make your acquaintance and to introduce you into our community for as long as you stay here."

Rocket coughed. "Pleased to make your acquaintance," he said, "this is Jill, Kyle Williams and I am Rocket Propellant Precip—" Rocket paused, and seemed to think better of it, "well, I am known simply as Rocket."

"If it be your pleasure, let us take a morning promenade," said Lord Bygone.

"He means a walk," hissed Rocket to Jill. Jill nodded.

"I find it rewarding to take all visitors to this estate around the grounds," their host continued, and they followed him out into the gardens through the front door. The fog had lifted and they could see the morning's activity well under way. Gardeners strolled about pushing wheelbarrows, others carried tools and all were clearly busy keeping the vast grounds in order. The Road could be seen in the distance, forming a boundary to the gardens on its east side, but everywhere else, the bank and wall closed out the horizon, completely surrounding the house. The steps they had come down from the Road were just inside the beginning of the bank, where it butted up to the Road's ditch.

"How did we not notice that wall?" said Kyle, "it's huge!"

Lord Bygone smiled proudly, "The bank and its wall are impressive, are they not? Let us see it more closely," and he led them down and through the maze of paths, past roses, lavender, clematis, neat hedges of box and holly and a host of smaller, fragrant blooms. They reached the bank, climbed a flight of stone steps up to the top of the wall and in the end were looking south over the Moor.

"From this point you can see all of our estate," Lord Bygone said with a sweep of his arm. "We've been building for some time. Although we have yet to complete this house, this is our refuge from the outside world."

The view of the grounds was superb, the sky was blue, and there was hardly a cloud in the sky, except the one above the mountain, dark to the northwest.

"Who, may I ask, do you refer to as 'we'?" Rocket asked, hands behind his back.

"All those you see here."

"But these are your servants, surely?"

Jill had never seen Rocket so keen to talk to a complete stranger.

"Nay, these are my brothers and sisters, not my servants."

"These are your brothers and sisters? How? In what family?"

Lord Bygone smiled. "In seeking the Lord of the Way, of course."

Rocket frowned, but seemed lost for words.

"May I ask you to repeat the question in two or three days? Then I might be able to answer you more completely," said the lord, "now may we continue our tour?" He turned on and started pointing out landmarks on the Moor, bringing the conversation to an end.

As she walked, Jill found herself not looking out, but back at the house. The walls were plain and the windows were placed in symmetric rows and columns, each window being above another. The highest windows were the smallest and above these were things that looked a little like wedding cake decorations. Tall, spiralling chimneys reached high above slate and lead roofs. Elegantly twisted tiny spires of stone pointed skyward and were encrusted in decoration. Plinths supported crests, carved shields ran along the top and everywhere shapes like flowers or piped royal icing confused the eye. It was all very grand. Jill noticed, by contrast, several small plain buildings down to one side and she asked what they were.

"Those are our stores, armoury, bakery and dairy. We have workshops there and a smithy. Would you like to see them?" asked Lord Bygone, pleased with her interest.

They descended the nearest steps and as they made their way over, Jill could not help staring at the gardeners and maids she met. There was a healthy open look to their eyes and face, but not an adventurous one. She wondered how they could look so well. She wondered how their ancestors had ever got this far.

One of the gardeners ran past them with a bow and arrow. The gardener shot and his aim was good. A crow fell to the ground and disappeared.

"Do you need to fight often?" Kyle asked, clearly nervous.

"Fear not. They have never yet proved too much for us." Said the lord and they walked on without another word.

The armoury was dark, cool and stuffy, with shelves and racks full of weapons. It was well stocked with staves very much like Rocket's, purple brown and rough. There were bows and arrows, lamps and even a few swords, but these blades were much shorter and lacked the same pattern of words as Jill's.

The bakery contained delicious smells and even more delicious breads, cakes and biscuits. It was all wholesome and simple. Jill found some gingerbread, and as the cooks loaded her down with it, the moist and spicy cakes brought memories of Dad flooding back. He liked gingerbread too. Rocket used fresh butter from the dairy on his assortment of French breads and in the storerooms;

Kyle managed to find the only chocolate on the estate. Jill had been stroking a cow in the milking parlour when she realised that the others had moved on. She caught up with them in the workshop. This room was huge and Lord Bygone noticed the glint in Rocket's eyes. "Feel free to explore and use anything here."

"My word, this is the royal treatment!" exclaimed Rocket, and they lost him for the rest of the day, into the depths of a machine-packed room.

Kyle was friendly and quiet, so much so, that it was with a shock that Jill realised that he too had disappeared.

"Where's Kyle gone?" Jill asked.

"He is, I believe, inspecting the archery range with one of my best shots. I thought that his nerves would benefit from the distraction. Would you like to take a little tea with me?" The lord bent with a stiff bow from his waist, and offered his hand in invitation.

So it was that a teenage girl and an ancient aristocrat walked arm in arm back to the house to take elevenses.

It was a grand spread of food on several small tables, enough for the many people gathered in the library, for that was where Lord Bygone had led them, and Jill remarked that she had not seen as much food in one place since Mrs. Lazybee's.

"Few manage to find the Road again after dining with her. Did you sleep there?" enquired the lord. They took the only empty seats hard against a bookcase, which seemed to have been left for the Lord and his guest.

"Just three nights, and not for more than a few hours, but Kyle slept there at least a week without waking." Jill glanced up to see everyone else was now sitting down.

"My friend, I would watch him carefully," said a grave Lord Bygone. "He may yet have acquired more than a few nightmares in that dreamless place. I wonder my dear, are your thoughts peaceful?" Jill was a little startled as the Lord peered into Jill's eyes. "Good!" he smiled, "I do believe they are. Now, to our business."

Everyone seemed to take this as a cue to eat and all took modest amounts of food, including Jill who eyed the gathered audience as she bit into a cake. Lord Bygone stood to his full height, reached down to a heavy book and cleared his throat. Finding his place, he started to read out loud.

"The Road before us lies,
Soft ribboned stone of old,
That sounds its clarion call,
To every heart that's bold,
'Come walk my every foot,
Come take to freedom's strides,
For following my path,
Answers every anguish cried.

There stands the ancient truth,
That all who would him see,
Abandon all their comfort,
And must follow after me,
For as I rise and fall,
Over mountain, moor and hill,
I'll teach them all the secret,
Of laying down their will.

The will that turns from good,
And seeks the other part,
That twists the high intent,
And hardens any heart,
Instead find my desire,
Lay hold my company,
For if you take my way,
Then he will take to thee.'"

Lord Bygone closed the book and sat back.

Now, Jill was not one for poetry, but she felt very peaceful listening to this, and though she thought that it might not be any good, she wanted to understand what was read. "Is the Road supposed to be talking?" she asked shyly.

"Yes," said Lord Bygone, "It is a verse we love, that tells of why people must travel the Road."

"So do you read this sort of thing all the time?"

"These and other poems, yes. They encourage us and teach us about our life."

Jill frowned. "Does anyone travel down the Road from here any more?"

For the first time that day, Lord Bygone looked uncomfortable. "No," he said, "it has become too dangerous. Some travellers make it here, but none for many a year. And none succeed in going further on."

"Oh well, I suppose we'll be the first then," said Jill.

Lord Bygone looked horrified and glanced around at the others in the library. He sipped heavily at his tea, and then ate a scone. Once he had calmed himself, he spoke, loud enough for everyone to hear. "That will be impossible. At best, it is ill advised — at worst, suicidal. We have lost too many who have tried to break the blockade recently. The best we can hope for is that the Lord of the Way comes with an army to rescue us."

"When would that be?" Jill asked.

The Lord turned his face to the bookshelf and spoke fiercely, but in a whisper only Jill could here. "I've pleaded with him many times, but he only says that it's not a matter of numbers, but of the right weapon. We have tried to improve our weapons in the Armoury, but have not found out yet what he means. We do not seem to have your luck with crows." He turned with a smile on his face once more and raised his voice again. "Nevertheless, we have held on here for years, and we will continue to wait." Lord Bygone stalked away from the chair, his chin high and his hands behind his back.

"But why did people try to go on if they didn't stand a chance?"

"There was a time when light shone from the north, and our

books were alive," he said sadly. The aristocrat spun around and faced Jill, real anger turning his cheeks red. "My people heard rumours of where this light could be found, a tower powerful enough to disperse the fog, to withstand the crows or even dragons and to deal with the ragged soldiers. Many thought it must be to do with the needed weapon." The old man shook his head. "The Tower of Fire and Light has not stood for years, if it ever stood, and if it remains till now it must be a stronghold of the enemy. I think it is a myth and I will not permit any more folk to be lost looking for it."

Lord Bygone composed himself and returned to the table. Smiling gently, he offered her more tea. Jill thought it best not to argue.

At lunch, dinner and supper, the same procedure was followed: in the dining room and all over the house and grounds people read as others ate, and everyone thoughtfully listened. Over the next few days, Jill observed little knots of gardeners and maids eagerly hanging on every word of the old poetry. Sometimes she would hear passionate discussion between the workers as to what different passages meant. She had never been with people who shared life together, who believed in something, who believed in each other. To Jill, it was wonderful, but something still reminded her of the Village.

One evening, a week later, Jill, Rocket and Kyle were sitting at dinner together.

"How are things in the workshop, Rocket?" asked Kyle.

"I seem to be getting along well. I've worked out how to produce cogs better and faster than they do, and so they'll have all their timepieces repaired by the end of the week. I say, you two seem to have been pretty busy too. What have you been doing?"

"I've been going out with hunting parties," said Kyle, "It's great fun, except when we run into crows. So far the archers have killed them all before they knew we were there."

Jill had been listening to Kyle and seemed deep in thought. She realised Rocket was looking at her and expecting a reply from her as well.

"I've been with Bygone," said Jill, for they had stopped using the 'Lord' part of his name when speaking amongst themselves, "He's great."

"And what's bothering you?" asked Rocket, who seemed able to read Jill well.

She toyed with her food. "It's just, well, just . . . just like I've been saying. They spend all their time telling each other to follow the Road, and they never do. They never do anything. They simply talk about it. It's just like Nowhere when it comes to that. When are we going to do something? When are we going to lift the blockade?"

"I know what you mean," said Kyle, "All this poetry is driving me mad."

"Look, we know the Wayfarer sent us here to lift the blockade," Rocket cut in, "but he didn't tell us how, except to use the Sword. Has the Sword responded to your questions?" Jill shook her head. "Then we have no instructions. Like I said a few days ago, we just have to be patient."

"I'm not so sure," Jill replied. "He said to press on to a tower, no matter what this lot say. Well, the only time I've seen Bygone angry was when he forbade me to look for the Tower of Fire and Light. I think we've got to move forward now, and I think the Sword is the weapon they're waiting for. Not that I want to tell Bygone that. He scares me a little."

"But we've got to lift the siege here first, not to mention the gifts you're supposed to receive," Rocket said.

Kyle's ears pricked up, "Where was I when this was discussed?" Jill ignored him.

"You had gone to your room, old boy," said Rocket, who hated anyone, especially Jill, being rude.

Jill continued with her idea. "Well, I'm not sure why you two are here, but I've got to see the Lord of the Way on business that is very important to me. Let me go hunting tomorrow and I'll 'stir the pot' a little. I can't use the Sword to lift the siege if Lord Bygone won't let anyone travel, but I might be able to attract some attention. Something's got to change, gifts or no gifts. I don't think the military gentleman knows where we are. After the Lodge, I'm sure he'd like to catch up with us."

"Catch up with you, more like," said Kyle. "I just watched."

"If you must, dear," said Rocket, "but please be careful what you blast. Let's not singe any of our hosts."

Jill just smiled.

Early the next morning Jill passed out of the door in the bank, with a gardener who intended to show her how to shoot mountain hares. They had not gone more than five minutes onto the Moor, when a crow flapped in sight. The gardener dropped to the floor and pulled Jill with him. He placed his finger to his lips. Jill sat up and shouted.

"Oi! You mangy clump of feathers!"

"What are you doing?" the gardener hissed.

"Getting a better shot, of course," said Jill and stood. She pointed her staff.

The crow changed direction and flew toward her.

"If you think I'm going to be caged by you, forget it," she shouted at the bird. "By the authority of the Wayfarer, GET LOST!" The crow disappeared in a puff of feathers, which blew back and up, away from Jill.

Two more crows immediately appeared low over the gorse. A third dropped out of the sky from high behind their heads.

"Like I said, be gone!" Jill said, shouting less and much more confidently.

Lightning leapt out of the walking stick and took out the two crows in front. The third crow flew off toward the north west. Jill let it go.

"Tell them that Jill's at the Mansion. M-A-N-S-I-O-N," she shouted after the fleeing bird.

"Can we go now?" the gardener asked, and started to guide Jill back to the walls. "How did you manage to do that?"

"What do you mean? You've got lots of staves in the armoury, don't you use them?"

"Only to strike the enemy, not to shoot thunder and lightning. The legends speak of such power, but we've not been able to use it for years," the gardener panted, for they were running back to the wall now. "Could anyone learn to master such power?"

Jill grinned. "It's a matter of knowing who you are and what you're about. I'll show you some time."

Rocket paused for a second, pressed his hands and fingertips together and bowed his head in concentration. "I do not wish to disparage your hospitality, yet we do not know why such a fine house exists alongside the Road. Surely, the Wayfarer, the Warden of the Road, wishes all to finish their journey on the Road? How can we if we build such magnificent edifices as this, that invite us to stop and stay, and luxuriate in such comfort?"

It was early morning and both he and Lord Bygone were standing on the wall, taking the air in the crisp light. Neither noticed the gardener and Jill slip back through the wall.

Lord Bygone bristled. "What we do is surely a matter of our own policy and counsel." The old lord's face became strained, but he quickly controlled his anger. "Yet I think I might perceive the cause of your confusion. I am their leader, not their master, and if they do not follow, or are not able to, I cannot force them. I know that we should be following the Road; however, we have an opponent, a fierce enemy who drove us out of our ancestral home and caused us to move here. He harries us when we try to send explorers and messengers down the Road. Consequently, therefore, there are those who are here and feel unable to travel. I wish—" he was at this point interrupted by Rocket.

"I wonder perhaps if you weren't meant to settle at the Lodge in the first place."

"What do you know of that?" Lord Bygone had become loud again, "Speak, sir!"

"Perhaps the disaster there was one that was inevitable, because you shouldn't have been there in the first place . . ." Rocket tailed off and seemed to shrink as the lord turned crimson and pulled himself up to his full height.

Jill had quietly approached the two men, and had been listening. She decided that now would be a good time to distract Lord Bygone.

"Excuse me my Lord," she said, "but I think that you might need to know something."

"I took you for a more civil young lady," the lord said, not unkindly.

"There's been a development that you might need to know about . . ."

The lord cut across her, "Please my dear, not now! Wait for a minute."

Jill pointed across to the distant mountain, and said one word, "Crows."

The cloud over the dark peak was swelling. The storm that had hung there was heading toward them. Lord Bygone turned toward the sound of a tolling bell. Far along the wall, on a raised platform, a groundsman was shouting and pointing across the Moor. He was vigorously pulling the clapper of the bell and more men were joining him by the moment.

"The storm finally breaks. It seems that we shall have to delay finishing our conversation. It is strange, do you not think, that we should be discussing the fall of the Lodge when our enemy masses again. The Lord of the Way said this day would come, but I find it odd that it should be upon your arrival." The old aristocrat had turned white as a sheet, and stared angrily at Rocket and then at Jill in turn. He remembered himself, and bowed stiffly. "It appears our enemy has fully mobilised against us. Excuse me sir, madam, but we have no time to lose," and with that, Lord Bygone strode off.

Preparations for the assault were feverish: men were running; beacons on the wall were lit; women were rushing to take their predetermined positions; and staves were handed out to everyone. The few, wearing what little armour they possessed, had drawn their short swords, which glinted in the light, and the entire company at the Mansion was assembling on the wall.

"What have you done, old girl?" asked Rocket. "What have

you done?"

Jill drew the Sword. It was pulsating with light and hummed gently.

A silver horn sounded. Another and another echoed from the wall's watchmen. Lord Bygone was on the westerly most point of the wall and started shouting orders. He turned and ran back to where Jill was standing and eyed her sword suspiciously. Although he was stiff and unbending, his face showed fear and his voice quivered. "Be prepared, the assault will be fierce. On yonder hill sits our tormentor, and next to him march his deluded captives. I suppose that he reckons to oversee our demise."

On the brow of a nearby ridge, a rider was sitting astride a dark horse. He was wearing a dark blue coat with long black boots and a large triangular hat. A crowd of tattered people was marching past him in ragged ranks. The Moor around became full of the enemy. Squares of men and women stamped into position; drums rattled out a steady beat. Thousands were arriving and changing the colour of the Moor from green to grey. Crows circled overhead, and dark clouds were billowing and massing behind them. Wolves from the military gentleman bounded from their master's side to the front lines, their yelps activating the lifeless ranks. The front rows started walking slowly toward the wall.

"I see where they intend to attack!" Lord Bygone announced. "Let us meet our uninvited visitors and whatever fate the Lord of the Way sends. Pray, stay here, where you should be safe."

Jill watched as the Lord ran away. "Uggh!" she shuddered. "Doesn't it give you the creeps?"

"How do you mean old girl?" Jill stared at him in disbelief. "All right," Rocket conceded, "it is all a bit odd. What I meant was, what bothered you in particular?"

"The fact that that weirdo and Bygone are both hundreds of years old. I'd sort of forgotten about it until I just saw him. He looks just like he did in that horrible painting; he obviously hasn't changed for centuries."

"Ah, yes, well I find that quite invigorating now," said Rocket, "it's all fascinating, just fascinating, don't you agree?" Jill said nothing. She shivered as the wind blew cold into her face.

Someone called, "Ladders!" Lord Bygone ran to where the shout had come from, a place where the wall was low and being repaired. He drew the sabre hanging at his side and called, "Rally to me, defend the breach, safeguard the brethren." Ladders appeared at the wall there and the defenders pushed them back. More steps were thrown up to replace them, all too quickly for the defenders, and then ragged soldiers were on the wall. They attacked slowly and deliberately with shards of something transparent like ice.

Jill shouted, "Watch out!" as one young man brought up his sword. The enemy slumped to the floor and Jill covered her eyes. "Oh, no, it's horrible."

"Well, no it isn't, look," said Kyle, "in fact, he looks much better, if you ask me." He insisted later that he had not sounded disappointed.

Jill peered out from behind her hands and saw the attacker on the ground, his normal colour returned and comfortably asleep.

There were jubilant shouts from the defenders, and through the crowd, Lord Bygone could be seen, sword flashing, rallying his troops, as the enemy was driven back.

"He's really good at this," muttered Jill and started to smile with relief. People drifted from their positions to help him and the wall by the three friends became almost empty. The crowd around Lord Bygone defeated the invaders and threw their ladders down. Within seconds, everything changed.

All around, at every possible point around the grounds, ladders seemed to sprout like blades of grass. "Careful, watch the walls. Defend the flanks!" Rocket shouted. Jill looked over the wall and below the crowd swarmed like ants. Five or six hung onto ropes on each ladder, holding them firm to the wall as the ragged people climbed up. Rocket and Kyle were trying to push a ladder away but failed. As he did so, a ragged soldier near the top of the ladder struck him, with something sharp, long and wicked. He staggered back.

"Is it bad?" Kyle gasped.

Jill glanced at it. "Not sure. We've no time to sort it out now. Run!"

They retreated and Jill started to bandage Kyle's wounded shoulder with a clean handkerchief.

"Help us push the ladders back!" Rocket shouted, but no one came. He turned around, and yelled, but all over the defences, Lord Bygone's people were struggling to hold their own. The enemy swarm was taking hold, surrounding small knots of fighters. Slowly but surely the zombies climbed the wall, relentless as the rising tide.

Kyle, Rocket and Jill, automatically stood with their backs to each other. Rocket was already fighting. Kyle's training over the last weeks was starting to show, he was swinging his staff and shouting himself hoarse. The ragged soldiers were falling, but not fast enough. Jill's sword, with a life of its own, rose high over her head. It suddenly occurred to her that she might die, but Jill was certain that these targets were not going to simply disappear when she struck them, the idea of hurting, or even killing someone made her feel ill.

In front of her, a grim man raised an icy dagger, and then, in spite of herself, Jill rubbed her eyes.

There was not one attacker before her, but two. Where she expected to see an ordinary person, a ghost like form shimmered, covering her opponent. It twisted and slid, like a living picture projected on a billowing sheet. The picture snarled and barked over the blank face underneath. The Sword descended and fire sparked as its edge met the ghost. A wind blew past her. The ragged soldier rolled his eyes into unconsciousness and dropped to the floor. Jill glanced at where she had struck him, but she could see no mark.

"Watch out," came a voice and Jill felt the Sword pull upward. She allowed it to swing and felt an impact upon something. This time she could not keep her eyes open. Another icy breath blew past her and she heard the thump of a man keeling over.

A familiar acrid smell reached her nose accompanied by a shower of feathers. Rocket was behind her. "This 'magic stick' can be quite fun. I'll take care of the crows, old girl," said Rocket, dispatching another one with a grunt, "you take care of the zombies." Two flickering shapes moved toward her, each occupying a woman. She took a moment to roll up her sleeves and then advanced down the wall. The first haggard ghost departed with a hiss, but the second recoiled like a bungee jumper. It leapt into the woman whose face changed from panic to horror; she ran screaming. Jill took the opportunity to fling down a ladder, and tried to push one away from the wall. It was too heavy. "Kyle, give me a hand," she shouted. She looked around, but he was gone.

"Where's Kyle?" she shouted to Rocket.

"He went to help Bygone." Rocket said, "He'll have to take his chances with the old man." The staves worked more slowly than the swords and Rocket was locked in conflict with three opponents. "Looks like you really have stirred things up here," shouted Rocket.

Jill stopped and stared. "This can't continue," she shouted back, "It's hopeless."

Chaos was all around now. Crows like a black blanket were covering the gardens tearing anything or anyone they could, men and women were falling as the zombies pierced them with ice. Rocket backed up to her. "What are you doing old girl? Can't you do any more than this? What's the Sword for?" he blurted between gasps.

"Of course, ask the Sword, you dumb girl," Jill said to herself, and hoped that it was not too late.

"What do I do?" she panted. Writing appeared and flickered on the hilt. The words resolved more quickly this time and she breathed them to herself,

"In the day of battle, at the moment of war,
His always is the victory; his the warrior's call,
Proclaim his mighty triumph; shout with all your heart,
Celebrate his majesty and he will do his part."

"What? More poetry?" She frowned and glanced around. "I'm

supposed to jump, shout and holler in front of ghost infested tramps? I'll look ridiculous! Can't I just kill a few instead?" The letters on the hilt flickered silently back, unblinking. She pursed her lips, then yelled in frustration and stamped her foot. "Okay! Stop being a wimp, Jill, just do it."

Remembering a video that she and Kathy's brother's best friend had once watched, she imitated its heroine, a cheerleader. With both clenched fists raised high, she held the Sword above her head. Jill started to holler like she had done once at a basketball match and jumped up and down.

"The Wayfarer's got it,
The Wayfarer's cool,
If you don't know it,
then you're the fool,"

For a second it seemed that dozens of heads turned to see what she was doing. Her cheeks burnt scarlet red. Rocket had picked up a sword and was firing the staff from his hip in between flashing swings, keeping her safe. She closed her eyes and tried again, this time words seemed to flow fuzzy and indistinct through her sword arm.

"The Lord of the Way has won,
The Prince has overcome,
He will open up the path,
They flee before his wrath."

The Sword started to hum and glow more strongly. "They're not fleeing yet," Rocket snorted. "I wish I had my lamp with me now. Every raven around here is heading here with all your hullabaloo. Can you hurry?"

Jill appeared to ignore his question, but she let the Sword drop to her side and closed her eyes as if listening. Cold sweat covered Jill's face and then a smile. She started to rap; her eyes closed, half frowning, half smiling.

"The Wayfarer's triumph rolls in today,
Before him all others fall away,
The end of the blockade now awaits,
All who will trust him with their fates."

The Sword started to shine. Jill grasped it with both hands now as it straightened up, the blade ringing with a high, bell-like sound. The light started to flicker, and it looked as if she was holding a vertical column of flame. Words and song were tumbling through her head, and others around the walls could hear it too. Wraiths abandoned their victims; other attackers had their fingers in their ears, doubled up by pain. Many of the defenders were looking around with awe, frantically searching for the source of the sound.

As all this happened, Jill knew where the source was; the source was the Road. The songs she had heard at the Lodge, and many others, flowed up through her arm from the Sword as if they were raging waters. Cool, liquid sensations tingled on her skin and flooded her brain. Jill could feel the song's power and volume rising and she hung on for dear life, gritting her teeth. It was as if she was on a mountaintop in the middle of a hurricane, but the hurricane was inside her.

Without warning, lightning leapt out from the blade, and impacted all the ladders in turn. The last of the attackers on the walls either slumped to the ground or tumbled back over the wall as temporarily the lightning passed through each of them. The lightning coursed outward, and the massed ranks of besiegers outside the walls began to be scattered. It was beginning to make a difference, but not enough yet, nowhere near enough. Though she could see this, her thoughts were beginning to tumble out of control. Everything was frightening; she was not going to hang on. She closed her eyes to shut out the outside. "I need help, please help me. For these people too."

The sounds inside Jill's head were now deafening and increased like a jet's roar at take off. Songs flowed like powerful currents of water and seemed to pour like a waterfall cascading upwards through her head. Words and sentences exploded inside her eyes and colours surged through her. It was all getting louder, and she was beginning to lose her grip on both the Sword and the delicious river of glory that coursed through her. Sweat covered her hands and began to trickle down her neck. Jill weakened.

A thought swung out of the mainstream and she felt it head for her, straight as an arrow. It struck home and she absorbed it. *Harmonise with me,* she heard. *How do I do that?* Another thought came that seemed to say, *Find out what I am singing.*

Suddenly, inside herself, she dove into the waterfall of song and tried to sing it, into a roaring stream of reality flowing through her and the sword hilt. The force of it left her breathless, and she stumbled as if on slippery stones. She struggled to reach the surface, gasping for breath, the surging flow stealing her thoughts. It was wonderful; it was dangerous.

Jill found her mind tumbling, eyes shut into shining brilliance, then regained her feet. She sometimes fell, but now her grip on the Sword was tightening. *I will flow with it. I'll let go!* Jill dived through breakers of harmony, surfed her own thoughts on the swell of the raging truth. She mixed with the power and felt stripped of all pretending. Her real self was naked in the words and she sang the desires of her heart, words for a father and mother, songs of longing, songs for healing.

After some time the surging currents stopped. She broke surface in her mind, no longer aware of the presence of power. Jill smiled and opened her eyes.

The outside of her body had not moved. Everyone was staring at her, and 'everyone' no longer included anyone who was attacking anyone else. There were no more crows. Jill remembered to stop singing, but did so reluctantly. The feeling of invincible life moved to the back of her mind.

Everyone had heard him, the Lord of the Way, through her. Everyone had heard her soul bared. She blushed, glancing to either side. A few of the gardeners stood slack jawed, swords limp in their hands. She brought the still vibrating blade down, placed it into its scabbard, and shook out her aching arm. She waved at the blank staring faces, blushed, and hissed at Rocket, "Let's get inside. Now!"

"Whatever you say, little storm maiden," he smirked, "If I wasn't getting used to this, I wouldn't be anywhere near you. Don't worry, I don't think anyone will try to stop you."

She found out in the next couple of days that battle had been impossible while she had her eyes closed. The lightning had increased to such a ferocity that people lay flat on their faces to avoid it and those struck had been set free from their ghosts. The community had more than doubled in size, and the military gentleman had galloped off at great speed, abandoning what was left of his forces.

Rocket later described for Jill how she had been bathed in blue-white light and as he remarked later, "The strangest thing was, there was this song, not just your voice you understand, echoing through the bell-like sound. No thunder, just that song."

Once she was in the house, Jill searched for Kyle everywhere. She eventually found him on a stretcher in the Library, with what looked like a piece of ice lodged in his shoulder. "Don't let me fall asleep again," was all he said.

Jill took out her lettered pebbles and placed all five on the transparent shard. The ice melted and Kyle immediately fell asleep, into a healthy sort of slumber.

"I tried that, with some of the pebbles around here, but it didn't work for me," said Rocket.

Jill shrugged as they both stared at Kyle. Rocket spoke, "I'm sure he'll be all right now," but Jill did not move. "There are other casualties, come on."

Rocket led her off to look after the other wounded, but Jill kept asking people to check on Kyle's health. Each time they would report back that he was still asleep and still smiling. One errand boy eventually said that the maids wanted to know how to stop him snoring, and at this, Jill laughed.

More pebbles were fetched, this time from the Road, and unlettered, and Jill would place them on the wounds. Each time she did, she heard a faint sound of music and song, far away, at the edge of her mind and shiver would run down her back. Much to Rocket and Jill's surprise there was little blood in the wounds, even wounds to the heart. Wearily, the rest of the day was taken in restoring things as much as possible, and when the sun started to become low, all the community gathered in the main hall of the House.

Jill had not stopped to rest that day, and like everyone else was dirty and weary. She had finally decided it was safe to remove the lettered stones from Kyle's shoulder. He stirred and started to open his eyes. "You let me fall asleep!" Kyle said and pushed himself up on one elbow. "Is there any food round here?" he asked and then fully sat up.

"Stop complaining. It's your lucky day. Rocket's getting hungry too, and I said we couldn't eat until we fetched you. You coming?" Kyle shrugged, swung his legs out of bed, and walked with them to the hall.

Jill sighed, sat down and started looking forward to supper being placed in front of them. She was surprised to find that several men stepped forward into the middle of the large hall. They began to sing. The first song was a little old fashioned and seemed to be all about how the Road had been made. The next song was sung by everyone and was about keeping the house friendly. Then three ladies stepped forward.

"I hope this finishes before my stomach starts to grumble," whispered Rocket. Jill gave him a kick.

The song was the one that Jill had been singing, in the heat of battle. It was not as alive as before, not as wild, but it was still beautiful. Jill could only say, "Ohh," and then Lord Bygone stepped up after they had finished and spent several boring minutes thanking them. Jill's mind was elsewhere. *I wonder what's going on at home.* She had pulled the stones out of her pocket and examined the worn 'G' carved in the sandstone. It was clearly cut. It knew what it was doing. *Why am I with these people?* She tried to think of the Wayfarer but somehow could not bring his face to mind. The droning voice cut through her thoughts for a moment, ". . . and will restore the historic peace of our existence. We look forward to their continued help in the life of this community . . ." *I didn't want to start a movement, I just want to help my Mum.* The stones clicked against each other in her hands. *Why does it always have to involve other people?* Jill wearily put the stones away and Lord Bygone finished outlining his plans for their future. Rocket spluttered into his drink and Kyle nodded in Lord Bygone's direction with a wild expression of disbelief. They looked at Jill, who shrugged and looked away. Then they ate.

Several days were spent in celebratory meals, poetry readings, and much hand shaking. There seemed to be lots of gifts, too many to put in a rucksack and Jill decided to ask Lord Bygone to look after them for her. Everywhere they went someone would thank them and say something like, "Could you sing again?"

Jill took to hiding in her room, which Kyle could not understand.

"The strains of fame are many," Lord Bygone would tell him every time he complained.

Days later, Jill was sitting in a secluded grove of bay trees on the far side of the dairy, watching the cows being brought in to milk when the gardener who had taken her out on the Moor emerged, shears in hand. He stopped and stared at her, with an embarrassed grin.

"Hello," said Jill, "I'm sorry but I've forgotten your name."

"Sye, my lady."

"Oh, don't make a fuss, I'm no lady. I can't stand people treating me differently."

Sye smiled. "That's hard not to do, if someone is special."

Jill became red and started speaking very quickly. "Look, I just sang what the Sword gave me, that's it. It wasn't anything I did."

"Most people would say that was pretty special. There's no siege now and people are already pressing to go down the Road. You still chose to sing, and I could hear your life in the words."

"Is that what the fuss was about last night, people wanting to travel the Road?" asked Jill.

"Yes, some have been harried by the enemy when they've tried to press on to the Tower of Fire and Light. Lord Bygone has put a ban on any more leaving, except those with special permission."

"I thought Bygone said . . . sorry, Lord Bygone said the Tower didn't exist? And what do you mean 'harried'?" Jill sat up and gripped the edge of the bench. Her frown had gone and her eyes were wide.

"Some do not agree with our Lord, but they'll have to speak for themselves, as will my Lord." Sye frowned, then spoke again. "As for myself, I'm not sure you should be here, not how things are changing. No matter who tries to keep you here, I think you're needed elsewhere."

"Does Bygone mean to ban me from leaving too?"

"What I mean, Ma'am, is that although the siege is lifted, there are attacks on our people. Some say it's a dragon."

Jill frowned. "Do you really think there are dragons?" Sye did not say anything. "Well, even if there are, I still need to get to the Tower of Fire and Light. You're right; I need to get out of here. And if I'm going to do that, there's someone I need to talk to, dragon or no dragon."

"Well that'll make a change from the last fortnight," said Sye with a smile. "Just remember to keep that sword of yours handy, I think you'll been needing it. I'll be seeing you, ma'am." He tugged his hat and left.

Jill rose and went inside and found Lord Bygone at his desk, composing verse. She stood at the door and hesitated. Jill found that she was shaking. *What is it with me? I win a battle and then go to pieces! Steady does it.*

"Sir, since the danger has greatly lessened, I was thinking that I needed to continue my journey . . ."

The lord turned and faced her, somewhat taken aback. He took off his spectacles and looked down into his lap, as he fiddled with his pen. "My dear, why do you propose to do such a thing? It is dangerous, and we have become fond of you." He looked up from under bushy eyebrows. "Besides, your gifting is needed here. What if our enemy reorganises to attack again? Stay here and help us. I will shortly be permitting a small scouting group to search out the area. But, I have to admit, that I am full of foreboding for them. But if you went with them, my heart would be greatly eased."

Jill bit her lip. It was several seconds before she answered. "It is not that I want to leave here, but I must complete my journey whatever happens. The Wayfarer said so." She emphasised the last few words.

The old aristocrat drew himself up to his full sitting height. "I'm sorry, but I cannot permit such recklessness. You will do as the Sword enables you I am sure, but I will not help. If you were my son, perhaps you would persuade me and I would send you with my authority. I had always wanted someone to give my treasures to," the old Lord tailed off into thought, but then looked up sharply. "But even if you could, I cannot risk losing more people. My answer is, 'no'. I have instructed the gatekeepers to let none pass, save the few I choose."

Jill opened her mouth, and then closed it. She fumed, clenched her fists, and then ran out of the room. The Lord Bygone was stammering, and went to follow her, but then checked himself. So Jill ran unhindered to her room and cried. She was almost completely finished when she had to answer a quiet knock at her door. "What do you want?"

A slightly shy looking Sye handed her a hand-carved tulip brooch. He said, "I'm leaving, thanks to you. Thank you again ma'am," then he quietly left. Jill turned the brooch over in her hands and saw there was something written on the back. "Don't be afraid. Let what is hidden bloom," it said.

Later that day Jill was thinking and looking out of her window when she saw a small party, equipped with coats, boots and staves, climb a set of steps onto the Road, wave cheerily to some friends and leave. She felt tense, and a little sick in her stomach, and although unsure what she was going to say, decided to find Rocket. Jill pinned the tulip to her coat, gathered up all her bits and then went downstairs.

"We've been here nearly three weeks and I'm getting fed up staying in my room," she blurted out when she finally caught up with him in the main hall, where he was fixing clocks.

He looked up over his half-moon spectacles. "That's not my fault dear. You've been in your room. We all thought you seemed tired."

Jill snapped. Heads turned in unison in the adjoining rooms and maids passing nearby stopped to listen and then decided to hurry on. Rocket went first white and then bright red as she raged. "I want to go now and if I have to, I'll use the Sword on this house too. I can't stand this place any more," she concluded. She said this more loudly than she intended and then dissolved into tears.

Rocket gently took her elbow and led Jill over to one side. "If you wish to leave, dear, Kyle and I have been itching to get going for several days now. We didn't want to disturb you too much. You didn't want to talk to anyone, not even us. Now if you get your things together, we will make our plans. It won't take much to find a way out."

Kyle wandered in to find out what the crying was about, and found Jill sobbing into Rocket's shoulder.

"What she crying about?" Kyle said, thumbing in Jill's direction. "Do we get to go now?" Rocket nodded and shushed him. Kyle chirped. "Great! I'll go and get my stuff sorted."

"'Great'?" said Jill, "I don't think he cares for anyone," still leaning her forehead on his now wet shoulder. She sniffed loudly. Rocket patted her neck in a way that would normally have been unbearable; however, Jill decided that it was acceptable for the moment and was quite disappointed when Lord Bygone came in. She walked over to the window, staring as if at distant trees while she cleaned her face with a handkerchief.

"Please forgive me, my dear. I knew you had to leave in the end, but I wished that it wasn't quite so soon," he said, downcast.

"I'm sorry to make such a fuss," said Jill, "I didn't mean to make so much noise . . ."

"No, my dear, I didn't hear you just now. Whatever it was you said, although," the lord chuckled, "the maids seem to be talking about it already. I have just been visited by the Wayfarer and he has told me that you are leaving, by his approval, whether I like it or not. I need to arrange one or two things." The lord left looking deflated, but much better for it.

Jill had blankly stopped mid-sentence and quietly closed her mouth. *Why didn't he talk to me?*

Rocket said a few 'thank-you's and both left to organise themselves.

For the rest of the day, Jill was packing in her room. The door was constantly being knocked on, and Jill had to work at not losing her temper over the interruptions, most of them being farewells or thanks.

At the front door, there was a huge crowd of well-wishers. They were all brightly dressed in their best clothes and decorated with bright silk ribbons and fresh flowers. People were waving handkerchiefs and cheering.

"It seems they really appreciated you," Rocket said.

Jill quietly walked down the path with Rocket and Kyle. She forced out smiles and said a few kind things, but soon subsided into silence. Kyle took the cheers as a conquering hero, and even Rocket glowed with pride.

They stopped as Lord Bygone stepped in front of them, holding a large iron key, hanging on a scarlet ribbon. Two gardeners stood on either side with swords and scabbards on purple cushions.

"This House has certain privileges inherited from our forebears, including the presentation of gifts. First, these are for the men." The gardeners stepped forward with the short swords and gave them to Kyle and Rocket. The lord then turned to Jill. "This key unlocks any closed door on the estate, and it is said that it opens many other places far from here too. May your journey be safe and may you stand before the Lord of the Way with joy in your hearts."

Rocket thanked everyone in a short and surprisingly un-boring speech and they walked happily to the steps. Kyle glanced over his shoulder.

"They're still waving and cheering," he said, and stopped to wave back. "I said, 'They're still waving,' — didn't you hear me guys?" He turned round and found that neither Jill nor Rocket showed any sign of stopping. "Oi! You two, I was talking." He started to trot to catch up. "You're supposed to listen." By the time he did catch up, he was panting. Jill smiled from the corners of her mouth; her eyes fixed on the way ahead.

"Let's go. I need to sort things out," was all she said. Not even Rocket could get her to say anything else for the rest of the day.

15

———

STAYING FREE

"But they've been so nice to us, why didn't you turn around and wave?" They were drinking hot chocolate, relaxing after a hard day's hike, but Kyle would not rest. He had been on the same tack now for several hours, even as they pitched their tents. Kyle's mind had been calm at the Mansion; however, being back on the Road seemed to have stirred him up.

The sandstone circle that Kyle was sitting next to gave him the creeps; even so, Jill and Rocket had woken the flames in the carved letters and looked far afield. Although they now had a much better knowledge of the Moor, the westerly mountains and the Sea, they had not been able to discover anything about the way ahead on the Road.

Kyle had said to Rocket that it must be because the Lord of the Way had not wanted them to see further down the Road. Rocket had said this was rot and was all for dismantling the paving to "fix the mechanism." It took an embarrassing incident, involving Jill reminding Rocket of the last time he tried to do this, before the red-faced scientist backed down.

This Vantage Point was under a semicircle of yew trees. The eternally green boughs sheltered them from a cold night breeze and the stars sparkled above the shimmering haze of lamp light. Kyle had finally worked out how to build the fire himself and the meal was cooked before Jill realised. They had eaten and she had stretched herself out and stared upward into the crystal skies, while the 'boys' planned and discussed. It had been then that Kyle had started to become personal and push his blunt enquiries. The stars seemed so far away and Jill wished to have their angelic perspective for once. She sighed and finally spoke.

"They were too nice. There is a reason for my journey, and I'm going to get to the end of this Road one way or another. I've got the gifts, we're going to the Tower, we'll lift the blockade fully, and then I can see the Lord of the Way." Jill had sat up and was staring into the fire. "And then, well, we'll see."

"But, but they were only being friendly. I can't believe you could be that rude, especially after all they had done for us"

"'All they've done for us'? That's great, that is, all they could talk about was what I'd done for them," Jill kicked the ground.

"What's the problem with that?" Kyle was becoming irate, in a way only possible for an angry eleven-year-old: a wrinkle-less scowl and a pouting lip.

"Leave her alone, old chap," Rocket said.

Kyle skewed around to face Rocket, "Why?"

Jill then looked up. "I didn't want to stay there, because I was too comfortable."

Kyle now exploded. "What? I don't get it. We waited around for days because of you, and now you say that all we needed was to make you feel really at home and we could have cleared out? If it was that good there, you should have waved at least." He was waving his hands, and squinting through the flickering light and smoke.

"I thought that if I looked back that I might not want to leave. It almost felt like Mrs. Lazybee's. I nearly forgot about Mum there." Jill leant back, propped up on straight arms, "I'm supposed to be out here."

"Kyle, she's right. I almost thought like that myself." Rocket warmed his hands, watching Kyle from the corner of his eye.

Kyle's eyes were wide open in disbelief, "That's it, both of you are going to pick on me now. I just think they're really nice people," he glanced between his two mute companions who were looking away, and threw up his hands, "Huh! I'll go and read, it'll be better company," he said and sloped off to his tent.

"Why's he so stirred up? He couldn't wait to leave this morning." Rocket didn't answer, but just prodded the fire with a stick. Jill waited for a response, but none was forthcoming. "Thanks for backing me up anyway," she muttered.

"Don't thank me, old girl. I'm not on your side, I just understand a bit better than he does. Comes with age you know."

"Here we go," muttered Jill.

"Kyle's just mixed up, and not used to anyone being nice to him. Can't handle it when it's happening, then misses it when it's gone. That's easy to work out. But you've been very odd to be with ever since you won that battle at the Mansion, almost as if you thought people were after you. I'd say that there's something you want to get off your chest."

Rocket pursed his lips and waited.

"Well I, I . . . I'm not sure how to say it."

"I am listening, old girl. Take your time."

Whenever Rocket was like this, Jill thought that this was how her Dad should have been, even though she could hardly remember him. She liked it.

"All those people wanted to get to know me. It wasn't me winning that battle, I just closed my eyes and sang, it wasn't even from me, it flowed through me from the Sword." Jill fidgeted.

"You picked up the Sword when we needed it, then the power flowed. That all takes courage and strength of character." A shower of sparks flew upward and Rocket's features were lit by the orange flare.

Jill objected. "It doesn't feel like that. In the Village, I'm powerless, but when I demolished the rotten halls at the Lodge, or when I was zapping the crows, I was angry and could feel I was doing something. At Lord Bygone's, it was like everyone adored me for doing nothing. I didn't come on this walk to win battles and I can't get tied up with too many people on the way. I just want to find whoever built this Road." She sagged, her stomach starting to knot.

"You mean you don't want to get to like people too much, or that you don't want them to like you? That's going to be difficult for you to stick to. My dear, there's no shame in letting what's been put in you come out, and a great many people never have the honesty to do so. Why be ashamed of that, eh? What other people think of the Road, or the Sword, or whatever else the Lord of the Way gives you, is up to them." Rocket finished drinking from his cup and placed it between them. It looked like three bronze leaves wrapped around each other, and like everything else the Wayfarer had provided, was exquisitely made.

"This cup didn't ask to be made beautiful, or useful, it didn't have any say in the matter. Now, it's not up to me to say what or who you are, but you can't change how you've been made any more than this cup can. You can mess things up, bottle up inside who you are, or you can choose to let it out. If people like it, that's not because they're saying you've done anything good, they just think the cup's pretty. Don't you think?"

"Think what?" said an unconvinced little girl.

"Think that the cup's pretty, old girl. Well, don't you?" Rocket tapped its rim with the end of his staff, and it rang, like a bell.

Jill smiled slowly, laughed and then nodded.

Rocket sat back. "Now why don't you go and apologise to that young firebrand who's all for manners and being polite and we'll see what these books can rustle up."

"What?"

"It is 'Pardon', young lady. Go, apologise, and see if Kyle will apologise to you as well. Fetch him and his map—oh, and your books as well. I'm not going to let a faulty observation station prevent us preparing."

Rocket's change of mood left Jill happy. However, a good ten minutes of argument with Kyle finally led to blows; only when he begged for mercy were apologies finally accepted.

Jill came back, bringing Kyle, his maps and the green book. "I can't find the blue book; it must have jumped out, or something."

"Yeah, I'm sure that's not all you'd like to get rid of either," said Kyle.

"That's not fair, Kyle. Sit down, please," Rocket scolded. Kyle slunk over to his place.

"As for the book, you could say that it jumped out," said Rocket and produced the book, "I noticed you weren't reading it, so I sort of borrowed it."

Jill gave him a reproachful look, "Rocket! I say, old boy —"

Kyle grinned, "I think he shows potential, at least that's what my social worker would say. A few more lifts like that and you'd fit into that boy's home I ran away from."

Rocket blushed, "It was in the interests of research, but I won't do it again."

Kyle placed a hand on his hip and wagged his finger, "Oh yeah, that's what they all say at first."

"Well, I won't. The book told me off."

"What?" Kyle's mood seemed to disappear in outraged amusement.

"Apparently it didn't like being borrowed, and kept on falling open at a bit that said, "No traveller will take any other's equipment.""

Jill shrugged as she looked down and tried to hide her smile while let out a triumphant, "Ha!"

Rocket suggested that they read over things together, mentioning any useful bits that they found.

They laid out the books in an arc, each under their own lamps and read aloud occasionally; Kyle with the maps; Jill with her history and Rocket with the blue tome. Kyle was distracted by a ticking sound. He was about to look for the cricket that he thought was making the noise when Rocket had to explain that it was his book was tutting at him.

"Why?" said Kyle, with a sly grin.

"It's still telling him off. Why do you think?" said Jill and talked to the book nicely to persuade it not to distract 'poor' Rocket. As she said, "We need him to think clearly about the way ahead." Kyle thought the whole thing was hilarious. He swore later on that the book purred for minutes after she finished talking to it.

Finally, there was a concentrated hush and they settled to read. Some time later Jill broke the silence.

"It says here that there used to be just one main Road ahead, but there was an earthquake and the Moor dropped down in one or two places. They built a bridge sort of thing, a 'viaduct'. Look, there's a picture." The other two readers got up, leaned over her shoulder, and saw a flat bridge with multiple arches.

"It looks like it's stood on stone stilts," said Kyle.

"Well that's good," said Rocket, "at least someone's doing maintenance."

"No, it doesn't stop there," Jill said, "It says that the 'commander of the carrion fowl —'"

Kyle interrupted. "Who? What's that stupid thing going on about?"

Rocket's voice was as gentle as Kyle's had been harsh. "Now Kyle come on . . ."

"Well who do you think tells the crows what to do, you plank?" Jill retorted.

"Jill, that's uncalled for, both of you," Rocket suddenly felt pity for his friends with teenage children. "Please carry on, my dear."

Jill's sulk was a pouting bout of three seconds, then, honour satisfied, she continued to read, "The commander of the carrion fowl, the usurper, sent his soldiers to pull down the Viaduct. The travellers presumed that the Road could not be harmed and did not try to stop them. However, the attack was successful in parting the stones and the Viaduct collapsed. The Road was not destroyed, but as the bridge fell, the stones formed a broken path, now splintered into three ways across the valley floor. Each one is considered to have merits, and each contains an element of the Road, but the traveller must now beware the attacks of the enemy."

"Weird," said Kyle.

"If each is only a part, then our weapons may not work properly," said Rocket.

"Great," said Kyle, staring ahead.

Rocket eyed Jill thoughtfully. "Jill, what's bothering you? Something is going on in that mind of yours, isn't it?"

Jill pointed at the book. "This is where the blockade has been imposed by the enemy. Like the Lodge, he scored a victory and he has used it. The Wayfarer didn't say how we would break through, he didn't explain how to do it," said Jill.

"What do you mean?" said Kyle.

"Don't you see? This part of the Road is where the enemy has built up forces to seal the Road to all travellers; his stronghold must be there, where the Road is weakest. We need to go through him, or sneak past, to finish the Road."

"Are you sure?" Rocket asked.

Jill nodded. "I'm sure that's what the Wayfarer was telling me."

"So you're leading us into a trap? One where our weapons might not work?" asked Kyle, "Great, just great."

"What do your maps say, Kyle?" asked Jill.

Kyle looked at the vellum. "Here's that bridge thing,"

"Viaduct," said Rocket.

"Yeah, the bridge thing is not far ahead, it crosses—"

"Crossed," said Rocket.

"Yeah, right, it crosses a valley with all sorts of marshes, woods and little rivers, and a bit marked, 'here be dragons'." Jill and Rocket leant over to have a look. "That does it," said Kyle, "if I'm going anywhere near there, then I'm definitely going the long way around."

"You don't think they just put that bit about dragons in to fill up an empty bit on the map, do you?" asked Jill.

Rocket's eyebrows had disappeared under his hair, and he chewed his lip. He said nothing.

"What does the modern map say?" Jill leant over to the other chart.

There was a rustling sound and the map flattened itself and partly covered the old velum manuscript.

"See, where the Road meets the valley it splits into three paths," Kyle spoke loudly and pointed.

"That one, the one that skirts to the right, to the east, climbs back up to the Moor quickly," said Rocket, who was standing up, stroking his chin. "It seems to avoid all the, er, tricky bits."

"It's a very long way. It tracks up one side of the valley, crosses the head, then back down again. It could take days, weeks even," Kyle said.

"We could nip across the shortest route, in an afternoon, right across the middle," suggested Jill

"And past, 'here be dragons'?" queried Rocket.

"What about the western, left hand turn?" said Kyle.

Jill was pouring over it closely, "It winds about through narrow, low, passing places. There's marsh and a building marked as the 'Questionable House' that looks like its enemy occupied from the inscription here."

"Perfect for an ambush," said Kyle, "Like I said, a trap."

"I think the choice is obvious," said Rocket, "The Viaduct was built to keep people out of the valley, so we'd better go east up the moorland path. We can all camp, there's a Vantage Point where we can see people coming."

"They can see us too," said Kyle, "all the time." Then more quietly, "Or maybe that's your plan."

"But you forget, my friend, we have our lamps, our weapons, and of course, most importantly, we have Jill," said Rocket through forced cheerfulness.

Kyle shook his head.

Jill snorted and looked up at Kyle with a grin, "Watch it, buddy. I don't need any pyrotechnics to sort you. Mind you, I certainly don't want to tangle with ambushes or dragons."

"Aw, I always wanted to catch a live dragon," moaned Kyle playfully. He acted out grabbing one in his arms and knocked Rocket over in the process.

"Will you two behave?" protested Jill.

Rocket sat up determinedly and bundled Kyle into a protesting heap.

"Excuse *me*," he said, rising and fetching the slim blue volume. "What do you think Jill?"

Jill had tucked her knees under her chin and was staring at the maps. "I don't know. I was thinking how long it will take to walk to the valley. Seven or eight days is my guess, light or heavy-loaded. And we shouldn't forget what the Wayfarer said. We are supposed to get through to a Tower; otherwise, we will not have the strength to lift the blockade. I think he meant this Tower of Fire and Light that Bygone got so steamed up about. We have something important to do there that will let Lord Bygone's lot get along the Road."

"Where have we got to go now?" asked Kyle.

"I'm not totally sure but there's a large building marked on the modern map before we get to the viaduct, I think it must be the Tower. We should take a look at it. I mean, it can't hurt, if the Wayfarer was right."

"I don't like always having to work on his say-so, I'm not sure I see the logic in it." Rocket's hands were in his pocket and he slouched unenthusiastically.

"I'm not sure I want to look at the place either," Kyle mumbled.

"What does the blue book say?" said Jill, changing the subject.

"It fell open somewhere interesting earlier on," Rocket thumbed through the book quickly, occasionally licking his fingertip so as to turn over individual pages. "Here it is," he said and proceeded to read it out:

"The Lord of the Way requires that all who travel his Road should travel light. No one can complete the journey with heavy weights in their backpack."

"Well that's obvious," Kyle said.

"Will you please not interrupt, young man," said Rocket. "I'm not sure it just means our equipment. In fact, I'm certain it doesn't, there's a list of things that weigh a traveller down. Fear, bitterness, anger . . .”

Kyle snorted.

“What else does it say?” Jill asked.

Rocket flipped it open.

“Well?” Jill and Kyle both leaned forward.

“'A traveller should be careful not to desire the good things his companions have', oh this is ridiculous,” snapped Rocket and clapped shut the book between his hands.

Jill grinned at Kyle and put a finger to her lips. Kyle looked away and snorted into his hand.

“As I was saying, where was I? Ah yes . . .”

Both children collapsed into laughter.

Further discussion was impossible, so Rocket said goodnight. Jill went to bed gazing upward into the clear sky. “Tell me what you know,” she whispered to the stars. “You must know what's going on, you see everything up there. What am I doing with these people? I hate having to cope with their . . . weirdness; with this journey's weirdness. Why can't I have just caught a bus or something, taken a ticket at the Lord of the Way's Palace and just stood in line?” The stars blinked back, uncomprehendingly. “And why have I got to save other people? I'm the one in trouble here, what's with this whole thing? It seemed fun to start with but now . . . And we haven't seen *him* in weeks.” Jill fidgeted and then reached into the tent. She picked up the carved tulip Sye had given her and traced her fingers around its outline. *Rocket seems to agree with the inscription, 'Let what's hidden bloom,' but I'm not sure I do.* Jill raised herself on one elbow. “What if I don't want to?” she asked herself. Jill looked up. “What if I don't want to care for other people, get involved in all that junk? What if I don't like myself any more than anyone at the Village?” The stars made no reply that she could hear. “Maybe they're too far away to care,” Jill said and rolled over, settling down under the splendour of a clear night sky and a shimmering canopy of light.

The next day, before dawn, they awoke under intensely cold, clear skies. Jill wrapped her sleeping bag around herself and wormed her way out of the tent. She hopped across the sandstone pavement to where Rocket was brewing coffee. Kyle was appearing at his tent door, bleary eyed and complaining about where his blankets were. He disappeared back into the tent. Rocket offered her a strong sweet coffee, which Jill took with pleasure, as she watched old, dry sticks crackle and dance with flames.

"Not using the stove?" she said as she warmed her hands by the fire.

"No, the embers from last night were still hot, and there is so much firewood around here. There are so many broken branches lying about. I can't imagine that anyone has camped here for years."

The little grove of trees was the only stand of wood for miles, and no one seemed to have moved the branches and their piles of soft needles until they had come.

"If campers had needed a fire they would have certainly taken their fuel from here," Rocket continued, "and all the moss our feet kicked off the stone almost cleaned it up. No one has walked here for years."

"Do you think there's hope? If no-one has been this way for so long then maybe we can't make it either," Jill said. "It could all be a waste of time . . ."

"My dear girl," said Rocket, "you can't think like that . . ."

"I found my blankets," came a muffled voice, "they were on top of my sleeping bag; I just couldn't feel them."

Rocket and Jill turned to see a very befuddled boy appear, eyes puffy and barely open. Now that Jill looked at him properly, she could see he was wearing a pair of shorts over his travel stained trousers and several layers of jumpers and shirts in random order. Both Rocket and Jill burst out laughing.

"What? What is it now? It was very cold last night." he protested, and was given a steaming mug of hot coffee. He sat down, muttering under his breath. Rocket and Jill decided to stifle their laughter.

The sun was about to come up and as they sat and looked north, Kyle said, "Look at that really bright star over there."

This was such an unusual thing for Kyle to say that both Jill and Rocket followed his pointing arm.

Low over the northern horizon, a piercing light was blazing. It started to reach downward, a shaft of fire trying to touch the earth.

Then, the sun came up.

They looked around to watch the dawn, silent in the glory. Jill looked back after what seemed an eternity.

"That star of yours is a bit taller now," said Jill.

When they looked around, they saw the red star had become a shining pillar.

"I wonder what that could be?" said Rocket.

Kyle grunted something about not wanting to find out, and stumbled back to his tent. The column of light on the horizon sank quickly into the earth and the sun began to climb the sky. "Well if it is a star," said Jill, "it's the strangest one I've ever seen."

Breakfast this day was especially good; Rocket seemed to be trying to lift their spirits with waffles made in a waffle iron he had produced as if from nowhere.

"Lord Bygone had metal smiths too," he said with a smile. "I found this when I was looking for parts to fix the clocks. It's as light as a feather, and turns out delicious waffles. I hardly notice it with the other pans and the stove."

They ate until they could eat no more, syrup thick on the plate.

The chores of the day; breakfast; washing up; washing in the western bank stream; and dressing for the day's hike and breaking camp; were all completed with the ease and speed of people who had got to know their tasks and each other's ways.

The walk started well, but today was different, as none of them wanted to talk. Jill normally started the conversation; however, she just scowled and looked down at her feet. *He's always getting in the way.* She stopped for a moment. Jill wasn't sure which 'he' she meant. *But if I'm always with these people how do I get to be myself?* A glare that could burn through leather was turned onto the back of the heads in front. *Maybe that's why the Lord of the Way hasn't shown himself yet, he's waiting for me to get rid of these jokers.*

Kyle again pointed just to the left of the Road. "Something keeps winking at me," he said.

"Well it's not me," said Jill.

Rocket looked, and could not see anything.

Several strides later Kyle cried, "There it is!" and Rocket saw it this time. These two spent their time spotting scintillations and then would stop and stare, but Jill never seemed to be able to look at just the right time.

"Pack it in, will you! I'm getting tired of this. I'll just get on without you if I have to." Jill turned white as she spat the words out, her face flat but her words dripping with contempt.

Something got the better of Kyle and he ran at her.

After a scrabble that Kyle had been winning, Rocket pulled him off, ear first.

"Now apologise, both of you," he said.

Rocket's manner was normally quite reassuring, however this time both children glowered at each other. They apologised, but in the end, they were walking on opposite sides of the Road.

Rocket was just murmuring to himself, "What would the Wayfarer do now? What would he say if he was here?" when a buzzard circled calling from above. They all stopped. The cry sounded so sad, almost heartbroken, that something made Jill nearly apologise then and there.

On the west, a breeze stirred up clouds and the cloudless day started to darken. The buzzard circled high above, apparently out of reach of the freshening wind. Kyle looked up. He could see a black-winged shape in the clouds, far above the buzzard. He tried not to listen, but there it was still; a faint hiss in the recesses of his mind.

"Go away," said Kyle.

Rocket looked sidelong at him, then back at the sky. "Yes, those clouds seem very black," he said.

"They're changing shape very quickly too," said Jill.

"Too quickly if you ask me," said Rocket.

"And from the north west," said Kyle. They agreed to keep watch on this as they walked, but Kyle could feel their approach, he knew what it was. "It's the crows again."

The others stared upwards following Kyle's gaze.

"Weapons out," said Rocket.

"I wonder why they want a licking today?" said Kyle, nervous and sweating.

"Why should you care?" said Jill.

"Quiet you two. Wits about you, these ones are coming in quickly."

The lamps failed to light and they tried to plant the staff into the Road, but it would not go in. Even the stove did not light.

The dark flock started to circle above.

"What's going on?" said a rapidly panicking Kyle.

"Be quiet, I'll sort this," said Jill and pulled out the Sword. It hung lifeless in her hands and nothing happened when she spoke to it.

The first of the carrion crows started to land on the Road. They seemed unharmed. Wolves could be heard howling.

"I don't like this." said Jill and took a swing at the nearest one. The Sword wounded it but it resolutely refused to vanish in the usual way. "We're done for."

The friends backed together and crouched down, fending off attacks that were beginning to come thick and fast. They worked in a bloody mess, the weapons now only having the power that their muscles gave them. Battered birds leapt at them; tangled mounds of sticky black feathers started to pile around them. They started to bleed themselves. A screech made them look up. The crows on the Road scattered.

"It's that buzzard again," said Kyle.

They watched as the buzzard collided with the flock, tore his way through the centre and then descended to the Road. The bird screeched loud and long, and made repeated passes over the knot of friends. They were crouching and after a few moments, Kyle went pale.

"I can hear words. Can you?"

The others' blank stares indicated that they could not.

"Oh, I really must be losing it," he moaned, "I knew this was all too good to last. I should have stayed at the Mansion. It was quiet there. Lovely and quiet."

"What's it saying, old boy?" Rocket grabbed his shoulder so hard it nearly knocked him over.

"I just keep hearing, 'Put down the heavy weights! Forgive!'"

"What?" said Jill, for once, honestly scared.

Rocket's eyes narrowed. He looked up at the tawny bird guarding them and smiled slowly. "I don't think that you're going mad, old thing. In fact, my guess is that your hearing couldn't be better. "

Kyle was in floods of tears by now and seemed to take no notice.

The buzzard stopped calling to avoid a posse of crows who had regrouped and set upon him.

"Kyle, I'm sorry," said Jill, "I really didn't mean to be so nasty to you."

"Oh yeah," Kyle sneered, "I really think we've got more important things to do."

"Can you hear the crows yet?" said Rocket, "Because if you can, then now would be a good time to lock their voices out again."

Kyle stopped and listened, and his eyes grew round like saucers.

"Steady, steady, old boy. 'Forgive', is what our friend said." Rocket glanced up. "It's fighting for us; maybe we should take its advice."

Kyle swallowed and his eyes widened. "I'm sorry," he said, looking her in the eye.

The lamp came on, and the dome returned. The nearest crows suddenly lifted off the Road, wisps of smoke rising from where they had been standing.

Jill looked up and saw the flock boiling. She seized her chance. "Clear the way! You've no right to try and stop us. We're here to stop your work!" Her staff was pointed up and she was holding it as firmly as she knew how.

Lightning struck upwards.

They walked for the rest of the morning with black feathers blowing past them in the air. Occasionally one would skid across the Road hissing as it went. No one saw the buzzard fly off.

In the afternoon, they sat and made tea. Rocket blew across his cup. "What has been going on with you, old boy?"

Kyle picked up a stone and threw it. "I kept seeing crows yesterday, but you didn't. Right?" Rocket nodded. "I wasn't sure what you'd think so I kept quiet. When I see them, I get these ideas that Jill hates me, wants to get rid of me. They kind of called at me until I was really jittery, sort of dropped feelings in my ears. I was just beginning to hear their voices properly, when I realised that my anger had the same taste as their words, if you know what I mean. Oh, this sound nuts." Kyle paused long enough to send another stone skittering. "Well, that's when the buzzard flew up, and it all got crazy. I'm making sense aren't I? Do you know what I mean?"

Jill said that she thought she did.

Kyle looked embarrassed, "I couldn't see it till then, I just couldn't."

Jill said, "At least you had a reason, I was just in a bad mood. Sorry."

Rocket smiled. "Anything else we should know?"

"Nah," said Kyle, "Not really."

That seemed to settle the issue.

It was half way through the last stint of walking before they camped that Jill turned around, walked backwards, and started talking excitedly. "That's it. I've got it."

"Got what, old girl?"

"Our weapons wouldn't work because we were disagreeing with the Road, kind of out of line."

"Uhh?" said Kyle, "I've already said sorry—"

"It's okay," the scientist said, "I think Jill's talking about something else."

"That's right," she said, doing a double skip to stay ahead of them, "the argument between us put us out of line with the attitude the Road has. When I disagree with what's coming through me, the power stops, so we unplugged ourselves from the Truth when we were angry."

"And you were both out of line with what the living book had told us about how to walk the Road," concluded Rocket. "It had warned us."

"And I was too stupid to hear it," said Kyle miserably.

After this, the other two kept being so nice to him to cheer him up, that he had to beg them to stop.

They made camp that evening on a wild pitch, cutting away at the bushes.

Kyle looked up. "There it is again."

The sun was setting through clouds, and this time, quite near, a tall spire of flames seemed to flash out of the evening mist, almost due north. It did not last long, and seemed dull compared to the day before.

"Remarkable, quite remarkable," Rocket mumbled.

This evening's mood was so much different that Jill nearly fell over Kyle trying to help him as he helped her put Rocket's tent up. Rocket sensibly kept a safe distance.

After some near arguments that started, "No, let me do it," they ate and then sat around and read under the stars again.

The good weather had lasted well and Jill wondered how long it would continue. She asked Rocket what his blue book had said today.

He mentioned something that seemed to do with the weather to Jill.

"It seems to be talking about looking down from the clouds, but the clouds bring power to the earth."

"Doesn't make any sense to me," said Kyle.

"It doesn't to me either, old boy," replied Rocket.

Next morning, Jill's eyes had snapped open and she marvelled at the sunlight on the canvas, brightly illuminating the tent. "Why didn't they wake me? It must be late," she mumbled as she got dressed quickly. Jill stumbled out, and found that it was not as late as she had thought. It was a crystal dawn.

Kyle and Rocket were standing together, dressed and staring north. Kyle simply watched, slack jawed, however his companion was talking to whoever would listen and share the moment with him. "Absolutely amazing, I haven't seen anything like it in all my born days. No, nothing like this."

There stood the outline of a tower, as tall as the clouds, shining like the sun itself.

There stood the Tower of Fire and Light.

16

The Tower of Fire and Light

The Tower was broad at the base, its outline sweeping upwards in two smooth symmetrical curves, which finished in a burning pinnacle, too bright to look at. It was less bright lower down and as the sun climbed, a strip of fiery reflection stretched further down the surface of the tower.

"It must catch and reflect the sun's rays. But how is it so bright at the top?" Rocket wondered. Everyone was shading their eyes.

Rays of light were thrown off the top of the tower in different directions, and Kyle was quick to point out that the shadows in the camp-site were not stretching west away from the sun, but south, away from the tower.

"We must be in a spotlight, or something," he said. Rocket commented that this would explain why they could not look at the top. They would be looking straight down the beam.

"'Restore the light to Lord Bygone's people'," Jill mused. "That's what the Wayfarer said. That looks like a good place to do that."

They stood quietly and let the sun rise in peace. The colours from the tower turned from reds to golds and became brighter until they thought they could bear it no more. Then the light started to fade at the top and reflections quickly slipped down the tower. Soon the tower was almost invisible, the same colours as the sky and clouds around it.

They ate excitedly, and started to hike in high spirits.

"How long will it take to get there, do you think?" Jill asked.

"Not long if we walk quickly," Kyle replied examining the map.

Unusually, they needed the map. Frequently they could not see this huge structure as they walked and it must have been taller than they had originally thought, for even Rocket became impatient with the journey.

By mid-morning, they came across a large path deviating from the Road. There was a sign that hung from an arched frame. It was being blown by the wind, spinning in space, decorated with a brightly coloured ball of red and gold flames. Shooting from behind this were blue-white beams of inlaid silver. A pointer with strange letters indicated the path.

"What do you think it says?" said Rocket.

"Let's give it the usual go," said Jill, "stare until it starts to make sense."

"I still don't like this," Rocket moaned, "very rum. Where's the mechanism, the causality?"

"Shh, I think I'm getting it," said Kyle, "if I have to hear birds and books talk, I may as well get to do something fun too."

"Okay, you go first," said Jill, "and I'll write what I've got. Let's see if it comes out the same." Rocket peered over her shoulder as she wrote and Kyle squinted at the words, frowning. "Ready," she said.

"This way to the Tower of Fire and Light," Kyle said, beaming.

Jill showed him her neatly printed words: 'Here is the Tower of Fire and Light.' She shrugged, "Close enough."

"Most odd," said Rocket, and spent the next fifteen minutes cross-examining both of them as they walked toward the Tower down the path.

It all ended in a water fight.

A full hour later, they were standing at the base of the tower. It was like a huge green house, perfectly round and pulled up to dizzying heights at its centre. There was no outside wall reaching the ground, but the roof, which was almost flat at its edge, was held up on arched pillars. They walked in and were amongst trees.

First, they met apples, pears, peach, plum and apricot. The fruit hung as brightly coloured baubles. The smell was over-whelming and made Jill's mind run back to dim memories of when she was very young. Rich sweetness first tasted on her mother's knee. She sighed. The air was warm and began to be hot as they walked in toward the centre. The orchards gave way to plantations of banana, guava and dozens of other fruits that even Rocket did not recognise. "I wonder what I'm supposed to do with the key?" Jill said.

"I doubt it has much to do with fruit farming," Rocket said dryly.

Kyle was hungry and their path was littered with discarded peels and cores. "Wouldn't be bad if it was. Hey, maybe it opens a barn door," he said through a mouthful of sweet pulp. They pushed through the fronds of the trees and vines and found themselves in the central atrium.

No trees grew here; instead, there was a circular sandstone pavement. Three white pillars sprang up as if to support the sky; light and glass dominated the air. They looked up. The roof swept upward. It was a little like looking into a bath plughole as the water spirals out. Directly above their heads the roof was still shallow, but as it approached the centre, it turned skywards in a stunning rise. The top of the glass spire was lost in a haze of brightness.

Kyle was noisily slurping a custard apple, pulling the flesh off its pips with his teeth, his hands and knife a sticky mess. As he stared up, juice running down his chin, he spat out a huge seed. "My Mum would have loved this."

"So would my Mum," muttered Jill, under her breath. *I wonder how she is?* Jill sighed. *I wonder how everyone else is? I wonder what they think's happened to me?*

Kyle paused thoughtfully. "Who do you think looks after it all?"

Another voice came in. "I'm glad to hear you like it. To answer your question, I do."

They all jumped.

"You're not the Wayfarer," Jill said.

"Well spotted. No I'm not," said the newcomer, "were you expecting him?"

"Well, no not really, it's just we're getting used to being surprised." Jill paused, "Oh, sorry I'm Jill and we've had a long journey, and the Wayfarer usually turns up when you least expect, and . . ."

"What she means to say is, 'Pleased to meet you'," said Rocket.

"Me too," said Kyle, wiping his chin. He quickly put the dripping mess of fruit behind his back and rubbing his right hand on his trousers, he held his empty hand out. The newcomer shook their hands with a smile. He looked at Kyle, "You're not called Adam by any chance?"

Kyle frowned, "Er, no, should I be?"

Rocket looked alarmed. "The fruit's not forbidden, poisoned or very expensive, is it?"

The newcomer laughed. "No, but it is polite to ask first, before eating your fill." Kyle looked shamefaced. "Welcome to my dominion, friend, and no long faces here. I am the steward of the power collected here. You have come to ascend the tower?"

"Well, that all depends," said Jill, "Do you know the Wayfarer?"

"More than that, we are of the same family. I am called the Steward by some, but others prefer to call me the 'Helper.'"

"Steward of what, may I ask?" asked Rocket.

"Of the Light, of the Truth."

"That's a rather tall task," said Rocket.

"Hence the Tower." The Steward smiled, "When you wish to ascend the Tower, come to see me in the centre." He walked away and disappeared underground, near the centre of the tower base.

"Shall we?" said Rocket, making a sweeping gesture toward

the centre of the Tower. "Let us examine this more closely."

They wandered over toward where the Steward disappeared, and came to the edge of the central circle of paving.

"You'd think they'd have chosen a different design," said Kyle. The sandstone was covered with script. The letters were bigger and bolder than at the Lookout, but the design was the same otherwise.

Rocket noticed the pavement's centre. It was alive with shining, living letters. He went to investigate, only to hear the Steward call out. "Do not stand on the central disc, please, you will find it far too hot."

Rocket frowned, and threw forward some lint and dust from his pocket. The lint was immediately reduced to ash. The dust made arcs of fire, shining like miniature suns and disappeared before it reached the paving.

The Steward had come back. "The light is perfectly focussed and there is normally no dust at this point. So there is nothing to indicate the power focussed here, save the fiery words; nothing to let you know."

"Really, how is all that done? Where is the power going? Is it solar?" Rocket was shooting off questions faster than the others thought possible.

"My friend, why don't you take a look?" said the Steward, gesturing upwards.

"How high is it?" asked Jill, looking pale.

"It varies; not much today, only a couple of kilometres," the Steward replied.

"Not as high as I wanted to go in the RAVE, but it should give an excellent view of the Road." Rocket mused.

"How high do you want it to be?" the Steward inquired.

Jill blanched.

"I think that will do," said Kyle, quietly smiling.

"Is there a good reason to go up there?" asked Rocket.

"You have been sent by the Wayfarer and bear a gift, the key, from the Lord Bygone. He needs to receive more light; he needs the beacon restored; his Library needs to be made alive again. All this can be accomplished with the key at the top. But only by someone with purpose." The Steward looked at Jill.

"Well er . . . yes. I'm not sure I know what I'm supposed to be doing," Jill stammered, "but from what you've said maybe I should go up. Then again, it is very high . . . and very exposed."

"There is also the ability to know your enemy's mind and his disposition from such a vantage point," the Steward continued gently, "even if that leaves you exposed. It is often true that you can not have the one without the other. The tower has the purpose of bringing all things out into the light."

"How do we get up there?" asked Rocket, apparently having decided for them.

"Er, I Umm, It's just that . . . well . . . Heights don't b-bother me exactly it's just that . . ." Jill was becoming quite incoherent, but none of the others seemed to want to notice. She sank into tense silence.

"I'm up for it," said Kyle, brightly.

"That's a terrible pun," Jill muttered. She was now very white.

"What? What did I say?" Kyle replied.

"Never mind."

"I thought you might never ask," said the Steward, politely ignoring the children's argument, "this way please."

Kyle, Rocket and Jill followed the Steward over to the edge of the clearing, to one of three slender pillars that descended from the roof. In its side were set three huge levers, rather like those in old-fashioned signal boxes. The Steward pulled the first lever. If they could have watched from above they would have seen the fiery writing on the central stone fade and three smaller spots of bright letters appear between the pillars.

The second lever was pulled and three cords dropped straight down from the spire above. These attached themselves to the central sandstone slab.

Jill stiffened herself and breathed in deeply in an effort to still her rising fear. Jill also noticed that the more afraid she was, the more angry she became with the others. "That's odd," she said.

Rocket was watching the machinery. "Yes, remarkable!" he said, with what seemed to have become his catch phrase.

"Please stand on the central stone. If you leave your equipment here, it will be best." They left their staves and bags. The men removed their swords, but Jill refused to take hers off. The Steward gestured to the area that had been so hot a few moments ago. They walked over and cautiously looked at the stilled inscription. "It's quite safe now," the Steward reassured them.

"Come on, you two," said Rocket. He stepped onto the circle of stone, inside the three silken ropes.

"Stand quite still, please," the Steward said and pulled the third lever.

They saw the ropes tighten slightly; then noiselessly the circle of stone lifted smoothly in the air.

"Cool," said Kyle.

"That's original . . . for once," said Jill. The pit of her stomach churned. Her mind was jostled by unwelcome thoughts.

In fact, it was far from cool. They all started to sweat. Although there was a stiff breeze blowing upward into the spire, the air was humid and it blew hotter and stronger as they rose. They were lifted slowly over the foliage. Jill stared as birds flitted between forest and glass and tried to forget what was happening. Other images asserted themselves. She thought of her Mum as she left her that day, she thought of her despair, of being crushed, of wanting everyone's problems behind. *Get a grip, girl!*

Rocket's eyes were everywhere and he was taking notes.

"There's no hand rail," said Jill, going grey.

"You may sit down if you wish," said Rocket, and then actually turned to look at her. "My dear girl, let's all sit together."

Well, I suppose he's not so bad. The knots in Jill's stomach unwound slightly.

They sat in the centre, or at least as far from the edge as Jill could manage to get.

"It's going to take all day," said Kyle.

"Yes," said Jill a little more happily, "I think I might just enjoy this," and she probably would have, if the ropes had not finished their run.

They were pulled up into the spire like a cork into the neck of a bottle from the inside. The stone slab fitted perfectly into a glass tube in the centre of the spire and clicked onto guides from which the ropes had come. Between the main glass spire and their tube three sails were furled, which connected to the guides through narrow slots. They could hear the wind howl through the gaps. It was unbearably hot.

"Thank goodness this stone stays so cool," said Rocket. They sat and waited, wondering what would happen next, straining every sense.

I'm trapped. I've always been trapped. Jill looked at the other two. *They're just the people in the Village. Rocket keeps telling me what to do, and Kyle's a pain.* A voice inside her head, distant but clear, seemed to be calling out, shouting sometimes, then whispering, "Lies, lies, they always lie." Nausea began to return. *What's with this?* The voice changed. "They always want something from you, then they leave you. They never keep their promises, they take and don't give." Jill felt tugged to the voice, but something was wrong about it, and she resisted.

A final click and the sails started to open out. They caught the breeze, and filled out, taking shape and tack. They started to spin like a horizontal windmill, each blade flat and taut. The stone moved up at once, slowly at first like an elevator, but it became clear that everything was gathering pace.

"Oh," Jill groaned, "Oh dear, Oh dear." Jill was worried as much by what was going on inside of her as what was happening outside.

Kyle, who had not cared much for Jill's health before, was suddenly very concerned. He was also completely unused to praying, but now found himself uttering urgent petitions under his breath, to whom he was not sure, ". . . And I'll be nice to her, just as long as I'm not scrubbing off this flying platform by the end of the trip." He finished muttering, opened one eye and checked Jill again. "Er, Rocket," Kyle tugged his shirt, "Jill doesn't look too good."

Rocket weighed up the situation and produced a flask that neither of them had seen before, and gave her a swig. It was bitter sweet, and stank like her uncle's breath in the evening, but seemed to settle her stomach a little. A strange flavoured lozenge was popped in her mouth and she was told to suck.

"It will relieve the pressure in your ears." And so it did, her ears popping with a satisfying thwack, which made her want to scratch inside her jawbone.

The sails slowly swelled out as the speed increased and they were soon flying upwards, like a galleon before a gale. Rocket stood and admired the view. To the south, all the terrain they had seen was coming back into view, until in the dim distance the suggestions of the Road near the hut could be seen. Mrs Lazybee's wood was a greenish-blue blur behind.

As Jill looked she remembered all that she and Rocket and Kyle had gone through; the way Rocket had saved her life, twice. For a moment, she clearly saw the Wayfarer's face. The voice in her head receded. *Rocket's helped me, like the Wayfarer has.* The nausea lessened still more. *Maybe I'm supposed to help the Kyle, even Rocket, like the Wayfarer's helped me.* The voice did not go away, but was very far off now, and Jill could ignore it if she concentrated.

Rocket turned to look to the north; green gave way to brown and to either side the blue of an ocean glimmered. From above, the shadows of huge rotating blades flickered across them and Kyle was looking concerned. "I think we're about to hit the top . . . very hard."

He need not have worried, the sails pulled back into blades and rotated against their original direction. They slowed. They stopped.

Invisible ropes lifted the stone clear of their sails, and the tube in which they were rising thickened out into the tail of a giant tear-drop. Shadows swept impressively over them. Rocket stared into the glare of the sun, squinting against the light.

"The air rushes up and away to drive the blades of a huge fan. It's still above our heads. Remarkable," he said, shading his eyes under his hand.

They were becalmed. It was still and cool here.

"Weird," said Kyle.

"Humph," said Jill. She stared at Kyle. *Perhaps he might need a break. Maybe that's my purpose.*

"I see you two are feeling like your usual selves again," said Rocket.

They had reached the great spinning blades and the air outside the tear-drop surged past the fan and tumbled out into the freezing cold air. This made a plume of cloud, billowing up like steam pouring from a kettle.

Out of the grey heights of the cloud, lightning struck the spire. A rumble of thunder accompanied their arrival in the centre of the tear-drop; the stone circle rose and fitted perfectly into the floor of a huge space. Rocket immediately started to explore. The room was about as wide as a house, circular, and was hollowed out of the huge tear drop shaped top of the tower. Only the floor was level, everything else was a continuous curve. There was the sound of running water as drinking fountains bubbled gently and the room was filled with a haze of bright light. Rocket started scurrying around, peering, inspecting. Jill looked around. She decided she liked the light. The distant voice went; the nausea went; and peace settled over her. She sat, smiling.

Kyle fidgeted. He twitched. He rose and started to pace around. He had enjoyed the ride up, but he was now upset. He could hear hissing. He could hear whispering. He was sure that somehow it was his fault.

"What is it with this light?" Kyle said.

"It makes my eyes sting, but it's wonderful," Jill sighed, "And I don't want to leave. Sort of makes things clearer."

"Fascinating, old boy, just fascinating," said Rocket. He was staring at amber and scarlet writing, in no language Jill had ever seen.

"What?" spat Kyle, still pacing on the stone.

"The writing tells of how this is an observation platform, a place to gather power and a place to send it out."

Jill said, "I thought you didn't like understanding things that you couldn't read?"

"Go on, tell us anyhow, I know you're just bursting to," said Kyle and started to shiver. He sat down on the stone again, dropping heavily, as Jill rose to join Rocket.

Rocket ignored his tone and delightedly read. "It says that the light, the fiery wind, and the storm all energise the top of the tower, which beams power down that shaft we came up. It also lists places that it beams light straight to." He pointed to a series of symbols around the room. "There are pictures of all the locations on the wall. If they're glowing they're working, but others, it seems," he wrinkled his nose in concentration, " are 'offline.'"

Jill and Rocket inspected the walls. There were pictures, woven in coloured glass, of places they had already been. Below these, strange looking scientific instruments were formed out of the transparent wall.

"Here's the Lodge," said Jill.

"I've found the Lookout and two other Vantage Points," said Rocket, "They're all lit."

"This one isn't," said Jill, "And it looks like Lord Bygone's to me. Maybe this has something to do with what the Wayfarer wants me to do here. How do you get it to turn on?"

Rocket hurried over. Kyle, still sitting, turned his back to them.

Jill reached up and touched the cool, raised amber lines of the Mansion with her fingertips.

The glass in front of her nose dissolved and a keyhole formed. She slipped out the large iron key from around her neck and placed it in the hole. Jill had to lean on the key to make it go in properly, and as she did so, the glass recoiled to form an oval doorway, and Jill stumbled and fell through it.

She was in a side room. The wind tousled her hair. The cold air was blasting in gusts from an opening in the outer wall, and before that was something Jill took to be a glass tree.

"Curious," said Rocket, "Looks like a search light growing from the floor."

What looked like a glass sculpture of a vine was wrapped

around a crystal cylinder. Jill walked toward it.

Several things happened at once. The key around Jill's neck jumped, being pulled out toward the twisted glass, and at the same time a huge dark shadow flashed past Jill's line of sight. "I want to go down," said Kyle, very loudly in an odd voice.

Both Jill and Rocket turned to face him.

Now Kyle looked grey.

Kyle looked very grey, and seemed to shimmer slightly.

The Sword was humming.

Jill closed her eyes. "Wayfarer, I don't want to use the Sword on him. He's a friend. Please, come now, we need you."

The mist was thickening over Kyle and he started to moan, "It isn't true, but I can't get their lies away. Can't get away, it's too much." His eyes were closed. Sweat trickled down his face. "Oh, it hurts!"

Both Jill and Rocket had seen too much to go near him at this moment.

"What's happening?" whispered Jill to Rocket.

"I was hoping that you could tell me," hissed Rocket, "but my guess is that the intensity of light is affecting him."

A horrible scream shook the tower.

Jill looked up to see a huge ragged bat-like thing flying back into the cloud. "A dragon!" she yelled.

"Don't be hysterical, there's no such thing," said Rocket. "You can't see anything clearly through these walls anyway."

For a second, Jill began to raise her hand to slap him, but hesitated.

"I want to go, I want TO GO!" Kyle's moan turned into a shout.

"If there was a dragon," said Jill, forcing herself to speak evenly, and pointing her upraised hand and finger at Rocket, "it might be causing Kyle's problems. He's only been like this near crows and I can't see anything like that up here except for that . . . that black thing."

The tower shook again as something dark and ragged covered

its top. Jill reached for the Sword; however, before she could draw it, lightning struck the black shape and it fell off screeching.

Jill felt the key twist toward the glass device.

"Let's get on with the job while we still can," said Jill. She turned back and let herself be pulled over to the glass sculpture in the middle of the floor, and saw a small piece of brass metal fitted to its side. It bore the indent of a key — of her key, which was being drawn like a magnet to the metal.

Jill heard Rocket drawn his sheath knife and she could hear him telling someone to calm down. There was fear in his voice. Jill looked up.

Kyle was walking toward them. His expression was blank and a mist was billowing over his face. He had ice in his hand.

"Rocket, don't hurt him!" Jill shouted. She fell as the Tower quivered under another blow.

They both backed away from Kyle, unsure what to do. Jill instinctively reached out behind and laid her hand on the outer wall.

Singing entered her head.

Jill pulled her hand back as if she had been burnt: it stopped.

Kyle was still coming.

She tried touching the wall again.

It was definitely the same song as the Road, but it was loud, so loud. The light she could see in the air pulsated to it as she touched the wall.

"Rocket, I can hear the Road here."

"What? What are you talking about?"

"The song I heard at the house. I hear it when I touch the wall."

"I WANT TO GO DOWN, NOW!" howled Kyle.

"Well, sing it, Jill," her older companion urged.

Jill looked at the Sword. "Sing" glowed on the hilt.

"Okay, okay," she muttered. Jill swallowed hard, laid her hands on the wall behind and closed her eyes.

The stream of power lit her mind like fireworks. It drowned her angers and struggles. She hesitated for a moment, wavering on the edge. The songs and words surged through her; she dove into the cataract. Jill opened her mouth and let the words fill it. Jill started to sing.

Kyle reacted immediately. He raised the ice up in both hands. Screaming, he rushed at her.

"No more," said Jill quietly.

Kyle dropped to the floor at her feet, as if dead. Her mind stood panting; she had pulled herself out of the song. "I've killed him," she thought. But the song rose in her heart, louder than her fear and she heard, "Tell the lies to leave." Her mind recoiled, "How can you do that?"

The words came again, and she decided to trust them.

"He doesn't belong to you, leave him alone."

There was a scream of rage from outside, and smoke and burning howled in through the window. Rocket had his eyes closed, and was shaking like a leaf. "There's no such things as dragons. There's no such things as dragons," he muttered over and over again.

The greyness stood back from Kyle's head, like silk in a gale.

Jill's voice rose in a command, "Lies, leave now and never return!"

The threads snapped and the grey mist shot back and out of the glass into the sky. Kyle slumped flat onto the floor. There was a crack of thunder and another bright flash and the sound of screaming from outside started to diminish. The flapping of great wings could be heard moving away. Jill allowed herself to look around, and saw something black slide into the bank of clouds.

Rocket opened his eyes. He rushed over to Kyle. The boy was asleep, smiling. Nothing, however, could induce him to wake up. Rocket shook him uselessly and Kyle simply mumbled something about leaving the light on when he went to bed. He started to snore.

"Jill he's asleep again! We need to wake him!" Rocket's voice rising in alarm.

"I don't think it's a problem this time. I think it's the right kind of sleep."

Jill took the key from around her neck and walked over to the glass tree. "And I think you go in here," she said. The key pulled itself out of her hand and clicked into the brass. Light flowed inside the glass from the vine's roots up, twisting and swirling like smoke. As it did so, there were creaks and groans and all sorts if high pitched sounds. The glass started to move. The cylindrical crystal, that Jill had thought was a barrel, was lifted up on two glass boughs, like the fingers of a hand, and it was pointed through the open window. Light streamed out of it. There was a clicking, a sort of crackling noise and then all movement stopped. Light filled the room. A tinkling noise told Jill that the key had dropped onto the floor, so Jill picked it up and slipped it back on.

"So it needed the key to know where to point," said Rocket. "What now?"

Jill yawned. "I don't know about you, but I can hear a lullaby at the moment." She slipped down the smooth wall and sat on the floor. "I think I might," she yawned deeply again, "just take forty winks." Jill was starting to slur her words, "just for a . . . oh dear me, for a few minutes." She slipped sideways, placed her head on her hands, and fell sound asleep.

Rocket looked up and around, trying to work out what to do. He rose to look out of the window, and found a timer built into the wall. As he bent down to examine it, he decided to try to set it and found luminous letters instructing him in exactly what to do. He proceeded part way, and then realised that he had stopped, but could not remember why. He nodded forward, and woke again as his head bumped the glass wall. He shook his head and finished setting the timer. He turned around. The other two were happily snoring. He smiled, and then in spite of himself, fell asleep.

Jill woke up in a state of extreme happiness. The light was certainly strong but no longer made her eyes sting. She sat up. It felt as if she had slept for a thousand years, but had woken at the right time of morning, without that heavy feeling of cotton wool between the ears that 'sleeping-in' can produce.

"Rocket, how are you?" Rocket answered by waking, opening his eyes and smiling. He un-slumped himself. Kyle stirred, but rolled over and went back to sleep.

"Well, it seems some things don't change," said Rocket, and checked the timer. "Only three hours. And what a sleep for three hours! I had such dreams too, all jumbled up, but all making sense."

"I think I dreamt of dancers, or dancing or singing or something like that. Everything was twisting together without tangling up in knots," said Jill.

"Hmpherity talsss in twent mmmin . . . uh," said Kyle, then started to snore.

Jill started to laugh, the first real laugh since she had met Rocket. She started giggling and soon Rocket was laughing too, uncontrollable, senseless laughing. When her sides hurt too much, she stopped. Kyle then rolled over again, and Rocket started giggling, which set Jill off again.

It took a good half an hour of this before Kyle woke up, and the first effects of his sleep in this room of light immediately became obvious. He started to laugh with them. Eventually, they all stood up and moved to the main chamber, where they found windows that looked north.

The valley, which was marked "here be dragons" on their map, lay spread out before them. Everything was picked out in fine detail.

"Look at that. You can see the whole world!" exclaimed Kyle.

They could clearly see a detour, far around to the east. In fact, that route disappeared out of sight into a far horizon, even from this height. The straightforward route ran into fog. Jill decided to find out more about the fog, so she started to examine the equipment built into the walls.

There were a series of lenses, stretched undulating things, forming part of the wall, and layered one in front of each other. Jill sat and stared at the strange symbols around it.

After a while she read, "Sit and stare, and you shall see what and where." So Jill sat and looked at the convoluted layers of glass. Initially all she could see were warped fields of colour, like looking through the bottom of a thick glass. But glancing round, she caught a clear image out of the corner of her eye. It took at least another fifteen minutes before she had reclaimed that glimpse. If she placed her head at the right place and looked in the correct direction, it became like looking through a telescope. This was quite a hard trick to perfect. She tried looking straight ahead, as if she was looking into binoculars instead. Another view of another place appeared.

Eventually Jill found the fog. She noticed the way it swirled, and details that she had not seen when walking through it; peculiar patterns and colours appeared before her eyes. Then a knowing grew within her that inside the dulling confusion something hated her. Pure rage, distilled and methodical, flowed up to her. Jill broke her gaze.

Jill looked at something else. The other route through the twisted lands to the west confirmed her suspicions. She could see the terrain in great detail; the unnatural crows roosted in angry groups and it was stiff, not only with bands of ragged soldiers, but also with part ruined houses where these people lived. One house was much bigger than the rest. "The Questionable House I suppose," Jill said to herself, and the word "Headquarters" came to her. The Road, or at least part of it, ran through the middle of the enemy's soldiers. She could feel their minds there too. She could feel arms and hands raised against her, pushing her away to . . . anywhere but there. Jill suddenly recognised the emotion they seemed to be trying to hide; it was fear. Were they afraid of her?

She sat back, exhausted and concerned. What was Rocket doing? She looked around and found that Rocket and Kyle were engaged with other devices. Rocket had flexible glass tubes in his ears and was looking at some sort of map, which overlaid the view. Kyle had his hands placed on two glass spheres and his eyes tight shut. The view was pretty and Jill felt no hurry to do anything, certainly not to disturb her friends.

Jill found a door and opened it, out onto a balcony. The wind whistled past and she decided to take a stroll outside. She wandered out and felt as if she was standing in half a wineglass. Jill looked down. Curiously, the dizzying sickness was gone. Now she came to think about it, her exhaustion had fled too.

The wind was icy; light warmed her from above. So this was what it was like to see things from an angel's back. All creation seemed stretched out before her, but everything was too far away to see what it was. Not as much help as she had thought. Even the living maps they had only told them so much, the rest had to be figured out as they went. "I wonder if everything we do is like that?" she thought.

She wandered back and got a drink from the fountains. Rocket had finished examining the instruments and had taken copious notes of everything. Kyle still had his eyes tightly shut.

"What did you find out Rocket?" Jill asked.

"I had a most remarkable view of history, or at least parts of history that had lodged in the view," he said, very matter-of-factly.

"What?" Jill stared at him and saw his eyebrows arch. "Sorry, err. Pardon me," Jill said with a smile, "But that sounds strange."

"Well, I'll tell you, since you've asked so nicely." Rocket stared into the distance, and then suddenly fixed Jill with his eye. "I looked at things, and then over the top, images of what had happened in the past all popped up. There were some maps of time too."

Jill looked confused, but said, "What did you see? Battles? Bits of the Road that are hidden? How it was built?"

"My dear girl, you're beginning to sound like Kyle," said Rocket.

Jill pouted.

"I didn't mean it, but look here, I have it all noted down. One thing that you might be interested in is that the military gentleman used to be a herald for the Lord of the Way."

"What's a herald?"

"He goes in front, blows a trumpet and declares the king's about to arrive, acts as a messenger too. What do you learn in school?"

"Whatever the teacher can squeeze in; in between riots," said Jill, and giggled as Rocket's jaw dropped.

"Shall we disturb Kyle?" said Jill, changing the subject.

Kyle was blissfully swaying from side to side, and as they walked over to him, he did not flinch.

"Ahem," said Rocket.

Jill hummed loudly.

There was no response.

Rocket spoke more loudly, "I say, is it good, your apparatus?"

Kyle had flicker of recognition, but then returned to blissful ignorance.

"Wake up, Kyle, time to get up," said Jill tapping his shoulder. Nothing.

Rocket shook him, and Jill took the opportunity to stand on his toes a little harder than necessary, although she did feel a little sorry this time.

Kyle swayed a little uncertainly.

"Doesn't seem sensible to us," said Rocket, "Perhaps a different approach?" Rocket lifted Kyle's hands off the glass globes.

Kyle appeared very relaxed, but immediately frowned. He opened his eyes and stumbled back slightly.

"Uhh, what did you do that for? I was just listening to a little wood." Kyle bent over as if his head was spinning.

"Pardon?" said Rocket.

"It was like, you could hear everything," said Kyle, "I started off listening to some crows. They sounded pitiful, so I tuned the globes to listen to some travellers. I heard some things like we can normally, and some things like we can never hear."

"Like what?" said Jill.

"I could hear the wind rush past clouds, water surging through rocks underground, and ants scurrying in an ant hill, and . . . and . . ."

"Go on dear boy."

"I think I even heard the grass grow."

Rocket managed to keep his eyebrows on his head.

"I was listening to some walkers on the Road, and I tuned to hear their boots crunch, it sounded so . . . so . . ."

"Earthy?" asked Jill.

"No, like breakfast cereal crackling. Anyway, my hand slipped and tuned into what was beneath the Road. I heard what Jill was singing that other day; it was amazing. I heard all sorts of stuff," tears stood in his eyes. "I could hear the songs flowing out from here. It goes all sorts of places. It ends up in the air and water, even in the plants. I was listening to some big old trees when you, well, brought me back," Kyle was beginning to straighten up now, "It was so cool though, they sounded so strong, so alive, like you could depend on them. I wish you hadn't woken me."

"Sorry old boy, but we were finished up here I think."

Jill nodded her agreement.

"Okay, so how do we get down?" asked Kyle.

"I think we should try this," said Jill and stepped off the glass onto the edge of the sandstone disk.

Around the rim, the letters lit up once more.

"Come on," she waved her hands and the other two stepped onto the edge.

Nothing happened.

Jill stepped forward.

The disk lit up further in.

"Oh I see," said Rocket, and strode toward the centre. The disk lit up fully and slowly started to sink. They all gathered in the centre, sitting down, back to back.

"I'd like to come back again," said Kyle.

"Do you remember what happened when you . . ." Jill stopped as Rocket nudged her in the small of her back.

"It's all right," he said to Rocket. "Actually, I do Jill, but I don't think it will be a problem again," said Kyle, "I think I've woken up for good this time." He flashed a grin of intense happiness.

Except when the watchers spotted something of interest in the panorama around them, they said little else. Mechanical wings whirling, wind whispering and howling, air hot and stone cold; they plummeted to the earth below.

The ropes dropped them into their place and returned upwards. The friends walked off their transport and as they did, a crackling of burning dust told them the power had returned.

The Steward appeared.

"Did you find what you were looking for?" he asked.

"I think so," Jill replied, "and some more, I think."

"It clears your mind up there," said Kyle, "something 'bout the wind being so clean," he said, looking up.

"You speak more than you know," said the Steward, "can I help in any other way?"

"Yes," said Kyle "What's the best way to carry guavas? Umph."

He said 'Umph' because both Jill and Rocket were conveniently positioned and had both elbowed his ribs. "Will you guys stop that? I was only joking. Anyway, I thought you were on my side. I was going to ask another question."

Everyone stopped and looked at Kyle.

"Okay, I'm getting there," he gathered his dignity and addressed the Steward once more.

"I could hear a song in the Road, but it came from up there. It…err . . . helped clear my mind, if you know what I mean?"

"Yes I do. Come with me," said the Steward, who seemed even more unfamiliar with the rules of conversation than before. He turned around walked toward the steps. The travellers exchanged glances, and Jill shrugged her shoulders. They started to follow.

He led them over to the steps and disappeared into the ground. The friends stomped down a spiral staircase, expecting cold air and damp dark places. Instead, hot dry air struck up from where yellow-white shadows danced. They reached the bottom and saw the Steward step through a brilliantly lit arch. "These," he said as they caught up with him, "are the Furnaces of Light."

Before them stood three bottle-shaped structures, each about the size of a garage, from which light blazed from small open doorways. Some rather sweaty looking men were throwing sand and dirt in with shovels. It turned into sparks as it flew around.

"What are you making?" said Rocket, "Glass?"

"No, something far more transparent, the Truth," the Steward replied.

"How can you do that?" Kyle said, shielding his eyes.

"The light carries the song that you heard and we mix it with the earth, so that it doesn't just fly back into space. From here it becomes something that ordinary people can hear, something that can go into the Road."

Kyle became excited. "So from here the song gets blasted into the earth and is sent out into the Road, and from the Road into the air and the trees and water."

"And into everything that can or wants to receive it," finished the Steward. "It strengthens the Road, empowers those who travel it."

"You mean that an angel's song is no use until it's brought down and mixed with ordinary stuff?" said Jill.

The Steward gave her an intrigued smile. "That's not how I would have put it, but that is not far from reality. Please," he bowed and gestured, "this way."

They continued to play the game of 'follow-my-leader', Jill first, then Kyle and then an ever-watchful Rocket bringing up the rear. They came to a small brightly lit stairwell that led up to a stone amphitheatre, surrounded by palms under the glass roof.

"This is where I adjust the light we send out from the tower without mixing with the earth. One beam always alights on the Lodge. I think you've been there?"

"Yes. Is that why it always extra bright there?' asked Rocket, "in the Living Library, anyway."

"It is. Excuse me, I have something to attend to."

He stood still and held out his hand to the spire, as if trying to feel the rays of the sun.

He glowed bright, and shone. The friends fell back in fear. For a few seconds he disappeared, then reappeared, walking back to them through some invisible doorway. He examined their startled faces.

"Oh excuse me, I thought that you understood. There isn't always a lot of difference between me and light that flows through here."

"Is that why I recognise you?" said Jill. "I haven't seen you before, but there *is* something about you . . ."

"Yes, I have followed your journey with much interest," said the Steward, "It's been a pleasure accompanying you, most of the time."

"I think I need to sit down," said Rocket, as he slumped onto the stone steps of the amphitheatre. He held his head in his hands. Jill asked him if he had a headache, and started to ask the steward for a painkiller and some water.

"No, I haven't got a headache, not yet. I *was* enjoying all this. But how can someone be thoughts, or truth, or light?"

"What is Truth?" said the Steward.

"That's my question," said Rocket, "And I'd thank you not to steal it."

The Steward stopped for a second, looking at him patiently. "All right. What do you think is Truth?"

"There is no such thing," said Rocket, "It's just opinions, no one really knows."

"What if there is always one opinion that is correct, amongst all of them? In a universe as vast as this, there might just be a correct opinion somewhere."

"Well, I suppose that might be so," said Rocket, irritably knocking Jill's hand off his shoulder.

"What if there was someone who had access to all that could be seen, to all those opinions and compared them? What if there was someone who could see all that is under the light?" The Steward's words were gentle but persistent.

"Well, I suppose, then he would always be right, but no-one can see all that," Rocket was not as aggressive as before.

"Then that one's opinion would always be true. Could you call that person the Truth?" the Steward asked.

"Yes, I suppose this imaginary person could be called the Truth."

"Look at me," came words that could not be easily disobeyed. The Steward blazed. "Who wrote your life in the books of the

Living Library? Who watched you on the Vantage Point and persuaded Jill to dislodge you? Who showed you secrets, but has withheld what would harm you? Who gave you aid against the lies? The crows? The Ragged Soldiers? Who lets the Sword flow with power? Now go! Face your destiny and remember me."

He was shining, and just as the light obscured every feature, it faded and he was no longer there.

"I knew I should've asked him how to carry the most guavas," said Kyle. The others looked at him. "Oh come on, I mean, he *must* know."

They left the tower, Kyle laden with fruit. He had asked this time. The men by the furnaces (who said they were volunteers) said they thought it was all right, but Kyle still stood in the middle of the amphitheatre and bellowed, "If it's okay, I'll have about five kilos." They took the silence as permission.

In no time at all, they reached the open Road again.

"What's a destiny?" said Kyle.

"I think we're about to find out," said Jill.

17

———

RAISING THE BLOCKADE

The group had checked their maps, set their course and arrived at the valley. Where was the viaduct? Lord Bygone's maps said it should be there. The travellers fell to arguing and split, one group went straight ahead, one to the left. They had no living maps, no living books and had not wanted to stop at the Tower of Fire and Light, and now they were about to discover at first-hand what lay in wait.

"Come on Jill, sleepy head, time to get moving."

Kyle was up early she thought. *How come he's this cheerful?* Kyle hadn't wiped that smile off his face all day yesterday, and was persisting in being his new, abnormal self.

Jill stuck her head out of the tent. The sky was barely lightening, and this was now high summer. *Ugh! It must be the middle of the night still!*

"It's going to be a beautiful day. Fancy a guava?" Kyle beamed. She was glad that Kyle was so much happier; she just hoped that she would be able to cope with his new disposition.

Breakfast came and went with Kyle cracking jokes. They packed

282

up the tents while he whistled. He was even in tune. They made sure that all their rucksacks were in place, and the equipment was secure, while Kyle kept saying, "What a beautiful day." Rocket was bleary-eyed and the sun had not yet risen.

"I say, old boy, could we listen to the dawn chorus?" Rocket said, "Only, I do so enjoy the song of the birds. It stirs me, sets me up for the day. It is especially good when heard in silence. No offence, I hope, it's just I do so enjoy it."

Kyle wavered for a second, then said, "I understand. You like birds 'n things like that. It's a great sound." He kept smiling. They walked with only the birds and the squeak of boots and packs, much to Jill and Rocket's relief.

Stopping for a break, Jill quietly caught Rocket while Kyle filled his canteen by the stream. "Is he all right? I've never seen him act so strangely, it's giving me the creeps."

"I know what you mean," Rocket said, "but I think we might just be beginning to see the real Kyle show through."

Jill groaned, "I'm not sure I can take much more of this."

"Don't worry, I'm sure he'll relapse occasionally, but don't begrudge him a little joy in his life."

"I'll try," she said, tightened her belt and straightened her hat.

The beaming boy reappeared up the bank, "Have you ever noticed how good this stuff tastes?" he said holding up a full bottle of water.

Rocket and Jill looked at each other, but said nothing. It was going to be a long day.

The march went well. Kyle shot a game bird, which the small brown notebook identified as mountain grouse. In the evening, he cooked, cleaned and served a delicious stew, and even Jill concluded that there were some compensations to his new attitude.

Kyle rose early again the next day, but by this time, his cheerfulness was becoming infectious. Rocket appeared bright and early and even Jill rose and entered into the spirit of the day.

The tower of Fire and Light could still be seen in the distance at dawn and dusk, and the next two days were gloriously hot. The number of crows started to increase, but stayed high and wide off the Road.

By the middle of the morning of the third day, they found themselves looking out over a cliff. The Road switched back and forth down the near-rock face and the three paths diverged below, converging again on the opposite side of the valley and then climbing the cliffs facing them, several miles away.

"Even in this sunshine, that fog persists in the hollow," said Rocket.

"It looks black in there," Kyle commented. "It must go deeper than we thought."

"Let's avoid it then, if you want. If we descend the cliff path, then turn right, we can climb back out of the valley and be heading east up to the moorland quite quickly. The great way 'round is waiting for us," said Jill, "if we're certain that's the way to go."

"What do you mean?" said Rocket.

"Well, I'm still not sure. We're meant to lift the blockade aren't we? I don't like being bullied away from where I'm supposed to be and it could take weeks going the long way around. It would only be an afternoon's walk to cross by the central path."

"We'll go east, the long way around, and be safe," said Rocket.

It was surprisingly easy walking down the switchbacked Road, and cool in the shadow of the cliffs. Jill said the walk reminded her of last summer and her holiday with her Mum.

"Uh, wish I'd been able to go on holiday with my Mum," said Kyle, and he walked alongside Jill. Neither of them said any more.

They arrived at the base without incident.

"Those crows are loud," Rocket said in a flat tone, as he stared into the distance. Jill thought that if he had a pipe, he would be chewing it. She smiled at him and then spoke up.

"I hope they don't want a fight," she said, squinting in the light, "it'll spoil a good afternoon." Even as she said so, her stomach was knotting up, although she had no idea why.

They tracked up the hillside heading east, the path leaving the parting of the ways, and slanting up the slope. It slowly regained the height just lost. This was in the full glare of the sun, and hot work. They reached a Vantage Point; a sun-bleached stone platform covered with lichen, just to one side of the Road.

"My turn," Jill said, and slipped off her backpack and boots, standing upright and bare-toed on the comfortably hot rock. She traced her big toe across the rough surface.

Without warning fire curled up around her legs, but didn't burn. Shafts of light broke out of the alive letters dancing on the paving. She was immediately somewhere else. Jill was now seeing more than she ever wanted, and seemed to have no control over where or what she was observing. The world around her faded and she had the strangest feeling that she was plunging down from the high diving board at the Town swimming pool.

Fog. Thick, curling, choking fog. It covered her, and chilled her to the bone. She was moving quickly, almost like a sparrow — flitting, swooping, turning. She could see nothing except broken paving beneath her. Now she was not a sparrow flying, but a stumbling runner, breathing hard and unafraid. Jill could hear something, someone ahead. She had to reach them before it was too late. She could see the light of a weak lamp ahead and hear three voices. Blackness loomed before her, and she stopped. The voices seemed to be off the Road now, to her right, how could she reach them? The voices stopped talking and the muffled sound of a huge door could be heard slamming.

Without warning, Jill was rising up, moving through the mists and bursting into the light. She was suspended over the valley, over the fog they had seen earlier. Moving now, slowly at first, then the rush of wind past her face. She was being hurled as if caught by the hairs of her head. Faster and faster she flew until she could see the Vantage Point. She could see an empty platform on fire, the letters dancing. Closer, faster, nearer and nearer. No, too fast. She would hit it and she was still speeding up.

Rocket watched with some alarm as Jill shot backward out of the fire and landed on her bottom in a small cloud of dust.

"Are you hurt, my dear?" he asked.

"No, but we've got to rescue some friends," Jill was almost breathless, "now, no time to waste."

"Who? What happened?" Kyle said.

Kyle and Rocket had watched with alarm as the fire had almost engulfed her, but had not been able to decide what to do. Jill had stood unmoved, unaffected, so they had not interfered, until she seemed to be thrown backwards off the stone. The violence that ended her vision left Kyle a little shaken.

"We need to go now. I recognised some of their voices," Jill panted, "in the fog, lost, trapped. I could feel them, they're losing their minds in there, their lives too if we don't act now."

"What can we do?" protested Kyle.

"We survived the fog before, for most of a day, I think we could do it again," Rocket replied. "Who are they, my dear?"

"They're the group that left the House the day before we did. I heard three voices, two gardeners and a maid. I think one might be Sye."

"There were seven in that group," Kyle added, "I wonder where the rest are?" He stared back over the valley scanning for signs of life.

"No time to lose. We need to go now," Jill was still out of breath from her vision, but was lacing up her boots as they spoke. They shouldered their loads and started to run. The men found that they had to run hard to keep up with Jill. She hopped precariously from rock to rock, even though the path was uneven and difficult to traverse. Jill almost turned her ankle several times.

They reached the base of the cliff in quick time, and immediately turned down the central path. Rocket was taking it the hardest, but they were all sweating in the midday sun as they headed to the mist. Regular exercise can transform your strength, and whereas they would have all found running for half an hour impossible three weeks before, now they ran hard for forty minutes before they reached the fog bank.

They pulled out lamps and attached them to their staves. A brief flurry of activity; lamps on, blades out and Jill checking, "All ready?" They entered in.

The beads of sweat cooled on their arms and head. They became cold and Jill sneezed. Rocket shivered. "Keep moving old girl," he said as he took the lead, "we'll keep warm that way."

The letters in the bark of the staves glowed brightly in the lamplight and Kyle thought he could begin to read some meaning in them.

"Though the way be broken, watch ahead, not below," he mused. He was following up the rear, "dumpty dumpt dumpt, up it will be flung, dumpty dump dump dump, raised never to return."

"Keep up, old chap. Watch this Road, it's all broken."

"No, watch ahead," Kyle shouted and sprinted over the broken and churned slabs. "Read the words on the staffs! Look ahead!" he called over his shoulder as he flew past his friends.

The other two quickly followed, trusting and running as hard as they could. None of them stumbled once. The Road turned down hill, into a hollow, the air becoming icy as they become hot once more. The pounding of feet marked their descent into the grey, and Jill noticed something ahead.

"Watch out for the blackness!" Kyle slid to a halt. There was a huge rock wall in front of him, crossing the Road. It did not touch the Road at any point, but seemed suspended above the ground just high enough to slide his boot underneath. Kyle set his lamp on the ground and struck the wall with his staff. The blast knocked him to the ground, but hardly dented the black mass in front of him. He stood up disorientated and partly outside the dome of light from his lamp. Jill arrived first and guided him back to safety.

"Will it move?" she asked.

"Move? I don't know. Not if we can't blast it, I guess . . ." Kyle looked at the staff. "Of course, that's what it was saying. Thanks." Kyle held up his walking stick and peered at the glowing letters.

"Though the way be broken, watch ahead, not below,
Use the staff on which these letters glow,
Extend your strength beneath and up it will be flung,
This blockade will be raised, never to return."

Rocket had caught up and was searching the wall to either side.

He returned panting. "It's secured by thick buttresses, and it's thicker at the top than at the bottom, as if it was an upside down bridge or something. There's also a door to our right, tight shut with no handle."

"That must be where I heard those three disappear, and the door slam," Jill frowned, "What do you mean about the wall being an upside down bridge?"

"If it was a bridge carrying its own weight, you might expect it to be thicker and stronger across the bottom to hold the weight of the stones above. This is the other way around, almost if the higher stones are holding the rest of the wall down, not up."

Kyle stepped back staring at the stick, and then looked up, muttering the words to himself. He fell backwards, over a large broken stone.

"That's it! How do I do this?" He placed the staff on a notch in the stone and angled it to point at the bottom of the wall, "Extend, er lengthen, er —"

"What is it old boy?"

"The wall is needs to hold itself down, because the Road is pushing it up. It's being repelled by the Road, just like the crows and the wolves and everything else that hates it. We've got to get the staves under the wall and lever it up," Kyle was frantically trying any command he could think of.

Jill leaned over and touched the staff, "I believe it," she said.

The walking stick shot out becoming three times as long, and wedged under the front of the wall.

"Help me," said Kyle and all three placed their weight on the far end of what looked like a spindly seesaw. There were slight cracking noises from the wall, the pole bending to the ground, sweat breaking out with grunts and gasps. But the wall did not move.

"Let's try mine," Jill said, Rocket unhooked his lamp to do the same. Soon three walking sticks extended under the wall. They leant on the levers, and this time it was the wall that groaned.

"The wall's got to give with all of us," said Kyle.

"Yeah," panted Jill, "Be removed. Now!"

There was a wrenching, crashing sound. Blocks of dark stone flew up. The three friends fell headlong and lay completely still as they listened to black basalt returning to earth. None of it struck the Road, but they had a very nervous thirty seconds.

"Right, let's go," said Kyle, and they moved through the gap.

Jill gasped, "This Sword's alive again and it's taking me off the Road."

The party moved down the bank through a ditch and dry scrub. The ground was dusty, in spite of the constant damp of the cloud.

Within a minute of wading through dead bushes, they came across a path.

"What's this, coal?" asked Kyle, picking up a piece of the gravel they were now walking on.

"Already part burnt, if it is," said Rocket, crumbling some in his hands.

"We have to go further down this path," said Jill. "And careful of any attacks, we don't know how the weapons will hold up off the Road. Listen for voices."

They started to trot down the Road.

"Stop," whispered Kyle Williams, "hhhsh." They stood still for a second.

Vague sounds could be heard ahead, muffled words rolled through the blank whiteness. They started to run. Words broke on them, words full of fear. Light showed through the mist, and they sped up.

There was an angry sound that they had heard in the fog before. It ripped the air in two. They stopped and listened.

"What was that?" panted Kyle, "It certainly sounded big and mean."

"That is our 'not-a-dragon'," said Jill, "We've already met it, when you were a little distracted. I hope it's not our destiny." She was crouching low and speaking gently.

"It will be for our friends, if we don't hurry. Assuming of course that it *is* a dragon." said Rocket.

"Are we ready? Make sure you've got all you need," said Jill.

They checked their equipment, put everything in place and moved forward, jogging with sword points first.

They found their friends dressed in their old-fashioned garb, wandering back and forth across the sooty gravel.

"Where am I?" said the maid. Jill recognised the sweet old lady. "Where's the Road gone? I followed the friendly voice through the door, but I can't hear him now."

"We need to go back, but I think you're sropping me," the first man slurred. The burly gardener looked quite dangerous and was angry. "They don't slam doors on fren's. We mus' 'urn around." He glared at Jill. "'Ware attackers. Knives out my fren's." He finished his words with a bellow and lifted up a cruel-looking blade. Rocket knocked the weapon from his hands with a single sweep of the flat of his blade.

The second man's lamp had gone out completely. It was Sye. All he said was, "Whom am I, friend?" He sat down as they arrived.

"Get up, please," said Jill, pity in her voice. "You need to come with us."

"Where's the voice gone?" asked the maid.

"What voice?" said Kyle.

"It was with us until just before you arrived, my dear."

At that point, the sound they had heard before came again. It was an enraged roar, heartbroken and furious. It sounded very big.

"Where's it coming from?" said Jill.

"In front," said Kyle.

"Behind," said Rocket.

"Inside my head," said the befuddled gardener gruffly, who was still smarting from the blow to his hand. His eyes were closed in pained concentration, but all he could do was mutter.

Jill tried to steady him and asked, "What's inside your head? Please tell me." Rocket propped him up.

"I think I see something ahead," Kyle shouted. To Rocket and Jill's amazement he ran forward into the fog.

"Come back," Rocket shouted. He and Jill ran after him, leaving the confused folk to stagger around on their own.

Two shaggy heads, indistinct and smoky, rose up before Kyle.

He ran forward, underneath the towering black monstrosities. The necks seemed to be going up forever, twitching like snakes and rising from a single body as large as a bus. Low, crooked, lizard-like legs held up the front and the low body's hindquarters disappeared into the fog. What's more, it was almost impossible to fix your eyes on the beast, because something like scales kept falling off its black bulk, and as this cinder snow hit the ground, it came back up as thick mist.

"My word! A dragon. A real dragon," was all Rocket could say, slowing to a halt. He stood transfixed in the middle of the path. Jill ran past Rocket and so he saw what happened next better than anyone else. Jill was trying to catch and stop Kyle, but somehow Kyle had found wings for his feet. She could not catch him, and he was sprinting headlong, leaving her behind. She kept glancing up at the twin heads high above. It became evident the dragon was bigger than it had first appeared as Kyle seemed to shrink as as he got closer. He had not reached it yet. Maybe there was still time.

One head had seemed to see Kyle, but the other was fixed on Rocket. The beast seemed confused, and did not respond quickly.

"Get out of his head!" screamed Kyle, and swung his sword at the beast's breast, reaching as high as he could.

Kyle's blade shone as he struck, and blood poured out. The tip of his sword had just been able to catch the dragon where his breastbone turned under his belly. The blood stank, and he stumbled back coughing.

Kyle had got the dragon's attention. It focused on him, four eyes glaring down at him. As Kyle stumbled sideways, the dragon stretched out a front claw as if to stamp on him. It missed its mark. Instead, Kyle was pushed backward and flicked into a ditch.

Rocket came to his senses. He stepped forward, lowered his staff, and commanded the beast. "Away! Leave the boy! He is under the protection of the Lord of the Way." Although no visible lightning sprang from the stick, the dragon's scales twisted and buckled and streamed from him, black confetti driven before the wind. Kyle didn't move.

Rocket's words drew the dragon's hatred to him. It answered with blasts of dark smoke and heat from both its mouths. Rocket swayed. He screamed fierce commands for the dragon to leave. The dragon recoiled, roaring in pain, and counter-blasted. It took a second or two for Rocket to recover his feet this time and he was already beginning to sound tired. He fought to focus his words.

"Clear your head, old boy, come on now."

Rocket looked back.

The man sitting on the ground was weeping, unmoved by what was happening around him. The burly gardener, so aggressive before, was cowering in fear and confusion and the maid could not be seen.

Jill had stopped running as Kyle had reached the great beast. She stared, beginning to back away, caught in the open between Rocket and Kyle. The Sword still glowed in her hands.

"What should I do? What to do? What to do?" Jill whined out loud, fear stretching her voice. The sword hilt glowed, and words appeared in fire on the hilt. The flickering caught her eye. She read.

"Use the pommel not the blade,
Strike the ground, make it unmade,
For where he stands, he has no right,
Banish darkness from the realms of light."

"How on earth am I supposed to know what that means?" Jill shouted, "I need to know what to do now! Please! You helped before."

She gasped as thoughts burst from the Sword. Words and images ran like a wave up a beach. Calm streamed up her arm and enveloped her head. The Sword had showed her what to do.

Rocket was on one knee now, hoarse and struggling for breath. The dragon showed no signs of relenting, paying no attention to a young girl. The old scientist called out, but Jill did not hear what he said, it was lost in the roar of the beast. Jill ran in to where Kyle had stood, raised her sword as high over her head as she could. She brought it down with all her might, both her hands grasping the hilt.

She missed the dragon. The sword hilt slammed into the black rock as she threw herself flat. Light from the Sword grip flashed into the dust. She saw the terrible, rotten underbelly of the dragon as the pebbled path was lit from below ground by brilliant light. Dust and stones were thrown into the air and the ground started to shake. Jill lay still, driving the hilt into the black volcanic rock as hard as she could. Rocket fell over and struggled to get up again as thunder from the deep could be heard and felt. The heavens spoke back to the earth as lightning split the sky and froze the scene in white light from above and beneath.

The dragon looked up, using both heads to scan the sky, completely ignoring Jill. "He hasn't seen me. For the moment, anyway."

The split started to open under the dragon. An horrendous red light shone up from the fissure as it started to spread. Then the cracking stopped and, for a second, so did Jill's heart.

She lifted the Sword and drove it with both hands into the ground again. The ground shook and heaved. Rocks fell into the widening chasm. The dragon finally started to pay attention to its feet. Jill looked up to see two heads staring down, focussed on her. Anger smouldered in its hissing breath. She watched the fissure slowly grow.

"Come on, get it done," Jill hissed. She had never been more terrified on the outside or peaceful inside in all her life. The dragon lifted a heavy clawed foot, as if about to bring it down on Jill. It hung in the air, poised like some gigantic hammer. Jill heard Rocket shouting and the dragon roared with pain. Now her sense of peace became overwhelmed by the knotting in her guts.

Writing flickered and changed on the hilt. "Strike the earth again. Now!"

"Of course," muttered Jill and started to pound the ground frantically with her sword handle. The rock vibrated, the beast above swayed, its paw still raised. The earth started to open quickly. The split reached its back legs, and she glanced up to see scales being stripped from the dragon's neck as leaves in the wind.

"Keep him off balance, Rocket. I need more time," Jill yelled. She could still hear Rocket shouting himself hoarse, but only in snatches.

The pounding of the Sword was slowing now as Jill tired. The dragon's back feet were slipping into the widening crack, and it made one last attempt to steady itself. Jill felt pain sear her body as hot breath raked her from end to end.

Rocket watched in horror as the teetering beast started to bring the raised foot down, its claws extended like spear points. "No, NO!" he shouted, forgetting to point the staff in his hand. He fell sideways with the effort.

Jill stared up again, into her approaching doom. She cried out in fear and turned away, burying her face in the rough stones. Jill heard a screaming roar, the slithering of scales on stones and earth. There was a moment of silence, and then a familiar voice saying, "Are you okay?"

As she slowly realised that she was not dead, Jill found that she could not get up due to her shaking knees. The feeling that if she had not already lost her stomach, she was about to, kept her attention. She lay shivering for a long moment and then murmured, "I think so."

A boy's hand reached down and cradled her arm as tenderly as he could. He helped to her feet. She heard a voice pinched with pain say, "We got him, didn't we?"

Rocket had watched in disbelief as a smoke-wreathed figure came between Jill and the descending claws. It brought a sword scything across the dragon's paw. The dragon had pulled back immediately. Indeed, Rocket said afterwards that he saw at least two of the claws sliced off. Stumbling backwards, recoiling in agony, it found that it no longer had anywhere to stand. The dragon had fallen, sliding into the fiery light with one last, awful scream.

"Kyle, is that you?" Jill asked. A slightly crooked figure helped her up.

"Yeah, and my side hurts like crazy," he said.

They both stared into the pit.

"Let's find Rocket, and get the other three out of here," wheezed Kyle. The ground was still shaking as it began to heal over, closing out the light and heat from below. The fog was being sucked into the closing fissure, and more daylight was spilling through the mist every second. The three friends stumbled toward one another. They stood for a moment and checked each other's wounds. Kyle's head was bleeding and he permitted Jill to dress it. Bandages and moss from the provisions soon dealt with the gash, but Rocket insisted that he show him his side.

"I don't think he's broken a rib, but he's already starting to turn purple from the bruising. Let's get some ointment on it. We'll have to strap it to prevent it spreading." Jill wasn't sure this was the right thing to do, but they all agreed to proceed with Rocket's idea. Rocket gathered Lord Bygone's three travellers.

"I'm sorry, my lord, for inconveniencing you, but where are we?" asked the maid. The gardeners glanced nervously about.

"We're on the Road, the middle path of three ways across the valley, and we just fought a dragon," said Kyle.

"A dragon?!" Sye exclaimed.

"Yes," he said quite flatly, and pulled out a map, "we're just there where it says, 'Here be . . .'"

Their friend stared at the map, "Well, I can't remember much of the last few hours, and what I can is very odd. I do recall being helped in some way by your good selves, but after that, all of it's a blank."

The other gardener pushed forward to look over his shoulders.

"I do remember one thing. Our friends went westerly, and if we've nearly been eaten, what's happened to them?" He stuck a broad finger into the chart. "That westerly path winds through the bog and past that house," said the burly man, "Sye, do you still think you recognise it?"

Sye, although rather shaken, looked closely. "It certainly looks like the Questionable House, more so on this map than ours back at the Mansion," he said, "I've seen it in the history books. Our guides were not clear whether it still existed. It was the reason that I did not follow my kin down that path." Jill's friend turned pale. "By the Lord himself, I can see words appearing next to the picture! The more I look, the more I see . . . What is this devilry?"

"It's okay," said Kyle, "they're Living Books. They gave me the creeps too the first time I came across them."

"Excuse me, but you said 'Questionable House'?" asked Rocket.

"Yes, it was a place from which the Lord Bygone's ancestors once ventured forth, to help the inhabitants around-abouts, to get them to walk the Road. But it was captured by the ragged soldiers."

Rocket frowned, "Would it still be in their hands?"

"That's what this map says, 'Captured by the military gentleman,'" Sye replied.

"And that's what I saw from the Tower too. All his soldiers pushing me away from them. Uggh!" said Jill, shuddering. "As far as I could tell, it's their main base. They won't be putting out the welcome mat."

"Upon my word!" the maid said, "Jonathan's party went that way, what will become of them? They're walking into the enemy's lair."

Sye turned to Rocket. "Will you help them, sir? We will retrace our steps to go to their aid, whatever you decide. However, we could do with all the help we can get." He stood stiffly, steadily holding Rocket's gaze. Rocket extended his hand to Sye.

"We need to move quickly then," said Rocket as Sye grasped his hand and shook it.

"I'll need to take the lead in this pursuit," said Jill. "Are we all agreed?"

Kyle winced as he nodded, "I'll do my best, but I'm not sure

I'll be able to move as fast as you lot."

"Nor I", said the maid.

Jill turned to her. "What weapon can you wield: a knife, the bow, staff or sword?"

"With the wars at home I've learnt to use all of them in some manner, but I'll warrant I'm best off with a bow, at least if it's small . . ."

Kyle unslung his bow and quiver and handed it to her.

"We can use a rear guard," said Rocket. "With all this enemy attention, we might need someone to follow on behind and relieve us if we're in a spot. Do you think you might be able to accompany Kyle, my dear lady, and assist him?"

"I'm no lady, sir," the maid replied, chuckling, "but I will do my best."

They quickly organised. It turned out that the second gardener was called Frank, and he was the maid's brother. The group of friends that Frank and Sye wished to rescue was led by his best friend Jonathan, whose sister Frank hoped to marry. Frank was very keen to try Jill's sword himself, but she explained that this was not possible, and Frank relented only when Sye assured him that it was useless to argue with Jill.

Rocket and Jill took off at a run, working their way back to the Road, past the ruins of the blockade wall and up the hill. From this slight rise, the view down their new path was clear. In what seemed no time, they had turned west.

They streamed sweat and blew hard. The gardeners kept up well, but Jill could not help thinking that it was unfair to have to be doing the same thing again, never mind twice in one day. Still it would lift the blockade, if she stayed alive, and then she could get help for Mum. *She fought the nagging question, "Why me?"* by pushing it out an imaginary door in her head. It was hard to keep focussed on the effort of running with doubts pestering her.

She glanced over her shoulder to see the 'rear guard' crest the hill they were descending, at least a mile behind.

The weapons jingled and the Road resounded with the dull thuds of their feet. They were slowing, pounding the metaled surface with heavy feet.

Jill wiped the sting of sweat from her eyes.

They found themselves in the folds of jagged hills. The slopes were only the height of a house, and the valley the width of a street. The terrain had dropped down and the Road began to wind around outcrops of stone. Patches of bare rock showed through the turf, often forming small cliffs facing the Road. Several sets of eyes scanned the heights as they jogged around the natural fortifications, watching for any signs of soldiers. The valley twisted, never allowing more than a stone's throw of clear sight. They could discover no opposition at any time.

As they rounded one corner, they came upon a low, stained building. It would have been white originally; however, water had spilled down the front letting green stains run rampant. The whitewash was flaking off in patches. Only the windows were intact.

"I can't see anyone," said Sye. "We should have been stopped long before reaching here."

"The Questionable House?" Jill asked.

"I'm certain," Sye replied. "It looks in worse shape than in the drawings I've seen, but it must be the place we're looking for."

Rocket spoke soft and low. "Take care, old girl. They must know we're here, after all the noise we've made today. I expect they'll be preparing a welcoming committee, after all."

"Aye," said Frank, "it may be a lobster pot."

"What?" said Jill.

The burly man smiled, "Easy to enter, hard to leave; for a lobster anyway."

"And our friends inside would be the bait." said Rocket, nodding.

"Only one way to find out," Sye added.

"Then it's time to draw our swords, again," Jill said. She pointed with her blade to a place outside the door. "Do you think one of you two gentlemen could stand the watch for us?"

Sye stood outside as they entered. They passed through an empty room. Dirt and old paper littered the room behind it; one or two new-looking oil lamps were smashed on the floor.

"Those are Jonathan's, I'll wager." Frank's voice was cracking. This room looked out of the back of the house, and the afternoon sun was streaming through the window.

"They may be nearby. We'll have to look around," breathed Jill, "quietly."

They started to explore. A door stood at the back corner of the room next to a flight of stairs and Jill noticed signs of fresh damage to the wood and plaster walls. She went over to examine the door more closely. There was writing above it in the same kind of letters that she had seen in a diary in the Lodge. She mouthed the words. They were old and awkward to read.

Rocket was glancing nervously into the next room to the left, which the gardener was exploring.

"Jill, what are you doing?" he said in a low voice.

"Shhh, these things nearly always turn out useful; let me finish." She waved a free hand behind her, shushing Rocket. She fixed her eyes above the door, frowning in concentration, looking as if she were absent-mindedly swatting flies behind her back

A sound came from the top of the staircase. Jill spun around and lowered her staff, pointing blade and stick up the stairs. Rocket stiffened.

There was the sound of shuffling feet. A voice spoke, as if straight out of the air.

"Who are you? Nothing! This place is mine. What rights have you here? None! You know nothing, because there is nothing to be known except me! I shall be all you know. Bow and you may yet live."

A ragged soldier appeared on the stairs, and started walking down. Before Jill could respond, a jagged shard of ice flew from behind his shoulder and smashed by Jill's feet. Obviously, he was not alone. She stepped back unsure how to respond, and remembered to ask the Sword in her hand. "What this time?" she shouted, running back to Rocket. Small letters flamed into life.

"Count the cost and cut the fetter,

Then his power will end,
Buy the key to your future
When you free your friends."

Jill stopped and stared at the hilt. She was absorbing the words, concentrating on another reality.

"Look out," Rocket shouted, as the ragged soldier threw an ice dagger of his own.

Frank reappeared and immediately cried out, "It's Alfred!"

Jill raised her head. "Okay, you first," Jill cried. She ran forward and swung the Sword.

A blinding flash of white fire filled the room and the ragged soldier slumped. Seconds later, a stunned Alfred rose and was supported by Frank.

"You're looking a little better, friend," said Frank. Alfred merely groaned, shading his eyes and trying to find his feet.

"Where are the others?" asked Jill.

Alfred could not reply. The Voice from the air spoke again instead. This time it came from the next soldier descending from above.

"I have those you speak of, and who are you? You have no rights here! Leave now. You will not finish your quest. There is no Lord of this Road but me."

"Liar! Be quiet!" Jill said, pointing her staff at the soldier. The blast knocked him over, and he lay senseless at the foot of the stairs.

"A friend of yours?" Rocket asked Frank.

"No one I know, sir."

Sye shouted from outside, "There are more coming."

The Voice came from the top of the stairs again. It sounded precisely the same as before, but the soldier still lay at the bottom of the stairs.

"What's going on?" said Frank, "I thought you knocked him out?"

"I'm not sure the Voice belongs to the soldiers," said Rocket,

"I suggest we clear out of this building, unless the Sword has told you otherwise?"

"Er, no, it hasn't." Jill bit her lip. "What about the others? Might they be in here too?"

A chunk of ice impacted the wall behind them.

"They are mine. I will not let them go. I will keep them."

"That Voice is definitely getting on my nerves," said Jill. She brought up the Sword and batted away the next projectile.

"If you don't come out soon, we won't be able to leave!" Sye shouted from outside.

"Okay, let's go," Jill said. She defended Rocket and Frank as they carried their friend.

The scene outside had changed, the sky now darkening with cloud. Sye was standing halfway into the Road and was staring at the gentle sloping lands behind the house. Crows were circling in large numbers; the pack could be heard howling not far away.

"The wolves sound like they are trying to come in behind us," said Sye, "but it's the legions advancing yonder that bother me. I think us lobsters are in a valley-sized pot."

Large numbers of ragged soldiers could be seen descending from the westerly slopes. Many were already on the Road the friends had come down and were beginning to climb the low hills beyond.

"It looks as if our enemy has access to this divided part of the Road," said Rocket, "That's going to complicate matters."

Jill scanned the scene. Where was their commander? A sudden movement drew her eye. There, on the crest of a hill near them, was a small knot of figures. Trees behind disguised them and a low cliff in front defended their position.

"It's definitely a trap; our opponent is just up there. I bet he's been watching us from the start." Jill pointed to the spectators only a bow shot away.

Sye followed the line of her arm. "I can see Martha, Jonathan and Felicity up there. They're bound by ropes, next to the deceiver on the horse. If it were not for his army, it would be easy. They are only lightly guarded."

Rocket looked up. "But there is an army and we will be hard pressed to escape even now. We need to leave."

"I'm not leaving without Martha!" blurted out Frank.

Jill stepped back a little as the other three started to argue.

She held the Sword up and was able to see her face in the blade. "Okay, you've got me here. I'm sorry for my bad attitude. Frank needs to help his friends, and you've said I should set them free. What should I do?" Jill asked.

The fire glowed and the familiar writing appeared once more. It said,

"You already know."

"Oh well, I was just hoping that was my over-active imagination. Here goes." Jill strode past the three argumentative men and the rapidly recovering Alfred, and simply said, "This way."

After a few moments, the men realised that Jill was striding down the Road, towards the rider. She lit her lamp and held it high above her head. The Sword she had been holding was now sheathed and she was knocking over the front ranks of the advancing troops with blasts from her staff. The sounds of her shouts began to sound faint and echo off the rocks and cliffs.

Frank and Sye drew their swords and rushed after her. Alfred reached for his weapon and, finding he had none, pulled out Rocket's blade from its sheath and followed his friends.

Rocket threw up his hands. "What is the matter with these people?"

He watched as they proceeded to walk away.

"I'd feel a sight better when she gets that Sword back out," he said, and followed as quickly as possible.

The military gentleman motioned with his hand and three huge hour glasses were brought forward by his servants and placed next to the three prisoners who were bound and gagged and sitting on the ground next to him.

His face stretched about his mouth, almost as if he was smiling.

The number of dazed soldiers lying in front of the advancing troops was beginning to slow them down. They stumbled and tripped. By the time they reached the house, Jill was already standing at the base of the cliff. A narrow strip of turf ran up its left-hand side, and she began to scramble up. If she had had time to look, the view would have let her assess the size of the army below and any escape routes. However, she did not stop to look. Neither did the four men scurrying up behind her. Several times she lost her footing, and several times sent loose stones upon the heads of those under her, but in a few heart-pounding minutes of climb, Jill found herself standing on the edge of a grassy knoll, at the head of the cliff. She struck her staff into the ground and drew the Sword.

Lamp in hand, she took a few moments to survey the scene.

There was a great brown-black horse with rider. He was dressed like military commanders she had seen in history books. Five or six ragged soldiers accompanied him and began to advance toward her. Two Maids and a Gardener sat bound and gagged on the ground, and a rope around all of them was tied to the pommel of the rider's saddle. Three huge egg timers trickled sand down into their base.

The rider's eyes bored into her and for a moment, she forgot where she was and what she was supposed to do.

Jill stepped forward, and raised the Sword. It shone, lightning crackling, the air trembling with power.

The ragged soldiers moved forward.

Jill knew the power the Sword was charged with was for the rider, not these poor wretches. She hesitated, unsure what to do.

Still the words burned on the hilt, "You already know."

Her four friends burst up the slope from behind her and ran past. Battle was joined as her friends immediately attacked the soldiers. Rocket and Sye shouted at her, but she could not seem to hear them any more. Jill was watching the rider, unsure whom was the hunter and whom the hunted. She made darting looks to see what was going on. Frank seemed to be down but Rocket had already dealt with two of the enemy. More ragged fighters came from the trees and Sye ran to block their advance. Alfred was bellowing fiercely from somewhere out of sight. Frank rose unsteadily. She allowed herself a moment's relief.

The military gentleman leered at her. Again she glanced about, to either side. There was no one to stop her; all his slaves were occupied fighting her friends. Jill started to walk ahead through a clear path. She looked up to see the eyes of the rider still staring at her.

The sound of struggles, of life and death, were all around her. The rider moved his horse over to the hourglasses. He was almost expressionless; all Jill could read in his eyes was arrogance. The top of the hourglasses stood about as high as a man's shoulders and Jill now noticed something in them that she had not seen before. In the upper sand pile, a figure was twisting and turning, struggling against its captivity. It was transparent, as if the glass was reflecting video pictures from a television. But there was no television and the people looked really trapped and frightened.

The rider drew a cavalry sword, and without warning smashed the nearest hourglass. A sudden scream was heard from behind her, and she turned her head. One of the ragged soldiers fighting Frank dropped lifeless to the floor. She turned again. The remaining hourglasses contained a man and a woman. They were both familiar. Jill was sure the man was one of the ragged soldiers behind her. She knew the woman, but could not catch the image of her face clearly.

All this time she had been steadily walking forward, the Sword sparking noisily in the air. Now disquiet rose in her mind. Why was it that the military gentleman had killed one of his own? Why not one of the hostages? Why were the hostages not ragged soldiers like their other friend had become? What was he doing?

The curved sabre in the hand of the rider smashed down on the next hourglass. Even as he did so, he did not take his eyes off Jill. Another scream rent the air behind her and she turned to see another soldier collapse. He looked just like the video image that had been inside the glass.

Jill looked from the hostages to the assassin. "Live bait for us lobsters, hey?" Jill's voice quavered and she hardly recognised it. "Why kill your own, you plank?"

She turned again and this time recognised the woman who was now staring at her calmly from inside her sandy prison. Jill took a sharp intake of breath, she trembled, she screamed.

"Mum! You've got my Mum!" The rider moved behind the last hourglass, his sword raised high. Rage started to rise within Jill, "You wouldn't? Don't touch her," then a pleading voice, "Please don't touch her. Please?"

Now it was clear. He wanted Jill. He wanted her Sword. The trap was for her. Who else could oppose him?

"Count the cost and cut the fetter," she said faintly. "Buy the key to your future . . ." Surely, this cost was too high. The Lord of the Way would not let it happen, would he?

She glanced at the Sword in her hand, now pulsating with power. The words were still dancing on the hilt, "You already know."

Jill glanced up and looked at the rider again. The military gentleman had apparently not taken his eyes off her, and still the sabre was poised.

The rider's shallow eyes showed death. They almost smiled as the only words anyone had ever heard come out his mouth hissed through his teeth, "Don't listen to him, he doesn't love you."

Jill remembered the Wayfarer; she remembered his eyes. She remembered whom she had promised. Jill raised the Sword high above her head and screamed. She brought it down. With one swift motion, the military gentleman did the same. The Sword contacted the rope between the saddle and the hostages.

Power like she had never felt before exploded around her. Lightning and wind burst before her and flung her back. Jill lay still on the grass and closed her eyes; it was too much to do any-thing else. The light surged through her eyelids and penetrated her skull. She shouted, she laughed; she felt as though she was dissolving into light. She started to become someone she had never been before.

As quickly as it had come, the storm left, casting her back into normality. The light faded and Jill was abandoned to the grass, shipwrecked and exhausted. When she was able to see, the hostages were greeting their friends. The rider was nowhere to be seen, and neither were his ropes. Jill sat up.

The third hourglass was smashed.

Jill wept.

No one could comfort her. She sat there wailing like a wounded animal, tears and loud cries being her only responses to questions. The Sword lay on the grass. No one else dared touch it.

Rocket persuaded the others to leave her alone. This was in reality not difficult. All across the battlefield old friends were waking up to liberty. Greetings from brothers, sisters, fathers and daughters rang across the Moor. Shouts of grateful praise rang out as people looked for someone to thank. Some, who had been in the military gentleman's service many years, started to clean the Questionable House, although they called it the Questing Hall. A few had to avoid a mad man or crazed woman, who did not welcome the return of sanity. They mostly ran to the north and the west, cowering and snarling as they went.

Through all of this, Jill wept, and all that Rocket could discern was the occasional cry of one word.

"Mummy."

They found tents stored in the Questing Hall. Somehow, they were miraculously intact after all those years of storage. The giant party of friendly strangers and restored families also found beer and biscuits. The barrels in the Hall's cellars were rolled out and these also turned out to be still good. Fires were lit as evening descended. Rocket could be heard saying that there was no way that foodstuff that old could still be edible, and that the beer had to be off. Mostly people toasted his good health and offered him something to eat. This seemed so to exasperate him that he fell silent. The good mood affected everyone, so that by the time Kyle had persuaded Jill to come down from the hill, she had mellowed.

"You've been drinking beer," she said, "you stink."

He led her, a little unsteadily, back to her tent. He always claimed later that it was only due to the two cracked ribs that he was wobbling, and everyone would politely agree. The night passed with a great murmuring contentment across the heath, with happy people in every tent.

Voices laughed in every tent.

Every tent, that is, except one.

18

————

No Turning Back

The air was crisp. The tent was filled with light. It was going to be a wonderful morning, or maybe even a wonderful day.

"It's going to be a great day for everyone." Jill sighed. "Everyone who has something to look forward to, anyway." Jill had sat up on her bed and was speaking out to the air. "Where are you? You kept turning up before, but I haven't seen you in weeks." Jill paused, then shouted out, "I did what you wanted!" She would have cried if she was able to. Quietly now, she talked to the tent walls. "Why? I am so confused. Where are you?"

The air hung cold and clear.

Jill drew the Sword, letting it lie flat on her blanket.

"Where is the Wayfarer?" she asked. Nothing happened.

"Where is the Wayfarer?" she repeated, louder than before. She held it in both hands, straight up in front of her and shouted at the hilt. "Where is he?"

No flicker of fire appeared anywhere on the weapon. She dropped it and it lay lifeless on the groundsheet. Jill dropped herself back onto the pillow, and now found a few tears.

"Is Mum okay?" No reply came.

"It's just not fair," and she almost decided to have another good cry, but something tugged inside her and made her feel that that was not the thing to do. She could hear her own voice in her head saying the words, 'not fair' and she sounded like one of her more annoying friends. "Okay, so the Wayfarer helps me, the songs and ideas in the Road power the weapons, and that all comes from the Tower and the Steward. But why the other people? Why all the fights? Why my Mum?"

The silence seemed for a moment solid and personal, like an old friend.

"I'm sorry," she said, "but I would like to know, if you can hear me. I came searching as much for her as for me. I thought you might make the difference."

The solid silence gently evaporated. Nothing but little specks of dust hung in the air. The sounds of breakfast, morning washing and packing up filtered lazily through the thin tent walls, and that was all.

Jill decided to get up.

The camp was breaking up. A few people had decided to go back to the Mansion House, mainly to find family members long lost to them. However, most people were heading out onto the Road, away from the world they had known.

A large crowd had gathered and as soon as Jill appeared, Rocket ushered her forward into the middle. A space had been cleared, and a dignified man (who they found out later had been Lord Bygone's chief assistant and his secretary) stepped forward.

"Madame," he began, "we who are gathered here today are all indebted to you, in a manner beyond calculation. We wish to thank you, but you seem to have all you could need, certainly beyond our means to supply here. Nevertheless, in the store rooms of the Questing Hall we have found something precious that the enemy could never value or appreciate."

From behind the speaker out stepped two of his assistants.

They had not yet found clothes to replace their tatters, but they carried a scarlet, velvet cushion. The cushion was huge and needed two people to carry it; in the centre was an ornate bronze holder cradling a short dark bar of metal. Jill thought that she had seen a gun barrel the same colour. The whole thing was minute in the middle of the cushion, and although the bronze was worked to look like the intertwining branches of a tree, Jill could not help let out a little disappointment as she said, "Oh, thank you. It's very nice."

"It is a lodestone, used by our people when exploring the western wilds," the dignified man continued, who had completely forgotten to introduce himself, "It will always point to the Lord of the Way, which here is due north. It will always point in the direction you should go."

"Uh, thanks, but I've already got . . ." and she tailed off as she saw Rocket shake his head, and Kyle look down in embarrassment. She allowed Lord Bygone's secretary to place the delicate silver chain over her neck, and felt the lodestone settle on her chest, next to the key. It was half as wide and half as long as her thumb, and almost felt warm. As it nestled next to her skin, she felt comforted.

The crowd swept her away to the head of a makeshift feast. The chefs amongst those she had set free had spent most of the night organising the festivities. The food was quite remarkable. Wild game and berries had been roasted, boiled, stewed, steamed, fried and prepared in ways that defied description. Baked goods were spread out, desserts were brought over from the Hall, steaming and scenting the breeze with sweet odours. Hams, salted beef, salted fish and pickles of every kind accompanied the food, and over the rough tables, white linen had been laid.

Someone gave a short speech and everyone waited for Jill to start eating. She crunched down on a pickled onion and even yesterday's fear still gnawing at her did not take away the flavour. The morning feast exploded around her and she found herself enjoying the occasion despite her mood.

Inside herself, she patiently out-waited all the interest from thankful people, while they shook her hand and talked, not letting her desire to be elsewhere show. Eventually Jill said goodbye to the crowd. She remembered to wave this time.

She, Rocket, and Kyle were standing at the edge of the Road when Kyle turned to her with a question in his face.

"Do we keep going? Which way now?"

Jill thought of turning around, of running back, but if her mother was dead, what would be the point? She had still not told anyone what she had seen. In answer, she held the lodestone out in front of her, letting it swing on its chain. It revolved slowly then stopped. It was pointing North, a crystalline fruit on one of the branches showing the way.

"Jolly good," said Rocket, as they stepped up onto the Road, "should be plain sailing now."

They settled into the rhythm of the Road and moved along at an even pace. As they hiked, the broken cliffs and hills that haunched low over them flattened out and the Road rose up once more. A few hours' good progress allowed them a rest and it was decided to inspect the maps. The valley appeared bright beneath them.

"Look", said Kyle, "there's something new on the modern map." He pointed at where it had shown the dragon. It now was completely different.

"Ruins of the Beast of Confusion," read Jill.

"And next to it," said Rocket, "it says that the Road leads to the 'Sunlit Uplands'. It used not to say that, did it?"

"These Living Books, I love 'em. They're great, always telling you new stuff 'n all. I love staring at bits in the evening to see what pops out," said Kyle. They were beginning to get used to his enthusiasm, so Jill and Rocket did not say anything, but only smiled.

The moment passed and Rocket pointed something out to Kyle. "Look," he said, "the old map now describes the Hall as, 'Founded as the Questing House, having undergone a period as the Questionable House.'"

"Up here we seem to make a difference," said Jill, "I wish that was true back home too."

Kyle was about to say something but Rocket signalled not to. Jill stared off across the valley, sighed and stood up, not noticing their pantomime of gestures.

"Time to be getting on, old boy," said Rocket.

The Road wound up onto warm grasslands. A few low trees, bent by the wind, swept the air in the distance as the cool breeze toyed with their hair.

They now had enough fresh food from the feast to last two or three days, and the freedom from needing to hunt made them feel as if they were on holiday. Their backs were warm as the sun shone gently on a green ocean stretching before them, and the sensation of an easy time lifted hearts.

The men walked with their shoulders back, arms swinging freely, exchanging jokes and talking about what they had done before.

"I've never seen you two like this," Jill said.

Rocket did not seem to have heard her, while Kyle just turned and grinned, and then skipped in front of her to catch up to Rocket. She watched them talk as if 'before' was a different place and what they had done had been done by totally different people. "Just as if they had read about themselves in a book," she thought. Jill kept on finding herself falling back and looking over her shoulder.

When Rocket had waited for her to catch up for the fifth time, he asked her if there was anything on her mind.

"We haven't seen the Wayfarer for quite a while," she said. "Why do you think that is?"

Rocket did not answer straight away but started walking. He stared at a distant tree, rather like it was a long lost friend he could not quite recognise.

Jill wondered whether he had heard the question.

Eventually, he broke the silence. "I don't really know, but I suppose that there have been other things to keep him busy. Now, with that Sword of yours, we haven't needed him."

"Not needed him for fighting, no." Jill bit her lip. "Do you think he's left us?"

"I think he has been with us through the Sword."

"But he said he needed someone like me to lift the blockade. Do you think he'll come back now that the enemy's been defeated, or do you think he'll lose interest?"

Rocket stopped. Jill walked a few paces past and had to pause and twist around to see what he would say. She found it hard to look Rocket in the eye.

"Do you really think that?"

"No," she looked down and then up at some passing clouds.

"Then why are you so downhearted? You are constantly looking back along the Road today. Are you expecting to see anything in particular, old girl?"

"Well, no. Yes. Maybe I'm thinking of home, and maybe I'm wondering where HE's got to." Jill placed a real emphasis on the 'HE', kicking the ground with her toe as she said it.

"There's something you haven't told us, isn't there? Look, I know you don't like praise and being made a fuss of and the rest, but you haven't said a word about the battle since yesterday. It was odd the way you just wouldn't stop blubbing . . ." Rocket was cut short by Jill.

"Oh, do stop being so blimmin' stuck-up," she said, and strode after Kyle, catching him quickly. "What was that you were saying?" said Jill.

"Uh," said Kyle, "just that I thought the plain looked like it dipped down over there. You c'n see all the birds hanging around over there, where it drops off, like."

"Really, *do tell*, old boy," said Jill, partly over her shoulder. She was speaking in a voice that Kyle would have found annoying, except for the fact that he had already launched into his own story.

Rocket just walked behind.

Sometimes, no matter how much you want to tell someone they are wrong, it is better to wait to give your reply. Rocket decided that this was one such occasion. He reached for a pipe, and realised that he had given up smoking years ago. Jill would let him know what was bothering her in time.

A pair of huge mountains dominated the view. A great misty

mount, apparently covered in ice and shimmering in the far north, emerged from the pale blue of the horizon, and hung like a mirage in their view. The other was darker and much nearer, off to the Northwest. It was covered with forest, and crows circled it in huge numbers.

The afternoon wore on, and they became aware that the Road was about to drop off this bright sunny plain and down into thick forest extending from the westerly mountain. The Road descended into the trees before them. As the sun dropped lower, the scene before them came into stark relief, every edge paper-sharp at their feet, the journey beyond the forest valley, still hazy and indistinct.

They descended from the plateau as evening was beginning to draw on, and even Kyle expressed worry about where they might camp.

"I think it would be wiser," said Kyle, "if we lit our lamps. There are still wolves and crows out there, and I don't fancy having a scrap with them tonight. Not if I can help it." So they lit their lamps.

As the day's light reddened around them Rocket called out, "Hullo, what's this?"

They could see a cave in the slope of the hill, just off the path. It was a sandstone cave, with a large overhanging stone ledge jutting out over the entrance.

"It looks a bit like a door," said Jill.

"And it's made of sandstone, just like the Road," said Kyle.

"Very unusual," said Rocket, scratching his stubble, "Caves are usually limestone. Could we have a closer look?"

"Let's camp here," said Jill, "with the lamps on in the mouth of the cave. Nothing will be able to get in if we do that."

So they did. They settled down, after a delicious meal of cold delicacies, the boys reading their books, and Jill studying the maps.

They had camped on a narrow dirt floor, between rough ledges. The cave walls curved over and deeper into the hill, the floor rose in uneven folds to meet them. Once they had set out their beds and built a fire in the entrance, there was very little space.

"It says here," stated Rocket, perched up on one of the ledges, "that that two-headed dragon generated the Fog of Unknowing, so that shouldn't be a problem any more. What do you think Jill?"

"Humm," said Jill, "'spect so." She did not look up.

Kyle found a bit in the thin green book about checking out caves, as they were not exposed to the light, and therefore dangerous. He took his lamp and explored the back of the cave. Kyle made a big issue of taking his knife out, "It's easier to use in a confined space than a sword."

Jill mumbled under her breath, "Boys' toys," just loud enough for Rocket to hear, but he said nothing.

"All clear," said Kyle returning after several minutes, "nothing back there except a low entrance to some sort of tunnel. It seems dry as anything, but I can hear water running somewhere. Must be miles down." Rocket made a comment about it being 'rum' and the two started to talk about caves. When Rocket got to the part about how limestone normally formed caves and started to describe how it happened, Jill put away her maps.

"Good night!" she said and slipped into her bed. Jill rolled over with such vehemence that she nearly kicked the fire with her sleeping bag, and spent a few minutes sorting herself out with lots of straightening, slapping, muttering and quick energetic movements. Kyle and Rocket lowered their voices, and the sound would have normally lulled her to sleep. Tonight, however, she tossed and turned. Long after the sound of deep breathing and gentle snores filed the cavern, Jill's mind wandered along worn paths of worry, back to her Mother's house, back to Nowhere. Jill tried to focus her mind elsewhere, and she could see nothing except the broken hourglass, shattered and hopeless.

A new thought came to her. She had not asked about whether the two ragged soldiers had actually died. Perhaps they had lived.

"But my mother wasn't a ragged soldier, was she?" Jill's mind boiled dry trying to think it through. All that seemed to be left behind was that HE had not been there. The thought left a dull red ache.

After a longer time than Jill thought possible, a sound interrupted her thoughts. It was the sound of a running stream. Jill was thirsty, and the canteens only had a little warm, stale water left in them. The stream sounded closer than she thought possible. It laughed at her, tinkling like a thousand bells. She turned her head and found that the sound was coming from the back of the cave.

Jill pulled on her skirt, top and coat, picked up her lamp and found her shoes.

"I'll get myself a drink and then I'll be able to sleep. Oh, maybe I'll take a water bottle with me as well," she whispered to herself. Now that she had decided to get the drink, all the worries seemed to have disappeared, and the thrill of a little midnight adventure cheered her up. Jill straightened up after collecting everything. As an afterthought, she drew her own knife and gingerly picked her way over her sleeping companions. She stumbled on the uneven floor. "Go on, a bad ankle and a stretcher ride would be a great way to finish the week," she scolded herself, but was now feeling quite elated, and turned from looking over their campfire to the back of the cave.

The embers of the fire cast a glow over the back wall, except for one dark space. She lifted her lamp higher and caught a glimpse of a tunnel wall behind, twisting downward.

Making her way over to the hole, the sound of the water became much louder, and leaning in she saw that the tunnel went down further than she could see. It looked as if two ragged slabs of stone had leant up against each other, forming a tunnel where they hadn't quite met. She started to climb down, over tumbled boulders and rubble that must have dropped from the inward slanting walls. Once or twice she slipped, for it was very steep, and a shower of stones spilled down into the dark. She kept moving, and always down. Leaning out, Jill stood up onto her toes and steadied herself with her fingertips on the slanting ceiling, trying to see if there was a bottom to the shaft. She was as far forward as she dared.

"When will this come to an end?" Jill wondered out loud. The stones gave way under her, and she shot down on a cascade of loose rocks. She bounced off one wall and then over a boulder. She crashed onto the floor again, barrelling down as if on some crazy fairground ride.

"Got . . . to . . . stop." Jill winced, dug in her toes and fingers and slid to a halt.

The lamp still worked. Good. Her fingers and palms bled.

"About right for today, typical!" she said and started to pick out gravel embedded in the skin.

She began to shift her weight to get at the little stones and reached out to steady herself. Her hand did not close on the stones to her right, but on empty air. Jill screamed and had a moment's sickening unbalance. Then she lifted up the dusty lamp. Next to her, a hole swallowed up the rest of the tunnel floor. It looked deep. She rolled onto her back, then sat up and knocked some pebbles over the edge as she did so. The lamp showed that the passage fell vertically hundreds of feet. The stones that had fallen in bounced off the sides of the shaft, and rattled hollowly down. She not able hear them hit the bottom.

"That was a bit lucky."

The lamplight revealed that the passage no longer sloped, but either turned vertically down into the abyss next to her, or horizontally through a cleft in the rock that was on the other side of the hole. A faint green light shone through this gap in the slabs, and Jill saw a thin shelf running around the hole to this rough door.

She decided to take this route, although she now remembered what Kyle had read from the book, the dangers of being so far from the light. A strange stubbornness had settled on her and Jill dismissed the idea of climbing back up, the stream had to be so close now.

The sloping walls forced her to crouch and move carefully, and she nearly fell. When she ducked through the gap, she knew that she had found the water. The cave, for that was where she found herself, was humid and dank. A stream flowed down the centre, which was the lowest part, splashing over round pebbles that covered the whole floor. The walls shone with light from a dripping green slime.

Now that Jill had finally found what she wanted, she realised it would be difficult to get back up. Still, the water looked good, and she was thirsty.

She carefully descended over the slippery stones to the water, and winced every time she placed her hands on anything firm. Jill thought she understood why the Village workmen swore all the time and she felt a kind of anger at life rising up.

Jill reached the water and looked up, resting from the soreness of her hands. For the second time that night, she received a heart-stopping scare. Opposite was a skeleton. Jill looked around, and found that there was more than one collection of white bones. The rib cages were easy to see now that she looked for them and she thought with a shudder that each of them had once been wrapped around someone's heart.

Something piqued her curiosity and Jill looked closer, over-coming her revulsion. In between the ribs, there was a strangely shaped dark lump. Jill had never been a nervous child, but now part of her wanted to scream. She quietened herself, lifted the lamp high and turned it up. There must have been over two dozen sets of bones, maybe more; some of the stones toward the edge of the light shone very white indeed.

"Well, I've never seen real bones before. I'll take a look, why shouldn't I?" Jill's voice was unsteady and a little louder than it should have been. She splashed over the stream; the water was ice-cold on her legs.

She clambered up the hill of pebbles in front of her to the nearest heap of bones. The skull's empty grin was fascinating and horrible. However the bones had got there, they were laid out as if the person were asleep. She looked more closely, bending down. There were no marks on the bones, none of them was broken, none rotten. The lumpy object in the ribs struck her as very peculiar. It was shaped to a kind of rounded point at the bottom, and twisted into several branching tubes at the top.

"It's about where the heart should be," she said out loud. Jill laid her hand on her heart and felt it beat faintly. She could hardly feel it all. Her thirst returned, and she found herself talking to the bones.

"I'll just get a drink; I'll be back in a minute."

Descending to the stream, she emptied out the canteen and crouched down, plunged it into the water. Jill lifted it up to her lips and steadied herself. There was a crashing noise and the sound of stones grinding and falling; the cavern rocked.

Jill fell on to the stone bank. "Earthquakes?" said Jill. "Can't a girl be left alone?"

"Don't drink it!" boomed a voice, even as the dust settled.

She had dropped the canteen, and Jill tried to see who was speaking even as she groped for her water. Now she could feel her heart beat: no-one could be seen. She tried standing, but quickly ducked down again, wanting to hide. The echo made it hard to tell where the voice had come from.

Her mouth had become very dry.

A little more slowly, she lifted the canteen up again.

"Don't drink it!"

"Who's there?"

"I will speak if you will listen. Put the canteen down, please."

Jill swallowed hard. She was so dry it hurt. She crouched down, and placed the canteen on the pebbles.

"You're not, not one of the, er, the bones are you?"

"No, but if they could speak, they would say the same thing to you as I have."

Jill frowned, "Why? Who are you?"

"Don't you recognise me yet?" the voice replied, soft as a breeze.

She stood bolt upright, spinning this way and that. "It's YOU! Oh Wayfarer, where are you? I've missed you, you didn't come."

"First, pour the water out of the canister."

"But why? I'm so thirsty"

"Do you trust me?"

Jill, sighed, smiled a tired smile, and poured out the water from the bottle.

The Wayfarer stepped out of the shadows and started to walk down to where Jill was. She felt odd, and started to cry.

"Oh, I'm always crying at the moment. I just can't get used to it," she sniffed, and burst out weeping again. "You didn't come. My Mum needed you and you didn't come. Why didn't you? Why?" Jill's tears fell into the stream at her feet as she kept repeating her questions. The Wayfarer crossed over to where she was sitting and sat by her, saying nothing. They sat together, him silent, her weeping, for what seemed like fifteen minutes, until at last Jill stopped. She only had one question now. "Is my Mum dead?" she said, and in speaking it out, the last of the resentment went. Jill felt completely empty.

"Try tasting the water now. Just a little on the tip of your tongue," was all the Wayfarer said. Jill brushed back her hair from her red eyes, and leaned forward. The water was chilling on her finger, and she placed it on her tongue.

"Ugh! It's so bitter! That's the most horrible taste I can imagine."

"And yet a little while ago, it would have tasted sweet to you."

Jill looked at him, not quite straight on, the belief draining from her face. The Wayfarer gazed back. Jill had to admit that she was not angry any more, all the fury that had been knotting up her insides had drained away with her tears.

My head hurts and my nose is blocked, but it was worth it.

"What would have happened to me if I had drunk from the stream?"

"The same as happened to those poor unfortunate bones," the Wayfarer said.

"What was that?"

"You're full of questions!" He paused, examining her eyes and then as if making up his mind he said, his voice low and soft, "Their hearts turned to stone."

Jill's face turned white as she remembered the strange shaped object in the bones, and she shivered.

"You're cold. Here, have my sweater to keep you warm."

Jill did not argue, but looked back at the bones.

"Why didn't you come? Why didn't you save my Mum? Why did you leave me alone?"

The Wayfarer held her at arm's length, and looked intently at her. "Do you trust me?"

"Yes, I think—I used to," Jill dropped her gaze. "But, you haven't been around recently."

"I have come now. Do you trust me?"

She looked up again, her voice soft now. "Yes, I do."

"Do you remember what I said about the enemy twisting words, twisting reality?"

Jill stopped breathing for a moment. She hardly let herself think it. "Mum's not dead then, she's okay?" Jill's voice rose up at the end with all the confidence and strength of a sparrow.

"All you need know is that things are not as he makes them seem, and never are. If you believe him, he starts to win."

Jill started, "He's winning? How come?"

"You'll be no good to Mum down here, will you? That is if you want to help her."

"You're right," said Jill, visibly brightening, "Let's go."

She marched back up the way she came. Jill reached the place where she had got into the cave and looked around, searching frantically. She stopped, sat down, looked at the Wayfarer and her face crumpled again. "It's not fair, the door's gone," she sobbed, "the earthquake must have closed it over."

"You will never be able simply to walk out of one of his traps, but you do have the tools to get out."

By this point Jill did not care what she looked like. She dragged the back of her hand across her wet nose and the other hand over her eyes and wiped them on her trousers. She stopped crying. "What have I got to do?" a very bunged-up girl asked, "If I had my Sword, I could ask it and blast my way out probably."

"It is not for personal use, but for helping to save others. It does help you when you use it, but that is not its purpose. Remember? Anyway, in the state you're in, I'm not sure you could wield it. Has it been active since the last fight?"

"No."

"Well, it's just as well I gave you a blade for personal use," said the Wayfarer, smiling.

"The knife. What can that do?" she said.

"Don't retrace your steps, up is out every time." He lifted Jill's lamp to illuminate the cave above their heads. "By the way, if I hadn't stopped your slide you would have plunged down a very deep hole already, so please try to cheer up. I do love you."

Jill looked up. "Stopped my slide? But you weren't there."

The Wayfarer had gone again.

"Up is always out every time? I suppose it is if he says so." She smiled. "He said he loved me," the smiled broadened, "I'm just glad it's not in a magazine sort of way." Jill sighed.

She stood up, gathered all her things, and inspected where the Wayfarer had indicated with her lamp. A narrow path gently sloped upwards from the back of the cave. Jill made her way across the cave, and started to walk up. As she ducked around outcrops and overhangs, Jill thought about the dagger. She held it and her fingers worked around its delicate tracery. *It is so beautiful, but how could it set me free?* She remembered the day they had received it as a gift, a gift to use when the Wayfarer was not there. *What did that note say?* Jill thought, *'Its edge will divide anything.' Could it, really? Huh,* she smiled in spite of herself, *I suppose I'm about to find out.*

She stepped up onto a broad ledge and held the lamp up to the find the end of her climb. The cave was cleaved down the middle, the two smashed edges of the rock running at a slant across the wall. Jill held the knife up to the joint between the two stone masses. The letters on the blade glowed. She took the dagger away. The glow faded. Jill returned it to the cleft and with both hands; she started to press the blade into the rock. Thoughts shone from the blade and she stepped back with her hand in front of her eyes.

"Ow, who opened the curtains too fast?" she said out loud. "How come I don't get to choose when this thing works?"

Jill shook herself and prepared herself for a shock, like a man about to step out from beside the fire into the blizzard. She stepped up to the unyielding surface and pushed the dagger toward it. It plunged in. Thoughts streamed through her. Light shone from the rock around the blade; shadows stood out sharp behind the cave's strange rock formations.

Jill decided to keep her eyes open to see what might happen. Light was pouring out from the dagger's handle, illuminating her hand from within. She could see all the bones in her hand. Jill changed her mind and closed her eyes again.

Now the thoughts pressed in: ideas of letting go, forgiveness, forgetting grudges, thankfulness and thinking about good things. A cascade of words swept through her. "It sort of hurt at first," she said later, "but I knew I couldn't let the knife go."

The rock started to tremble, and then a strange high-pitched note struck through her. The note rose and so did the stream of ideas—both were painfully sweet. She became used to the words and as she agreed with what they said, it did not hurt any more. Then without warning, both stopped.

She could no longer see red light through her eyelids, so Jill opened them. There was a gap in the wall. At least, she thought there was, it was hard to see through the green blotches that moved into the way whenever she wanted to look at something. She groped forward and felt the hole and a cool breeze. Relieved, Jill fetched the lamp and moved forward, returning the dagger to its scabbard.

Once her eyes had re-adjusted to the gloom, it did not take her long to ascend the smooth path ahead of her. She emerged into the back of the cave to hear Kyle snoring. Rocket was propped up on one elbow, watching her.

"I convinced Kyle to go back to sleep after the earth tremor," the scientist said, "and that you had just gone for a stroll and not to worry. Are you well?"

Jill nodded and yawned. She never found out whether the Wayfarer had talked to Rocket that night. He would not speak to me about it either.

"Then let's get some proper sleep, old girl, I have the feeling we'll need it tomorrow. Things are afoot, my dear, things are afoot."

19

———

PART WAY ALONG

Jill slept soundly again, but woke from a confused dream with feeling that she had lost something. She wondered if the encounter with the Wayfarer in the cave had been real, and took a long time to get up as the others prepared breakfast. Her nose twitched with a delicious smell. Where had they got bacon from?

"Did you enjoy your midnight walk?" Kyle asked cheerfully.

Jill looked to the rear of the cave and saw the new passage the dagger had opened up. She shuddered.

"No, not really, but I slept well afterwards," she said hesitantly.

"Oh, you look so good this morning," said Kyle, "you feeling okay?"

"Yeah, much better thanks."

Rocket had finished cooking and cleaning and handed Jill a bacon sandwich. "Shall we get going now? Time to get on, I think."

They checked their maps, consulted their books, but neither gave them any useful information.

"It just says, 'Part way along,'" said Kyle.

"Intriguing, don't you think?" said Rocket.

"Uh?" said Kyle.

"He means it's interesting, in a kind of mysterious way Kyle," Jill whispered loudly.

Kyle said, "Thanks," and blushed slightly.

They all packed up the camp, and continued their walk down the hill. It had rained overnight and the air was chilled. It would be a cold day if it continued to rain, and since they had started journeying north things had got distinctly cooler. The summer's heat was fading, the scent of the air was wetter each morning and although they were all thinking it, it was Kyle who raised the question first.

"If we are still walking in the Autumn, how are we going to get on when the snow starts falling? That rain before the Lodge was really bad, and I don't think I could handle snow, you know what mean?" Kyle was frowning and looking at his boots as he said this.

"I don't know, old boy. But we've tested this Road and found it's real. It's always given us what we need to keep going, I expect that the Wayfarer's got something up his sleeve, eh?" Rocket's eyes twinkled, and although Kyle looked unconvinced, Jill remembered what Rocket had said last night.

"What do you think he might do?" she asked.

"Oh, I think it's best to wait and see, don't you, old girl?" Rocket said.

Jill was going to say something more but stopped herself and the next few hours passed in almost complete silence, the travellers content with the morning and each other's company.

The Road had led them downhill, and now wound level through the tall pine forest around them. The surrounding darkness was filled with the smell of pine needles; not much light penetrated the canopy of the forest here. In the distance, they thought they saw a grey form against the carpet of brown needles and occasionally someone pointed out a black-winged bird far above, but they never thought themselves under threat.

"It's like they're afraid of us now," said Jill. The other two agreed.

The Road straightened up and climbed the hill and the pines started to become shorter and more sparse. They took frequent breaks, as it was thirsty work, and by lunchtime they were able to look back over the valley behind them. The pines were unbroken in every direction, and now they were much higher up than it had seemed possible when they had viewed this side from the Sunlit Uplands. The Dark Mountain lay to their west, the woods sweeping up and smothering its sides.

Jill looked back down the Road, looking elsewhere after a second so that the others would not notice. She even caught Kyle looking back once, as if he too might be searching for something.

"Time to move on," said Rocket in an unusually eager way.

He does know something. But if he did, he didn't let slip.

They continued their climb.

The trees quickly changed to silver-barked birches, and even these became shorter and more widely spread. Eventually, nothing but brown grass waved in the cold gusts of wind.

They climbed still higher.

The sky had become threatening; dull clouds covered any hint of blue. The slope began to level off and the horizon they now saw was a bright white haze. The White Mountain seemed as far away as ever.

"What concerns me," said Rocket, "is that it looks to me as if snow has already fallen."

Pulling their cloaks around themselves, they fell into their own thoughts and no one said much for a few minutes.

Jill stopped and the party paused for a second.

"I was thinking," said Jill.

"Yeah," said Kyle, "You were thinking what?"

"I was thinking that I don't want to get you two into trouble if you don't want to go on." Jill looked over her shoulder. "We have a lot of friends back there. We could over winter at Lord Bygone's. We could, even go, well . . ."

"Go on, old girl," said Rocket faintly.

"We could even go home. You know, back to a normal life."

Kyle frowned and spoke slowly, "I think it's a bit late for that. You should have said so already. I wouldn't want to be normal now, and, anyway, I've been thinking about going back too . . . but I made a promise to finish this walk, right? To get to the end of the Road, all the way, no bottling out."

"I think that's the most sense I've ever heard," said Rocket, "I'll walk you back as far as you need to go, but I'm not turning back. Not for all the tea in China."

Jill looked back over her shoulder once more. "Okay, as long as you're certain."

"No," said Rocket, "as long as you're certain."

Jill stood stock still, nothing showing on her face. "Yes, I've decided. I promised too." She started walking and the boys let her go ahead, watching the way she strode, her head held high. "Come on, slow coaches," Jill said. Giggling bubbled up and she started to run. The others followed laughing.

The chase lasted a few minutes and as Jill panted steam into the air, she decided that something very heavy had been sitting on her shoulders and head. Whatever it was, it was great now it had gone. "Let's keep it that way, old girl," she said to herself and laughed.

The Road flattened out before them. They had finally crested the rise and Rocket let out a low whistle. "Well, now, would you look at that? My word, would you look at that?"

He was looking backward, at a most amazing view. It was the entire Road so far. If you can imagine sitting on a very tall tower, or even perching on a satellite, then looking away towards the curve of the earth as far as you could, you might get some idea of what it looked like. They could even see the Wayfarer's Hut and the coil of smoke from Mrs. Lazybee's fire and oven.

"We can't be that high," said Jill

"No way's that natural," said Kyle, "Weird."

"Precisely, old boy, precisely," said Rocket, "Fascinating, absolutely fascinating." Rocket seemed to be really enjoying himself.

"You always wanted to get higher up, didn't you?" said Jill.

Rocket did not say anything, he just grinned from ear to ear.

They kept walking.

A short distance on they came to a low milestone, rather like the ones you might see by the sides of ancient roads in Britain or Europe. It was sandstone, curved at the top, and about forty centimetres high. It had only three words carved on it.

"Part Way Along," read Kyle.

"Wish they'd give us some idea of how far that is, or how far it is to go," said Jill. "I never was any good on long car journeys. I always asked whether we were nearly there yet. Usually after about five minutes."

"No numbers," Rocket murmured to himself, "Fascinating. Absolutely fascinating."

Rocket cocked his head at Jill. "There's one thing that I'd like to know before we move on."

He does look like a squirrel! she thought, and then told herself that this was not the time or place. "Ask me," said Jill.

"What's your name, your last name?" queried Rocket.

"She's Jill Walker," said Kyle, "Everyone in the Village knows that."

"No, that's my Mum's name before she married. She went back to it after Dad left," Rocket was watching her with a piercing gaze, and Jill knew she had to be precise. "On my birth certificate I have my Dad's name. It's Kinsey."

Rocket nodded and he seemed content with that. "Now we're really getting somewhere," was all he said.

They soon came across small pockets of snow, and the breeze had become an icy wind. They were wearing all the clothes they could find, and had begun to lean into the wind. It cut through them. Their eyes watered, they kept their heads down. When they did look up, small flakes of snow stung their faces. They could see the White Mountain more distinctly now. The white cloud underneath it stretched out sideways as far as the eye could see.

Rocket stopped and held out his hand to stop the others.

"Look," he said, "look at the Road."

Before them, the Road stretched straight and unvarying. Snow was beginning to pile up in scattered heaps amongst the brown windswept tussocks on either side, but oddly, there was no snow on the Road. The view generally was dismal. However, what held their attention was not the clear sandstone surface of the pavement, but the light and shadows cast upon it.

Instead of the even grey and yellow light of the snow clouds, the bright sunlight of a hot summer's day shone down. It was nowhere else, just on the Road and the ditch. The Road shone hot and luminous under the heat of midday.

"It goes on for miles like that," said Kyle. He was shading his eyes and staring into the gap between the sky and earth, "As far as I can see, anyway."

"It's not behind us at all," said Rocket, who was staring at the light and then flicking a glance over his shoulder.

The effect was unvarying, until, without warning, it faded away rapidly, just in front of them. Dull ground suddenly ate up the lit area of the Road like a carpet being unrolled. Jill let out a sigh. Then, at her feet, the light returned as quickly as it had gone, and followed the galloping dimness down the Road. Jill noticed that the shade that was running along the Road had blurred edges. "So does the wave of brightness that followed," she thought. Another thought struck her and she pointed. "The front edge of the darkness is slowing down," she said, "and the back edge is catching it up."

"It's a cloud's shadow!" said Kyle.

They looked up, but nothing in the clouds could give an explanation of what they were seeing.

When they studied the Road again, it had changed.

If anything, it was brighter than before, but there were jagged shadows pushing into the Road from the sides. They moved back and forth randomly against each other. The light reflecting off the Road was almost too bright to look at.

A few wisps of snow blew past. The wind had dropped and so had the temperature; even so, no one noticed.

A few moments went by, and Jill shouted, "Palm branches! They're the shadows of palm branches."

"In a gentle tropical breeze," said Rocket.

"Yeah, on a *really* hot day," said Kyle, blowing a stream of breath, like smoke, into the freezing air.

They stood there, peaceful as they watched, no one wanting this strange sight to cease. A minute later it changed again, and this time they saw it happen.

The bright apparition diminished, and another pattern of light grew in its place. This sight was a familiar one, with the milky sunlight of an early spring day filling the path before them. The shadows of clouds slipped across the Road, like orphaned ghosts with nothing above to make them in the first place. They raced each other in endless competition, obstructing the light of a morning sun that was not gently shining where they were. If they could have seen the sun it would have been in the afternoon sky; as it was, the sky was still and leaden.

They watched other forms of time and place parade their shadow puppets for them. Dusk and dawn; rain making the stones wet and one of nearly complete blackness. Kyle leant close to inspect this particular one.

"It's night time, you can just see the stones if you stare hard and shade your eyes," he said.

As they started to stamp their feet, Rocket suggested they started to walk again. Jill and Kyle were still not sure about moving onto the strangely lit Road.

As the three friends talked, Jill pulled out the lodestone. The gem on the point was glowing and the tiny rod could not be turned in any direction but ahead. It hung stiffly in the air as Jill wrapped its ribbon around her wrist.

"The little compass wants us to go on," Rocket said.

"Do you think it's safe?" asked Kyle.

"It may be dangerous," Rocket mused. "I have a distinct feeling about this and I'm sure it's a risk."

"Do you think we're supposed to?" queried Jill. "It seems almost private here."

"I don't know." Rocket shrugged. "But *he* said, 'to the very end of the Road.'" Rocket's eyes shone with the energy of his decision. He moved forward.

Kyle looked at Jill with a question in his face and Jill simply shrugged. "We may as well go with him," she said, as they watched the scientist move forward. Jill followed quickly and Kyle eventually came along behind; they walked like this for several miles.

The wind had dropped to almost nothing, and besides the sound of the running feet of a startled hare, there was a complete silence. It was such a loud silence that they felt that if they had spoken, they would have not been able to hear one another. Even the hare's crunching steps faded quickly into the surrounding noiselessness. Each of them felt elated, too happy to speak even if they wanted to, but none was sure why. No one wanted to break the quiet taboo. Finally, Jill spoke up, hoarse with the effort. It felt as if she would have broken in two if she had not.

"We're being disconnected from here and being plugged into somewhere else."

The mist that had always been far off now seemed only a mile away. They walked on, giddy and sleepy and generally odd all over. The mist either moved toward them or they toward the mist, they could not tell. It seemed only moments later when they arrived.

Neither Jill, Rocket nor Kyle could say later when it happened, but the mist had turned into a wall of light as they approached. It was standing like a breaking wave, which had been frozen in time. It scintillated with light. Flecks of intensity ran up its face and tumbled in the foam peak. Pale, rainbow-siphoned colours moved inside it — time, movement and thought seemed to shine out from it. The lodestone was surrounded by a halo of the same light and the ribbon hung at an angle as the rod very gently strained forward. Their thoughts thickened again, the unbearable joy they were feeling lessened and they could speak once more.

"Do we go into it?" Kyle asked, "I'm sure it's not safe." His voice was not frightened, simply calm in the falling snow.

"I know it's not safe," said Jill. "But I'm going to go in."

"The Road leads to it, and runs through it, so I'm going," said Rocket, his eyes shining.

Kyle started to lift his foot, but never finished the step. The wall of light broke like surf over them.

Jill was abruptly in the wave. The ground dissolved from under her, the world from around her, but she felt no motion on her skin; no feeling of height, none of speed.

The light bubbled around her. What she saw was like looking through a camera as you dive through the turmoil of a breaking wave. She saw it far more clearly than your eyes can, without the feel of water, salt sting, cold or force. Jill's sight stretched into the wave far further than it would in the normal world, she could see every detail.

Blueness, the colour of early morning surrounded her. No one else was there, at least no one she could see. Jill could hear the song of the Road again now, high and lilting and singing for sheer joy. One voice or thousands? She could not tell. Man's voice or woman's? Who could care, it was so beautiful?

Then, almost close enough to touch, a slab of her life slid by. Everything she saw, tasted or felt, moved past as a piece of solid video, like a window in the air. Everything about the experience was wrapped in and contained in the slab. Then there appeared another, and then another, until windows filled her view. Most of her life was there, running on invisible railway lines from the horizon, shooting past all around her. Soon she was seeing her walk down the Road, and all the events that had happened to her these last few weeks.

She felt a breeze. A voice asked her, "Who are you?"

Jill was a little startled, but spoke back "I'm Jill Walker," she said.

"That's what you do. Who are you?" said the voice.

Let's try again. "I'm Jill Kinsey?" It sounded like Jill was asking the question.

The voice came again, "Yes, what does that mean? WHO are you?"z

"I am a young girl." Jill's hair moved slightly in the breeze.

"Yes. What more?"

"I am from Nowhere?"

"And?"

"I have been walking this Road." Jill realised that she was not even convincing herself.

"Now we are at the beginning again. Do you not know yourself better than that now? Why are you a Walker?"

"Well that's just my . . ." Jill was silent for a second as she realised the question had more than one answer. "I decided to leave, to get away from everyone, to look for help."

"Better, but Walker is a word you know, what does Kinsey mean? Do you know that?"

She thought the voice was teasing her.

"What has that got to do with anything?"

"No names are accidents," it whispered. "Do you want to understand?"

Without hesitation, her desire answered an unspoken 'yes'.

"Kinsey means 'Royal Victory', and no victory is won on your own, no King governs for just himself. That, at least, is a part of you."

Jill's hair whipped about her face in a stiff gust. She thought hard, and found her mind opening up smoothly, unfolding meaning. She started to realise what the voice was saying.

"I am Jill Kinsey, Walker of the Road, Wielder of the Sword, Victor in Battle, defeating dragons, Freer of Hostages, and most of all, Friend of the Wayfarer."

Warm winds surrounded her, and the voice whispered, "Good, very good. That will do for the moment." The voice's tone changed slightly, it became brisker, more businesslike, "Jill, Royal Victor, what boon do you wish for?"

"What do I wish for?" repeated Jill.

"Yes," the voice became low and soft, "What do you want? What do you really want? What do you long for with all your heart?"

"If my mother is alive, I want her to be well," said Jill, trying not to start crying again. Then she remembered herself and added, "Please."

The wind swirled around her. The blueness did not change. There was silence again.

"I want my mother to be well, please," Jill said much more loudly than before.

She waited as the wind rose. Her coat started to flap around her.

"I want my Mum to live, I WANT HER TO GET WELL!" Jill was shouting now and tears were running, but not in self-pity; not in sobs. The wind rose in fierce blasts now. Jill steadied herself.

"Please, whoever you are, if you are the Lord of the Way, if you can help, I want my Mum to be free of her illness."

The wind turned into a storm and the light around her shook. There was a sound like thunder, a brilliant flash of light, then calm swept over her and the blueness left.

Jill's eyes adjusted to the change in light. Rocket was standing on her left, Kyle to her right, and they were all on the Road, but not the Road on the Moor. Kyle was removing his coat, and Rocket had a small pile of outer garments next to him — scarf, gloves, hat and now his coat. The air was stiff with heat, and Jill was beginning to sweat. She started to peel off her heavy winter clothes too. They were soon down to silks and a few remaining wool garments, which were light, but still uncomfortable in the heat.

"Why do you think we're here?" asked Rocket. Both the children found it hard to know what to say to him at first; in the end, Jill said, "The Road must have brought us here for a reason."

Kyle said, "It certainly solves the problem of freezing, maybe the Road, or the Lord of the Way or whoever, has a sense of humour."

"How so?" said Rocket.

"Well, I complain about freezing, so I get steam-baked instead."

"Did you all get here straight away?" asked Jill.

The other two looked flustered, and said that they hadn't. Jill said that she did not want to know what had happened, and Rocket and Kyle looked relieved. "Some things are meant to stay private. But it does show," she continued, "that a mind, a person has brought us here, if we all — well, we were all talked to. Maybe being here is the answer to that conversation."

The others agreed and an awkward silence ensued. They all looked about their new surroundings. Bright green foliage leaned over imposing sandstone walls, low buildings surrounded them and behind them stood some sort of fortified gateway. The sun was high, and the sky dotted with bright clouds. It was a beautiful tropical day. It looked like a picture from a tourist brochure. However, what took their attention was directly ahead of them.

Before them stood a huge building. Its lowest levels were sandstone, then directly above that the next layers were made of a polished deep blue stone. The whole building rose in a succession of bands of rock, each flowing into the other without a break. The lower layers were dark colours often striped with brighter hues. Whites, oranges, browns, greens, pale blues and reds tumbled around the foundation and then swept up. Above the height of the windows, which were made from coloured panes of crystal, the stone became transparent. Deep red, green and blue gave way to light blue and then colourless crystal, clear and sparkling.

"Are those gemstones?" said Kyle in awe. "They're huge."

"All except the lowest foundation stones," said Rocket.

"What are they?" asked Jill

They were all standing and staring: Rocket scratched his head.

"Well . . . the deep blue at the bottom is polished granite, and the next layer of royal blue with the gold flecks, that's lapis lazuli. I don't know all the rest, but I think I can see Tiger's Eye Agate, that's the black and orange rock. There's olivine; the deep green band over there." Rocket had pointed at a layer of rich, earthy green on one of the side halls.

He continued to point out minerals, semiprecious and precious gems. Agate, chalcedony, sardonyx and carnelian built up an array of rich colours in fine layers. Jill lost track of which ones were which, but she did remember rather liking the ring of deep red Jasper that topped the walls off.

Pinnacles of pure Quartz crystal sparkled in the light, and the roof rose as curving domes and flat expanses of continuous crystal stone. Jill had only seen rocks like that in her Mum's rings.

"The first of the clear layers is Beryl," said Rocket.

"I know a Beryl," said Kyle, "one of my social workers is called Beryl."

"If I said the green Beryl is called Emerald and Aquamarine is the light blue gem stone above it, would you understand that?"

"That's Emerald?" said Kyle, his eyes nearly falling out of his head, "are you sure?"

"Pretty sure, it's the colour, the crystal angles and the way it scatters the light that lets you know," Rocket said with a mellow enthusiasm. "Yes, and above that, the main part of the dome over there, is . . ."

"Ruby and Sapphire?" said Jill.

"Yes," said Rocket, "which are both types of Corundum, and the clear bits that shine with little rainbows, are . . ."

"Diamonds?" said Jill.

"Yes, can't a man finish his . . ."

"Sentences?" said Kyle.

Jill giggled and Rocket almost frowned; the laughter echoed around the walls and across the deserted compound.

"Perhaps the people are in the palace," said Kyle.

"Palaces are the best places to find princes or kings, or lords I suppose," said Jill. "I know the legends say the Lord of the Way is a prince, but I get the feeling he's a king as well." She stood and stared and then started to speak. "Let's go . . ."

"In?" finished Rocket with a grin, and bowed low with a flourish, "Ladies first."

Jill accepted his invitation with a playful huff, and they moved toward the low steps, walking up to a wide level space that in turn led through a huge doorway. Pillars of a single colour ran up around the portal, and they passed under an arch as they entered into brilliance. Columns holding up the roof ran down either side of a central aisle and were covered in light of every conceivable hue.

The hall they were walking through reminded Jill of a huge church, although there were no seats or pews. There were side passages leading into many different rooms, or other parts of the complex. The riot of colour and light, the scattering rainbows from the crystals, and the long vistas left and right captivated their attention, so it is no wonder that they did not notice the main reason for the palace until they had walked half way down the aisle.

"There's a big platform and a huge seat on it," said Kyle, "at the end." He was pointing and Jill and Rocket followed his directions. "You can see it; look just there, in the middle with all the rainbows around it. S'ppose they must come from that diamond the size of a car, up there, on top of that glass dome."

"If I'm correct, that dome is also diamond, even though it's not shaped like the traditional gem," Rocket said.

"Oh, I see it," Jill exclaimed and scampered off like a small girl. "It's where the prince will be! Come on!"

They set off quite quickly and did not feel the need for caution until they arrived breathless on the edge of the huge open space next to the throne.

"We ought to approach the prince's throne carefully," said Rocket, "We may be here to set him free."

Reluctantly, they drew their swords. Jill was watchful, confident, she knew how to win now, and this final test should not be a problem.

The throne was set in the centre of a large circle of sandstone pavement. In it, at random angles, and in every possible size of letter, were carved words from the languages of the world. This circle was bigger than the Vantage Point, more massive even than the pavement in the Tower of Fire and Light and the carved letters ran into and over each other, hardly allowing any space between them.

They paused a second before stepping onto the pavement.

Jill stepped on and the letters glowed under her feet. The fire rippled around the circle. Flame rippled through her mind: words and phrases that told of the wonderful Prince, the Lord of the Way, lifted her. *So this is his palace, I've arrived!* Her mouth began to go dry. The outer slabs were ablaze with light. Jill stepped forward again and the fire spread inward with her. When she stopped, so did the flames.

Rocket and Kyle caught up with her.

"Go on," Rocket whispered, "this is your moment."

Jill strode forward and in toward the throne. The words in her mind leapt into song, and she hummed along with a high lilting melody, one she had not heard before. *This is odd — shouldn't a king's throne, or even a prince's, be surrounded with trumpet blasts, and loud proclamations?* Her heart beat wildly. Would the Lord of the Way be here? Would he give her request? Would Mum get well? Surely, the Lord of the Way would answer her. *Oh, where is he?* Jill reached the centre of the pavement, the stone dais, and then stopped and looked around.

Colours shone, the building opened up along several impressive side passages, all leading away from the throne. She walked all the way around the bottom of the steps; looking, searching. Behind the throne there was a great wall filled with multi-coloured alcoves and a huge clear window. Jill squinted against the sunlight and returned to the front of the dais. She looked down the avenue of pillars, out to a view of vivid green hills, with the ribbon of the Road running through it.

The pavement was only flickering with embers now; the words in Jill's mind only quiet poetry. Rocket and Kyle met her and sat on the lowest steps of the throne's ascent. "I'll just get off the pavement for a moment," Kyle said. "No offence, but I don't seem to be able to handle the stereo in my head like you can. I'll be seeing things next if I don't move."

Rocket smiled and looked up. There was a faint sound of movement.

"Hello, is anyone here?" Jill called.

Words formed in her head, "Look for me with all your heart."

Jill scowled. Of course, she was on a huge seeing platform. Immediately she used the skills she had learnt and 'looked' out from the Vantage Point.

Her mind ranged over the hills around the palace, through villages and small towns, past statues and monuments to previous ages. She felt people and trees, heard the hum of a beehive, the bray of donkeys and the grind of machines. Growth, life, anger and even love flowed about her, but there was no great prince out here; she was convinced. Jill found she could look further. Fields and roads and houses flashed by, soon plains and valleys and mountains whirled past. She could see very little in detail, but she could feel that he was not there. Jill reached out beyond this. Oceans and islands, continents and seas passed under her gaze. Where was he?

"With all your heart," the voice spoke again. Longing rose up inside Jill, she felt herself breaking inside, finally breaking in two. The feeling could not be kept down, it flooded up and out. Her attention swung around. She wanted to keep searching, but could not hold herself to it; her feelings mastered her mind. She spiralled in. Closer and closer to the centre, faster and faster her sight. Inward to the very middle. She sensed the urgency, the nearing arrival. Her heart was breaking. Faster than the flux of thought, quicker than sight, she was back in herself with all the power of the seeing station focussed on her. She opened the eyes. She saw him.

"It's YOU!"

Opposite Jill stood the Wayfarer, leaning against a column by the entrance to a side hall. He was smiling.

"What are you doing here? What's going on?" Jill shouted her questions. She would have run to him, but she found that she was still in the main current of the Vantage Point's power, and anyone who has tried that kind of thing would tell you that to move suddenly is inadvisable. But that was odd, she was still in the seeing stone's power—why was she seeing with her eyes open? She was looking for her prize, the end of her journey, but staring at the Wayfarer.

He stood up straight and walked toward them. Rocket burst out with loud greetings and Kyle waved.

"It's good to see you, my friends. How did you come to be here?" The Wayfarer's eyes twinkled in amusement.

Rocket spoke up, "I was hoping you might be able to help us there. We were just walking along the Road and had the most peculiar experience."

"Please, continue friend," smiled the Wayfarer.

"Well, we'd just got past 'Part Way Along', when shadows from foreign parts appeared on the Road," the Wayfarer nodded knowingly, "and then we lost track of quite when or where we were. Got swallowed by a blue light, some sort of wave I suppose, and then found ourselves here."

"And do you know where you are yet?"

"If I'm hearing right, this is the Palace of the Lord of the Way," Kyle put in.

"You have learnt much about the Road if you can easily hear the Songs of Greeting. Did you hear anything else?" The Wayfarer had walked to the edge of the circle and as they talked, their voices reverberated around the dome and pillared halls.

"When we were in the blue light, I heard a voice ask me questions," said Jill, feeling a little shy.

"Will you all tell me what it said?" the Road's Warden asked them, "it could turn out to be important."

"I'd rather not, if you don't mind." Rocket spoke gently, and met the Wayfarer's gaze.

"I understand. And you Kyle?"

Kyle's eyes misted over and he was staring out the door. He looked at the ceiling, then the floor. "No, er, not really. Sorry."

"No problem, you need to think, don't you?" The weathered traveller's voice was soft and accepting. Kyle shrugged, but did not look up.

Jill looked at the Wayfarer, who met her gaze. His face was a picture of friendly curiosity. "Well, I was asked who I was," she said.

"What did you say, storm maiden?" As the Wayfarer used her pet name, Jill was sure he giggled. Still, he seemed far too serious for that.

"I said I was Jill Kinsey."

"And?"

"I said I was someone who wouldn't stop, and didn't let anything get in the way," Jill was choosing her words carefully.

"Modestly put. And that's exactly what drew you to the Road." The Wayfarer definitely chuckled this time. "But what did the light say to that?"

Jill was curious herself, and she was falling into the Wayfarer's eyes again.

"It said that no King governs for himself, and that no victory is really won alone. What did the voice mean by that?"

"How should I know, little storm maiden? But perhaps when you decided not to die, but to fight, not to lie down under your fate, you needed to know that victory depends on other people."

"Do you mean that I'm not strong enough to win on my own?"

"No, you're strong enough, but then there would be no victory if it was only for you that you fought."

After a second Jill frowned. "I don't understand."

"Do you remember the people in the Cave, with the bitter water, and hearts turned to stone? They sought themselves first, and separated themselves from everyone else, even if it was for others they came." Jill was frowning. "Let me ask you another question. The books, the Steward, the Songs, the Truth—what do you think makes them all work?"

Rocket cocked his head in interest. "Ah, at last!" he whispered to Kyle.

"It all seems to have to do with what's inside people, what they're made for, how they think and act." Jill was looking off to one side staring into space very hard, and talking slowly. She suddenly looked up. "And it seems that some have more Truth than others."

"Yes, it depends how much they stay in the light, how much they choose to see, and to see yourself you need other people to reflect the light back. No one sees themselves well, how much they are in the light, how much in darkness. Your friends reflect back what you are like. The Road and the Living books also reflect the way of the light. They show how people should be. To win, you needed friends, other people, not to run from them."

"Friends like you?"

"Yes," the Wayfarer paused, "And others who need your help, even people in the Village. Have you still got those lettered stones?"

"The ones you used to wake up Kyle after the crow's attack?"

"Yes, those. What do they spell?"

Jill pulled the battered stones out of her pocket and held them in her hand. "I never worked that out. The best I could do was, 'A page'."

"Come look at this, little storm maiden." The Wayfarer ascended up to the highest step on the dais, just under the throne. He knelt and pointed at the stone surface and at a sentence in a language that Jill did not recognise. Jill stared for a moment and then realised that there were several holes, roughly hewn in the stone where five letters should be. "Try your pebbles here." Jill hesitated, looking at the dirty rocks in her hand. "It's all right; I want you to keep them."

The stones dropped into the holes and spelled out 'Agape'.

"What does it mean?" Jill asked.

"That I will never stop watching, listening, waiting for you to ask for my help. That I never go away or become disappointed. That I never will leave you, no matter what I see."

Jill gasped. "That's how I read them the first time I looked at them, but it didn't make any sense," Jill said.

"Sometimes you see more with the first glance than with all the staring in the world. Not everything can be seen by you Jill, not even from a Seeing Stone."

Jill blushed. "Is there anyone who sees it all?"

"Pick the stones up," the Wayfarer instructed. "I want you to keep them."

"Why?"

"You see them as 'A page'. Good. Let this be the first page of our story together." The Wayfarer grinned. "The light asked you another question, didn't he?"

"It asked me what I wanted."

"And what did you say?" the old guide replied.

"I said that . . . that," Jill swallowed hard, her heart beating in her throat, "that I wanted my Mum to get well."

"I thought you just wanted to find the Lord of the Way?"

"I do, that's why I wanted to find him." Jill exclaimed. "That's why I ran away. I never wanted to fight or leave everyone behind, but I thought that if he could make the Road, and if the Road was indestructible then he could help people. He can help sick people, can't he?" She had started to cry, but only a little.

Jill was no longer thinking about herself. She was turned out onto one person, pleading for another. "Where is he? You must know. I've looked for him, and it's brought me here. Please, if you know, could you bring me to the prince, to the Lord of the Way?"

There was silence.

The Wayfarer strode across the pavement toward them. Flames leapt up around his legs and blazed behind him. A breeze stirred the still air. The whole of the circle lit up, the gold letters shimmering. The words in her head were so loud that Jill stepped off the circle, and upon the steps.

He swept past them up the stairs to the throne. He reached the chair at the top, turned and looked back down at them.

"Do you not know me yet, friends?" His clothes started to shine with light and his face grew brighter. "I am the Lord of the Way, and I keep faith with all who come to me. All who forget themselves find me."

He sat on the throne, and the room shook with a low bass note. Several other notes followed, rising in pitch till the palace was filled with a terrible and rich blast of trumpets.

"I speak and all is done." He was too bright to look at now. "I speak and all listen. Listen now. Your journey will continue, although you will return to your beginning. All who ask me will be answered, and, if I have heard, you know you have what you ask for." The rock around them was trembling, and still the sound rose.

"Jill, be my Keeper at the Gate. Rocket, be the Warden at the Sea. Kyle, be my Man at Arms."

None of the three friends were still upright; the waves of power that emanated from the throne threw them on their faces; the light was almost unbearable, even with their eyes tight shut.

Reality began to break over them. All of them felt they would die.

As suddenly as it had begun, with the sound ringing in their ears and as they still blinked against the light, it was all over. They now stood looking over the Village, in the centre of the Vantage Point. The sun was setting, crimson and orange through the City's smog.

"I didn't want to leave," said Kyle. He was, however, grinning from ear to ear.

"Nor I, my friend, nor I," said Rocket sadly.

Jill was standing looking dazed.

"Did you guess?" said Kyle.

"No. Well, not until earlier today," Rocket mused, "I knew something last night, but I never expected it to be quite like this. He seemed just like us, besides the turning up unexpectedly and the sudden disappearances. All I can say is that today I woke up knowing that the Road led to him, the Wayfarer that is. Shall we start to walk down, old girl?"

Jill managed a weak smile and the men said nothing. She turned and walked down to the Road, and the other two followed.

"How long do you think we've been away for?" said Kyle, "'Cause I don't think this weather is fall weather. Look at it. It's like no one's back at school yet."

"I think you're right you know," said Rocket. Then, sounding remarkably humble for once, asked, "Do you think he might be able to send us through time as well as space?"

They were talking loudly, and in good spirits. From what Jill could hear, Kyle seemed to accept without question that his situation was taken care of, and Rocket was intrigued by what a letter at home would tell him.

Jill was not sure what to think. He had said that those whom he heard would have what they asked for. He also had given them titles and talked about continuing their journey. "What was that all about?" she thought, turning over her thoughts like the sea churning sand.

They were at the bottom of the hill now, turning into the Village, and Jill was inspecting the dryness of the lawns, and the children running in the streets.

"Still not at school, uhm, about three weeks into the holidays I'd guess," she ruminated to herself, "That means I'll have to stay with Mrs. Varney for the next three weeks. Boy, will I cop it. Everyone will know I've run away and be looking for me."

Rocket interrupted her inside conversation. "Now, I'm sure from what HE said that we'll need to keep in touch. Let's make sure we each have phone numbers, email addresses and all that. Look, here's some of my cards to write on." Rocket pulled out his business cards and Jill suddenly realised that he was not wearing his hiking gear, but was back in his flying jacket and lab coat. She was not wearing her beautiful wool clothes either and she had an unusual leather backpack on. She slipped it off and discovered the Wayfarer's gifts all neatly packed away, and cleaner than she had seen them for weeks.

"Well, now that we've got that sorted, on with the Road," said Rocket.

Jill grabbed him with the keenness of a desperate and condemned woman.

Kyle, hugged her too, and sounded croaky. He sniffed loudly.

"I'll take Kyle back to where he thinks he should be," said Rocket and the two walked off waving. "See you soon, I'll contact you," were Rocket's last words.

Jill stared after them for what seemed an age, and then turned down to the Merrison's.

The Merrisons answered the door quickly, and Jill was swept up into the house by Mrs. Merrison. Much to Jill's surprise, she was beaming a smile as she did so.

"How are you?" said Mrs. Merrison as Jill stood awkwardly in the hall.

"Uh, I'm okay," Jill havered for a few seconds, and then said, "I'm sorry for, for . . ."

"For disappearing for three and half weeks without confiding in me, or anyone else?" The parent before her was doing her best to look stern.

Jill thought two things. The first was, "Not bad, only a half week out," and her second thought was, "What does she mean, 'Not confiding in me?' Why would I talk to her?"

Mrs. Merrison was apparently quite good at reading faces, because she immediately said, "It's amazing what an oldie like me can know. I was young once too."

Jill hung her head, taking comfort in ordinary trials and mundane trouble.

"You're not in trouble. I told Mrs. Varney that you and Cathy had suddenly got the chance to go on a three week camping expedition on the Moor. I said that you'd gone with a camping group. I think you might call them the 'Wayfarers'."

Jill looked up, completely mystified.

Mrs. Merrison was standing with crossed arms, head and hips tilted to one side and a broad smirk.

The Road had not prepared her for this, life in general had not prepared her for this. Why was her friend's Mum playing mind games with her? Why could she not get into some old fashioned trouble? What was Mrs. Merrison talking about? "I am sorry, but I'm not sure I understand. Why did you say that?"

"We have an old family friend," said Mrs. Varney, "He popped in on the first evening that you should have been here. He said that you had started to talk to him as you walked up the Hill, and not to expect you for about three weeks."

Jill's eyes narrowed. "How do you know I went up onto the Moor? I didn't talk to anyone when I left the Village, I just went."

Mrs. Merrison raised her eyebrows. "Really? Let me give you a clue. He said that you were trying to hack his Road apart, and then said you had the cheek to ask for his help."

Mrs. Merrison's tongue was poking a lump in her cheek. She was clearly enjoying herself, and stood stock still, waiting.

Jill's eyes widened. "You mean—you're—you know—HE comes here?"

"Yes," Mrs, Merrison's eyes flicked skyward, "we moved here to be nearer the Moor, but as it turned out that wasn't necessary."

Mrs. Merrison became more serious, "You have nothing to worry about with Mrs. Varney; she was delighted that you had such an horizon-expanding opportunity."

"Where's Cathy?" asked Jill.

"She's been travelling on the Wayfarer's business like you," said Mrs. Merrison. "Well, don't look so surprised, she always was just like you."

Jill tried to stammer something out but was not able to keep her words on her tongue.

"Now, there's no need to go back to Mrs. Varney's either, there's someone waiting at home."

Jill flew out the door and up the street. She sprinted down the main thoroughfare of the Village and into her own home stretch. A light was on at home. She leant on the door with all her weight and it burst open.

Her Mum was sitting in the front room looking very pale. Jill nearly ran out in fear, for she had never seen her Mum looking so bad, never so sick. She caught herself. Did she trust the Wayfarer, even if it was bad? What had he said, now? If HE had heard her, then it would be done if she believed it. Did she really trust him?

Her Mum looked up from the couch, "Hello dear, how are you?"

Yes, she believed him, and before she changed her mind, Jill ran over to her and buried her head in her Mum's hair.

"It's going to be all right, Mum, it's going to be all right."
"Yes, dear."

Jill watched her mother over the next few weeks. It seemed that whatever the doctors tried, it worked now. Even when Jill's Mum had a violent allergic reaction against several of the drugs and could not take them, she continued to get well. Jill seemed totally relaxed in a way her counsellor could not understand, which made him mutter darkly about 'repression', but Jill did not care.

Jill tells me that her mother asked her nothing about her three weeks away, but when Jill asked her Mum about why her stay at the Capital had been cut short, she talked again and again about two things.

"I was getting worse and worse, and I had tubes and wires into me, all high tech stuff, but not comfortable at night. It must have been that that brought on this strange dream. It was a nightmare; I was trapped in an hourglass, and I could feel my feet slipping down the hole with the sand. I saw you outside, in strange clothes, you were filthy dirty and I know how you like to stay clean. Anyway, I was wondering what it was you had in your hand; it was all fuzzy, when this sword smashed through the glass. I could see it coming toward me, and all I could think was how sharp it looked. I must have had a fever, as I suddenly saw a tall tanned man in the glass with me. He stood between me and this slow motion blade and then there was nothing but red, and I woke up. I sat up in bed so hard that I jerked all the wires and tubes out and then, without the pain, I went back to sleep.

"Well, they fussed about me, and put one or two back in, but then the head doctor ordered that I be left alone. He said, in that sad doctors voice that they have, 'It's not going to make much difference now.' Why he happened to be there I do not know, but I was thankful not to have those tubes in me any more. Well, that was all I thought about it, and beside the painkilling drugs, they almost stopped treating me. I thought they would have to fetch you, and I was going to ask to sign the papers for my own funeral, to save bothering other people, when this new doctor came in. He was tall, had dark curly hair and had the most beautiful eyes, you should have seen them Jill, and I thought I'd seen him somewhere before. He walked straight over to my bed, looked at my notes, and said, 'You're going to get well.' Then he produced my suitcase already packed and handed me my dismissal papers. He showed me out in a wheelchair and paid for my taxi home. Then he said, 'Give my regards to Jill,' and I haven't seen him since. But you know what? I thought on the way home that I remembered where I'd seen him before. He was in my dream, in the hourglass with me, I'm sure. Isn't that strange? I must have seen him around before, and that's how he got into my nightmare, but I didn't think that they'd put your name in the notes. I'm sure they didn't."

Jill would smile each time Mum told the story and say, "No, I'm sure they didn't have my name in the notes. Why would they? Do you want a cup of tea Mum?" and then go in to put the kettle on to boil.

ABOUT THE AUTHOR

Matthew loves to tell stories. He has worked as a social worker, teacher and building physicist, and presently runs a physics consultancy. He loves building computers, building up the local church, cooking curries and talking about what matters in life. He is very proud of his wife and four children. After being born in Liverpool, he learnt to walk aboard ship on the way to Africa, where his parents worked before returning to the UK. He has fixed an ancient building and a 1970's campervan, and found that the world is full of connections which really matter. He presently lives in the South West of England, and loves the hills and moors of his homeland. He draws on all these experiences to vividly tell stories that draw the reader in.